Praise for Ann Wadsworth's *Light, Coming Back*

"Mrs. Medina's story is a touching one, mostly grounded in the hard realities of lovers coming together out of terribly mismatched circumstances and of options taken up terribly late in the game." —*The Advocate*

"Wadsworth's refinement of style is impressive." —*Boston Sunday Globe*

"Keenly observed and illuminating. In many ways, reading *Light, Coming Back* is like reading a novel by Virginia Woolf, and it's one of the best works of 'lesbian fiction' in a long time." —*Echo*

"Mrs. Medina becomes more human as events compel her to deal with abandonment and loss. By the end of *Light, Coming Back*, she is on the brink of becoming a heroine worthy of the term." —*Boston Sunday Herald*

"Wadsworth's writing style is both spry and graceful. With a poetic flow she pays detailed attention to the cultural differences between characters. Through simple yet powerful phrasing, she allows the power of the reader's imagination to draw conclusions." —*Bay Windows*

"For all of Wadsworth's characters, age really doesn't matter in their desires and their capacity to give love, but it does in their actions and their outcomes. The workings of time are both with and against them, like a wave smoothing, then abandoning, the shoreline. Wadsworth's ability to describe this tide is breathtaking and beautiful, showing us the fullness of a life captured." —*ForeWord*

"Superb. Wadsworth is the magician here, summoning up a novel that enfolds the reader in a singular spell. Honest, heartbreaking and, ultimately, hopeful, *Light, Coming Back* is a smashing debut."
—*Courier-Post*

"Ann Wadsworth fleshes it out with uncommon skill and a perfect pitch for how mature people deal with the emotions of lust, love, and death, to say nothing of the awkwardness of a sudden triangle. Wadsworth's characters are honest, authentic, and memorable. Just like this book." —*Front Page*

Light, Coming Back

Light, Coming Back

a novel

A N N   W A D S W O R T H

alyson books
los angeles | new york

© 2001 BY ANN WADSWORTH. ALL RIGHTS RESERVED.

MANUFACTURED IN CANADA.

THIS TRADE PAPERBACK ORIGINAL IS PUBLISHED BY ALYSON PUBLICATIONS, P.O. BOX 4371, LOS ANGELES, CALIFORNIA 90078-4371.

FIRST EDITION: OCTOBER 2001
FIRST TRADE PAPERBACK EDITION: OCTOBER 2002

02 03 04 05 06 **a** 10 9 8 7 6 5 4 3 2 1

ISBN 1-55583-767-0
(ALSO PUBLISHED IN HARDCOVER WITH ISBN 1-55583-633-X.)

LIBRARY OF CONGRESS CATALOGING-IN-PUBLICATION DATA
WADSWORTH, ANN.
    LIGHT, COMING BACK : A NOVEL / ANN WADSWORTH.
    ISBN 155583-633-X (HARDCOVER); ISBN 1-55583-767-0 (PAPERBACK)
    1. MARRIED WOMEN—FICTION. 2. HOSPITAL PATIENTS—FICTION.
    3. TERMINALLY ILL—FICTION. 4. LESBIANS—FICTION. I. TITLE.
    PS3623.A39 L54 2001
    813'.6—DC21   2001033581

CREDITS
COVER DESIGN BY MATT SAMS.
COVER PHOTOGRAPHY BY PHILIP PIROLO.

FOR ALICE ROBINSON
1948–1999

{ I }

In Hospital

~ one ~

In the hospital, at the beginning, I used to sit and watch out the window. Sometimes I did this for entire days, or great parts of them. As my room faced the street, there were things I could see, and I found that after an hour or so there appeared a regularity of incident, a sort of balance.

A car turns the corner, stops, backs, parks. A door slams. A woman walks away (she is tall, thin, her skin the creamy color of cappuccino), and her trajectory is balanced by a man who cuts diagonally across the street to catch up with her. He is waving a small package wrapped in red paper. They meet; they speak. She kisses his cheek. They start off again together.

During this adventure a bus pauses on the main thoroughfare, half a block away. Two young boys, caps in hand, descend in a flurry of legs and distant shouts.

A breeze blows down the street, lifting the curtains of a room in a brick building just across from mine. An old sheet of newspaper skitters and turns along the sidewalk. A car passes, its muffler porous and noisy. I hear a brief thump of music.

Two women come down the street, heavy with shopping bags; they meet a third. They stop and talk. Put down their bags. They laugh. Across the street another woman emerges from a building, looks up and down the street, and puts her hands on her hips. She looks up in my direction, removes her glasses. (Does she see me?) Strands of gray escape from a pink scarf she has wound around her head. Does she think of the crazy people over here behind the wired windows?

I followed these events with a disinterested curiosity, thinking of wheels, clocks, the orderliness of dials and numbers. Am I crazy? Was I?

~

My own life at that time was standing to the side in a shadowy corner, quietly, but with a certain air of menace, waiting for me to meet its gaze. I was trying to put that moment off as long as I could. I kept my eyes on the street and my hand on my watch. (The street was Eule Avenue, in one of the more modest Boston suburbs.) We are told that our universe is expanding into chaos, but in that street I saw the reassurance of order, as long as I didn't look too intently. In the same way the bleachers at Fenway Park on a hot July afternoon used to seem miraculously balanced in color—the red shirts, the white shirts, the green dress, the bare chest. As long as you didn't look too closely. And I had to be careful; if I looked too hard at the street, I might see the ugly tobacco stains on the teeth of the woman with the pink scarf, or the man waving the red package stealing on tiptoe into his daughter's room at midnight, slipping into her bed as she waited, feigning sleep, wishing for death.

From the still center of chaos I was watching, patiently trying to relearn how to go about living a life.

Much of my own life had been—until the most recent four or five months—as superficially balanced as this street. I suppose this was the disease from which I was supposed to be recovering, but I am suspicious of facile parallels such as this. I was not stupid. My actual experiences had been of a regulated and hedgy type, however, much as, say, a tour of the Greek islands that allows only fifteen minutes per island, and everyone is ordered to be back on the boat by five-thirty, ready to depart. I am ready to believe that one of the reasons I was attracted to Patrick was that he had such a clear idea of what he wanted, what he liked. He would have decided on one Greek island and told the tour to leave him there. With him I no longer had to make up my mind. Then of course after he died I had to make a lifetime of decisions right away. And by that time most of my options were gone. Or the most important one, perhaps.

Certainly being in that hospital was an unsettling experience, although, happily, the others didn't seem to notice. The principal reason I gave for having signed myself in was that I needed someone to cook for me for a while. I didn't believe I was severely disturbed. However, the body can go crazy—completely on its own—while the mind still thinks clearly. I don't think I would have eaten if someone else hadn't cooked. Taylor Bond, my therapist, had some comments to make about that. We don't always agree, but we go along. It doesn't matter, really, which of us is right.

At first, in my hospital room, there were only the bed, a straight wooden table, a metal lamp with a segmented gooseneck. An over-stuffed chair in which I might read. A framed painting of flowers on the wall, I didn't know what kind—I could not look at flowers then long enough to determine what they were. Reds and yellows. On my table was one book, a dictionary. I didn't wonder about this at first. Later, as I began to stay awake longer, I would look through the dictionary to pass the time. I found one page had been horribly crumpled and then straightened out, not too successfully. On this page the word *dull* was circled heavily with a black felt pen:

> *dull (adj) [ME dul; akin to OE dol, foolish, and prob. to*
> *L fumus, smoke] 1. mentally slow; stupid. 2. lacking sharpness*
> *of edge or point. 3. lacking brilliance or color. 4. not*
> *resonant or ringing. 5. low in lightness. 6. cloudy, overcast.*
> *7. tedious, uninteresting.*

I immediately recognized myself in all these definitions, and knew I had been the one to circle the word and then attack the page. When this had happened I could not remember.

When I was not observing the street I would lie in my bed and watch the tree and the sky (a common story, from those in jails or hospitals, but I didn't really "watch"; after a while I hardly even "saw"). I finally asked them to remove the flower painting, and soon after that Bond brought me something else, a little reproduction of one of Canaletto's paintings of the Piazzetta in Venice.

"Here," he said. "I didn't much care for the flowers myself. I want you to just look at this every day."

"I'll try to remember."

"Look at it. There's a lot to see. Try to see something new every day."

"I know this painting very well. I've looked at it often." I smiled. "I don't think I'll see anything new."

"Just try it."

"Is this a practice for something?"

I came to have a feeling about this painting, never substantiated, that it had been left by another patient. So I looked at it; Canaletto can be wonderful with details. But I own a Whistler etching of Venice that is much better, much moodier, like the city itself.

When I saw that drawing I remembered that once I could be moved by views, sunsets, by a convivial meal; once I had played, even laughed, and did not dwell on whether I was happy. I think Bond may have had the idea that this "former" person I was might be re-created simply from one small memory of it, much as a hologram is able to produce its total image from a tiny piece of itself, even when most of the rest of it has been destroyed. But I wanted nothing to do with this plan. I have to live out the rest of my life, and although I don't know how I'm going to do it, I don't want this "former" persona to be involved.

One night I woke, hearing the March wind in the trees, and thought I could smell the pungent aroma of a fall wood fire, as Patrick and I had smelled it walking in the fields around Assisi years ago. I clearly thought I heard the voice of a young man who was harvesting olives call out to warn us about several scythes he had left strewn along the path. We had paused, startled, not wanting to take another step—Patrick for some reason thought he was going to shoot us—but the young man laughed and pointed to where the blades were lying, and motioned us forward. It was silly, such a sudden, small misunderstanding, but Patrick and I clung to each other in relief and stopped and had a cup of wine with this man, for whom we instantly felt undying friendship. It was a glorious afternoon, hazy with sweet autumn smoke.

We are always homesick for places where we cannot be. What are we longing for? Some feeling of wholeness or peace, something that's never possible right where we are? Some feel they are cut loose at birth and flung through time without any clue to where they belong, or with whom, and their life's obsession is to land somewhere, to find that missing person, or place, or spirit. "That imbecilic passion of the part for the whole," as Sartre has written. Yes.

A waste, isn't it, that sort of search? You can waste your entire life. I have had that imbecilic surge of recognition only one other time in my life. That is probably my allotment.

~

In the hospital they left me alone for the most part and just let me do what I needed to do. I'm sure they couldn't imagine why I was there. Bond came in once a day. We finally began to talk.

"I know I've betrayed your trust," I said to him, which had absolutely nothing to do with what was really the trouble. "And you'll probably never let me have any sleeping pills again."

He looked at me blankly. "Is that the first thing that comes to your mind?"

It was.

And that was odd, because I hadn't taken any pills. Pills had nothing to do with it.

Santino Cassieri from the Trio Riviera, Patrick's former chamber group, came to see me while I was in that ward. He came and played his violin for a while. Then he left. We didn't talk much; I sense that he misses Patrick even more painfully than I do, and that to look upon me causes him immense grief. And who could blame him? He did mention that the Riviera's pianist, Barbara Wu, had decided to abandon her playing career altogether because of the seriousness of her arthritis. Her decision was not unexpected. We were both silent, thinking of what this would do to her life. Patrick had loved her very much.

Santino was wearing jeans and a white shirt, sleeves rolled to the elbows, and these clothes smelled fresh out of the laundry. At fifty, he still looks like a college boy.

~

Patrick was one of the most beautiful men I have ever known. His black hair (when he was younger) was brushed severely back from the great expanse of his forehead, a forehead like a mountain face. By contrast, his features seemed soft; he had dreamy green eyes and full, but not loose, lips. He used to sit at the window some nights, resting his cheek against the great curve of his cello, his arms loosely around its waist. I seldom interrupted these erotic moments with his instrument. But he played with the pain and virility of an obsessed man. The singing he brought forth from that box of wood and gut!

Patrick knew the music directly; he entered it. I have seen for myself what playing the andante movement of the Schubert B flat piano trio could do to him, for example. As for me, I believe this music can be moving, but I am not one for romantic indulgence. I prefer the first movement myself, the allegro, which "strides forth with brilliant and passionate spirit." These are my own words, spoken in bed with Patrick one night, when we were drinking champagne and making up phrases for imagined reviews. (Nicely put, I thought.)

In recollecting this time (*re-collecting* is an appropriate word) I have a tendency to swerve from the narrative, to drift away to minor considerations (the Schubert trio, for example). To set my life in order, as I should be trying to do, I should have only facts, their form should be easily comprehended and not confused by subtleties.

Although subtleties, I am told, are what give texture to one's life.

People are generally uncomfortable around those with mental problems; they find them fascinating and, at the same time, disgusting. This is not an unusual human conflict. We feel the same about exotic foods such as eel livers and haggis, and certain violent crimes. My own illness was constructed of the material designed to conceal it, so for a long while others did not have to deal with it and neither did I. But the drama grew bigger and more complex. I was playing more than one role, especially after Lennie came into my life. (There, I have written her name for the first time.) I had different scripts for different occasions, different people. I should have known this situation couldn't go on indefinitely.

What pushed me over the edge was lying to Patrick, or perhaps *dissembling* would be the better word, a slyer, more dishonest action.

After that point, everything in my life became completely without substance, ready to betray. In any life, I think, there must be one person to whom you never lie, who folds you in. Patrick was that person for me. Until the last three or four years of his life, when everything began to fall away from him, Patrick was always completely there when we were together; he was always *with* me. He folded me in, always. My dissembling sickened me, but I rationalized my actions by telling myself that he wasn't well, that I was protecting him from distress he might not be able to handle. But lying to Patrick not only broke my heart, it broke my will. Craziness is what happens when there is no one left to whom you can tell the truth. You are left with all of it, alone.

In the hospital, after a couple of days, they wanted me to associate with others, even though I was only to be there for a short time. I didn't mind. One of the women in our circular ward said to me, "My daughter is Queen of Miami." A man passing by overheard. "Not possible," he said, shaking his head seriously. "Castro is Queen of Miami." (It could be true.) I didn't mind. I loved these stories. No one was lying. These were stories from a life I had ignored for most of my years. They were authentic.

At the end of ten minutes, or an hour, I could return to my room and shut the door, return to my chair by the window, or to my bed. At eleven-thirty my lunch would be brought, then taken away; at five-thirty dinner. After dinner I could come out and watch television with the others if I wished (I didn't), and I could have milk or juice at ten.

~

"Would you like a radio?" Bond asked me. I said I wouldn't. He opened his hands. "Books?" "Not yet." After a moment he said, "Soon we've got to talk." I smiled and looked away. I knew that.

My room was painted in two shades of a color of green that was not inclined to excite the imagination. My window faced southeast.

"Now, can we just get to..." Bond said. The roles of patient and doctor are not entirely comfortable for either of us. I started to talk with him when Patrick's mind began to go, and for a very long while I convinced myself that my visits to his office were to assist me in dealing with Patrick's deteriorating condition. Bond was never fooled, however, as has become apparent. I've known him for a while, and I like him. He waited until I grew tired of that game. Now I think he believes he waited too long.

"I think it's time we talked about, began to talk about, what happened to you," he said. "You were not thinking of suicide."

This was not a question, but I said, "No." He watched me and waited. "You feel I betrayed you because I stopped seeing you. Because I didn't keep appointments." That was all I could think of to add. *Betrayed* was, of course, an inappropriate word.

"On the contrary, I feel I should have anticipated your reaction."

"Things like this are that predictable?"

"Well." He smiled. "I wasn't surprised."

Others, perhaps, had felt what I had, their days one long gray afternoon after another, the loss of taste, the disinclination to eat, the unwashed clothes, the uncared-for body. The attraction of the gin bottle. Staring into the dark.

"It wasn't just Patrick, you know."

He nodded.

"In fact, I am very angry at him just now."

"And the girl..."

"Lennie. And she is not a girl, as I have pointed out to you often enough."

"She is involved in this too."

"I feel cheated."

"By..."

"Not by her."

"Have you heard from her?"

"I don't know where she is. And she certainly has no idea where I am."

Bond watched me for a moment. He sees too much with those eyes, I thought. Patrick used to comment on Bond's skin, which was rich and brown, and had a tint of gold in it. I was much more affected by his eyes.

"Do you hope?" he said finally.

"I don't have specific thoughts about it."

"In general terms, then. Do you hope?"

I thought about this question. "No," I said, "I don't hope in general terms. Neither specific nor general. I thought I had a hope about Lennie, but that turned out to be a rather self-indulgent fantasy."

"I would guess that you probably still have a hope about Lennie. Things were never really settled between you. That leaves room for hope."

"Well, perhaps you're wrong."

After a moment he said, "Have you thought of where you'd like to begin again?"

"Do you mean where, or at what point?"

"Either. Both."

"No. I haven't considered that. I'm having a difficult time with specific things."

He nodded. "Well, one thing at a time."

"It's hard, you know…"

"Yes…"

"When both of the people…"

"Yes…"

"Let me finish!" I looked at him, startled at my tone. "Please."

"Sorry."

"Never mind. I'd like to start again on an island somewhere, if you want to know. One small room. No possessions. No fancy aspirations."

"No people."

"Right. No people from my past. No one who needs me to care about them, to feed them, to help them grow up. No assurances of life everlasting, no pietàs, no fighting side by side at the barricades, no champagne at midnight, no breathless descent in the elevator."

He looked startled, but he didn't interrupt.

"Don't worry, Bond," I said. "It'll work out. I'm all right." I looked at my watch.

"You used to do that, when we were first meeting. Look at your watch."

"Yes, I was worried I'd run out of things to tell you."

"And after a while—"

"You couldn't shut me up."

"Who has cheated you?" he said. "How have you been cheated?"

I put my eye up close to the Canaletto. Bond said to look at it, so I cooperated. The tiny people seemed dwarfed by the architecture—the pink and white marble of the Ducal Palace, Sansovino's noble library. The expanse of the Piazzetta itself. They all had something particular they were doing, but their surroundings made them almost insignificant. Pointless.

That is what I saw on the first day. But I'd seen it before.

~

I remember the first time I lied to Patrick. I make myself think of that evening sometimes because it helps to anchor my mind to what followed. It was a night in late October, but still warm. That afternoon I had spent with Lennie, and I simply couldn't leave her until it was very late, nearly six. I knew several friends were coming by for dinner, and that Patrick and Santino and Barbara—the old Trio Riviera—were to play for them, an occasion rare enough at that point. The meal was more or less organized, but I should have been back by four. I arrived back at the apartment to find Patrick sitting in the living room with his shaky arms clasping his cello. On this night he had put on a dark blue linen blazer and a lighter blue shirt with thin white stripes and one of his paisley ties. It had obviously taken him a great deal of time to dress. He smelled faintly of his familiar cologne. His spacious forehead was covered in a fine film of sweat, and two little tears were poised in the corners of his eyes. As I looked around the room I saw that he had been attempting to get things ready; a trail of ice chips led back toward the kitchen, and on the coffee table lay a plate of broken crackers and some old cheese I had intended to throw out. My late arrival suddenly became too monstrous for any words, so without meeting his eyes I removed the handkerchief from his breast pocket—the large, light blue handkerchief that matched his shirt—and, in a familiar and intimate manner that I called up from recent memory, I patted his forehead dry. This was not an act of affection, or even remorse, although I did feel terribly guilty. I had come to him straight from Lennie's bed, and he knew where I had been. That was not the lie. The lie was that the gesture was not for him. The gesture was made because my body was still longing for her, and I needed to touch flesh. The flesh I touched was his, but my mind remembered her body. And that was the first deception.

But he was relieved I was home, and the evening went well after that. I don't think he dwelled too much on this deception. But he began again to try to play his cello at home soon after that evening, and because he had grown so frail he wasn't able to play with the vigor he once had, although the sweetness was still there. For vigor he substituted brief spasms of furiousness, which were painful to hear because he was trying too hard. I gradually took to moving farther and farther away—first to the living room, then to the kitchen, eventually to my own room, and my own bathroom. I became as angry with him as I had ever been in our years together. But when he tracked me down one evening I emerged smiling from the bathroom, where I had been reading Edith Wharton, my dry hair in a towel, to meet his steady gaze, his cello in his hand.

"Of course your playing doesn't bother me," I said lightly. Lie follows lie. I slipped past him into the bedroom.

I did not dream at first when I came to the hospital. I felt I had lost everything that anchored me in dreams, much as someone using a computer hits one key and destroys all memory. I was content. What there had been to feed dreams was bloodless now, a sightless grub. I no longer suffered for the cat I imagined out alone on a bitter January night. I no longer went over and over the final hours of my mother's death, her hollow voice saying "I'm afraid." I no longer tried to enter the mind of every passenger trapped in a falling jet. (What were they thinking? What did they see?) In short, I abandoned the role of suffering god. I felt nothing.

"Would you like to go home?" Bond asked me. "There's really no reason for you to stay."

I tried quickly to think of one.

"I'm not ready."

"What exactly are we waiting for?"

"Are you anxious to get me out of here?"

"People who are here cannot take care of themselves. You are responsible, you can take care of yourself, you are aware of your situation."

"It's my situation that scares me."

"We can have our meetings in my office. Being scared is no reason to stay."

"Give me another week."

"We can give you five days."

I nodded.

Pots and pans. Patrick's things, his music scores, his clothes, his cologne. The living room curtains, with the cigarette burn. My bed. My sheets, the one I saved in the bottom drawer from a night with Lennie. An empty bottle of San Gimignano under the sink. The empty air. The dust motes floating in the late afternoon. The complete silence.

The rest of my life.

~

This was not actually a hospital, where I was. Well, it was, but there was a section of it for those who weren't in extreme crisis—a "holding" area, I suppose one would call it. I checked myself in, and they could not keep me. In fact, they now seemed anxious to see me go. Bond got me in. I think he wanted to keep his eye on me. He had given me a few sleeping pills, and I happened to miss an appointment with him, and so he just appeared at my door. Tina Bird called him, I think; she was more aware of my deteriorating state of mind. I could never have called him myself; our relationship was quite formal. I couldn't imagine him in my house until he was suddenly there. I had never cried in his presence. I looked him in the eye as often as I could, but I generally spoke about the interpretation of dreams and how to deal with Patrick's growing senility.

Patrick had thought Bond was a "charlatan," but Patrick thought of all medical people that way.

I did talk with Bond about Lennie, but I presented my case as something to be examined: a fifty-nine-year-old woman, happily married, infatuated with a woman half her age. That was the case, simply put. I remember casually laughing about the situation as I talked with him, while my entire body quaked as if it were in a freezer chest.

"What was the attraction?" he asked me at one point, a query that was too far from the clinical to suit me. "Was there any warning?"

"What sort of warning? Do you mean was it love at first sight? No, I don't believe in that. She—" I threw open my hands "—made herself available, I suppose. I found it a bit exotic, began to dwell on it a bit too much. I suppose it became inevitable, something I had to try, eventually."

"That sounds pretty coldhearted, Mercedes—in view of your response when she left your life."

"Well, it did get a bit more complicated, Bond. I'm not denying that. I can't figure it out. She was there. On a certain day when I was ready for something like that, she was there and somebody else wasn't. Are you looking for something more sensational?"

He didn't seem to think there was anything sensational about my situation, however, which did little to reassure me. I did not speak with him about my sexual confusion, although he might have helped me with that. The phenomenon of being fully aroused, sexually, for the first time in my life was not something I could "share" with him. I gloated about it to myself but hid it, or tried to hide it, even from Lennie. Patrick, on the other hand, probably understood best what I was experiencing, but at the end he slipped away from me with great speed, and there were a number of important things I hadn't talked with him about.

I am tired of saying, "Patrick knew." Of course he knew. I discussed Lennie with him. But I must be honest again; he knew the facts but not the extremes. Or he suspected the extremes, but his failing mind only registered fear. Sex came naturally to Patrick—he always welcomed it—but he was basically a conservative man. The extremes of his life went into his music. Sex for him was like beef and potatoes; he knew nothing of crème brûlée and Dom Perignon. Well, perhaps I am unfair. I enjoyed Patrick sexually, but I was never completely involved. What I really liked was the comfort of being with him, sleeping with him, waking up, having breakfast. Walking with him in the street, arm in arm. Our conversations. We had an extraordinary friendship. I never imagined myself in a state of persistent sexual arousal about anyone, much less another woman. I think, before I met Lennie, I would have viewed such a state with bemusement, perhaps even a bit of distaste.

How ill-equipped words are to convey extremes of passion; their business is that of control.

"Let's start, where?" Bond said.

"In an orderly way, if I must leave here soon."

"All right. Start where you want."

"Much of it you know."

He nodded. "Don't let that bother you. I don't mind."

For a few moments I thought about what I wanted to say. What I needed to say. What was the trouble?

"I loved my husband," I said.

We tried again.

"There must not be a problem," I said. "Everything seems fine. I miss Patrick, that's natural. I miss Lennie, that's natural. These are things I need to get used to. They're not problems."

"All right. How do you see your life proceeding?"

A gulf opened. Closed quickly.

"Just answer quickly, Mercedes. Don't think about it."

"I see my life proceeding in a careful way."

"Careful?"

"I don't know why I used that word. I'll have to go slowly, that's all, look around me. I don't know where I'm going."

"That might become tiresome."

"So be it."

"Are you angry now?"

I rose and left the room. Without a word. I am not a rude person; I had never behaved that way with anyone. In the day room I went over to a spot behind the piano and stood watching the door. Bond didn't follow me. Perhaps our time together as doctor and patient was at an end.

The next day I apologized for walking out. We sat facing each other in a far corner of the day room. It was a quiet time, after lunch.

He smiled. "You've never done that before."

"Well, no, I wouldn't. Are you happy about it? Is it a sign of something?"

"A sign would help, wouldn't it?"

Tears sprang into my eyes, inexplicably. "Yes, it would."

He waited for a moment, very patient. Glad, I suppose, that I was finally shedding tears. But there were not enough to shed, as it turned out. "Can you give me a hint about where I should start?"

"You have lost your husband, for whom you cared a great deal."

"Yes."

"And your lover is also gone. Somewhere. We do not know."

"*We* don't and I don't."

"Your lover who introduced you to some rather surprising parts of yourself, parts that caused you considerable conflict."

"There was no conflict about the way I felt."

"And you say you signed yourself into this hospital because you wanted someone to cook for you for a while."

I couldn't suppress a laugh.

"Why the laugh?"

"I was thinking about Jean Harris."

"Jean Harris?"

"The headmistress who shot the diet doctor. She reportedly said something like that as she was taken into prison: 'At least someone else will be doing the cooking for a while.' "

"Do you plan to look for Lennie?"

"Of course not. She can look for me, if she wants me."

"See, we're clearing some things up. Does she know that Patrick is dead?"

"How would she know?"

"She might know."

"She might. I don't know how, unless she's been reading the obituaries, which seems unlikely."

"Do you imagine your life with her or without her now?"

"I never imagined my life with her before."

"Is that true?"

Of course it wasn't true. "We never spoke about it. I never expected it."

"No, you never spoke—"

"Let's talk about now. I don't imagine my life with her now."

"But—"

"I miss her."

"Yes."

"I miss her."

He nodded.

"The possibility of her." The vulnerability of my position was very clear now.

"Don't get angry, Mercedes. Just try to follow this through."

"I can follow it through. I miss her, but I'm angry at her. She woke me up—these words are impossible—she got me out there and then she just...walked away, left me there."

"Do you understand why she left?"

"Patrick came after her with his Confederate sword."

Bond smiled.

"No, I don't know why she left."

"She knew Patrick was dying. She knew her presence in your life caused him some anxiety."

"She left because she was tired of me. It was me, not him."

He looked at me calmly.

"Patrick was weakening, but he died because he allowed himself to," I said. "He was eighty-five, remember?"

"Do you feel your relationship with Lennie pushed him to that choice?"

"What melodramas you have to deal with every day," I said. "How do you keep from laughing?"

"The point is now, now you have to continue. You have to find a way to continue, and denial cannot be a part of it."

"Cannot, you say?"

"Well, of course it's your choice."

"I'm not stupid enough to deny that Patrick and Lennie are no longer in my life."

"Your physical life. No, you won't have trouble with that part."

"What else can I deny?"

"Well, what do you think? Patrick is still very much a part of your emotional memory. Do you have trouble with that?"

"No."

"And Lennie? Will you deny her a place as well?"

"It's difficult to determine where she would fit." I stood up. "And that's all I'm going to say today. I want a nap."

How many days were left?

Back in my room I took off my clothes and arranged my body before the long mirror behind the door. I remembered the days when I had actually been able to vault over a tennis net. Why I thought of that particular feat, I don't know. I did it once; more than once, often. My thighs were firm; even now they have little flab. My concern was always my bones. I peered at myself in the mirror. I was blessed with high cheekbones, but my shoulder bones are like pipes soldered together. My hips have broadened—there is no denying that—but my waistline is still eminently discernible. My breasts? I appraised them unflinchingly, hefted them in my hands. Lennie loved to lay her head between them. So did Patrick. Sagging a bit now. Average, probably. My hair was graying nicely, nearly white now, but it would be fine if I kept it short. And my face—it still had the mild look of a schoolgirl, as if everything that had happened over the last six months had simply passed it by.

It was bewildering. I had never thought about my body much, except in terms of aches and pains. Certainly I never thought of what might attract other women sexually. The possibility had never occurred to me. Lennie's body, on the other hand, had been so casually sexual and so clearly female that I was sometimes bewildered by the inevitability of my feelings about it. However, thinking about her body now is not a luxury I should allow myself.

Lennie said to me once, "I'm tired of people who don't know what they want, who have to be *coaxed*. I want somebody who'll see a light in my eye and come to me." I thought I was that person. I came to her.

I don't believe I shall ever love another person again, male or female. And that is sad. One can adjust to not being loved, but not loving is a profound deprivation.

Late that night I wandered into the day room (so-called, even at night) to see if the nurses could get me a cup of tea. No one was at the station, so I walked on into the darkness of the bigger room and went, as I often did, to stand by the window. I was hoping for a bit of fresh air; my skin felt damp and old, unpleasant. It looked like a nice night—you could tell by the brilliance of the stars that it was cold. I wondered, in a simple and curious way, where Patrick was.

"You like the stars?" A voice came from one of the chairs.

"Who's that?"

"Fumio." He emerged into the reflected light from the nurses' station.

"Oh, yes." I had seen him about. "I thought you were a doctor."

"I was."

He was in his middle forties, I had guessed, that vast playground in which death taps you on the shoulder now and then while you are still smiling toward your youth. His short, spiky hair rose like an enormous surprise straight up from his forehead and was sprinkled with gray. He was wearing glasses with small round lenses.

"I don't feel like talking," I said. "I was looking for tea. I don't mean to be rude."

"I understand," he said. "You see, these nurses go off. There are problems elsewhere, I think. They're not really needed here. They call this the housekeeping ward."

"They do?" I smiled. "Well, it is. One would think, though, maybe someone might require some help. Someone should be here."

"Yes. I require some help, and I cannot find them."

"What do you need?"

"I need to talk to someone. I understand you cannot, and that is all right. I will wait here in the dark for someone to come back."

"I think I'll go in search of some tea." The cat in the cold, the passengers in the falling jet. "I'll look for the nurses."

I heard him settle back down on the vinyl sofa, which heaved forth a crumple and a sigh. He said nothing. When I came back with two paper cups of tea, lukewarm, he hadn't moved.

"You know *Star Trek?*" he said. "The television show?"

"Yes, I know of it."

"They say space is the final frontier."

"You can talk, Fumio, but I don't want to talk. My name is Mercedes Medina, and you can go on without hearing from me."

"Space is not the final frontier. The mind is the final frontier. And it is final, because it is endless."

I heard one of the nurses come back into the station and pick up the phone. I wondered whether he would prefer talking with a nurse.

He sipped his tea. "Have you heard of the tarantula wasp?" he asked. "When the tarantula wasp is ready to lay an egg, she stings a tarantula spider, but does not kill it, just paralyzes it. The egg is deposited on top of the spider. Then the wasp puts everything in a hole in the ground. When the larva hatches it has live food to eat."

Good lord, I thought.

He held up a finger. "This is the mystery: Number one, how does the wasp know the exact spot to sting the spider so it will not die? So it will live to be food? And number two, how does the larva know how to eat the spider so it will remain alive and be good food for exactly as long as it takes for it to mature?" His teeth shone in the near darkness. "If food dies, larva dies also."

"And number three," I said, "what is the experience of the spider as it is slowly eaten alive?"

He rocked back and forth a little on the noisy couch. "History moves very slowly, as we see it. We look at that wasp and say: 'That is an efficient way to keep species going. Nature has evolved in this way, and so the spider must sacrifice itself.' And we think it has always been this way. Not true. At some point a first wasp had to sting in just the right place."

"I don't like nature," I said. "I am not entranced by flowers, or walks in the woods, or houses in the wilderness. I dislike people who are always rhapsodizing about nature."

"A rhapsody?"

"Sorry. What is your point?"

"My point is that something is going on."

"Yes." I glanced over at the nurses' station and saw that both attendants had returned. A great sadness suddenly rose in me for all those spiders who were picked, randomly, to be eaten alive, not knowing why or what purpose they served. Thinking of them, I found my eyes were full. I couldn't save them, I couldn't explain, there was no way to comfort them in their endless, torturous sacrifice.

Had the suffering god awakened?

Fumio's eyes burned out of the darkness behind his little glasses. "Think of a past crossroads in your life," he said to me. "Think of the road you took." He paused to allow me to choose this time, and I just made a motion with my hand. I had passed too many crossroads in recent years to choose one. "Now you chose one way. Somewhere in a parallel universe, the path you did not choose is evolving."

Suddenly I thought of the woman in the elevator at the Mark Hopkins in San Francisco. My honeymoon with Patrick. The woman in the gray suit in the elevator. Her pearls. Her scent. In what locked chamber of my heart was this memory still breathing, still watching me, still unwilling to disappear?

"And who is walking that path?" I asked him, because I had to say something.

"You. You are walking." His teeth gleamed again. "And some-time you may encounter this other life, in a dream, perhaps, or if you have a mental leap."

"I don't think that would be a good idea," I said, and stood up. "Give me your cup. I'll take it away."

He stood up also. "Perhaps we shall meet again. Thank you for sitting with me. I am troubled about the spiders. But it has evolved, so it must be right."

"Yes. And we must think that in a parallel life there must be spiders who got away."

He smiled and bowed slightly. I wondered whether he pondered these questions constantly. It must be exhausting.

The woman in the gray suit!

Patrick and I had been on our honeymoon, which was not significant in itself since we had been living together for several years. But I was enjoying him thoroughly. His trio was scheduled to play in Los Angeles at the end of April, and we had gone out to San Francisco ten days early.

I shared an elevator with this woman at the hotel the day after we arrived, a long slow ride down with just the two of us and the operator. I met her eyes just as I got in, then turned to face the front of the car, as we all do. There was a faint, complex scent, if I remember, not floral. Intoxicating. She wore a gray suit that fit the tall shape of her body, as was the style of the day, a white sort of shell underneath. Small, luminous pearls. I was acutely aware of her. At first I thought it was because I was wondering whether to exchange some pleasantry with her; two people alone in an elevator, after all, is not like being with a crowd. I suppose this made me tense, but I don't remember a tenseness. I remember a sort of aura that settled over us. I began to feel something was about to happen to us, something—I wouldn't have called it sexual then—physical, I suppose. I had no experience with feelings such as this. The sensation of her body next to mine made me breathe a little faster. How stupid I was not to realize what was happening. I was aware of her breathing, the sound of her body against her clothing, the slight rise and fall of her breasts, which I don't remember if I actually saw, or sensed. I almost felt myself swaying toward her (perhaps I did!) while the car moved slowly downward, humming through empty space. Our two bodies caught together in limbo.

I felt this woman's head turn to look at me, and I (the bravest thing I had ever done) turned and met her gaze. We smiled as if we secretly recognized each other. And I remember a feeling, a soft pull downward, that had nothing to do with the descending car.

We arrived in the lobby, the doors slid open, and there was Patrick, brimming with delight. For a moment I couldn't move, then I held out my hand to him, and the woman in the gray suit passed close behind my back and away. I wanted to follow her with my eyes, but instead I put my cheek on Patrick's shoulder and gripped him tightly, wondering what storm had passed so close and left me behind, clinging to driftwood.

The woman was usually alone, for I saw her several times in the dining room, absorbed in making tiny calculations in a leather notebook. Once, however, I spotted her in the bar, in the company of a large man with a sandy mustache who kept brushing her shortish blond hair away from her forehead with one of his large hands. I had the feeling they had not just met.

"Do you know her, Merce?" Patrick asked me at dinner. He saw me watching her table.

I told him we had ridden down in the elevator together. "Do *you* know her?"

Patrick looked hard. "Not my type."

The thought of this woman bothered me, I remember, and the possibility of meeting her again in the elevator made me anxious and excited. While I made love with Patrick that night, her face came into my mind once or twice, and I—without hesitation—groaned and clasped him tighter. Afterward I felt elated, sexually, and then troubled, because I felt I had created something false. And I don't think I analyzed it any other way.

Then it was time for us to go to Los Angeles. On the evening before our departure the woman was in the dining room with the man with the mustache. When I looked toward her table I saw her head bent close to his in intense conversation.

When Patrick got up to go and buy a cigar in the lobby I had an overwhelming urge to do something—I had no idea what—but the situation was completely foreign to me, I didn't know what was possible. I could have sat there all night simply looking at her, watching her move, watching her smile. Beyond that I could not imagine.

So she finally rose, said something to the man, and turned in the direction of our table. She had something in her hand. I was suddenly terrified, as if I had ventured too close to a battlefield and found myself in the midst of falling mortar fire. But she had no intention of confronting me in any way. As she passed my table she did not pause, but placed a single gardenia beside my hand. She and Patrick passed at the door.

I didn't attempt to conceal the flower, and for some reason Patrick made no mention of it—which was odd, because Patrick did not miss much. I took it back to New York with me, pressed between the pages of the program from the trio's concert. And somewhere, in my boxes in the closet, it still must be.

The memory of her lost its intensity during the months that followed, but never fully retreated. Certain sensations could bring her to my mind immediately: the scent of a gardenia (of course), a gray suit with a particular cut, the downward pull of a descending elevator. But I never quite figured out what part I had played in this experience. Or what part I could have played.

I was not naive at that age. I knew about women who loved other women, and felt this was their business and not a moral issue.

Certainly, traveling about with Patrick I had met several lesbians. Now I see that experience in San Francisco as an unmistakable indication of a powerful turn in the road. A turn I nearly missed.

Others have many lovers in their life; I am not the type. I do wonder sometimes what I may have missed. But Lennie came when I was ready for her, or for the experience she brought—that might be more accurate. She came when I was ready for her and left before we had finished. Then, of course, Patrick left permanently. These are the two in my life that I have loved unconditionally. I am not silly enough to imagine that the woman in the gray suit would have meant anything to me. But it is depressing to contemplate my life from this point on, without friends who might understand my longings, who might be dealing with the problems of romantic love as they approach sixty. Are there others? There must be. But no way to get to them. And would I want to, if truth were told? I would not be comfortable with groups of people who assembled together for no other reason than a shared sexual preference. Or any preference, for that matter. I don't count myself part of any of these groups.

I have always been strong and I must rely on that now. I am strong, I have interests, several projects in mind, and I can count on a few friends to fill the hours. There is still much to do about Patrick's things, his papers, his music.

And, of course, my own work.

"How many days do I have?" I asked Bond.

"This is Wednesday. You should plan to be out of here by Friday, if not before."

"Friday."

"Will you have trouble with that?"

"No. No."

Some time went by.

"You're quiet today," he said.

"Why don't you ask me some questions. Something you don't already know."

"All right." He gazed out the window for a moment. "What will you do with your time at home?"

"I'll find that out when I get there, I suppose."

"You told me once you were working on a translation of a novel by an Italian author. A major work, if I'm not mistaken."

"I can't remember why I should have spoken to you about that."

"It seemed important to you."

"It was important to me once that I finish it. Well, the first draft is nearly finished, in fact, but I have no real interest in it now."

"Perhaps you could get back to it."

"I don't feel compelled to create an agenda for myself."

"Do you understand why I'm concerned?"

"I suppose you feel you have to keep an eye on me, make sure I'm occupied. I assure you I'm not thinking of suicide."

"No, I'm not worried about that. There are ways to end your life other than killing yourself."

I watched him and said nothing. He would have to come to me with this one.

"Look." He leaned forward with his arms resting on his thighs. "You have lost a husband for whom you cared very much, and another relationship that you were just beginning to explore. You're being far too rational about it."

"My lack of emotion? Is that what's bothering you?"

"Well, I think the emotion's there. I don't believe you asked to come here because there wasn't emotion."

"There is nothing to be gained by letting emotion get in the way right now."

"Get in the way of what?"

"In the way of life."

He nodded. "You do plan to have a life, then."

"Don't patronize me."

"I'm asking you to look at the question."

"All right."

"Look at it before it sabotages you."

"All right." I got up. "Who is that Asian man I see about? I think he's a patient. Fumio is his name."

He looked at me a long while before answering. "Ask him who he is, he'll tell you."

"I just don't feel that anything you can say will have the slightest effect on how my so-called life will progress."

"I'm not interested in what I say. I'm interested in what you say."

"This is a very personal, very private matter."

"I understand that."

I paced over to the window. "I'll just say this, that if you're in some way trying to cast blame on me because I'm not raking my breast and crying over Patrick's death, you haven't been listening to me for the last year or so. I was grieving for him long before he died. Patrick was an old man, he was eighty-five, his mind was failing, and his body, but he'd had a good life. He did everything he'd ever wanted to do, he'd had his music, he'd loved well—and he'd had others besides me, I knew it. But we belonged together. And we were together. I stayed with him, right to the end. And I shall miss him dreadfully. But I can do that without grieving in paroxysms."

"Blame is not an issue here at all."

I leaned my back against the wall beside the window. "You never thought my relationship with Lennie amounted to much, did you?"

"Why do you say that?"

"Because when you talk to me about it, your tone changes. You talk to me as if I were a child."

"I certainly took it seriously because it was obvious you did. And we haven't talked about it much. You chose to tell me less than a month ago."

"I suppose you were interested in it from a pathological point of view, your patient returning to her pubescent years."

"Is that how you thought of it?"

"I'm talking about how you thought of it."

"My thoughts aren't the issue here."

"Of course they are. I long for you to approve of this girlish experience, don't you see? Validate it a bit."

"Why?"

So I can, I almost said. "In my life I have always finished what I began. I like to tie things up, and I don't believe this is a negative trait. Lennie is a mysterious thing that began and then simply stopped, without any sense of a real ending. I feel the need to end it, and I need her complicity in this. But it seems unlikely that I'll get it. So I'll have to find some way to close it up myself. I don't know how exactly, but day by day perhaps it will work out." I looked at him straight on. "Now, that's an adult way to handle things, isn't it?"

"It seems like an admirable goal."

"Not a solution a fourteen-year-old could come up with."

He smiled.

From my cradle, my knuckles in my mouth, I smiled back at him.

That night I watched a cold full moon rise through a snow mist into a black, bitter sky. Lennie hated the cold. Why was Bond forcing me to think about where she might be?

Sweetheart, I thought. *Where are you?*

Untidy words, like an unmade bed. I wanted to shut the door on that messy room.

My life had been a still life. Very still. Then Lennie came and a banquet became alive on that canvas; she was the banquet, and I seated myself at that table with joy. Now the table is abandoned, as in a painting by Vermeer; the bread lies in crumbles, the knife with a small crust of cheese along its blade. The tablecloth is rumpled, the plates quiet with the remains of bones. An orange peel is curled by the clear green wine glass with the twisted, graceful stem. The napkins, having scrubbed greasy mouths, are balled by the plates, the chairs pushed back, the blue water jug empty, the attendants gone. This banquet I had been foolish enough to believe would go on—for a while, at least—is concluded. I am not a fool. I do not believe in life after death. I do not expect kindness from strangers. Things are as they are.

But Lennie is gone. She woke me from a life of sleep, and now I discover I have no reason to stay awake.

I sat in the day room on Friday and waited for Bond to bring me my papers to sign. Fumio stood by the big window overlooking the courtyard, and I thought briefly of speaking to him; then I decided that our conversation had been one of those encounters one sometimes has in the night that should simply remain part of night's darkness.

Bond arrived with the papers, which I signed without reading. I accepted some prescriptions and prepared to depart.

"We have an appointment next Tuesday," he said.

"Yes."

"I want you to keep it."

I nodded.

"How are you getting home?"

"Valentina Bird. You met her at my apartment door, when you both came to rescue me."

He smiled. "Ah, yes."

"She's my dearest friend, Bond. She won't let me slip away from you."

"I'm not worried at all." He looked at me. "Ready to go?"

I wasn't. I imagined the ride back into the city, along the colorless, late-winter river, the filthy remains of snow lying along the roadsides in black, leather-like patches, the rooms of my apartment, dusty and airless, unless Tina, of course, in her great goodness, had gone in and brightened the place up. This would be like her, and I should probably steel myself to expect flowers, shining tables, and the smell of cinnamon. And fresh sheets.

"I don't suppose," I said, "there's anyplace else I can go?"

Bond had taken my elbow and was guiding me toward the elevators. "What did you say? Where would you like to go?"

"There's nothing at home," I said. "Nothing."

He turned me to face him. "I know this is a cliché," he said, "but try simply one hour at a time. Don't look forward. Don't imagine anything. I'll give you a call tonight."

Outside it was a pale day. Pale, March, still cold. I walked into it.

{ 11 }

In Love

P atrick noticed the damage to the Whistler first.

"Here," he said one morning. "This thing looks a little wacko."

Mrs. Medina came up behind him and took off her reading glasses. "Now, how did that glass get cracked?" she said.

"The painters."

"The painters were here last spring."

"You don't need to remind me, Merce. They woke me up every morning at six-thirty, and that Hungarian one stole a bottle of my Black Jack." He blew his nose loudly on his red-checked handkerchief. "You should have hidden that painting away, since it means so much to you."

"It's not a painting, Patrick. Look, they cracked the glass and the paper is torn. And they never said a thing."

"Your little Venetian trifle. Well, look at it now."

"Patrick, go get on some shoes or your slippers, or something."

"What's for lunch?"

"Lunch." She sighed. "Look at this, this dirt that's filtered through the crack in the glass." She put her glasses back on. "Well, I'll just have to have it repaired."

"Is the mail in, do you think? What time is it?"

"Nearly eleven." She stood and looked at the etching, then carefully removed it from the wall. "I don't know if anyone can repair the paper."

"Oh, forget it, Merce. Put some tape over it or something. Come over here and look at this bench across the street. Someone's painting it red."

"If I don't repair it, Patrick, it will just get worse."

"Throwing good money after bad."

"Bad money? A Whistler?" She carried it over to the window to see it in better light. "Look, already the paper is discolored."

"That trinket reminds me of a very bad period in my life. I thought you had left me when you went out across the canals to buy this thing. I don't think kindly of anything this Whistler ever did, because of that upsetting time."

She looked at him in amazement. "Well, don't blame Whistler," she said. "And I wasn't leaving you."

"Well, we won't argue about it."

"No. We won't." She walked into the dining room. "I'm going to call Bonnie Friedman at the Fogg. If you want your lunch, go get something on your feet." She stood for a moment in the kitchen door. *But I was thinking about leaving*, she remembered. *I was considering it.*

"Why are they painting that bench?" he said, following her.

Bonnie agreed to let one of her crew take a look at the damage. "Just wrap old Whistler up and bring him over here," she said. "We'll get you a report in a couple of weeks. If you come over tomorrow, I'll take you to lunch at the Faculty Club. How's that darling husband of yours?"

"Very well."

"Still full of pepper?"

"I think you could say that."

"Not playing much now, though, right?"

"Well, he plays, Bonnie, sometimes with friends, but he doesn't perform anymore."

"That's a loss for all of us."

~

It was a loss for her as well.

At the age of fifty-nine, not old at all in her book, Mercedes Medina was slowly coming to suspect that most of the important events of her life had come and gone. Patrick's failing health had a lot to do with her feeling, but in fact she had been relieved when Patrick decided to retire. She had loved their travels together, his music, the concerts in exotic cities, but she wanted to unpack for good now, and put the luggage away.

Patrick had saved her, she believed, from a life of self-indulgent loneliness. Their professional lives had been separate but shared, although there was certainly more of his to be generous with. During the months she was teaching he proclaimed interest, but his curiosity extended primarily to her students, young female ones especially; that was the way he was. Until recent years his trio was on the road for more than half the year, and she was with him as much as she could arrange to be. Now that life was over.

Lennie Visitor entered her life on a day she could not decide what to give Patrick for dinner, sole or macaroni and cheese.

She hadn't expected to end up at a florist's that Thursday; she didn't have anything on her mind, in fact, except anxiety about the etching. In later romantic moments she imagined that the entire morning had been a slow progression toward an inevitable door, which was standing just ajar. Afterward, that is, she thought this. Afterward, the Whistler became unimportant.

She was wearing her Harris tweed jacket for the first time that fall, and the red and gold Hermès scarf Patrick had bought her in Zurich.

~

"Well, Mercedes," Bonnie said at lunch. "Here we are again." They were working on a cream of mushroom soup that had heated up the spoons. "And don't think I'm going to let you avoid the issue."

Mrs. Medina smiled.

"When are you going to cross the river and teach over here? The Romance Language Department is full of holes right now. They'd probably hire you in a minute."

"They'd have me teaching Italian 101, wouldn't they, without a Ph.D. I'm spoiled. I can teach what I want now. My own schedule." She wiped her mouth. "In any case, my department head is a friend, she counts on me."

"Well, eventually..."

"Yes, eventually I may think about it." She thought of having nothing but her teaching, when Patrick was gone. That, no doubt, was the way things would proceed. But that part of her life hung ahead of her in the dark.

"Well," Bonnie said afterward, as they made their way back across the Yard toward Harvard Square. "I'll walk you as far as the gate." Bonnie was narrow and nearly six feet tall, and Mrs. Medina had to hurry her steps to keep up with her leggy pace. As they parted Bonnie said, "Check out the preposterous window display at Pittino's. I think Guido's already practicing for next year's flower show."

The day was soft, hazy, and full of wind. She walked along Church Street looking into the shops, and wandered on, although Patrick was on her mind. She felt oddly detached, as if it were the afternoon before a journey, and a long night flight lay ahead of her. The window display at Pittino's was even more disorienting, and featured what she thought was a 19th-century English drawing room interior in which a violent explosion of mums and zinnias had taken place. But it drew her in.

She had to push through nets of ferns and displays of rocks and falling water to get into the larger part of the flower shop. The aroma of fresh earth was overpowering, as if she had arrived on a lush, damp island that might at any moment spring forth with the echoing sound of macaws or the creak of bamboo.

And there was the heady scent of gardenias.

Behind the main counter Guido Pittino waved her forward. He was on the telephone. "Here, Len, help the lady," he said. "I've still got Waterman's on the line."

A young woman unfolded herself from underneath the counter. She was tall and clear-eyed and had a direct look about her. That is, her face was plainly pretty without frills or pretense. She had a wide mouth that was smiling as if she really had something to be happy about, as if she and Mrs. Medina were old friends and hadn't seen each other for a while. She had a flat box full of gardenias in her arms, and lifted it casually toward Mrs. Medina's nose for her to smell.

Mrs. Medina, startled, took a polite sniff.

"Too sweet, right?" the young woman said. "Too many. One gardenia is more than I can handle." She cocked her head. "Or maybe you like them."

"I don't know," Guido said into the telephone. "I don't know if I can *get* three dozen yellow roses by tonight."

The young woman looked around for a spot to put the gardenias down, and finally bent over and placed them back on the floor. "What'll it be?" she asked, straightening up. "Sorry you can't have the gardenias." She brushed her hands off. "I saw you looking. They're corsages for some big thing at the Faculty Club." She put her hands on her hips and smiled as if they were sharing a private joke.

What's this about? Mrs. Medina thought, returning her smile hesitantly. *Have I met her somewhere?*

Her hair featured several different shades of blond, with some darker evidences underneath, and wandered back over her ears to the nape of her neck, where it came to rest in a thick clump of curls. It had a sort of wet look. In her left ear was a gold hoop. Her complexion suggested that she was probably a real blond, and Mrs. Medina detected a faint spicy scent that either came from the girl or from some nearby floral arrangement; she couldn't be sure. She swayed, slightly, and put her hand on the counter to steady herself. The girl had on a white T-shirt under a gray cotton pullover.

"So, you want something delivered, or you want to take something away?" She met Mrs. Medina's gaze directly and her eyes seemed to be amused about something.

Mrs. Medina nodded, and cleared her throat. "Yes," she said.

"Yes...?" She opened her hands. "Yes?" She gave a little laugh.

A small card lay on the counter waiting to be put in with one of those overly cute arrangements that went out in footballs or red glass hearts. Someone had written, *Why did you leave without waking me up? Thanks for an unforgettable night.*

"Well, maybe you just came in to say hi," the girl said brightly.

"Lennie! Get the other phone, will you? I'll take care of the lady."

"Try the freesia. Just came in," Lennie whispered.

Guido came up behind Lennie and moved her toward the other telephone. "Phone," he said. "Sorry, madam. How may I help you?"

"The young..." Mrs. Medina began. "The young woman was saying...about the freesia..."

"The white roses are excellent," Guido said, smoothing his dark mustache with his forefinger and thumb. "Or a fall arrangement, perhaps? Japonica? Nerine?" He gestured to the large refrigerator behind him.

The young woman called Lennie was standing at the large back counter to the right of the refrigerator door. She stood with her weight on one foot, one hand on her hip, talking—quite a graceful pose, actually—and Mrs. Medina saw what she thought was a small pigtail hanging down beneath the bunch of curls at the nape of her neck. Now she bent over to write. She laughed. She looked over her shoulder and gave Mrs. Medina the briefest of looks.

"Madam?" Guido repeated.

"Freesia mix," Mrs. Medina said quickly.

"Freesia mix, certainly."

"Three."

"Three bunches, freesia mix. Cash or charge?"

"I'll write a check," Mrs. Medina said. "But—" she smiled. "Just—I'm curious, just for the future, of course, what exactly is nerine?" She fumbled in her bag for her checkbook. "Or is it nerines? What are nerines exactly?" She saw Lennie hang up the telephone and go through the door into the large refrigerator.

"Nerines, madam. Certainly. Nerines are these. These beautiful pinks here. Similar to a lily."

"Lovely, lovely," Mrs. Medina said. The nerines had tall stems and delicate, tongue-like petals. She touched one with the tip of her finger. "They're quite nice, aren't they?"

"Plus tax." Guido attacked the cash register with a flourish.

There was a crash behind him.

"*Ah, Dio!*" He threw up his hands and raced toward Lennie, who had emerged from the refrigerator with pieces of broken glass in her hands. "Careless, careless girl!" He disappeared inside, among the irises. "Go," he shouted from within, "finish with the lady. I will bring the freesia." He slammed the door furiously.

Lennie wiped her hands on a paper towel. "Cold in there," she said. "My hands slipped."

Mrs. Medina looked down at her own hands, fiddled with the clasp of her leather billfold. "Are you bleeding?" she asked. "Maybe you should get a bandage."

"Nah. Happens all the time. Cheap glass, breaks easy. How far did he get with you? Oh yeah, here's your check. I have to look at your license." She sang under her breath as she wrote down the numbers. "If I didn't know better, if I didn't know..." She took her full lower lip between her teeth, then looked up. "You Portuguese?" she asked.

Mrs. Medina shook her head.

"Your name." She handed the license back. "Medina."

"Oh, no. My husband's family was Spanish, but quite a while back."

Lennie lifted her hand to smooth her hair back behind her ears. There was a small cut on her index finger, and the tiny smear of blood suddenly seemed uncomfortably intimate.

"He's from Virginia, actually," Mrs. Medina said firmly.

"The sunny southland." The smell of the gardenias rose like ether. "See something else you like?" Lennie said. She leaned back from the counter and tilted her head.

Mrs. Medina looked at her, uncertain, irritated, beginning a strange unraveling. Then Guido swept by and left the wrapped package of freesia on the desk.

"Ever seen a blue rose? Look at this." Lennie held up a rose-like flower that was indeed a deep purplish blue, the color perhaps of a vibrant bruise, or the clouds that sometimes gather low on the horizon just after sunset.

"A blue rose," Mrs. Medina said. She cast about furiously for something else to say.

"Lisianthus," Lennie said professionally. "It isn't really a rose, just looks like one. A guy in one of my classes told me about how he used them in a couple of his gardens. So I told Guido to order some. Wait a minute." She reached under the counter and got out a dog-eared notebook of what looked like class notes. "Vase life, two weeks," she said after a moment. She put the notebook under her arm. "Here, take it." She twisted a bit of tissue and paper around the stem and held it out.

"Why," Mrs. Medina said, flustered, "thank you. But..."

"Go on, take it. Look, we've got two huge boxes here full of them. Things were a little crazy in here today. We want to keep the customers coming back, you know." She moved her torso from side to side. "Don't we?"

"Oh, yes," Mrs. Medina said. She was clutching the rose in her hand. "All right."

"All right—?"

"I'll come back."

"O-o-okay. That's cool." The phone rang. She turned away to answer it, and Mrs. Medina knew she had been immediately forgotten. "Well, hello," Lennie said in a lower voice. "Hello, hello. What're you up to?"

Mrs. Medina walked calmly through the ferns and out into the stupor of the Indian summer afternoon.

She moved quickly away from the shop as if she had some immediate purpose, walking steadily without knowing where she was going. She paused briefly and considered going back to explain why she had made that inane comment at the end—"I'll come back"—as if it were important! She still clutched the extraordinary blue flower tightly in her hand. Three-thirty, the clock in the Square said.

She strode toward Mount Auburn Street and went into Café Paradiso finally, and sat down. "What do I want?" she said to the waiter, and he responded with a smile, "You want a double vanilla latte." And so she got it. It was fate. She never ordered flavored coffees.

She lay the flower on the table in front of her. The freesia now were a burden. *Lennie*, she thought. *What kind of a name is that? Why did she speak to me so outrageously? As if she knew me?* She thought a moment. Well, perhaps she did know her. What was so familiar about this girl? Someone's daughter, a friend's daughter? She ran some names through her mind. *I would have remembered her*, she thought. *Surely.*

Near the cash register was a slowly revolving display of Italian pastries of various sorts—cannoli, cream puffs, and a lovely olive-colored pear tart. "How much for a couple of pieces of the tart?" she asked the woman behind the counter when she went to pay. "Oh, just give me the whole thing, why don't you?" She smiled. "It's a beautiful day."

She circled around the Square for a while, not really knowing why, and after a half hour finally went into Au Bon Pain and bought a cup of tea. She took it outside to the terrace. The afternoon was growing chilly as the sun fell, and she leaned over her black China tea, breathing the steam. When the girl appeared, Mrs. Medina realized she'd been expecting her, and she waited calmly for her to pass by. Carrying the flat box of gardenias, now covered, Lennie crossed the Square against the light, dodging the traffic. She had long legs; a long, even gait. She had put on a black leather jacket, not new, with some faded red stitching on the back that Mrs. Medina could not read. Her face was smooth and determined in the gathering dusk, and the last of the sun glowed against her curls.

She crossed Massachusetts Avenue as the traffic eased, and passed from sight.

Patrick was surprisingly calm about her late return.

"I wondered," he said. He seemed engrossed in plotting something on one of his Civil War maps. He looked up. "What have you got there? Flowers for me? What are these, freebles? What do you call them?"

"Freesia, Patrick."

"A delicate flower for the faint maidens of old. Look a bit wilted, Merce. Find 'em in a trash can? Oh, don't draw yourself up—I can see the wrapping, can't I?"

"Look what I've bought us for dinner." She displayed the tart.

Patrick had a sweet tooth. "Delizioso," he said. "What's the occasion?"

"No occasion."

"You're jazzed up all of a sudden. Who's up your sleeve?"

She peered up the sleeve of her blouse. "No one. Sorry."

"Well, calm down. Your vibrations are disturbing my deliberations about General Beau."

"Right," she said.

"Time for my snort anyway."

In the kitchen she put the tart on the counter and got out a crystal bud vase for her flower. She took it to her bedside table.

"There," she said.

She went and fixed herself a gin and bitters, and took it back to Patrick's room with his evening Black Jack.

"Good afternoon?" he asked her. "Get Whistler into surgery?"

"Yes. Prognosis good." This was the sort of conversation she needed. And the kind that she and Patrick were practiced at having.

"How much?" he said.

"How much—"

"Moolah. How much will they take you for?"

"Well, I'll have to wait to hear from Bonnie. They couldn't tell me anything today."

"There'll be visiting hours, no doubt." He sipped his whiskey almost daintily.

She hadn't considered that. "I suppose I could go back and check on how it's coming along."

"Given yourself a mission again. Well, look." He pointed at the television with his glass. "There's been snow already in Montana. Bad sign."

"Well, I see it as a good sign," she said. "The seasons change. It's nature, it's natural. We're lucky things change."

He gave her a skeptical look. "You're nuts," he said.

~ *two* ~

That was Thursday. During the night on Friday she was overtaken by a sudden flu that woke her in the night with a throat so sore she had to grip the sides of the bed to swallow. She got up and smashed some ice cubes with Patrick's silver ice hammer and took them back to bed. The pain was delicious, and the ice slid down her swollen throat with a silken quickness, like frozen, anesthetizing jewels. Once before she had had this experience with throat pain, when her tonsils had been removed, in those days a bloody and excruciating procedure. She had asked for buttered toast as soon as she could eat, to the bewilderment of her mother, and the feel of the salty crusts on her raw throat was half pain, half ecstasy.

By dawn her fever was up to 102, and the blue lisianthus by her bed had assumed an aura of stark, almost vocal intensity, as if it were a tiny cloud on the leading edge of a dark storm, and she lay on her side and watched it curiously. Patrick was worried. He paced around outside her room as if—she imagined in her stupor—he were a wolf waiting for her to die so he could tear off her flesh.

"Come in, Patrick," she croaked at him.

He put his hand on her brow and looked at his watch. She found this gesture wildly funny, and her laugh sounded bright and brilliant, like a strobe light in her head.

Slowly she gave Patrick instructions about his breakfast.

"I'm going to call Harry Max," he said. "Time for the doc."

She put up both her hands and shook her head. Her nightgown was soaked with sweat. If Harry came she would have to change. *Even a doctor deserves a clean nightgown*, she thought. In a small corner of her mind she was alert to the problem of Patrick wandering about the apartment on his own, possibly burning himself on the stove, or slipping.

"Don't turn on the stove," she whispered to him as he hung up the phone.

"I told him you had a fever of one-oh-four," he said. "That's about right, isn't it? He's going to call a prescription in to Phillips and ask them to send someone over with it." He bent down close to her face and stared into her eyes. "Somewhere you're in there, aren't you, Merce?"

She nodded.

"Don't go away too far." He looked at the lisianthus and sniffed it. "Well," he said, "I have to eat."

He brought his bowl of cereal into her room and sat and ate it and watched her slip in and out of sleep. Then he went and got his maps and spread them over her rug. He fetched her more crushed ice, which she heard him bashing away at, and every fifteen minutes or so he came and stared at her eyes, whether they were open or shut. She felt his dry hand on her forehead. Her dreams were filled with reds and blues and brilliant light. In one of them the woman in the gray suit made one of her periodic visits, smiling in a sort of golden aura, silently holding out a large book that was elaborately decorated with pages of flowers that seemed to be alive.

She rolled and tossed, first sweating with heat, then shaking with chills.

When the prescription was delivered Patrick brought in a cup of lukewarm chicken broth and some ginger ale. "I did this in the micro thing, but it didn't heat it right. You must have this medicine, Merce, and Harry says you have to take it with something in your stomach." He presented her with a large orange pill.

She was touched by his gestures, and rose on one elbow and forced herself to drink the broth, take the pill; the salt, in fact, soothed her throat. She drank it for Patrick. *I guess this is love too*, she thought. She sank back down on her pillow.

She was vaguely aware of the scent of tuna fish in the room and the smell of Patrick's whiskey. But she had no idea whatsoever about what time of day it was. When Patrick brought his cello in she realized it was dark again; he played a Bach cello suite sweetly for five or ten minutes, and she felt soothed and content and exhausted. She opened her eyes and saw him clearly for the first time that day. He stopped.

"Finish," she said weakly.

"I finish, you take your pill."

"Just play."

"Stubborn wench." But he went on, closing his eyes, his arm shaky but his fingers true.

When she looked again he was sitting in the chair with another bowl of cereal. He put it down. "Now another pill," he said, coming to the bed.

When that was finished, she said, "Patrick, you can't just eat cereal. There's some leftover macaroni and cheese in the icebox."

He shook his head. "Too much trouble."

Then she made a move to get up. "Down," he said. "I'm fine." But she began to worry, although not enough to get up and cook. Her legs could barely carry her to the bathroom. *Legs*, she thought, and without hesitation remembered the girl's legs in her jeans, her long legs. *What is this?* she wondered. *Has she made me ill?* And this thought frightened her.

That night she slept fitfully, with a dim lamp on. She could swallow now, and around four she woke with a great hunger. She tacked down the hall to the kitchen and ate the macaroni and cheese cold from the casserole dish, and drank a large glass of ginger ale. Afterward she brushed her teeth and changed her gown.

"Merce," Patrick's voice called from his room.

She went down the hall to him.

"Are you well now?"

"I'm better. The pills seem to be working."

"You frightened me."

"Thank you for taking care of me."

"I made a mess of your room. I had several picnics in there."

She smiled. "I didn't notice."

"I'll run the Hoover tomorrow."

"Don't worry, Patrick. I hope you don't get this too. Go to sleep now." She touched his cheek.

"What a relief," he said. "That's over."

"Yes," she agreed. "I think it is."

She went back to her room and picked her way among the maps and crumbs and plates, and fell back into bed. She felt the disease beginning to settle into her chest. *I guess it's Sunday now*, she thought.

In the morning she woke and lay quietly for a while, exhausted, completely peaceful. She had never been sick so suddenly before, never since she was a child and diseases came and went as a natural part of life, and she was granted those marvelous, long days tucked away among the blankets, reading, while everyone else was at school, and her mother had brought her hot lemonade. She touched her throat, her chest, which was now tightening up, her thighs, which were aching.

Beside her bed the flower was as fresh and lustrous as if it had just been painted.

She sat up and swung herself to the side of the bed and gathered her strength for a few moments. The remains of Patrick's picnics were strewn about on the far side of the room. It was early, about seven-thirty. She made her way slowly through the mess, picking up plates and glasses and napkins and a little pile of olive pits he had carefully arranged on the table.

He came into the kitchen as she was starting the coffee.

"So," he said, peering around at her face.

"I'm back," she smiled, but her voice caught and she began to cough.

"Coffee is my thing to do," he said. "I'll do it."

"I'll tell you what," she said, feeling the weakness in her legs again, "I'll fix us a bit of breakfast and you can serve me in bed."

"Good," he said. "Good. I don't need to get dressed, do I?"

Sleep pulled her softly down, but she propped herself up in bed, prepared to act like a queen. *How stale it is in here*, she noticed. She wrinkled her nose and got up again and threw open the window, and the air was mild and full of sun and galloped into the curtains.

"Merce!" Patrick said, who did not believe in fresh air. He put down the rickety tray and marched with purpose toward the open window.

"Don't touch it, Patrick," she said, getting back into bed. "I'm longing for air."

"Not wise, Signora."

"Come on, let's eat."

"You'll get pneumonia," he muttered. But he began to butter his toast. "It's your room," he added. "Your turf."

"Yes."

"Your body, as I have always said."

"Did Al bring up the papers?"

"I didn't look. You want me to read you the news of the world?" His face brightened. This was something he sometimes liked her to do for him.

"I'm going right back to sleep, I'm afraid." She began to cough a little and had to steady her coffee cup. "You're sweet to bring me my breakfast in bed. I don't know what happened to me. I haven't been that sick in years."

"Well, something attacked you. You brought it back with you from Cambridge. Probably something you ate." He lifted his head. "Shrimp, probably. Did you have shrimp?" Somewhere during his life he had acquired a bitter distrust of shrimp.

She smiled to herself. "No. No shrimp." Then she said, "What will you do with yourself today?" She placed her empty plate on her bedside table, beside the flower.

"It's my week to do the *Times* crossword."

"So it is."

"And Santino said he might come by." He scraped the last of his eggs up noisily. "He's looking for a new pianist. He wants my advice."

Mrs. Medina had the feeling that someone, somewhere, was putting together a jigsaw puzzle. The pieces were coming together with an inevitable but frightening rightness, and there no longer seemed to be so many loose voices whipping about, demanding her attention.

"So," Patrick said, "I told Santino you had a run-in with her one night and that you would give him all the dire details."

She opened her eyes. "A run in with whom?"

"Mags Krivatsy."

"Patrick, for heaven's sake, that was ages ago. Why does Santino need to know about that?"

"Pay attention, Merce, I've just been telling you! Santino's considering her for his new accompanist."

"Well, she's very good. Don't you think?"

"Merce, you nearly knocked her block off in the Ritz Bar! Santino will want to know this!"

"I was never ever close to knocking anyone's block off. We had a small disagreement. And she's a fine pianist, no matter how much she irritates me."

"I enjoyed every minute of that evening."

Mrs. Medina laughed weakly. "Yes, I imagine you did."

"You called her a mad Hungarian."

"Well, she was. She is. We'd both had a little too much to drink that night, if I recall. Patrick, Patrick, I must sleep now. You and Santino settle this—you don't need me."

He looked hurt but gathered his plate and cup and walked slowly toward the door.

"Take mine too, please, Patrick. And soak them."

"Women's work."

"Thanks for your company. If you get hungry, eat some of that pear tart."

"I'll give some to Santino. That window should be closed, Merce."

"I want it open, thank you, Patrick." Her cough was rough and loose now, and it didn't worry her. Her bed was warm and promised dreams.

She slept deeply. At one point Patrick stuck his head around the door and said, "Say hello to Santino, Merce." She smiled and waved her hand a little. "Hang in there, Mercedes," Santino said. Later Santino, who was a good cook, brought in a bowl of penne with his own homemade tomato sauce, and a large ginger ale with ice. "I'll just leave it," he said quietly. "Eat it when you want." He placed a cloth napkin over the bowl.

Sometime during the late afternoon she awoke again, quite lucid; the wind had died down, and there was a stillness about the light that reminded her of early summer.

The next morning she wanted simple things. She was hungry

again; she wanted fresh orange juice with pulp clinging to the glass, two slices of warm toast with melted butter, and tea with honey. She wanted to take a long shower with fragrant soap, and wash the fever out of her hair, and put on her mauve silk shirt, her thin black cotton trousers with the deep pockets.

She rose on one elbow. *I'll call Michael and have my hair cut*, she thought. She had slept all night with the windows wide open. She smiled, and then heard Patrick in the kitchen.

Mrs. Medina wafted unsteadily into the kitchen. Patrick was swearing at the coffeepot. She kissed him on the cheek.

"This goddamn thing has blown up," he said. He tapped its lid and studied it.

She reached around him and plugged it in. "Works better that way," she said.

He turned around to face her, frowning. "What are you doing up? Shouldn't you be ringing for room service? Look at you, all dressed and smelling like a reception at the French embassy."

She peered into the refrigerator as the coffee began to perk. "I'd like a peach, I think," she said. "Something juicy."

"Maybe I should go and shave." He rubbed his chin. "Do you think you'll cook?"

"What do you want?"

He affected a pensive look but then replied, "Eggs, I guess," as he always did.

"No need to shave before breakfast. Here's your juice."

"No peaches?"

"Not much of anything. You've cleaned us out. I'll go out and get some things after a bit." There was the pear tart. Patrick had cut a large wedge out of it, and this made it look real, no longer a work of art. That was fine.

He was twirling the cord of his pajama bottoms. "I don't get it," he said. "Yesterday I thought I might lose you to the vapors of eternity."

"Well," she patted his cheek. She put a couple of woven place mats on the kitchen table. "No more picnics in my room," she said. "What a mess, Patrick."

"I told Santino I would get you well." He sounded disappointed.

"And you did. You took very good care of me. I'm still weak, Patrick. You'll probably have to take care of me later today."

"I'll make you a cup of tea."

"Because I'm going over to Newbury Street to have my hair cut."

"What?" He came around to stand between her and the table. She was holding a fistful of knives and forks. "I won't have it. You can't go. You're just up from a bout with the plague."

"It's just a short walk. I'll see Michael and come straight home." She took the eggs from the refrigerator. "One egg or two?"

He put his hands on his hips. "Something's up with you, Merce. Are you still taking those orange pills Harry sent over? You have to take them until they run out."

"Yes. I am. The coffee's finished. Do the grounds, please, Patrick."

three

The girl, Lennie, kept creeping into Mrs. Medina's mind. Mainly her voice, the look she had given Mrs. Medina over her shoulder. She would be there, and Mrs. Medina would push her out, not allowing herself curiosity or speculation, a denial that in itself was unexplainable. This effort exhausted her after a while, but she was able to wait a week before she returned and walked into the shop, trusting that an excuse would occur to her. She had no idea what she was doing, or why. At first there seemed to be no one around, then Guido emerged from the refrigerator, his arms full of mums.

"Yes." He came toward her, smiling. "Yes?"

There was no sign of Lennie.

Guido put the flowers down on the counter and gave her a quizzical glance and waited. Beside the flowers was a stack of green pamphlets called "How to Grow Healthy Gesneriads."

"Madam would like—?" Guido offered.

"Yes," Mrs. Medina said. "Last week I was in and I wonder if I might have left my umbrella here. Blue, with green stripes."

Guido shook his head. "I'm sorry, no."

"I foolishly left it somewhere."

He took a perfunctory look under the counter, then smiled again and shrugged.

"All right, then. Thanks."

She walked away from the shop as quickly as possible. And then, improbably, Lennie emerged from the alley by the Coop and nearly ran her down.

"It's you," she said with a pleasant look. She shook a bunch of keys in her hand.

"Oh, yes, hello," Mrs. Medina said. "Hello."

They looked at each other. Mrs. Medina felt a soft weakening in her legs, a soft pull downward. As if...and then she knew, she knew it wasn't the girl she was familiar with, it was the feeling.

"I thought you might be back," Lennie said.

"Why?" Mrs. Medina said, almost defensively. "Why did you think I'd be back?"

"Hunch."

"Well, I was looking, actually, for something to tell me about gesneriads, how to grow them." *What were gesneriads?* "Not for me, actually, for a friend. I thought you might have something...something simple, easy to understand."

"We've got a whole stack of things. Come on."

"Well, I'm rushed now, I can't go back. I'll come in again when I don't have so much to do."

"Sure. I'm usually there." She smiled. "Sometimes I have a class. Then I go out."

Mrs. Medina nodded. "Well, nice to see you."

"The lisianthus alive and well?"

"Oh, yes. It's lovely still."

"See you." She raised her hand.

Keep walking, Mrs. Medina said to herself. *Keep walking.* Before she knew it she was well on the way out Brattle Street and could have walked all the way to Concord.

My flowered blouse, with the tiny roses, and the blue skirt? Mrs. Medina asked herself. *No, too Talbot's. Out of season, anyway, now. Let's see. I guess the tweed will have to do.*

She stepped back and surveyed her closet.

"Look at this stuff," she said aloud. "I'm an old lady."

She heard a movement and turned to find Patrick leaning against her door frame, a tiny bit of pink lobster caught in the corner of his mouth.

"Going to the prom?" he said.

She regarded him with some irritation, her hands on her hips. In spite of the lobster, he was not a child, he did not look like a child; in spite of his gradual decline, he still had a wonderful sense of style.

Today he was dressed in crisp khaki trousers and a canary yellow V-neck cashmere sweater over his multicolored striped "Saturday shirt" from L.L. Bean.

"You have lobster on your lip," she said, sagging onto the bed. From time to time the pale remnants of her flu ambushed her.

"So I do." He dabbed it with his handkerchief. "Very good lobster salad, but those creatures rattle around on the bottoms eating God knows what, so I only want the claws. The curved claw meat. You know that. Today you gave me some part of the head, I think."

"One does not eat a lobster head. They have no heads."

"I've seen their heads, they have heads with two big bulging eyes. I want no part of that or any of that stuff in the middle. The tail I will eat in a pinch."

"I know you prefer the claws, and that is what you generally get."

He put his handkerchief away. "Is it so much trouble to feed me?" he asked. "May I come in and sit down?"

"Of course. Sit. I try to find inventive ways to feed you, Patrick. It's getting harder. You used to eat almost everything."

"Well, yes. I did. I ate dog once."

"Please don't go on with that story."

"For dinner, I'll have dog Florentine."

"Did you come in here for some purpose?"

He nodded, leaning back in her reading chair with a sigh. "It's nearly two-thirty," he said.

"Yes."

"Are you off somewhere?"

"Yes, in fact I'm off to Cambridge."

"I thought we were going to read, Merce. We'll never get through that Trollope if we don't keep going." He threw up his hand. "What's in Cambridge that's so goddamned important? A bunch of hippie students and pretentious faculty wives studying nuts and berries. Souvenir stores. What the heck do you do over there?"

A thousand years ago her father had asked her a similar question, she remembered suddenly, a rainy Sunday afternoon, Graham Kilmer waiting for her in front of the house, at the foot of the wide expanse of summer lawn, in his father's block-long '53 Olds convertible with the pale green leatherette seats and the steering wheel with the big turning knob on it. *I am a child*, she thought furiously. *I am living my life in reverse. I was born ancient, and now I want to walk off a pier.*

"What's in Cambridge?" Patrick repeated. "You've been already this week."

She paused and considered. Perhaps she shouldn't go. She had only suggested that she might come by for that pamphlet on gesneriads. Sometime.

Patrick leaned forward. "What's the matter with you, Merce? Found yourself an afternoon fancy man?"

"Don't talk to me like that," she said, standing up. "Don't talk to me as if I were a wayward child."

"Children don't have fancy men." He grinned. "Now, sit down, get that buzz out of your voice, and tell me all about it. I'll give you the benefit of my long years of experience."

"I'm tired of your experiences, Patrick."

Had she really said this? Yes, she could see by his face, she had said it.

"I'll be back after a while," she said. "I'll be back." She backed out of the room, just managing to remember to pick up her bag and grab a sweater from the chair in the hall, and fled to the elevator. In the lobby Al gave her an odd look as she rushed past, yanking the sweater on over her head, but it was only on Berkeley Street, on the way to the subway, that she realized what she had on.

Under her old Brooks Brothers sweater, stretched and loose, one of Patrick's old white shirts, rolled up at the sleeves.

Her oldest pair of green corduroys, slightly knee-sprung, and speckled with faded white paint.

Some old black flats, which she had slipped on to make lunch.

And under her sweater she still had tied around her waist her dark blue Boston Symphony apron.

She sat on the outdoor terrace of Au Bon Pain. Harvard Square. It could have been any place. The afternoon was chilly, and clouds were sliding in across the Brattle Street rooftops, from the west. A large Earl Grey was quickly losing its heat in front of her. She stirred in one more little package of sugar and crumpled the paper into a tiny ball, dropped it into the ashtray. The students passed in a steady stream, still in shorts, some of them, still in tank tops, although the equinox had passed. They were clowns, they acted as if they had the rest of their lives to walk down Massachusetts Avenue and bump against each other and feel the blood pressing against their veins. At one of the solid stone chess tables the chess master waited for a game.

Her purse bulged with the apron, which she had folded and stuffed inside. The purse looked like a creature now, swollen abnormally with something it had eaten whole. She sipped her tea and smoothed her hair. The waiting was beginning to excite her. She had no idea what she would do—go into the shop, lurk around outside like an obsessed teenage boy and then pretend a coincidental meeting that would not be believed, or simply go on waiting. For something.

She wondered whether she actually wanted to be seen today, dressed as she was—she remembered there were two small mayonnaise stains on the shirt she was wearing—and she pulled herself down inside her sweater. But, looking around, she saw she was dressed much the same as everyone else around her—better than most, if one could use the word *better*. In a way she was camouflaged.

At the next table a middle-aged male professor was attempting to show off his knowledge of French to a clearly uninterested female student.

"Stop saying 'postcards.' If you're going to France you must think of them as *cartes postales. Cartes postales*."

The student twisted her straw and twined her feet around the chair. "*Cartes postales*," she repeated.

"Every time you perform any action, you must think of the verb, think of all its forms. This is what I did, and I had no trouble at all when I got there. No trouble at all." He pulled on his beard. "To push open a door: *Je pousse*. I push. Your boyfriend does it— if you have a boyfriend—*Tu pousses*, you say. Familiar. Some stranger, *Il pousse*. And so on. You're going in two weeks. Can you order a meal?"

Mrs. Medina looked quickly at him. He was desperate. He was nagging the young woman, and he was smiling only with his teeth.

The girl chewed on her cuticle.

"Once on a train to Paris—" he began, pronouncing the city "Pah-ree," in a pompous tone.

"*Coq au vin,*" the girl said. "*Café au lait. Vin rouge. Merci.*" A thin band of sunlight broke through the low cloud cover. She put on her dark glasses.

"I'm going to cry," the man said. "I want to go with you. I want to show you the truffles, *les truffes,* from Provence. Pigs are trained to find them. They're the most wonderful things on earth."

The student put her chin in her hands. "Pah-ree," she said pointedly.

"I lived there," he said.

Mrs. Medina had become intrigued by where this saga might go next. When Lennie slipped into the chair opposite her, it took her a moment to react. Then, much to her surprise, she didn't react, she was still in disguise, so she simply smiled.

"I saw you sitting here," Lennie said. "I just sat down. To say I didn't have the gesneriad pamphlet with me, I guess. I didn't think it was you at first."

"No tweed jacket."

Lennie raised an eyebrow.

"Napoleon's wife," Lennie said, "when she was laying out her gardens at one of her big houses in France, brought in all sorts of sensitive plants from her island, I forget the name."

"Josephine. She was from Martinique," Mrs. Medina said, then stopped herself. *Pah-ree,* she thought. The professor and his child student had departed.

"Yes. They had to be kept warm, so she built a greenhouse and put twelve big coal stoves in the basement to keep the temperature steady, keep the humidity right."

"So," Mrs. Medina said. "You're a student, then."

"Well, yes and no. I'm sitting in on a course at the Design School, but they don't exactly know about it." She smiled. "I'm a little old to be a student."

"You must know someone, then."

"Yeah, I do."

"What's your course?"

"It's called 'Plants in Design.' Next semester I might do a course on the environment." She looked around. "Or maybe I won't. I don't know what I'm trying to prove." She returned her gaze to Mrs. Medina. "Are you an artist?"

"No. Why?"

"Your cords."

She looked down. "From painting a piece of furniture, I think."

"That gesneriad pamphlet is back at the store."

"I don't need it today."

"But I can tell you about gesneriads. If you want."

They paused and looked at each other. Lennie's face seemed to soften, and she lifted her hands and ran them through her hair. Mrs. Medina was careful with her eyes. She kept them focused on Lennie's nose, a handsome, forceful, Greek-looking nose, one that might have been worn by Aphrodite.

Dusk was folding in.

"If you want privacy, I can get lost," Lennie said.

"Privacy here?" Mrs. Medina laughed.

Lennie smiled a little. "Anyway, I guess I'd better..."

"Would you like a coffee?" Mrs. Medina asked.

"Sure, I'll get it." She was gone quickly.

Mrs. Medina belatedly opened her purse to find some change, and the apron sprang out onto the bricks.

"What I'm doing now," Lennie said, "my own private little project, I'm working with the folks at the Zen Center in Watertown." She sucked on her plastic spoon. "They've got some land in the back of their house they're clearing out, and they want a garden. Sort of formal. Mostly herbs."

"You're a landscape gardener too?"

"Well, not big time." She twisted her little pigtail around one finger. "I've done some small jobs. Guido's mostly trained me. I did my own little yard, such as it is. But this Zen stuff, less is more, you know, that's their thing. They want room to walk, paths, places to rest and sort of think, I guess, not too much of anything. Lots of green. Space, space, space." She stopped. "I don't know. Simple can be complicated, you can't just throw in a bunch of flower beds and trellises. They've got me sitting with them, you know—*sitting*— that's when they all meditate together. I do that with them to get more of an idea of what would be right. It's hard, sitting, I can't do it yet. My mind runs all over the place." Lennie had ordered a large regular coffee and had brought a chocolate chip cookie back with her. She smiled at it. "This stuff is bad for me," she said.

Mrs. Medina swallowed down a dry throat. She turned her empty cup round and round between her fingers.

"They call it the waterfall of words," Lennie said.

"How much space do they have?" she asked.

"For the garden? Almost half an acre—it's more like a little field. It slopes down to a pond."

"Quite a challenge, then."

Lennie nodded. "I like it. I'd rather be doing that than arrangements for Guido, all the same, one after another." She spread her hands out on the table. Long, businesslike fingers, short, neat fingernails. "Look at that," she said. "I left some dirt." But she didn't try to get it out, and Mrs. Medina was relieved.

"Dirt is part of your job," Mrs. Medina smiled. She wondered at her calm, she wondered when she would break into pieces. And she couldn't explain.

"Yeah." Lennie stretched out her legs. She was in black jeans and had hung her leather jacket over the back of the chair. Underneath she had on a red cotton jersey shirt with three buttons at the neck, which were undone. A small pendant on a gold chain rested in the hollow of her throat. Her sleeves were long, and she had pushed them up around her elbows. "Nice evening," she said.

The street lights had come on. Behind them the chess master was involved in a fast and noisy challenge match. Hands crashed against the timer.

Patrick.

Mrs. Medina stood up. "I have to go," she said.

Lennie looked up at her. "Too bad."

Mrs. Medina's clothes did not protect her now from a blush that began just below her breasts and threatened to move up and inflame her hair. But she took a breath into her lungs and said, "I'd like to hear more about this Zen garden. Sometime, of course."

"Sure. You could come out to see it, if it's ever finished."

"That would be nice."

"That would be very nice." She stood up. "So. If I'm not there when you go in the shop, just ask Guido for the pamphlet. He knows where they are."

"Thank you."

Lennie slipped back into her jacket, and they stood with the table between them, looking at each other. Mrs. Medina flexed her fingers. She imagined Patrick standing by the window, watching for her. And yet the girl seemed to be drawing her closer. No time now for the subway. She looked toward the cab stand and saw the last one pull off in a cloud of black exhaust.

"I don't know what I'm doing here." She thought she had said these words to herself, but to her horror she realized she had actually spoken them aloud.

Lennie smiled. "Wait," she said. Then she walked quickly to the curb, raised her arm, and a passing Brattle Cab darted out of the stream of headlights and arrived at the curb with a small flourish.

"Do you know," she said later to Patrick as they ate the small steaks she had broiled, "that Josephine had a greenhouse, probably at Malmaison, with twelve stoves in the basement to keep her rare plants warm?"

"She wouldn't have called it a basement," he said, chewing hard. She probably should have cut up his meat in smaller bites. He put down his fork. "Don't run off like that again, don't just vanish on me like a chicken from the chopping block. If you're mad, stay and fight!"

She nodded. "All right, Patrick. I was upset."

He peered at her through the candles. "You're through with your menopause, aren't you?"

"Well past it," she said. "It has nothing to do with that."

~

Waiting for sleep she thought, *I don't want one day after another, separated by sunrise, sunset, winter, summer, plodding along. I want one wonderful moment that will last until I die, in which day will be indistinguishable from night, water from air, song from silence. Touch from breath.*

In the middle of the night she heard him come into her room and felt his weight on the side of her bed.

"I'm awake," she said. "Are you all right?"

"Yes."

"Do you want a light on?"

After a moment he said, "I never wanted to do solo work, you know. I was always happier with the trio."

"Yes, I know."

"But I did it. I had to. They won't take you seriously if you don't."

"You did some wonderful solo work. In fact, I remember the night you nearly decided to abandon the trio altogether."

"That was after Tomàs died, and I thought there was no other fiddler in the world that would fit in."

She patted his thigh and left her hand there. The window was open, but the air was completely still, and silent. Perhaps it had rained.

"Could I have made it as a soloist?"

"Have you had that dream again?"

"I don't just think about this once a year, Merce."

She felt him shiver, and drew back the covers. "Want to get in?"

"No, I won't stay long." He blew his nose. "I loathe the Dvořák concerto. It is cruelly obsequious."

She laughed.

"But in my dream I'm playing it with some hotsy-totsy orchestra behind me and I'm making it something it isn't, I'm making it wonderful. And I wake up happy."

"Better than a nightmare, Patrick."

"No. It isn't. Why should I be playing that half-baked piece? And why should I wake up happy about it?"

"Yes, I see," she said. "You're right."

"Cellists have a hard time going solo."

"Yes. Remember Moira Bernstein."

"No need for her to end that way," he said. "Stupid woman."

"And she was good."

"Well, I'm good too, toots. I'm still good."

A long time passed, and she felt him wondering about his life, how it might have been different. She stretched her legs and shifted her position slightly.

"Do you want some milk?" she asked him finally.

"Is that all that's left for me?"

At these words she saw with a quick start of happiness her own life opening up in front of her like a long, festive corridor, lamps lit, time, no need to run.

She swung herself out of bed. "Of course not," she said. *Guilty*, she thought. *Guilty of having more time left than he does. Guilty because this girl has come into my life.*

~ *four* ~

Gradually they began to meet once or twice a week for coffee or tea. Pretending their meetings were occurring only by chance had begun to irritate Mrs. Medina—why should she dissemble?—and she had gone in one day and simply asked Lennie if she'd like to take a break. This act had been spontaneous and nearly stopped her heart, and if Lennie had said no, this strange little farce might have concluded forever. But Lennie didn't seem to think it was unusual at all, and the farce became something less comic, at least to Mrs. Medina.

But their routine was established casually and without the need for much planning, much to Mrs. Medina's relief. But in its casualness was its fragility, and she feared that any moment she might be expected to explain some unknown thing, or be exposed as a fool. She was, in fact, beginning to feel a little foolish. Was she acting her age (for example)? Should she have been taking tea with other friends, women her own age, and talking of stocks, and books, and the Museum of Fine Arts?

"These guys want herbs," Lennie said one day. "Other things too, but lots of herbs."

"Well, herbs can be flowering," Mrs. Medina said. She tried quickly to think of one. "Lavender," she said. They were sitting outside at the Paradiso.

"Oh, sure. I don't mind the herbs. Sort of transcendental. I was talking to one guy—he's a monk out there, I think. They'll use these herbs, see, they cook for themselves, and they make things to sell, like, you know, scented bags—"

"Sachets."

"Yeah. To sell. They're mostly self-supporting. But I've just got to figure out—" She stopped talking and looked pensively at the sky, catching her full lower lip between her teeth.

Mrs. Medina removed her sunglasses.

Lennie shook her head and shrugged. A waiter came out, hugging his arms for warmth.

"Cappuccino, please," Mrs. Medina told him.

"Me too," Lennie said. "And not too much milk."

They sat quietly, Mrs. Medina watchful for a moment at which she should begin to talk. It was early afternoon. She was back to her tweed jacket.

"I'm thinking of geometric shapes," Lennie said. "But I have to find out about walking meditation...if they want gravel paths, or crushed shells, or grass for their walking." She looked at Mrs. Medina. "They do walking meditation. Ever heard of that?"

"They walk and meditate at the same time?"

"They do. Following each other, all in step. I see them all in step, walking along a path lined with maybe...silver king or yarrow. Then if they just want to sit down, there should be, you know, a sort of sitting area around the pond. Sage, rosemary. But," she paused, "I need a focal point, and I don't think it can be the pond."

The waiter arrived with the steaming coffee. He placed the bill under Mrs. Medina's saucer. She added some sugar to hers and her hand shook a bit.

Lennie looked up at her. "Ever wear hats?" she asked. "I see you in a hat. I mean a big hat, that might sort of come down over your face."

"I rarely wear hats now. I used to, when I was younger."

"You'd look great in a hat."

"I—"

But Lennie went on. "Quiet paths, or something that your feet can really contact. That's the question. I'll have to ask." She flexed her fingers, put them around the coffee cup. "I've done some gardens, but most people just want roses, right? Bo-ring. This one will be different. I want this one to smell—" she showed her teeth "—I don't know. I want to be able to smell the earth."

"I'm sure it will be wonderful. I wouldn't know where to begin."

"A few things I can put in now. But first I have to clear out all the brush, that sort of stuff. The grade down to the pond, that could be a problem." She sipped her coffee tentatively. "Formal plans." She nodded. "I'm not used to formal. I'm more used to not predictable." She smiled. "I'll have to calm down."

"Good training," Mrs. Medina said.

"I saw a great picture of a kitchen garden in a French book that Guido has, all geometrical spaces with paths between. I kind of like that."

"A *potager*," Mrs. Medina said. "Vegetables and herbs."

"Right."

"Yes, it must be wonderful, just to step outside and pick some basil, or dill. Mint."

"Mint," Lennie said. "*Mentha*." She began to show off a little. "*Anethum graveolens*. Dill."

Mrs. Medina laughed.

"I like these Latin names. *Salvia*, I like, that's sage, *galium odo*-something—sweet woodruff, smells like new-mown hay when it's dried." She looked into Mrs. Medina's face. "*Eruca vesicaria sativa,*" she said, suggestively.

"What's that?" Mrs. Medina asked cautiously.

"Arugula. Good for salads. Then *nepeta cataria*—"

"Catnip, I think," Mrs. Medina said.

"Catnip, right. Catnip, catnip, funny name."

Lennie's mouth was sensual, without being too full; it moved over and around words as if she were feeling them, tasting them.

Then Lennie said with a grin, "And *cannabis sativa,* the best of all."

"And what's that?"

"Why the evil weed, of course. Grass. Herb. Mari-juana," she said in a low voice.

"In a Zen center?"

"What better place to grow it?"

Mrs. Medina felt foolish.

"Just a joke," Lennie said. She paused. "Come on." Their eyes met and held for a moment. "Come on, all right?"

Now Mrs. Medina moved through the days with the fragrant names in her head: rosemary, chamomile, coriander, thyme. Lavender, mint. She went to the market and bought great bunches of basil, dill, and rosemary, and hung them around the kitchen tied with ribbons. The kitchen became a *potager*.

"Are you trying to kill me?" Patrick asked cautiously. "Are you concocting a secret brew to do me in?"

It was just a friendship, after all.

And the age difference—well, people could be friends at any age.

One day Lennie said, "Can't break now, we're too busy. But wait for me at the Paradiso. I'll meet you. I get off in half an hour."

Mrs. Medina would have waited half a day. Half a year. She had already waited more than half her life.

five

On the day she finally retrieved the Whistler from the Fogg, beautifully repaired, its vitality restored, she brought it back into the apartment almost surreptitiously and quietly rehung it. She had stopped using it as an excuse for her absences from the house, but if Patrick should see it, his agitation would be roused.

Of course he spotted it, with his sonar tuned to anything within his range that had changed, that might threaten him.

"When did that come back?" he said to her, just before lunch.

"Oh, a couple of days ago." She was searching through her bookshelves for an old volume on herbs. She did not turn around. "They did a good job, don't you think?"

"Did you mention it to me?"

She shrugged. "I can't remember."

"Well, you didn't mention it."

"I may have forgotten to tell you."

He came around to stand by her side. "There's something going on," he said.

She looked at him and removed her reading glasses. "Something?"

"Yes. You're avoiding me."

"Avoiding you, Patrick? I live with you, we have every meal together."

He took her by the elbow and led her to the couch. "You're nervous as a ferret," he said. "Some afternoons you can't wait to get out of the house. I am left to tend the fire. I could conk out at any instant. You are not naturally a devious person, and you're not doing this very well." He threw back his chest and looked down his nose at her.

"Patrick, I brought the print back last week sometime, and there must be some reason I didn't mention it to you, but I can't remember now."

"I'm going to have a cigar," he said.

"You've already had your cigar for this month."

"Goddamn it, who cares?" He stood up. "If you're trying to kill me, a cigar isn't going to hurt."

"Patrick!"

He stood looking down at her.

"Sit down," she said.

She wondered how to begin. Her mind was like a spilled suitcase, with seemingly unrelated pieces strewn about. Patrick was forcing her, finally, to put them all together.

"I think," she said after a few moments, "that I've allowed myself to become silly. Well, infatuated." That was what it was, then.

He snorted. "Well, that's not news to me. I spotted it before you did. Who is he? And it had better not be Santino."

She laughed a little. "No, not Santino. This is a person you have never met, Patrick."

"Should I run for my grandpop's sword? Defend my castle? Are you walking out the door?"

"I don't think it will come to that."

"Women always say that. Then on some winter night, they grab their furs and jewels, take their husband's wallet, and run off into the storm with some beach boy with no hair on his chest. Where do I stand here?" He ran his hand over his wispy hair. "Maybe I need a little snort before lunch."

"No, stay still for a minute. I am not leaving you. I will never leave you. I'm hoping you'll just let me get over it."

He scratched his ear. "But," he said, "if you're seeing someone, I should know who it is. It's my right. He's taking you out of my afternoons."

"I'm not seeing someone in the conventional sense, Patrick."

"Don't give me that psychiatrical cow poop! Do you want me to roll around at night imagining you with Ronald Colman?"

No, she thought, *I don't.* She moved over closer to him. Because the best explanation for all of this lay in a past he could remember.

"Do you remember our honeymoon?" she asked him. "At the hotel in San Francisco?"

He looked at her uncomprehendingly. "Someone you met *there*?" he said. "You've been waiting all these years?" She shook her head. "Of course I remember our honeymoon," he said with a huff.

"Do you remember a tall blond woman in a gray suit? Short blond hair? We saw her around the hotel, in the restaurant."

He frowned.

"We talked about her once or twice at dinner."

He raised his chin. "Ah, yes. The gardenia."

So he had noticed. "Yes," she said.

"Well, I remember. Get on with it."

"I found her very attractive." Mrs. Medina felt her palms begin to sweat. *How do people do this?* she thought.

"You're avoiding the issue."

"No, I'm not. This is difficult, Patrick. Help me a little. Your life wasn't spent under a bush."

"You're raving like a madwoman, talking about our honeymoon. How am I supposed to help you?"

She took a breath. "I was attracted to her, Patrick. Maybe in a physical way, I don't know. Now it's happened again." She leaned back. "I think." He would have to figure out the rest for himself.

And he did. But it took several moments. "A female person?" he said finally. "That's your infatuation?"

She nodded. To her dismay, she began to shiver. It was news to her too.

She watched him process this information. "Ha!" he said after a few moments, and stood up. "Well, is that all? You thought that would get my dander up?" He was attempting to give her a grin. "About time you had a little jazz in your life. I've told you that before." He took out his handkerchief and blew his nose again. He rubbed it hard. He took a shaky little breath. "Well. Well. Time for a Black Jack, I think. Maybe a double. I'll bring you something too." His voice trailed away behind him as he shuffled out into the kitchen. "A woman!" she heard him exclaim. "Mind your manners, bub."

Mrs. Medina let her head drop back against the couch cushions and listened to him banging at the ice with his silver ice hammer. *He wants to see what it's all about,* she thought. *It appeals to his sexual curiosity.* She wondered if it might be better if she thought of it that way herself, instead of dangerous, purely and simply terrifying.

When he came back into the room he was carrying his whiskey in a large glass with one enormous ice chunk in it. He brought her a whopping snifter of sherry.

What are we celebrating? She asked herself. And then she asked him.

He took a sip of whiskey and tilted his head toward the ceiling. "Well, you tell me," he said, without looking at her.

She slid her bracelet up her arm; back down. Her heart was pounding. Telling Patrick had been silly. It was an issue now, one that he would pursue with the passion of a hound. And she must let him do it, see her as a child, ask her questions for which she had no answers. It was the way they had always handled situations like this. Except this was something new.

Patrick had picked up a *New Yorker* and was examining the cover. "These covers are getting worse and worse," he said. "They aren't funny anymore."

"It doesn't seem to bother you," she said, turning the glass of sherry about on its stem. "What I've told you. You seem relieved."

He looked over at her. "Well, Merce, I thought you were going to take off. Sure, I'm relieved, darn tootin'. Do it, whatever you're going to do. Get it over with. Then we'll get back to normal." He put down the magazine. "Now," he said, and leaned forward, "let's become a little more particular. You're telling me that every moment of our honeymoon, room 821 of the Mark Hopkins Hotel, a very romantic place, and I remember every footstep in the hall, you were having lurid thoughts about this blond dame?"

"No, of course not. I noticed her. It was confusing."

"Did you sneak off silently down the carpet while I was snoring away? A little assignation?"

"We never spoke."

"Merce, that was nothing. A girlhood triviality."

"I wasn't a girl then, Patrick."

"Now your old man's over the hill and you're getting a little frisky. That's to be expected. It's to be expected, Merce! And you're a sweet, sweet person not to pick someone that might have made me worry."

"This doesn't worry you, then."

He took a delicate sip of his whiskey, and some of it remained on his upper lip. He wiped it with his index finger. "Not one damn bit," he said. "On one condition."

"Don't go setting up conditions. Conditions aren't appropriate here."

"Don't tell me that. I have to sit here through these afternoons when you're off mooning about all over Harvard Square or wherever you go. You have to be careful, Merce. I have many friends around there. Do you slink around corners, hide in alleys waiting for this— whoever it is—to appear?"

"I do not slink around. I'm appalled that you should say that."

"Yes, discretion has always been your middle name."

She laughed a little. "Yes. You could say that." She got up and moved to the window.

"Well, tell me about mine enemy. Some feminist professor?" He looked at his glass and shook the piece of ice around. "Time for a refill."

"Time for lunch," she said.

She gave him curry soup, which he adored, and half a tuna sandwich on whole wheat.

"Trying to soften me up," he mumbled into his spoon. "I can spot it a mile off."

"There's no need to soften you up," she said. She had not drunk much of the sherry, so she gave herself a glass of Orvieto. It did not go well with the curry. She sat with her chin in one hand.

"Talk to me," he said. "Answer my question. Then we'll get to my condition."

She wiped her mouth. "Understand me, Patrick, this is not a rela- tionship we're talking about. It's a simple, curious infatuation. An attraction to someone who reminds me of a stranger I never met. And I'm warning you—don't make a big thing out of it. If you do, I'll be forced to bring up the unfortunate affair of Beatriz Cortázar."

He slammed his spoon down. For a moment he simply glared

at her. Then he smiled alluringly. "This is war, then," he said.

"No, certainly not. Just don't go throwing your weight around without remembering your own peregrinations."

"Well," he said, "well—"

"Yes. I'll say no more."

"I do deserve some answers."

"You do. And you will get them, but not in the detail you probably want. How about some vanilla ice cream, with chocolate bits on top?" Her hands were freezing. Perhaps it *was* war.

"No."

"Suit yourself. Now, this person, with whom I am *not* having an affair, is a young woman I met at Pittino's flower shop on Brattle Street."

"How young?"

"Young, I don't know, about twenty-seven or eight. Maybe thirty."

"Jail bait! Jail bait, Merce, you fool!"

"Patrick, twenty-eight is not jail bait."

"Mercedes, you are nearly sixty years old."

"I am constantly aware of that fact."

"Does she know how old you are?"

"We've never discussed it. It's not an issue. We meet for coffee and talk, that's all."

"But you want more."

She sighed. "I don't know. Really, Patrick, I don't know. I can't even put a name to it."

"I can. Lesbo."

"That's not the word I would use."

"Most lesbos are fat and wear motorcycle jackets and have crew cuts. I've followed a few down the street. That's not you."

"It's not me, and it's probably not a multitude of others. It certainly wasn't Jean Natini."

"Jean Natini! Her?" He considered this revelation. "Wow. She was a dish."

"Yes. So was her lover."

"Are you a lesbo, then? Are you telling me that?"

"I don't like categories. I've been as clear with you as I can be."

"Not much to chew on."

They were eating in the kitchen, and she stacked the bowls and plates and carried them to the sink. "There may never be anything more to chew on than that. Disappointed?"

"Well, tell me about her, then. Is she blond, like the other one? Stacked like Rita Hayworth? Has she snared you with some drug? What do you have to talk about with a twenty-eight-year-old floozy?"

"Well, she wants to design gardens, I think. She's taking a course at the Design School. Garden design, landscape design, whatever they call it. She's studied computers at U Mass, but she wants to design gardens."

"Does she like music?"

"I don't know."

"Does she have a brain? Does she think?"

"I'm going to make some tea. How about some?"

"I never have tea until three."

While the water was heating for tea she heard him making his way down the hall to his bathroom. *It was a stupid move,* she thought. *To tell him about this silly business. And he never gave me his condition.*

She decided to use the Minton, and took down her mother's teapot, with the swags of colorful flowers trailing around its fat midsection, and the saucer, thin as air, and the delicate cup. She examined the flowers closely, as if she'd never seen them before, and smiled, thinking that Lennie would like their brightness. She ran some hot water and carefully filled the teapot, to warm it, then took down the canister of loose Hu-Kwa. She wondered what she would do with an entire pot of it. Patrick drank only Red Rose made with bags. But it didn't matter, did it? Extra tea? Did extra tea matter, after all?

She stood with her eyes closed breathing the acrid steam of the Chinese tea. And quite suddenly the clock in the living room struck two.

She turned. "Patrick!" she called, already moving down the long hall to his bedroom. She found him standing at the window, oddly propped against the sill, staring down at the street. The autumn sunshine fell across his head and made it shine.

"Patrick," she said, in a softer voice, "are you coming back out?"

When he did not answer her, she came to him and turned him around to face her. His eyes were puzzled and blinking rapidly, and he shook his head slightly as if to clear it. One hand gripped his loose trousers at the waist, and his open fly revealed his green boxer shorts with the tiny gold anchors.

"What's happened?" she said. "Come and sit down." She brought him to his reclining chair. "Let's zip up your pants first."

"I was pissing," he said, gripping the arm of the chair. "I looked into the toilet bowl and forgot who I was. Something sucked my brain out. I went to the mirror to see who I was, and there was no one there. I dripped on the floor."

She took his hand. "Do you know who you are now? Do you know who I am?"

"Yes." He leaned back. "I thought this wasn't going to happen again, Merce."

"It hasn't happened in a while."

He sighed. "I'm tired."

She fetched his lightweight brown blanket from the bed. "All right, time for a nap anyway." She tucked the blanket in around him and stood up. "Arms and legs okay?" He wiggled his hands and feet. His eyes were closed. "And what did we have for lunch?"

"I had some curry soup," he said. "I know what else, but I'm not going to tell you."

She smiled. "I'll be right back. I'm going to clean up your bathroom."

At the door he said, "Merce." She turned to face him. His eyes were still closed. "Don't blame your little confession for this."

She called Harry Max from the phone in her room.

"A little seizure, probably," he said when he finally called back. "Want me to come by?"

"Think you should?" Patrick liked to see his doctor for social gabbing, but having him there professionally made him irritable.

"Any other symptoms of late? Loss of attention, dizziness, anything like that?"

"His attention seems unusually acute."

"Well, I'll drop by anyway. He'd better stay in bed, if you can keep him there. Don't let him get agitated."

"No agitation," she said.

Four-fifteen. The fading golden light was still captured in the topmost branches of the trees along the avenue. She opened the window wider to let in the sweeter air. Perhaps it was the time of year; she always felt happier in the fall. Summer and winter were tedious in their sameness, their relentlessness. She had never been one for those extremes.

Her mind drifted, half listening for Patrick.

Lennie might be looking for her at this time of day. For coffee. Probably not. Well, she might be. What *did* she have to talk about with a twenty-eight-year-old floozy? Was that what Patrick had called her? She smiled. When she was working she met friends for coffee all the time, and they talked about a variety of things, nothing serious. Her meetings with Lennie were like that. Weren't they?

But she remembered Lennie's half-closed eyes as they met her own, and felt a startling clutch in her gut. There had been no conversation at all then.

~ *six* ~

For several days she stayed home with Patrick, and no mention was made of their discussion. Mrs. Medina wondered if his little "episode" had erased it from his memory. She doubted it.

"Maybe I should get one of those bracelets, with my name on it," he said one evening at dinner.

"Do you really think you need that?"

"I need it for myself, goddamn it. Have you ever looked into a toilet bowl and not known who you were?"

"I can't say I have."

"Well, then."

Days he would wander through the house, she could see him touching objects, hear him identifying them to himself. "This is the cigarette box I bought for Merce at Shreve's, her birthday, some year." He shook his head. "This is a picture of the trio at—" he peered closely "—at Aix." He straightened up. "Aix, that's it. Barbara had a cold." He gave a firm nod.

But one evening when they were watching the eleven o'clock news he turned to her and said, "Where's Mama?"

"She's dead, Patrick, long ago."

He turned back to the screen silently. After the news she put him to bed and held his hand for a while, sitting on the side of the bed.

When she went back into her room the telephone book lay open where she had left it, to the V's. There was no Lennie Visitor listed. And if there had been, she wouldn't have called. There was a point at which one had to accept the futility of certain paths. Perhaps she had reached that point.

She was preparing for a brief foray to DeLuca's for groceries the next morning when her answer came. She got the phone on the second ring, although she knew Patrick had not gone back to bed after breakfast.

"Mrs. M? It's Nikki. I'm back."

Mrs. Medina sank into a chair and put her hand over her eyes. *An angel from heaven*, she thought. *Thank you, thank you.*

But she responded, "Nikki! How wonderful! How was your summer?"

"Great. Totally cool. I was in school in Germany until the end of July, but I met some really neat people, and afterward we all went down to Greece. In Turkey I think someone shot at me!"

"What a tale to tell."

"Now, of course, I'm flat broke."

Yes, Mrs. Medina thought. *You're broke. You need money. Thank God, I've got it.* "How are your classes?"

"Great. I've got Tuesday and Friday afternoons free. I was wondering, could Patrick use some company, like last spring? I'd love to come and read to him again and talk and go for walks and stuff. Give you a break."

Nicola Rasmussen was a lively BU drama student Mrs. Medina had found to come in and keep Patrick company several afternoons a week last spring while she was teaching her course. She was earthy and buxom, with a shocking amount of hair that ran wild over her head. She was decidedly without attitude, rare for a twenty-year-old, and Mrs. Medina liked her because she seemed to have some genuine affection for Patrick. He fluffed up his feathers when he knew Nikki was coming. Mrs. Medina might have called her "robust"; Patrick called her "stacked," and he adored her.

"Nikki, you're a godsend. I'll give you as much time as you have."

"Super! When should I come?"

"Tomorrow. Can you come tomorrow? It's Friday."

"Sure. Not until two, though."

"That's fine. Now, Nikki, Patrick is very fond of you, I know, and he sometimes gets overly excited when you're around. I'm aware of that. But he's had a couple of little seizures recently, and his doctor wants him to stay as calm as possible." She paused. "Do you understand?" Mrs. Medina was aware that Nikki and Patrick's reading sessions sometimes got a little frisky ("extraterrestrial" was how Patrick explained it, without apology), and she wanted to head that off. Patrick's sexual adventures were mostly in his head now, but his head contained some vivid fantasies.

"I would never do anything to hurt him, Mrs. M."

"Well, I know that. I just wanted to mention it. So we'll see you tomorrow about two. Welcome back." She hung up.

There was a small pause of pure happiness. Then she thought, *Lennie probably won't be there. Or she'll be there and she won't be able to leave. Or she won't want to have coffee.* She paused. *Or she won't remember me. It's been nearly a week, after all.*

Tomorrow! she thought. *I'll go anyway.*

Patrick was working carefully on the crossword. He did not look up.

"Well," she said, "it seems that someone shot at Nikki when she was in Turkey."

Now he did raise his head. "Nikki!" he said, his eyes alert. "Is she alive?"

"Very much alive."

"That little vixen. Who fired on her, the police, or some jilted Romeo?"

"She'll tell you all about it, I'm sure. She's coming tomorrow."

"The Blessed Damozel has returned to me. About time." He threw his chest out a bit and ran his hand over his wispy hair. "Time for a haircut, Merce. Bring out the shears."

Mrs. Medina counted the steps from the subway to Guido's. She got to ninety-seven, and stopped in front of a little consignment shop next to the florist's. She peered without interest at a tedious collection of woolen afghans that were draped inside the window and thought seriously about turning around and going home.

"Well, hello," she murmured quietly. "I just came in to say hello." She shook her head. No. "Got time for a coffee?" Better. Oh, just do it.

Lennie was just hanging up the phone. "Hi!" she said. "Where've you been? Got time for a coffee?"

"Sorry your husband's been sick," Lennie said. They crossed toward the traffic island in front of the Coop, Mrs. Medina tripping along after Lennie, who was dodging cars. "I have to drop off this deposit at the bank for Guido. Do you mind?"

"No, of course not."

Mrs. Medina bought a copy of the *Corriere della sera* at Out of Town Newspapers, and waited for Lennie in front of the bank. She adjusted the collar of her tweed blazer. The day was promising rain. It was cool. She looked at the sky.

"Let's go somewhere different," Lennie said, coming out of the bank. "Let's go to Ernie's. It's quick."

Mrs. Medina faced her on the sidewalk. She was suddenly doubtful. She felt the fragility of the emotional boards beneath her feet. Her excitement had evaporated, the pointlessness of this adventure was creeping up on her.

"Look," she said, "if you don't have time for coffee..."

Lennie smiled. "Come on." She shouldered her way into the crowd milling along Massachusetts Avenue. She was wearing a cotton sweater in a shade of teal that reminded Mrs. Medina of deep, tropical water. And she moved like an exotic fish among the people.

Ernie's was on Mount Auburn Street, near the bottom of Holyoke, just before the Vietnamese restaurant. In the air was the strong aroma of hot frying oil.

Inside Lennie said, "No cappuccino here. Coffee, tea, juice. Big, fat doughnuts. I come here for breakfast sometimes." They sat down at a sticky booth with cracked wooden benches.

"Anything," Mrs. Medina said. "Tea. With milk." She fumbled around in her bag for her coin purse.

"My treat," Lennie said.

Putting her coin purse away, Mrs. Medina broke a fingernail on the clasp. She didn't have time to file it before Lennie was back with two steaming mugs of tea and two chocolate chip cookies.

"So does your husband have the flu?" Lennie asked. She pulled the sleeves of her sweater up over her forearms.

Mrs. Medina sighed, watching Lennie's arms. "No. He's older. He's sick sometimes."

"Is he retired?"

"More or less." Mrs. Medina smiled. "He doesn't want to be." She paused. "He's a musician."

"Played in a band?"

"He's a classical cellist. He played in a trio."

Lennie raised her eyebrows. "That's cool. Would I know him? I know that guy with the crutches, what's his name, he's played with the Pops."

"Itzhak Perlman. He plays the violin."

"Right."

"Patrick Medina."

"Excuse me?"

"My husband. Patrick Medina."

Lennie shook her head. "No, I don't think I've heard of him." She sipped her tea. "Been married a long time?"

"Over twenty years."

Lennie nodded. "That's pretty long. I don't know anyone who's had a long marriage, really. My folks split up when I was ten. We all had to move."

"Where did you go?"

"I went with my Mom to Inman Square. Know that neighborhood?"

"Not really."

"I was in the streets a lot. The apartment was a box."

Before Mrs. Medina could stop herself, she said, "Where do you live now?"

"Out past Porter Square. Not a neighborhood you frequent, I'll bet." She smiled.

"I guess I'm more familiar with Boston."

It was mid afternoon, and Ernie's was noisy and quiet by turns. Most people were picking up pizza slices and drinks to go at the long counter in the back.

"But," Lennie held up her finger, "the most beautiful garden for miles around. About the size of a little dance floor. Pride of the neighborhood." She looked at her watch.

Mrs. Medina was drinking her tea with her left hand to hide her broken nail. She was clumsy, the tea slopped out onto the table. *She's got to go back*, she thought. *Hurry, hurry.* She was tired of coming to Cambridge. Could she ask Lennie, could she possibly ask Lennie to have dinner? Or—she searched her mind—what else?

"Got to get back," Lennie said. "I have a delivery." She folded up the small green money bag, now empty, and flipped her pigtail back over her shoulder.

Mrs. Medina's heart lifted at this gesture, and she laughed. "Why did you grow that pigtail?" she asked.

"Like it?" Lennie said. "Kenny dared me to grow it. He has one too."

"Kenny—"

"Kenny Barrett. Except his is red. He's a redhead. Or more like orangehead. He shares my place."

"Oh," Mrs. Medina said. She had never liked redheads.

Lennie looked at her closely. "My friend Connie and I took him in while we were living together in Jamaica Plain. We needed the money. Then when she and I split up," she shrugged, "Kenny and I found a cheaper place. You know." She did not move her eyes from Mrs. Medina's. "We're not involved or anything."

Mrs. Medina colored slightly. "That's none of my business," she said, drawing herself up and smiling.

"I'm not rich. Kenny can be a jerk, but I need his bucks."

Mrs. Medina stood up. "Well, let's get you back to Guido."

As they left the restaurant, Mrs. Medina put her hand lightly on Lennie's back, just at her waist, for a moment, to move Lennie ahead of her through the door. *A social gesture*, she said to herself, as they walked up Holyoke Street. *That's all*. But her hand was already remembering the firmness of Lennie's back, the start of the swell of her buttocks, the rough texture of her sweater.

Lennie, on the other hand, was speculating aloud about whether she would have to put gas in Guido's truck before she took it to the Zen Center.

seven

T he television harangued her, but she tried to tune it out and went over the mail, keeping Patrick company with his first Black Jack of the evening. Late afternoon. And it wasn't his first, she had to remember; it was to be his only. She had watered it a bit, and so far he hadn't seemed to notice.

She looked out of the corner of her eye at Patrick, who was marking off one of his Civil War battle plans on a piece of graph paper.

"Want me to turn it off?" she asked hopefully.

"Nope," he said pointedly, without looking up. "Keeps me company these days."

"There is no cure for a negative self-image except from within," a plump woman in pink was saying to the talk show host. "Dare to love yourself! No matter what you've done in your life." She looked into the camera. "Dare to touch the fine inner parts of your spirit. You *can* be loved! The trick is to love yourself first!"

The host turned to a young dark-haired woman on his left. "Tell us your story, Gloria," he suggested unctuously.

"I married my own father," she said in a half whisper. The audience gasped.

"Ha!" Patrick said, again without looking up. "I love these things."

The woman in pink leaned forward. "Oh, sweetheart," she said to the girl.

The host stood up. "And we have him here. Please welcome Waldo Tex DeVane!"

The audience booed. Waldo doffed his Stetson and smiled. He was the girl's senior by at least twenty-five years. His salt-and-pepper crew cut exposed many bare patches, and he had a mouth full of tiny little teeth, which showed a great deal of gum. He sat down beside the young woman and took her hand. She looked off into the middle distance, her eyes expressionless.

"Now," said the host, "tell us your story. From the beginning." The story was long, and involved separation in infancy and a dramatic romance that began in a line dancing contest. There were several commercials.

Mrs. Medina went for a glass of wine. She was disgusted, but returned.

"And who told you," the host said into the face of Gloria, the young woman, "who told you you had married your daddy?"

"My mama," she said.

"Came after me with a shotgun," Waldo said proudly. The audience cheered.

"But she was a lousy shot," Patrick said, putting down his drawing and squinting at the screen.

"My little girl here told her to get lost," Waldo said, and leaned over and kissed her on the cheek.

"Can't help who you love," she said in a monotone.

The woman in pink rose in a cloud of rage. "Can't you see what he's done? Gloria, how do you feel? How do you feel about yourself?"

"I feel like a piece of shit," she said, and the network bleeped the four letter word. "But no one else will have me now."

"Go get 'im," Patrick said, and took a swig of his drink. He looked at the glass. "You've watered this drink," he said to Mrs. Medina.

"Honey," the woman in pink said, "was there issue from your union?"

The young woman seemed puzzled. "Issue?"

"Children," the host volunteered.

"I was pregnant, but it didn't take," she said.

"An unborn child doomed by perverted genes," the woman in pink hissed at the camera.

"Now, wait a minute!" Waldo said, releasing Gloria's hand. The audience cheered.

"I'm going to get this girl back on track," the woman in pink said. "She has to learn how to love herself."

"I love her, damn it," Waldo said. "That's enough."

"You watered my drink!" Patrick said in a louder voice.

Mrs. Medina's empty stomach was churning from the wine. "Yes, I did. And don't give me a problem about it."

"You're going to start your life anew. This man is your father. You married him in innocence, but it's time to close that door. Open another, and smell the fresh, clean air."

"The only air in here is from your ass! And it's hot!" Waldo shouted, jumping to his feet.

"You're keeping this little one chained in bondage," the woman in pink said, almost in Waldo's face. "Release her into her true self. Allow her to love herself. She has to get on with her life!"

"Let her go, Waldo!" a man in the audience shouted.

Patrick was struggling to lower his recliner, presumably to go after another drink.

"You sit right there," Mrs. Medina said. "Don't you move one more inch. You're a stubborn old man. I'm trying to keep you alive!"

"I'll go out on my own terms. Get me out of this chair." The chair, apparently, had become caught on his brown blanket.

No agitation, no agitation, Mrs. Medina thought. *What can I do? It's all around us.*

On the screen, Gloria shrieked, "Let me be! Daddy, let me be!" and fell sobbing into the arms of the woman in pink.

"We love you, Gloria," the woman in pink said, stroking her hair.

"We love you, Gloria!" the audience shouted.

The woman in pink looked over the top of Gloria's head at Waldo and said, "Get lost, prick," and caught the censors napping.

Patrick's chair crashed to a level position. "I'm not a child," he said, struggling to his feet.

"Patrick, please!" Mrs. Medina rose to her feet. "Jesus Christ, you are exhausting me! I am tired of policing you. I am tired of these awful television programs. Is this how we're going to spend the rest of our lives?" Then, to her horror, she burst into tears and sank back down on his bed, her head in her hands.

From the television came a roar of applause.

Patrick stopped in shock. After a moment he turned off the television and put his glass back down on the table. From the side of his bed he grabbed his box of blue Kleenex and sat down gently beside her. She showed no signs of stopping, so periodically he handed her a fresh Kleenex, then returned his hand to the back of her head, patting it every so often. His eyes stared quietly off into the gathering darkness.

Every time she thought she had finished, a fresh surge of tears came. She had no idea why she was crying. Her mind was full of Lennie, of orange-headed Kenny, sharing Lennie's life in a way she had no way of doing, of the dying plant she'd had to throw away that morning, its one bright leaf still struggling for life, of thoughts of her own hopeless life, of Patrick's imminent departure, of her own work, her notes neglected, in disarray. That betrayal. And the woman in the gray suit walking past her, out of the hotel dining room, forever.

She felt Patrick's hand shaking as he patted her back and tapped her forehead several times in an odd way, and she felt the heat of his leg against her thigh. He was very much alive, and this thought calmed her. When her tears finally stopped, her head was beating like a bomb, her chest ached, she felt completely exhausted. She took Patrick's hand and held it against her heart.

With his free hand he blew his nose.

"What a pair of fools," she said finally, in a croaky voice.

"Speak for yourself," Patrick said. "I'm no fool. You're in trouble." He got up and fetched his glass from the table. "Here, have a sip of this. Raise your head, Merce, or you'll plug up your sinuses. Let 'em drain."

She blew her nose again and took a sip of Patrick's whiskey. They sat side by side on his bed, their knees touching.

She smiled slightly. "I look a mess, don't I? My eyes feel like inner tubes."

"You look fine. Who cares about how you look? Look at this." He showed her his left hand. "I've got a new liver spot. That makes seventeen."

She was exhausted, and finally let her head drop onto his shoulder. His shoulder bone was sharp as a propeller blade. *He's lost more weight*, she thought, and her eyes filled with tears again. *What will I do without him?*

"What's this kid done to you?" he asked after a while. "Or is it only me? You'd better tell me. Is it blackmail?"

She burst out laughing, in spite of herself. "She's done nothing, Patrick. I've done nothing. That's the problem." She turned to face him. "I'm in trouble, you're right."

"I don't understand this," he said, shaking his head.

"Here." She handed him his glass back. She went into his bathroom and splashed some water on her face, then peered at herself in his mirror, where he had looked and seen no one, she remembered. She might have been happy to see no one at this point, but there were her blotchy skin, her puffed eyelids, glaring.

He was still sitting on the side of the bed. The room had grown chilly, so she went to turn up the thermostat. "Want your flannel shirt?" she asked him.

"Is the sun down?" he said.

"Yes, well down."

"Better have it, I guess."

In recent weeks the darkness had begun to confuse him. He loved his red-and-green plaid flannel shirt; it gave him a point of reference. In it, he knew who he was. She had nothing like that in her wardrobe.

She got him back into his recliner and went and got him another small drink, unwatered, with fresh ice.

"Here," she said. "I'm not deliberately trying to annoy you. I think Harry feels that some whiskey—*some*—relaxes you, but too much can do you harm. I agree with him." She sat down in his old wing chair, which he rarely used now. "But for the record, I also think that if you want to kill yourself, you should be free to do it. Just don't expect me to watch. Or help. I will deter you in any way I can."

He sipped his whiskey. After a little while he said, "I'm pretty tough." She waited for him to go on, for she sensed he had something else to add, but he didn't.

"I apologize for that little display," she said finally.

"No need."

"I wasn't crying entirely about her, Patrick. But she probably set it off."

He set his jaw.

"Can I talk to you about this?" she asked him.

"Go ahead. If you get carried away, I'll stop you."

She walked over to the window and opened it a bit more. Now that rush hour was over, it was quieter in the street. "This okay? Not too cold?"

He pulled his blanket up a bit.

On the corner playground below, she saw John Patel, who lived downstairs on the third floor, still pushing his small son on the swing, by the light of the street lamps. There was a great sense of care and affection in the way John placed his hands on his son's hips and sent him flying forward, not too high, but high enough to make the boy cry out in happiness, knowing he would always fall safely back into his father's arms. As she watched, John took him off the swing and they walked companionably toward the playground gate, hand in hand.

She came back and sat down. After a moment she said, "Would it have been better if we'd had children?"

He started. "Better? For who?"

"I was just watching John Patel down in the playground with his son."

"Tim."

"That's the son?"

"Tim. We're pals."

She nodded. "Should we have had children, Patrick?"

"It's a little late to open that topic."

"Well, I know that."

He sighed. "It wouldn't have been a good life for a kid. We were too busy. We were always tooting about. You would've had to stay home."

"Yes." Had she ever wanted a child? They had both enjoyed other people's children. But they had been happy enough with each other, with their freedom.

"My seeds were probably too weak anyway, by the time we got together."

She laughed a bit. "Not necessarily. Remember Strom Thurmond."

"That old coot." He paused. "Anyway, I was more than enough for you to take care of."

That much was true.

"Why are you circling round the barn?" he asked. "You're supposed to be enlightening me about your girlfriend, not crying about unspilt milk."

"Please don't refer to her as my girlfriend. She is not my girlfriend."

He sipped his drink and said nothing.

"If it's all right with you," she said quickly, quickly before she could consider it, "I think I'll ask Nikki to stay on for the evening sometime next week. I'd like to take Lennie to dinner."

"Is that her name?"

"Yes. That way you'd have my company during the afternoon and Nikki's at night. What do you think of that?"

He faced forward and said nothing.

"I'd like to be with her just a bit, to talk. To get to know her." She cleared her throat. "To know her better."

He reached over and put his whiskey glass down on the table. "She has a boy's name," he said.

"Well, so does Nikki, if you think about it in a certain way."

"Nikki's name is Nicola."

"Patrick, I'm not trying to compare Nikki with Lennie, not in any way."

"I thought you were going to get this girl over with in a hurry! You could have had a common ordinary affair with a man, couldn't you? If you needed sex? Gone to a sleazy motel and spent the afternoon? Wouldn't that have been enough?"

"Sex is not the issue."

She took a breath to try to explain how she felt—for now she wanted to talk to him about it—but he turned sideways to look at her, and she saw that his eyes were clouding over with a vagueness she had come to recognize. "Would Nikki fix my dinner?" he asked.

"Yes. Remember, she did it a couple of times last spring."

"Can she cook? I don't remember."

"You had no complaints. Veal marsala, remember?"

"Would you stay out all night?"

"Of course not. I'm talking about dinner, Patrick. Nothing more than that."

He leaned his head back and closed his eyes. "I wonder," he said after a moment, "what happened to the old Grosvenor Hotel in Manhattan. Fifth Avenue and—what? Did they tear it down?"

"I believe it closed. I don't know when."

"We had some good times there, Merce. Nice big rooms."

"Yes, we did."

He sighed. Then he said, "I suppose veal marsala would be all right."

~ *eight* ~

She went out into the morning to buy Patrick some new underwear. Green-and-blue boxers with gold patterns were his current favorite, and so she headed over toward Neiman's. The air was sweet and warm, with a mild tang of salt in the wind that gave a spine to the morning, and the sun was just present above the hazy building tops. The behemoth garbage trucks—for this was Thursday, a garbage day—were making their ponderous way along the Back Bay grids, and the flags turned in slow curls atop the Copley Plaza Hotel.

After leaving Neiman's she wandered along through Copley Place, where in a jewelry store window next to Louis Vuitton her eye was caught by a bracelet made up of links of small rectangular pieces of gold, not too thin, not too thick, and she imagined it on Lennie's wrist. She imagined it would look elegant, not like anything, probably, that Lennie would ever pick for herself. She considered it, walked away, turned back, and bought it. The salesman gave her a shiny gray box with lavender tissue inside. This present seemed to represent a lovely possibility, an assurance that *something* would happen.

She cut through the Marriott, across the walkway to the Prudential Center, and proceeded up Boylston Street to Tower Records to buy Patrick a copy of some Brahms trios the Riviera had recorded in London ten years ago, recently reissued on CD. On her way out she had a strange jolt: a thin young man with orangish hair and a pigtail wound in a tight coil on top of his head was standing on the street haranguing a young woman in black with gold rings piercing five different locations on her face and a man with pale skin and pens in his breast pocket who looked decidedly nervous.

Could this be Kenny? Mrs. Medina gave him a long look. How many other redheads with pigtails could possibly be around? She thought the odds were good. She disliked him instantly.

The young woman poked him in the chest. "Don't touch me, man," he said to her, and shoved her roughly in the shoulder. Mrs. Medina slipped quickly by. He looked up as she passed, and his eyes, below his pumpkin hair, were as vague as Patrick's had been yesterday. Mrs. Medina clutched her packages and moved off in a sweat toward the safety of Commonwealth Avenue. Halfway home she sat down on a bench.

There was no possible way he could have known who she was— or even that she existed—but she had looked back over her shoulder anyway, partly out of curiosity, she guessed. *That* was who Lennie lived with? She couldn't imagine it. But—and here she brushed some imaginary lint from the sleeve of her jacket—the two of them were friends. Or were they? Or rather, what kind of friends? People live in proximity—she pictured this scene—they have meals together, they talk, they argue about money, they sleep under the same roof. That is a kind of intimacy. And things happen. They drink, they smoke something. They're young. Maybe they give a party. Everyone goes home. They're tired, a little high. They find themselves in bed together. She closed her eyes. *It's happened to me. It can happen.*

But with that scruffy guy in black sneakers and sagging jeans? And that awful red hair?

"I think Tina called," Patrick said anxiously as she took off her jacket. He had met her at the door.

"You think it was Tina, or you think there was a call?"

"There was a call. I listened to a voice." He shook his head.

"No message?"

He wasn't sure.

She suddenly remembered that she hadn't given Tina her birthday present, or even sent a card. She walked into the kitchen shaking her head and ran into a wall of heat. All four electric burners on the stove were glowing like rocket engines. "Patrick, why are all these burners on?" she called to him.

He came through the door. "I wanted some tea. Then the phone rang."

"Did you need every burner?"

"I can't figure out these stoves," he muttered.

She switched them off and turned to face him. But she saw the anxiety in his face and stopped her tongue. She went back into the hall and collected her packages.

"Anything for me?" He followed her into her bedroom.

"Some new shorts. See if you like them." She handed him his bag and threw the rest on her bed. "Now, do you still want that tea?"

He walked down the hall toward his room, and this time she followed him. "Patrick?"

He seated himself in his chair, and she saw that he'd fixed himself a whiskey instead. She stood and watched him take a sip. "I don't like it," he said finally.

She knew he didn't mean the Jack Daniels. "What don't you like?" she asked him. She did not sit down, for she was now impatient for lunch. She thought of a cheese omelet. Her body in recent weeks was revealing new appetites of all sorts. She found herself desiring hot scented baths, Scriabin, Gershwin songs.

"What don't you like, Patrick?" she repeated. "Then I must fix us lunch."

"You can bring her here for dinner," he said abruptly.

"Bring—?"

"Yes. No sense tooting off somewhere and paying enormous sums. And paying Nikki."

She sighed. "Let's talk about it later," she said. "Aren't you hungry?"

"How much do you pay Nikki, exactly, to change my diapers?"

"Nikki enjoys her time with you," she said softly. "It's a pleasure for her."

"Money can't buy love, Merce." He frowned and sipped his drink. "Tina said something I can't remember."

"I'll call her. It's not a problem."

"I don't like it."

"Patrick."

"I don't like any of it."

Could he get no further than that? She realized she knew exactly what he meant, but she didn't want to hear him say it. And there was a way she could help him, but she couldn't let him ask her.

"Come on," she said. "Help me make lunch."

During lunch he looked up at her and said, "Can I buy my way out?"

Later, while Patrick was napping, she placed a call to Taylor Bond, a psychiatrist who had spoken with her on several occasions about Patrick's mental fluctuations. An hour later he called her back.

"Want to talk on the phone?" he asked her. "I have five or ten minutes."

"No, I'd rather come and see you, if it's all the same."

"Okay." She heard him turning over the pages of his appointment book. "Well, I'm booked until later next week, unless you want to come in for half an hour late tomorrow afternoon."

"I'll do that."

"Five-fifteen, then."

And then, since she had the phone in her hand, she looked up Lennie's number at the flower shop and dialed quickly without allowing herself to think.

Lennie answered the phone.

"Hi. It's Mercedes Medina."

There was a pause. *She doesn't know who I am,* Mrs. Medina thought for one terrified moment. Then she heard Lennie say, "Thanks very much. Come back again."

Mrs. Medina transferred the phone to her other ear.

"Hi," Lennie said. "Can't go for coffee today. Guido's arranging a wake."

"No, it's not that. I was wondering, do you want to have dinner sometime next week? Tuesday maybe?"

"Tuesday? Sure. Where?"

Where?

"Tired of Cambridge?" Lennie said.

"Well, yes, a change might be nice." But where? She hadn't thought.

"Okay, I'll meet you at Park Street down by the turnstiles, on the inbound Green Line side. We can decide. I can't make it before six-thirty."

"Six-thirty is just—six-thirty is good, yes."

"Okay. See you Tuesday. Got a customer now."

"Of course."

"Don't change your mind." She hung up.

Mrs. Medina sat with the receiver in her hand. The entire exchange had taken less than a minute.

~

"Have you read any of that book I gave you, Mercedes?" Taylor Bond asked the next afternoon. "The one by Maria Filer? She has a good section about dealing with the aging mind."

"I took a look at it. I'm still wondering, Bond, are you absolutely sure it's not Alzheimer's?"

"Harry Max and I did all those tests. Or as many as Patrick would submit to. There was no indication. We can do them again, if you can convince him to participate."

"He told me he'd figured out how to beat those tests, whatever that means." She made a little movement with her hand. "Yesterday he had all the stove burners on when I came in."

"He was trying to—"

"He said he was making tea."

"But he realized what he'd done."

She nodded. "But it didn't seem to bother him. His mind drifts off like that. And then there are these spells that have been happening again."

"What does Harry say?"

"Well, we know about the arteriosclerosis. Maybe they're small strokes."

"No loss of speech, no paralysis?"

"No."

"These dissociative episodes sound like what he was experiencing last winter. How long do they last?"

"It's hard to tell because sometimes he just sits there with them, you know, and it's only when he says something, or looks at me, that I catch on. I suppose there are times when they're going on and he doesn't say anything at all."

"Well, it doesn't sound completely like Alzheimer's. But to determine whether there's cognitive impairment we'd have to test. And there are some tests he can't beat."

"I won't have him tested again."

Bond watched her for a moment. "Why did you come in, Mercedes? What can I do for you?"

"Well, Patrick, of course. He seems to be worse, Bond."

"Then what can I do for him?" She looked at him. "He's nearing the end of his life, you know that."

"But he's not that near, I don't think."

"Yes, he's a surprising man." Bond got up and opened a small window behind him. She watched him walk. He had been an all-Ivy wide receiver at Brown and was still light on his feet. "But you have to watch him now."

"I do watch him." She paused. "But I can't *always* watch him."

"You sound angry."

"Don't start on me, Bond."

He smiled. "What's been going on recently?"

She looked at him quickly. "What do you mean?"

"Has he been unusually agitated?"

"Yes, I guess, a couple of times."

"And what's happened?"

"He gets overly excited—about one thing or another—and afterward goes into these fugue states, as I told you. He says he forgets who he is. He talks about his mother, who's long dead, and places from his past."

"Does he still remember the plans from his Civil War battles?"

"Of course. Those will be the last to go."

He laughed.

"I don't know what to do," she said.

"Be with him. Read to him, take him for walks. Anything that makes him happy. And watch him."

She looked at him.

"Harry's probably told you all this, Mercedes. I can't say anything more."

"I'm supposed to keep him calm."

"It would be better for him, yes."

She rubbed her eye with her forefinger. "In recent weeks I seem to be provoking him from time to time. Unintentionally, of course. Sometimes there's tension there. I don't think it's good for him." She rocked a little in her chair and drew her jacket closer around her. She noticed a small run in her stocking, just coming up from the heel.

"What provokes him? What do you imagine that you do?"

She cleared her throat. "I'll take the blame," she said.

"Blame isn't an issue here."

"Well, I seem to have the need to get out more. Spend more time away." She did not meet his eyes.

"Perfectly natural. Why are you talking about blame?"

She spread her hands. "I feel guilty."

"You have a life too."

She thought about that.

"You have a life, but you also have Patrick. The problem is to balance the two."

"I don't think he wants me to go out at all."

"Well, what are we talking about here? All day, every day, all night, every night?"

"No. Just—" She stopped, looked at her watch. "I probably should be going. You said half an hour."

"I have a while longer, if you want to talk."

She sighed. "I don't know if I do."

"I think you're perfectly clear about Patrick. I don't think that's the problem."

"What are you suggesting?"

He watched her thoughtfully and waited.

For a few minutes she considered what to say. Outside the window an outbound trolley clanged its bell and rattled past along the

Beacon Street tracks. *I'll catch the train back at Kent Street*, she decided. *Not at St. Paul. That'll save me a block.*

"Mercedes?"

"I have nothing to say, Bond. It's my problem. I'll just have to stay in more, watch him all the time, never bring up anything that will excite him, never do anything that will cause him to wonder about me."

"No more waltz evenings at the Plaza?"

"Yes. In a figurative sense. And it's not funny."

"No, it's not." He shook his head. "It's not funny. I will ask a question here, though. If you did all that, which you have done without question for several years, is there something now that you would have to give up? That you wouldn't want to give up?"

"Yes."

"That's the problem."

"Yes."

"All right." He leaned back and looked at her over the top of his half glasses. "Perhaps you should talk with someone, just on a short-term basis. It doesn't have to be me."

"I don't think that's necessary."

"Well, consider it, at least. Why don't you come back and we'll talk again. This is Friday. How about next week sometime?"

"You said you were booked."

"I sometimes have some space free around this time of day."

"Not Tuesday."

"Okay."

"Wednesday would be all right, if you really think it's necessary." She got to her feet and busied herself with some lint on her skirt.

He walked over to his desk and consulted his appointment book. "Wednesday, but not until six."

"Six is all right. But not much later. Patrick likes to eat by seven-thirty or so."

Bond nodded and walked her to the door. "Give him my greetings."

"I don't intend to tell him I've seen you."

nine

"**A** *bunch of the boys were whooping it up,*" Mrs. Medina began, "*in the Malamute saloon...*"

" 'The Shooting of Dan McGrew,' " Patrick interrupted. "By Robert W. Service."

"Yes," she said. "By Robert W. Service."

"If you're going to read it, you must read the whole thing, including author and title."

She was sitting propped up on pillows on her bed, and he was reclining on her chaise in his blue-and-green-striped cotton robe, his ankles crossed demurely. He had on his green socks. She looked at the phone and thought, *She'll probably call and cancel.*

"Well?" Patrick said.

"Well—"

"Let's have it."

"All right, all right." She leafed slowly through the volume, its weight comfortable in her lap, its musty pages foxed and brittle, well read. "One has to be in the right mood for this elevated piece of poesy." As she turned the pages, her hand rose to touch the areas of skin around her mouth, where she found the beginning signs of the dry patches that appeared each winter when the heat was turned on. *The mange has returned,* she thought.

"Come on, Merce. The kid on the music box..."

"Yes, it's just here. *The kid that handles the music-box was hitting a jag time tune...*"

He leaned back and held up one finger. "Now, once you were going to investigate jag time for me. What the hell does it mean?"

"I always assumed it was the same thing as ragtime, Patrick."

"Maybe it isn't. And it's very important to the poem. If the kid at the piano was playing ragtime, Service would have said so, don't you think?"

She looked up at him over the top of her glasses.

"If jag time refers to some sort of Alaskan Indian tune, that would change the whole gist of the poem," he said. "Was the kid an Eskimo?"

"My feeling is that Alaskan music would not include ragtime, or jag time, whatever that may be."

"Well, then, why say it?"

"It's the gold miners who are in the bar here, not the Alaskan natives, Patrick."

"Jag time, jag time," he mused. "It bothers me."

"Shall I continue?"

He nodded.

She went on, hoping he would tire soon. "The Shooting of Dan McGrew" made him laugh, and she read it to him once or twice a month. "*Back of the bar, in a solo game, sat Dangerous Dan McGrew, And watching his luck was his light-o'-love, the lady that's known as Lou.*"

"Stop right there," he said.

She looked up and removed her reading glasses.

"I just thought of something."

"What's that?"

"Do you remember a gal named Lola Winter, in New York? Tall, smoky-looking cha-cha. Used to hang around with what's-his-name that used to write our reviews for the *Times*."

"I can't place her."

"That critic, Merce, the one that ended up writing program notes for the Los Angeles Philharmonic."

"I do remember *him*."

"Well, Lola was his bed companion for many years."

She waited a moment. "So?"

"She was my idea of the lady that's known as Lou." He looked dreamily at the ceiling.

"I'm glad you have an idea of her. It makes the poem livelier."

"What's your idea of Lou, Merce?"

"I have a much clearer idea of the stranger, I think."

His eyes brightened. "*And such was he, and he looked to me like a man who had lived in hell.* Ha! You never told me that. What is your vision of the stranger?"

"Well, he's got red hair."

"What? A carrot head?"

"He's tall, with a sort of stubble, and has narrow slits for eyes. He has bad posture too—he slouches—and he has a hand-rolled cigarette between his bad teeth." She was making this up as she went along, and delighted that Kenny fit the role of villain with such ease.

"A redheaded Eskimo." He grinned. "No wonder Lou was tempted."

"She wasn't fooled, though. She pinched his poke in the end."

"Lou is my kind of gal. But we're not to that point yet." He leaned back. "You've got to get to it in the natural progress. *Then he clutched the keys with his talon hands...*"

"We're not to that point yet either." She put her glasses back on. "All right. Here we go." As she continued, she slowed down at the moments she knew he loved. "*While high overhead, green yellow and red, the North Lights swept in bars—Then you've got a hunch what the music meant...hunger and night and the stars.*" She tried to make her delivery as dramatic as possible, to suit his growing excitement. When she read "*then I ducked my head, and the lights went out, and two guns blazed in the dark,*" he gave a little whoop, as he always did, and said, "Blam! Blam!"

Finally, she finished softly, "*and the woman that kissed him—and pinched his poke—was the lady that's known as Lou.*"

He closed his eyes and smiled. "We decided what a poke was once, didn't we?"

"Yes, the little leather pouch he carried his gold dust in." She took off her glasses. For a moment the room was blurry. Her sight was getting worse and worse, but she didn't want bifocals, not yet. She took up the little mirror by her bedside table and looked at her eyes. Bloodshot. She had never believed her eyes were her best point. She pulled at one corner of her lid.

"So we must settle this jag time business."

"I'll do my best."

"Now, listen, Merce, I have something to say. This is the poem I want read at my memorial service, after I go. Forget about anything else I ever told you. This is the one. It will make everyone happy."

"All right." She was still examining her eyes in the mirror.

"Don't fail me, Merce. It's not in my will. I have to trust you with this."

"I said all right, Patrick." She glanced over at the window, where small rivulets had begun to ease their way down the glass. *Raining,* she thought. She touched her mouth again. *Perhaps I should call the Skin Salon for a facial. Not so extravagant. It's been six months or so.*

"The thing is," Patrick said, "I like to think of my memory service full of music and people laughing." The rain pushed against the glass with more insistence. "I'll just be sad to miss it myself, is all." He tilted his head to one side. "You'll be sad, won't you? Not to have me there?"

She tried to think of the name of the nice woman who had worked on her before.

"Merce!"

She jumped, and the book snapped together and fell off her lap onto the floor. The bookmark sailed out and slipped under the bed.

"Don't do that, Patrick," she said. "Of course I'll be sad. There's no need to shout at me."

"Yes, there is," he said. "There is a need." He teetered to his feet, gathered his robe about him, and marched off to his room.

Saturday morning was still and warm. By eleven it was hot, it felt like late June. It was not what one would call Indian summer, but something more like a temporary fever. By evening it would be damp and musty and humid.

"Are you speaking to me this morning?" she asked Patrick at breakfast.

"Why not?"

"I apologize for being distracted last night."

"You were not distracted. You were uninterested."

She rested her hands beneath her chin and looked at him. He was stirring raisins into his cereal with great concentration.

"Please forgive me," she said.

"The milk is sour," he said, sniffing it. "Here. You smell it." She had been forgiven. He always forgave her. Throughout their life together, he had forgiven her always—when she asked, when she hadn't asked, when she had nothing for which to be forgiven.

"Sour," she said to Patrick. "I'll get the fresh quart."

In the kitchen her Italian calendar for October pictured a colorful view of the grape harvest near San Gimignano. Today was Saturday. She looked at the clock. *Eighty-one hours*, she calculated, *and thirty minutes*. The weekend stretched out before her filled with hours, minutes as small as pomegranate seeds. But it was only a dinner. She had to remember that.

"Merce!" Patrick shouted. "Let's have the milk!"

Mrs. Medina finally reached Valentina Bird on Sunday evening. Tina was her department chair at Boston University, and Mrs. Medina hadn't talked with her in weeks. They were old friends. Mrs. Medina was wary.

"What in the world was going on with Patrick the other day?" Tina asked her.

"Yes, he told me you'd called."

"I knew he was there, he had said hello, but after that not a word. So I just kept talking, as usual."

"I think he was having one of his spells, Tina."

"Spells? Call it what it is, Mercedes. I hate that word, *spells*. Some sort of seizure? Has he had a stroke? He's one of my favorite people in the world. How is he?"

Mrs. Medina sighed. "Some days good, some days he's not all there. I don't think they know exactly what it is. He's just not young anymore. Don't blame me."

"Who's blaming you? Give him a kiss from me, all right? I'm sorry he's not feeling well. Now let's have some news about you."

"There's nothing much," Mrs. Medina said. "Sorry we seem— well, we've missed each other's calls."

"We have indeed. I have some papers here that need your signature. And I want to talk to you about your winter course. How about lunch?"

"Lunch?"

"Lunch. Remember lunch? We haven't had lunch since before the semester started. I want to see you!"

"Lunch would be fine."

"Okay, how about next Tuesday?"

"Tuesday's out."

"That was quick. Wednesday?"

Wednesday. She thought of Bond. "No, not Wednesday either."

"Well, you name a day, then."

"Could I call you, Tina? I'm having to watch Patrick more and more. Every day I have to just see what sort of shape he's in."

Tina paused. "Well, sure. You call me when you get a day free. But soon. I've missed you."

"And I've missed you."

"Something wrong, Mercedes? Don't want to pry."

"No, I'm fine. I'll call you soon."

"All right. Soon, then."

On Tuesday morning she rose at dawn, excited at the fog, which was still and watchful as breath among the partially leafless trees. The city seemed like a living creature of an unknown sort, poised at the peak of inhalation, a smile just appearing in its eyes.

And the day seemed to progress by inches, by moments that she savored as if they were parts of a joyous song, slowly ascending toward evening.

ten

The restaurant called Djuna was in the South End, across Tremont Street and up half a block from Hamersley's, where Mrs. Medina and Tina had come for dinner last winter and spent nearly sixty-five dollars apiece. Djuna was down five steps behind a window lit by an open book designed in green and blue neon. Sixty-five dollars here would probably buy a meal for three, including wine. The restaurant had been Lennie's choice. She greeted the woman who was seating customers, and while they were waiting for a table, ran off to the restroom, leaving Mrs. Medina sitting in a black plastic chair with a green padded seat, her fingers clasped tightly in her lap. She attempted not to look at any of the others talking and gesturing above her head. She hated waiting like this. Patrick had always swept her into any restaurant, and a table was always ready; he passed discreet, folded twenties to the maître d', and there was never a problem with anything.

But tonight she and Lennie had taken a packed 43 bus from Park Street, which rattled and slammed its way through rush hour with alarming ferocity. They stood all the way and were unable to converse because of the noise, a convenient situation that allowed Mrs. Medina some time to calm her nerves.

She had agonized all day about what to wear. She did not want to err on the side of conservatism. On the other hand, she had no idea where they would go to eat, and she had a horror of dressing inappropriately. She had finally put on dark green gabardine trousers and a white silk shirt buttoned at the neck. On her way out the door she realized she had on no jewelry and rushed back and threw on the silver and coral earrings Tina had brought her from Antigua.

The bus lurched to a stop at the Berkeley Street light and threw them against each other, and Lennie looked up and laughed. Mrs. Medina's hands were sweaty, the hand bars were sticky with someone else's residue, and she thought the earrings were probably wrong. They *were* wrong. The sickening smell of mothballs was no doubt seeping out of her short suede jacket with the rubbed elbows that she hadn't worn since last spring.

I tried too hard, she thought.

"Stop whining," a woman's voice said close to her ear.

Startled, Mrs. Medina turned to see a heavy-set woman shaking her child's arm.

All right. All right. She'd quit whining.

"This is a nice place," Lennie said as they sat down. "But don't expect the Ritz."

"Oh, I don't expect the Ritz," Mrs. Medina said quickly, "in fact, I'm glad it's not the Ritz. I don't like the Ritz much. They won't let Patrick into the bar without a tie."

Lennie shot her an amused glance. Mrs. Medina's leather purse, shaped like a small saddlebag, slipped off the back of her chair and onto the floor.

The restaurant was long and narrow, with an entrance to a little terrace in the back. The walls were hung with some pencil drawings of various female writers—Colette, Toni Morrison, and Djuna Barnes herself—and near their table was a photograph of a large-eyed gamine sitting on a bag of grain, inscribed, "Love to Madeleine from the heart of the souk. Jane Bowles."

They had one candle floating in a small cut-glass bowl. Its flickering light glanced like quick bright touches on Lennie's fingers, which were turning a fork over and over against the blue tablecloth. Mrs. Medina's hands were again clasped in her lap.

"Is your husband feeling better?" Lennie asked politely.

"What?"

"You said he wasn't feeling well."

"He's dying," Mrs. Medina said.

Lennie was wearing a black twill jacket with a simple white T-shirt underneath. She was not in the least masculine, or even particularly boyish, but her manner—even when she was seated—had a certain attractive bravado about it. Mrs. Medina realized that she had all evening simply to raise her eyes and look at her.

"A Beefeater martini, straight up," Mrs. Medina told the waitress.
"Rolling Rock," Lennie said. And added, "Straight up."

Mrs. Medina cleared her throat. "Do you come here often?" she said. Lennie burst into laughter.
"A joke?" Mrs. Medina asked her.
"It's the oldest pickup line in the world," Lennie said, leaning forward, her eyebrows drawn together in feigned intensity. "You never heard it?"
Mrs. Medina flushed. "Yes, I suppose so—"
"I know, I know. Sorry I laughed."
Mrs. Medina smiled.
"In fact, I used to come here a lot," Lennie said, "but it's a hike now from North Cambridge."
The martini finally arrived, and Mrs. Medina grasped it as if it were a communion chalice. A waiter passed with a plate of scampi, leaving a heady trail of garlic in his wake. Mrs. Medina's stomach gathered itself into a knot of hunger, but she was doubtful whether food was what she needed. She closed her eyes.
"So," Lennie said, smiling. "What looks good?"
"How is the sole?" Mrs. Medina asked, frowning at the menu.
"The sole? I don't know. Everything here is generally good, but don't get the chicken whatever—here it is—the chicken Kiev. The chef still doesn't get it. She puts peas in it."
"All right. I won't get the chicken Kiev."
"Always noisy in here," Lennie said.
Mrs. Medina was wary of looking around. She felt the room was filled with eyes, all waiting to meet her own. She straightened the collar of her blouse.
"What'll it be, ladies?" the waitress said.
"Hi, Sylvia," Lennie said to her.
"Oh, hi, Len. I was looking over your head. How've you been?"
"Pretty good."
"Connie's here," the waitress said. "Up near the front."

"Saw her," Lennie said. "I'll have the linguini with clams and a salad."

The waitress smiled at Mrs. Medina. "Refill?" she said. "Or you want to order?"

"The sole," Mrs. Medina said quickly, and shut the menu.

The sole was very good, moist, and came with grilled tomatoes and spinach. Mrs. Medina was very much aware that she was on her third gin, and Lennie had switched from Rolling Rock to white wine. The gin was decidedly bad with the spinach. Her head began to ache a bit. Over the din of voices, Kathleen Battle was singing something from *Cosi fan tutte*. She put down her fork, feeling the advent of despair.

Lennie wiped her mouth. She looked at Mrs. Medina for a long moment. "You're not comfortable here, are you?"

"Comfort," Mrs. Medina said, shrugging her shoulders.

"What is it? Did I use the wrong fork?" She stopped. "Sorry. I'm an asshole sometimes. Always the wrong joke."

Mrs. Medina longed to be able to think of the two of them as old friends, just having dinner. But they would never have been friends. Not in the natural course of things. They wouldn't be here if something else was not...supposed. Anticipated.

This meal was exhausting her.

"Connie," Mrs. Medina said suddenly, surprising herself, "was someone you lived with?" There was nothing to do but jump into it.

"Yeah, for a while. After I finished at U Mass. We still look out for each other."

"I don't mean to pry—"

"Not prying. You can ask me anything you want."

"I don't generally do that," Mrs. Medina said. She took a deep breath. "I'm just trying to make conversation, believe it or not."

"Why?" Lennie took a sip of her wine, then drained the glass. "We're doing all right."

Mrs. Medina took a graceful sip of her martini, but the glass was empty, had been for a while. So she put the glass down, again at a loss.

"Want another?" Lennie said.

"No."

Lennie moved her neck around, as if it were stiff. *Or perhaps she's bored*, Mrs. Medina thought. Lennie ran both her hands back through her hair and checked her little pigtail. Tonight she had braided three orange beads into it. "Do you ever trim that?" Mrs. Medina said quickly. "That braid?"

"This?" Lennie reached one hand back and gave it a few flips. "Doreen takes care of it. She cuts my hair. I'm thinking of changing my hairstyle, though." She ran her hand over the top of her head, where her hair was tousled. "This is getting sort of old now, I think. I'm tired of it."

Mrs. Medina smiled.

They looked at each other, and Lennie tilted her head to one side as if she wanted to ask a question. Mrs. Medina's hands were clasped in front of her on the table, and the little candle was burning low. She realized she could hear Lennie breathing. Or was it her own breath? Lennie seemed to be considering some action, and she finally reached across and cupped Mrs. Medina's hands with her own. She said nothing. Her eyes were clear and calm. Every tiny muscle in Mrs. Medina's body was primed to spring away, but in the midst of this tension her mind grew quiet, and she held Lennie's gaze with a courage she hadn't known she possessed. She supposed Lennie could see the fear in her face, but there was nothing to do but trust her with it.

There they sat. Lennie's hands pressed tightly against Patrick's ring, and Mrs. Medina felt this pressure with an odd sort of pleasure, as if he had his arm around her, urging her forward. Then Lennie withdrew her hands, and something new began.

Mrs. Medina gripped the seat of her chair. *I'm old enough to have a heart attack*, she thought, *or a stroke*. She hoped it wouldn't happen here. "Well," she said. "Is this a restaurant for women?"

"Do you mean for lesbians?"

"I suppose I do."

"No. Not exclusively. Lots of lesbians come here, but gay men do too, and neighborhood people. Look around you."

Mrs. Medina ventured a glance. She wondered which woman was Connie.

"Feel better now?" Lennie asked. "Want some coffee?"

"I'd better. Espresso if they have it."

"They have it."

"Dessert?"

Mrs. Medina didn't think she would ever eat again. A waiter arrived with the coffee and departed. "I guess we don't want dessert," Lennie said.

Mrs. Medina smiled. "I guess not."

"What is that music? Do you know it?"

Mrs. Medina listened. "Sounds like Mozart."

"You like that?"

Mrs. Medina nodded. She stirred her coffee. "What kind of music do you like?"

"Me? Oh, I don't know. Regular stuff."

"Rock?"

"Some rock, yeah—Aretha, Chrissie Hynde. And I like Kenny G." She took a sip of coffee. "You're mostly into classical, right?"

"Mostly. But I do like some jazz. I'm not familiar with Kenny G, but I actually heard Stan Getz in Paris once, years ago."

"That's cool. Some dark little club? Down three steps, lots of smoke? That's what I think about Paris."

"No, in fact it was in a very respectable little theater, no smoke at all!" She laughed. "Not the best place for jazz, I guess. But I loved it."

"I bet it was great." She drained the coffee from her cup.

"I guess I need to go to—" Mrs. Medina began, and turned toward her purse.

"Hi, Len."

Mrs. Medina smelled the perfume first, then when she turned around she saw the back of a dark head bent over Lennie's face. The front part of this head appeared to be giving Lennie a quick kiss.

Lennie pushed the visitor into a vertical position. "You could knock first," she said, looking up.

"I did. You were absorbed." She turned to Mrs. Medina with a lovely smile composed of teeth that had benefited from a lifetime of the most wholesome food and the highest-priced dental care. "Hi," she said, sticking out her hand. "I'm Connie Downs."

Mrs. Medina smiled. "Mercedes Medina." Mrs. Medina gripped Connie's hand with a firmness based on years of practice.

"That's an auspicious name," Connie said. "Should I know it?" She touched her hand to her hair, which was up in a sort of casual knot at the base of her neck. She was wearing a stylish black skirt that ended just barely beneath the level of the table, and the plunging neck of her matching jacket revealed a well-tanned expanse of chest. Pearls. One imagined shapely legs. She was in exquisite taste, and her eyes were bright with curiosity. She put her hands on her hips, and a waiter eased past her with a tray of desserts.

"You're blocking the way," Lennie said.

Connie looked around for a chair, but all in the vicinity were occupied. She smiled down in a genuine way at Mrs. Medina. "Lennie and I are old friends," she said. "Are you an old friend? Or a relative that's been out of the picture? I love those earrings, by the way." Mrs. Medina read this remark immediately. The earrings were wrong.

"A friend brought them to me from Antigua."

"I'm going to the Caribbean in February," she said. She turned to Lennie. "Dad's got the boat in St. Martin this winter. Want to come for a week?"

Lennie sighed as if this was an exchange they had had often.

"Maybe you're a client," Connie said to Mrs. Medina. "Lennie's going to grow something for you?"

"Do you ever shut up?" Lennie asked her.

"I guess I'm a new friend," Mrs. Medina said.

"Aha." Connie tilted her head and gave Mrs. Medina a long serious look. She was unusually pretty. No getting around it.

"Con, you are seriously in the way," Lennie said. "Why don't I call you tomorrow?"

"I'm going off to L.A. tomorrow. Trouble in paradise."

"Connie's at Fidelity," Lennie said. "She's a whiz at making sure other people's money is pampered."

"I could've made you rich," Connie said. "But you wouldn't let me."

"I'm happier living hand-to-mouth, I guess."

"That's such a silly point of view. You just don't trust anything you can't hold in your hands."

"That's about right."

"Do you know Harvey Bass?" Mrs. Medina said.

"Harvey, sure. We were at the B-school together. Great guy. How do you know him?"

"He's my husband's great-nephew."

"Your husband?" She looked at Lennie.

"Oh, well," Lennie said, laughing. "You'd better go back to your table, hotshot. Call me when you get back. Don't get burned on the beach."

"You still living with Kenny the creep?"

"He pays half the rent."

"When he thinks about it. I wish you'd get him out of there. Trouble's going to dump on him in a major way one of these days, and he's not one to go down alone."

"You see drama everywhere, don't you? Say good night, Connie."

"All right. Good night, Connie." She shook Mrs. Medina's hand again. "If I see Harvey, I'll tell him I met you," she said. "Keep an eye on this girl."

"I will," Mrs. Medina said.

Connie gave the top of Lennie's head a brief little rub and moved her shapely body back toward the front of the restaurant.

"She seems very nice," Mrs. Medina said.

"She went to school in Switzerland for a while."

"Did she."

"Yeah. It was her personal mission to smooth out my edges."

"Edges can be intriguing."

"Well, she wasn't one hundred percent successful." She stretched. "If I hadn't quit smoking, this is the moment I would light up."

Mrs. Medina looked at her watch. It was nearly ten-thirty.

"Got to go?" Lennie said.

"I should. Someone's with Patrick. She should get home." She spotted their waitress and said, "Check, please." At least that worked.

Lennie reached for her billfold.

"My treat," Mrs. Medina said.

"No need," Lennie said. "We can split it."

"No," Mrs. Medina said. "I hate to argue about checks."

"I won't argue, then," Lennie said. "Thanks."

The restaurant had cleared out somewhat, and when they arrived outside they found it had been raining. Connie had gone.

"How will you get home?" Mrs. Medina said. She thought of her bed, she thought of just collapsing into it and sleeping for a day without getting up. She just wanted to get away from Lennie now, away from the tension, and home. She wanted to sit with Patrick while he had his nightcap, watch the news, then fall into bed.

Lennie looked up and down the street. "I don't see a bus. I guess I'll walk over and take the Orange Line downtown."

"Let me send you in a cab." She opened her wallet and extracted a twenty, folded it in squares, just to be ready.

"It's only four or five blocks. No problem. You want a cab?" Her eyes searched the traffic. There were none in sight. Rainy night. "How far do you live?"

"Clarendon and Commonwealth. I'll go inside and call a cab."

"Why don't we walk?"

"At this time of night?"

"Sure. We can walk right across Dartmouth Street."

"No. Look, there's a cab."

Lennie gave a loud whistle and, miraculously, the cab veered to the curb. Lennie, it seemed, had a way with cabs.

"Come on," Mrs. Medina said. "I'll give you a ride to the subway." The ride would not be long.

"Something wrong?" Lennie said in the cab.

"What makes you think something's wrong?"

"You're mad."

"If I were mad, you'd know it."

"Everyone says that."

Mrs. Medina shook her head. "I'm tired. I drank too much."

"Well, something's wrong."

Mrs. Medina gripped the door harness. Too many years of straightforward conversation with Patrick. She did not know how to be evasive.

"Maybe I'm not into Mozart, but you didn't even ask me about my Zen garden."

"What, don't tell me *you're* mad?" Mrs. Medina said with a laugh. "I'm sorry. Your garden interests me very much."

"Well, we can't talk about it now."

Mrs. Medina felt herself being yanked from one emotional yardarm to another.

Nothing was settled, that was it.

"Back Bay Station," the driver said.

"I'm going on," Mrs. Medina said to him through the partition. She turned to Lennie. "I can easily send you to Cambridge in the cab."

"Cabs aren't my thing," Lennie said. It was very dark in the backseat. The orange neon circle over the portal of the station cast watery shadows through the window. "Thanks again for dinner."

"My pleasure."

They sat in silence.

"Back Bay Station, ladies," the cab driver repeated. The interior of the cab smelled of vanilla. A little vanilla Christmas tree, dangling from the back window.

Lennie put one hand on the door. Mrs. Medina felt as if she were sending her off on a troop ship, to war, that she might never see her again. "I'll see you soon," she said, with a sudden catch in her voice.

Lennie turned back and put one hand on Mrs. Medina's cheek, and her hand drew their faces closer until Mrs. Medina could smell a vague trace of Lennie's scent, and sensed with a sort of violent recognition the heat of Lennie's body. Lennie kissed her briefly; briefly, but not without a soft urgency, still holding Mrs. Medina's face with one hand. She felt the hard edge of Lennie's teeth, her full lower lip.

The cabbie raced his engine. The meter ticked over. And a burst of rain blew against the window.

Lennie put her cheek against Mrs. Medina's for an instant, then opened the door. "I'd better beat the rain," she said, and jogged off toward the station entrance.

Mrs. Medina was afraid to move. She could not for several moments even open her eyes. The tension that had held her together all evening was disintegrating as she felt Lennie move farther and farther away from her, into the neon rain. She put her hand to her forehead.

"Where am I going now?" the driver said. "Where *to*?"

eleven

"**D**id you shut the living room window?" Patrick asked her. "It's going to rain all night."

"It's shut."

This was where she'd wanted to be, only an hour ago. Patrick in his chair, drink in hand, the television tuned to a late Celtics game from Los Angeles. She stared at the set.

"Well, sit down, Merce. You're nearly in my way. What are you sipping on there?"

She sank into his wing chair. "Water." She looked at her watch. Lennie would be home by now.

"Are you drunk?" Patrick asked.

She smiled. "No."

"Well, you can tell me what you had to eat. Where did you go?"

"A little place in the South End." She had grabbed some matches on her way out the door of the restaurant, and now she felt for them in her pocket and took them gently into her fist. "I had sole, with a grilled tomato, and some spinach."

"Very healthy."

"And three large martinis."

He gave a low whistle and took a sip of his whiskey. He frowned at the Celtics on the screen for a moment. "No wonder you crept back here so late. Did you talk about me? Does she know all my habits now, all my ups and downs?"

"I do sometimes talk about you."

"What I mean, Merce, is are you going to be running out to see her, night and day?"

"Patrick, we only had dinner together."

He looked over at her. The hand that was holding his drink trembled a bit, so he put his glass down on the table.

Without returning his look, she said, "Do you remember, years ago, when we were in Paris, someone took us to hear Stan Getz?"

"Who?"

"Stan Getz, he plays the tenor saxophone. It wasn't at a bar, it was at a hall somewhere or a small theater, on the Left Bank, probably."

"That is completely gone from my memory. I only like Louis Armstrong."

"Yes, I know. But I wondered whether you remembered." She put her water glass down on the floor and leaned her head back against the chair. Exhaustion was loosening her limbs. She remembered Lennie's hand against her cheek, the contours of her mouth, the rush of rain as she had left the cab. She closed her eyes.

She knew Patrick was watching her, and it was all right. He finally turned out his table lamp. The commentary from the television suggested that the Celtics were beginning to score some points, she heard that over the sound of the rain, which was steady now. Patrick pulled up his brown blanket with the tiny gold threads. His drink was now mostly melted ice. Finally, he used his remote and shut off the game, leaving the room in darkness, and there was no sound but Mrs. Medina's deep, regular breathing.

In her dream it was, surprisingly, Connie who appeared, lithe and chic in an outfit of black silk. Mrs. Medina sat at a table attempting to have a conversation with Lennie, who was present only as sullen energy, unseen. She saw herself talking, the fear building in her belly, what should she say next? What riposte to make to Connie's brilliant bons mots, her fluid gestures, her obviously sexual familiarity with Lennie? In her dream Mrs. Medina imagined Connie was the perfect lover; she was reminding Lennie of particular ways she had pleased her, and in the dream Mrs. Medina herself stumbled and careened from one absolutely stupid remark to another.

The dream went on unbearably. Mrs. Medina was overwhelmed by a bitter sense of betrayal, and rose to depart.

She woke suddenly, as if she had been touched on the shoulder.

She was in darkness, not in her own bed, and as she moved, her shoulder and neck and her lower back protested painfully. Patrick, still in his chair, was snuffling and bubbling in his sleep, and she read his table clock as four-twenty. She wondered why he hadn't wakened her, as he usually did when she drifted off in his room.

She creaked her way into his bathroom and turned on the light. In the mirror she looked her age, she looked as if she had a hangover—which she did. *Do I look the same?* She touched her mouth with one finger. *Lennie kissed me*, she thought. She sat down on top of Patrick's laundry hamper and put her face in her hands. *I should be delirious.* Her eyes were full of grit. She felt weightless, almost; as if she were floating on her back, unable to move: pulled toward the shore, then toward the open sea.

She put some water on her face and went back out into the bedroom.

"You passed out on me," his voice came out of the dark.

She sighed. "I'm sorry, Patrick. I drank too much."

"It's now nineteen minutes to five."

"I didn't mean to wake you. I'm on my way to my own bed."

"Want some cocoa?"

"I'll make you some, if you like."

"Not for me, I don't drink that stuff. I was going to brew some for you."

"No need."

She heard him struggling out of his recliner. "Okay, I'll make some of my special soup for you," he said. "Pardon me if I don't shave first."

This soup was "special" only by virtue of the fact that Patrick had invented it himself and invested it with mystical curative powers. It was simply a can of chicken broth, a tablespoon of sherry, some pastina, chives, celery, a tomato—if there was one around—and several dashes of Tabasco. Parmesan to finish. She sat at the kitchen table watching him at the stove, just to be sure, but he used a church key on the broth instead of a can opener and was careful to keep the burner set on medium. She seemed to be observing him from a high point in one corner of the kitchen.

He looked over his shoulder at her. "I'm at my best at this hour of the day."

"Yes," she said dreamily. She poured herself a second glass of tomato juice. The salt was wonderful, brought tears to her eyes.

"Then it all goes to hell." He brought over the old blue cracked teapot that he liked to use and two white mugs with Tanglewood green tree logos. "I made up some tea too," he said. He pointed at her juice glass. "You are fooled by that stuff. It isn't healthy. And it's full of salt." He set her steaming broth before her with a little clump. "Your veins will shrivel up."

She put her hands around the bowl gently and stared across at him without really focusing. Finally, he said, "Ready," and poured the tea. He gave himself a little dollop of milk. He squinted his eyes as he sucked the tea up through the steam. He liked his tea nearly boiling.

The soup was wonderful, just what she needed. "This is good," she said. "Thank you."

Light was appearing in the kitchen window. It was Wednesday morning.

"Have you betrayed me?" he asked her.

She reached over to touch his hand and reassure him, that was her immediate instinct, but then she paused. She had, in a certain way, betrayed him. Right now she knew her duty to Patrick, she knew she loved him in a way that would endure, but there was at this moment no one in her heart, no one in her mind, but Lennie. If Lennie had called her she would have gone to her immediately.

"Aha," he said.

"I haven't slept with her, Patrick, if that's what you mean. But God knows I've thought about it. That may be a betrayal in your book." Now she did put her hand over his.

He raised his chin. "Well, in my book that might be on the verge."

She continued to eat.

"But—" He held up one finger.

"Wait," she said. She pushed her bowl to one side. She was tired of being on the defensive, and she didn't want to talk with him just yet; it was her own precarious heaven, and she wanted to stumble around for a while.

"Wait," she said again.

He put both hands on the table. "This is going to be a three-ring circus," he said. "And they will carry me off to the undertaker's slab alone."

"You will do me a great favor and not speak that way again."

"Well," he said, and looked at the ceiling, "I'm not going to the slab anyway, I'm going into the fiery furnace."

"Yes, you are. And so am I."

"We had a life, goddamn it," he said. "Why can't you be loyal to it?"

She thought about that for a long moment. "I am loyal to it," she said finally, having decided that that was the truth. "It's very precious to me."

He looked glumly at his empty tea mug. "You're wearing me out," he said after a moment. "I should have known better than to grab you when you were so young."

She smiled. "Look, the sun is up."

"The sun has nothing to do with it."

"You're right, it doesn't." She gathered the dishes together and put them into the sink. The wonderful exhaustion was creeping back into her limbs. And now the joy was coming with it.

He peered at her face. "Your face looks like those roaring dawns when we used to drink all night and then run down the middle of Fifth Avenue dodging cabs and slink between the sheets at the Grosvenor as the roosters were crowing."

"That bad?"

"You always looked as good as Dietrich."

She smiled. "I'm ready to slink between the sheets right now. I'll do up these dishes later."

"Yes. I may be a housewife, but I won't do dishes."

She got up and went around the table and kissed him on the head.

"Don't do that just now," he said.

"All right." At the kitchen door she said, "I'll sleep for two or three hours. If I'm not up by ten, wake me, all right?"

"Merce."

"Yes?"

"You should bring her here. She needs to meet me if she's my rival."

"Patrick, I am asleep on my feet."

"You shouldn't drink martinis at your age. You don't have the head for drink anymore. Go to bed."

So she did.

But she didn't sleep. In spite of the soup, the tea, and her several hours of restless unconsciousness in Patrick's chair, she still felt drunk. She put her head on her pillow, her body collapsed into the sheets, but the room circled her. She opened her eyes. *Did I kiss her back?* she thought. *I can't remember. It was such a shock.*

She groaned and turned over. She put her hand over her own mouth and the drunken feeling began again. Her lips felt dry and not in the least sensual. What had they felt like to Lennie? Last night she must have tasted overpoweringly of stale gin. Ghastly. Now she knew she had to sleep. But: *Will we go on, will we speak about it?* She opened her eyes quickly. *And there were the hands, earlier in the evening, I'd forgotten. She clasped my hands in hers and said—oh, what? Nothing! Nothing was said. But her eyes.*

And then there was Connie. Mrs. Medina pondered every bit of that conversation she could remember. "We still look out for each other," Lennie had said. Well, what? Did they sleep together still? How beautiful Connie was. Anyone would want to sleep with her. And young. And young.

All she knew now was that she wanted to see Lennie and kiss her again, and she didn't think she would be able to do anything until she could get to that moment.

~

Patrick opened her door, and she sensed him standing there but did not open her eyes.

Finally, he said, "Merce. Telephone."

She sat up with a start.

"I wouldn't have wakened you, Merce, but it's ten-thirty. You need to be up and about. Almost lunchtime."

She shook her head groggily. "I didn't hear it." She checked her phone. "Oh. The ringer's off. Who is it?" Hope rose quickly. For it must be Lennie. She was stupidly grateful that Lennie had called her first. "Patrick, shut the door, would you, please? I'm awake now, out in a minute."

"Good morning, Mercedes."

She sank back against her pillow, in blackness for a moment.

"Bond."

"Patrick tells me you're in bed. Not ill?"

"No. Just—" She sat up again. *She kissed me*, she thought. The day opened like wings.

"Mercedes, could we move our appointment up to five-thirty? I've had a cancellation."

Her mind searched about. Today? With Bond?

"If that's inconvenient, six is still fine."

"Perhaps it's not necessary after all, Bond."

"Whatever you want. Patrick better?"

She ran her fingers through her hair. "Yes. Yes, I'd say Patrick is acting better."

"And you?"

Without hesitation she responded, "Today I'm extremely happy."

Bond laughed. "Well, good. I wish more of the people I see had that complaint."

"I'd still like to talk with you about Patrick. I'd just rather not do it today, if that's all right."

"All right. You sound quite different today. I was concerned about you the other evening."

"I guess I've had time to think," she said quickly.

"Good. Good." He paused. "Call me when you'd like to talk, then."

"I will. Thanks."

She sat on the edge of the bed with the telephone in her lap. The question was, would Lennie call? Should she call?

Mrs. Medina started a pot of coffee, then went to the living room window overlooking the avenue. The sun was sailing along above some high overcast and a ragged carpet of leaves on the grass across the street still clung together in the damp from last night's rain. She hugged her own body in a stillness of excitement.

"Merce!" Patrick called from the kitchen.

She rushed in to find the coffee bubbling out in little squirts over the top of the stove. "I forgot to put the lid on!" she said happily, mopping it all up.

"You talk about *me*," Patrick said darkly from the kitchen door. Today, in a rare lapse of taste, he had put on a green-and-orange plaid tie with a pink shirt.

"Well, we need a new pot, one of those automatic-filter things."

"Doesn't taste right," he said. "And it's lunchtime—why are you making coffee?"

"I felt like some," she said. "Let's see if I can save some of this."

"Well, it's lunchtime."

She looked up at him with wide eyes. "No, not yet," she said slowly, with a smile in her voice. "We'll eat at one."

"You've made the day out of whack," he said, "sleeping like that. And you've got on a skirt."

She sat down at the table and sipped at the bitter coffee. "Yes, I do."

"Why?"

There was a tremendous crash of cymbals from her bedroom.

"What is that?" He listened intently. "Is it that pansy Mahler?"

"Yes, it's almost finished. And it is anything but a pansy work. That's an offensive word. Why do you use such words?"

"That does it." He marched away down the hall, then turned and came back. "I told the doc that you should talk to him."

"You told Bond I needed to talk with him?"

"Well, I let him probe around me with his little pencils and machines. And I beat 'em. Now the signs point to you. We can't have you raging around like this, all deranged, burning up the coffee."

She could not bring herself to be angry. "You're a sly one. I'd rather talk to you."

He squeaked across the floor in his sneakers and sat down at the table. "Let me have a taste of that," he said. "I'm hungry as hell." He made a face and put the cup down. "Can we get this day back on track? I'm getting mad. Do I have to fix my own lunch too?"

"You really want to eat this early?"

"I could eat a truck right now."

"Okay. Lunch it is."

~

She dreamed over the lunch dishes, letting Palmolive run gently over her yellow-gloved fingers like green gold, and thought: *I'll send her flowers.* She turned off the water and stood in the steam, gazing at the patterned tile behind the sink. "Oh, stupid," she said aloud, "she's surrounded by flowers." Then she laughed and spread her hands out, dripping over the floor, and gave a quiet little shout.

She took a cup of Hu-Kwa back to her room, where the Mahler had concluded. There was a certain air of *Rosenkavalier* hanging about in her room, so she put on the old Schwartzkopf recording and settled back on the chaise.

Some minutes passed. She drifted.

Her door creaked open. She lifted her eyelids slightly.

"Turn off those goddamned Huns," Patrick said, "and let me sleep."

She roused herself and switched off the machine. "Go back to bed, Patrick. Opera's over."

"Why do you listen to those Nazis?" he said. "The music is intolerable."

She turned her body to face him. "I understand that you want the music lowered," she said, "and that's fine. But I don't need a critique of what I'm listening to. Go back to bed."

"Mooning about." He clicked his tongue.

She stood up quickly, and saw him flinch back, and after that she was ashamed, her anger left her, and she smiled. "I guess I'll have a lie down too," she said, "so go on back."

After a moment he went silently back down the hall.

She looked at her watch. She would call Lennie at four.

"Lennie is not here," Guido said decisively. "Not here today."

She had imagined every scenario but this. "Not there—is she ill? This is Mercedes Medina, Guido."

"Yes, madam, I know. No, not ill. Out with the Buddhist fathers. With permission from me. They are doing bulbs today."

"I see."

Guido volunteered nothing more.

"Do you expect her back, then?" Mrs. Medina asked, disappointment beginning to creep toward her across the carpet.

"Who can say? She has keys, she may come back after I close. Do I leave her a message from you?"

"Yes, all right. Please just say that I called."

"Certainly."

She replaced the receiver and sat without moving until the light left her room and it was completely dark.

twelve

Patrick wanted a fire, so they had their evening drink in his room.

"First fire of the season," Patrick said with satisfaction. "Now, sit down here and enjoy it."

Mrs. Medina had called directory assistance for Lennie's home phone number and memorized it instantly. She looked into the fire and thought of these magic digits—two threes, a one, two sixes, two sevens—that could put Lennie's voice into her ear in ten seconds.

"You're sitting on that telephone cord," Patrick observed.

She smiled and untangled it.

"What is that smile?" he asked. "It's not for me, is it?"

She looked at him and could not think of what to say. "I'm here. Just a bit disoriented today, is all."

After a moment he said, "You'd better talk to me, Merce. I'm tired of waiting for you to sink my ship."

Mrs. Medina got up and closed the curtains, as if this closer privacy would make her task less difficult. Patrick slurped his whiskey, and the ice clattered against his teeth. She wondered how frightened he was, if he were as frightened as she was. The fire snapped and exploded sparks, burning last winter's dry wood.

"Noisy," she said, settling back into her chair.

Patrick looked over at her. "Can't help it. The ice creeps up the glass suddenly and bangs me in the mouth."

She smiled. "The fire," she said.

"Fires are noisy. That is their nature."

She took a deep breath. "First," she said, "there is no need to be nervous about me. About you, about me and you."

"Nerves are not involved."

"Patrick, just let me have my say, then you can make any comments you want."

He took another drink of whiskey and clutched at his blanket with an involuntary grasp.

Her mind seemed to fill with a sudden waterfall of random electrical confusion: She heard the Mahler symphony, then the cabbie's voice asking "Where to? Where *to*?" She felt Lennie's hands clasp her own, then imagined them deep in dark earth, setting bulbs, and saw her rising up, brushing her hands on her thighs, and imagined those thighs, and Lennie's mouth.

Patrick put his glass on his table and looked over at her.

"Last night," she began, "last night something happened, a small kiss, Patrick, is what it was, but I'm afraid it's put me round the bend."

He watched her steadily, obediently silent.

"Surely this must have happened in my life sometime before—" She shook her head. She knew it hadn't. She turned in her chair to face him more directly. "I'm sorry if this is painful for you to hear, but I have to talk to you. I can't just continue along in this state." His face was set and calm, and he turned toward the fire. "Did I tell you how old she was? That should stop me cold right there, shouldn't it? And we don't have a thing in common. Oh, hell," she added, and let her head fall against the back of the chair.

He raised his chin a bit, tilted his head, and observed her out of the corner of one eye. But he did not offer to help her negotiate the labyrinth through which she was threading her way.

"I don't know what my options are," she said without opening her eyes. "That's telling, I suppose. I suppose at my age I should be content just thinking about her. But...it may be too late." She opened her eyes and looked over at Patrick. A few moments went by, and a log fell with a surge of sparks. The muffled sound of rush hour horns rose from the street below. "That's it," she said finally. "I have no intention of leaving you, and what I feel for her does not diminish my love for you one whit. That's all I have to say."

She watched him pick at a frayed thread on his shirt cuff. Why he had chosen that old pink shirt today was still a mystery. He clearly hadn't been thinking about what he was putting on.

"I may speak now, I take it," he said after a few minutes.

"I hope you will."

He finished his drink and wiped his upper lip with his forefinger. "Women complicate things, the crazy fools, and screw up everyone around them. You're following right along the trail, Merce, right along the well-worn trail, and the coils are rising up around you. You're going to throw yourself into a pit and drag me with you. I will not go."

Yes, she could throw herself into a pit.

"My problem is easy. You are my wife. I count on you for companionship, and over these last weeks you have not been a companion. It makes me mad. I don't care if you're in love with a girl, a snake, or a Ford V-8. Makes no difference. I need you with me, and when you're not there I'm lost in the outfield. You're in love with this kid—so what? Great feeling. Enjoy it. Sleep with her if you can loosen up. I've prepared myself for this event, even if you've thrown me off the tracks a little here. I've been expecting a man to march up the path for a long time, not some girl. But don't take yourself off in the distance. Where I can't get to you. Makes me feel like you're trudging mud all over our life. And that's all I have to say."

They sat there together, and she heard him begin to wheeze a bit. The whiskey was affecting his sinuses, as it sometimes did.

"Patrick—"

"I have not been a saint in my life, Mercedes."

"No."

"But don't do this just to pay me back."

"Patrick!"

"All right. All right. If you want to and she's willing, don't worry about the age thing. I myself have never had a problem with younger fillies." God knows that was true. "And stop looking for things in common, because it doesn't matter. But be realistic, Merce. Her bones are younger, her mind is younger, and she's liable to flit about. Don't expect too much. Women have a hard time with that."

"Some men too, I think."

"Well, I never wanted any more than moment to moment. Except for you. I knew I wanted you for the long haul."

"Yes."

"You're smitten. Don't analyze it to shreds." He patted the top of his head in an abstract way. "I was smitten with you. I remember how I felt, clear as a day in May. I thought if I didn't bed you down immediately you'd float away from me."

"That first weekend in Balbano, it was all sex, then?"

"Don't be a fool. I was nearly sixty then, Merce. No, I wanted to get you close to me as soon as I could. Wrap you in and never let you go. You were young. Sex was just a way."

She had a quick memory of the first weekend Patrick had asked her to go away, waiting for him backstage at the Teatro Comunale in Florence, two weeks after they had been introduced, warm, heady days, during which they had seen each other nearly every day. It was May, and he and Santino and Barbara had played a brilliant recital at the Maggio Musicale, the Tchaikovsky, a Beethoven, and a new cycle of songs for mezzo-soprano and piano trio by Gina Bagni. In the darkened theater she had watched his arm moving with vigorous sensuality across his cello; he had held the instrument like a lover, and she had wondered about Patrick Medina, there in the dark, and thought of the bag containing her nightshirt, a skirt, some underwear, that was waiting in the checkroom. She was at the theater on this very warm May night because Patrick had telephoned her at the school—the Maestra had fetched her away from her students, with a disapproving look—to say, "Pack a bag and meet me after the concert. You won't be back until Monday morning."

And so, after the confusion backstage, he had taken her away in a rented, or borrowed, Alfa, and with the top down he drove masterfully over the autostrada to Lucca and five miles beyond, through the darkened hills to the village of Balbano and the Villa Casanova, a huge old stone farmhouse now become an inn, where the owners knew him, and kissed him, and didn't mind that it was one-thirty in the morning. They gave Patrick the room keys and a bottle of Prosecco, and Patrick took her hand and drew her across the gravel yard to a stone wall. Below them, among the dark hills, the immense night landscape of Tuscany lay under wheels of stars, and a sweet wind carried the aromas of wild sage and pine. In the darkness they talked of the small, ruined castle they had passed on the road and counted three falling stars; they watched a late train move like a speedy necklace across the valley floor. She looked sideways at Patrick and thought that she probably belonged with him, and it was easy and she was not frightened. And she was ready for him. But then they finished the wine and he took her elbow, guided her to her room—her own room!—and bid her good night.

When she awoke the next morning and threw open her windows, the first thing she saw was a golden horse at full gallop in the sunny field below, followed by a foal trying happily to keep up, and she almost exclaimed in delight. When she lifted her eyes she saw the gentle curves of the hills, still pooled in mist, and then Patrick had knocked at her door, with a waiter bearing a tray of golden crusted cornettos, fresh-squeezed orange juice, and foaming cappuccino.

Patrick said at breakfast, "I'm whisking you off to an illustrious villa, about an hour from here. They want the trio to play there in the fall, and I'd like to scout it out. We won't play with mosquitoes. What do you know about acoustics? I need your opinion." He seemed to be enfolding her into his life without asking, and yet without presumption, and she knew at that moment that their life together was beginning from that day. From that day. And that night, when he took her to his room, it seemed a natural extension of the day during which this knowledge had become clear to them both, the day in which small pieces fell together: the easy fit of their intellects, their palaver, the hot noon sun, the fiasco of local Chianti and the tomatoes and bread they bought from a market in Poggio a Caiano and ate near the flowering, glorious villa, their nap together on their backs in the deep grass under the cypresses, lulled by a stupefying uproar of cicadas. In bed she was astounded by his exuberance, and she was glad he seemed so satisfied with her, wanting already to give him back the happiness he had so generously awakened in her. Having him want her so terribly was fascinating and erotic, and as he slept afterward she could see again the amazing stars beyond the filmy movement of the curtains and the night air was full of roses and it was May and she was completely content. The difference in their ages did not seem apparent to her at all.

Now he sneezed and she jumped.

"What's the problem, Merce? Lost your drift?"

"I was thinking," she said. "About the horses."

"Ah, yes." He tapped his finger against his mouth. "At the Casanova. You loved those horses, didn't you? I could barely drag you inside."

"You never had a bit of trouble," she said with a little smile.

"Forget memory lane," Patrick said. "You'll just get confused."

"I am confused."

"Love or sex? I give you the green light."

She shook her head.

"Well, if it's love, it's out of your control. It's there or it isn't. Sex, now, you can do something about."

"This sort of conversation makes me uncomfortable, Patrick."

"That's the real problem, toots."

"It's not just sex."

"Better make up your mind."

"I'm happy to be in love with her. I would be happy even if I never saw her again," she said, then thought, *What a blatant untruth.*

He leaned back in his chair. "This is all making me tired," he said. "I don't even feel like another Black Jack—that's how tired this talk makes me. I wish I had your problems. You've won the lottery, that's what I think. Claim your prize."

"Well," she said. "Maybe." She sat with her hand still on the phone, as if it had a heartbeat, as if she could follow its rushing miles of red and blue arteries to Lennie's door, to her room. To her ear. To her heart.

"Get on with it, Merce!" he said. "For Christ's sake."

By ten-thirty she was in bed with a book. She had barely considered what to pull from the shelf; she was only hoping it would make her sleep. She had made sure Patrick's phone was turned off, but she knew Lennie would not call now.

Unless she had stayed at the Zen Center for dinner, perhaps, and not returned to Guido's. Unless—what? Unless she was in bed with Connie somewhere. Mrs. Medina closed her eyes, then opened them quickly. No, Connie was in Los Angeles. She didn't have to worry about Connie tonight.

She listened to the distant thud of her heart, the nearly silent thrusting of blood through her veins. Her body was taking care of business, even though her brain was asleep at the wheel. She slid down into the bedclothes and shivered, wondering whether she should change her silk gown for a flannel one. But she imagined Lennie arriving at her door at three in the morning and finding her in a flannel nightgown. Not very sexy. She opened her book and looked at the letters marching across the page, scrabbled all over like ants on some mysterious journey that had nothing to do with her. She closed it and put it on her bedside table. *Books are useless,* she thought. *I don't want words.*

thirteen

M rs. Medina woke late, to her astonishment. It was nearly nine. She felt uncomfortable, sweaty, and the sheets were tumbled.
She lay on her right side and brushed her hair away from her face and
focused on a long finger of sunlight that was making progress across
the rug. She had no desire to get up.

She wondered what Patrick was doing, so silently, then after a
pause she rose quickly and threw on her robe. Santino met her at
Patrick's door, his half glasses down over his nose.

Before she could speak he said, "I was just coming to get you. I
can't rouse him."

She moved quickly around him to Patrick's bed and sat down. He
lay on his back, breathing lightly. His eyes were not shut, but his eyelids were fluttering about. He did not really seem to be awake. His
hands were icy.

She turned to Santino without rising.

"He called me about eight," Santino said. "I could barely understand
him, Mercedes. He was, well, I couldn't tell if he was crying or gasping.
I kept asking him where you were, and the best I could understand was
that you had gone off somewhere. So I came right over. Used my key."

"Santino, I was asleep right down the hall."

"Well, I looked in, I saw that after I got here."

"Why didn't you wake me?"

"I was just coming to do that, Mercedes." He frowned and
pushed the sleeves of his blue V-neck sweater above his elbows. "He
just sounded anxious."

"Patrick," she said, shaking his shoulder. "Patrick, wake up. Time
to wake up."

"He said he needed someone."

"I was here. Patrick. Talk to me, you stubborn old man!" She gave him a good shake.

He opened his eyes and steadied them on her, but she could tell he didn't recognize her.

"Patrick, squeeze my hand, if you hear me. Squeeze it." His hand lay limply in hers. She sensed Santino bending over her, watching Patrick's face over the top of her head. She sat back with a sigh.

"How often is this happening now?" Santino asked.

"Too often."

"What is it? He was moving his hands and legs. I don't think it's a stroke."

"No, it's not a stroke. They don't know what exactly it is." She rubbed her chin. "If I can't get him to wake up in a few minutes, I'll call Harry Max." And with that, Patrick clutched her hand in a tight grip that startled her so much that she slid off the bed and sat down on the floor with a hard thump.

"Hey!" Santino said. "Hey, buddy, let's get with it! Let's rise and shine!"

Mrs. Medina stayed on the floor, Patrick's hand in hers.

"That's better," Santino said above her. "You recognize me now?"

"Yes, I do," Patrick said in a weak but irritated voice. "What are you doing here? Have you spent the night with my wife?"

"Yes," Santino said with a smile. "And she's a hot number, let me tell you."

"Bugger off," Patrick said. "I'm going back to sleep."

"No," Mrs. Medina said, struggling back onto the side of the bed. "No, Patrick, best for you to stay awake. Stay awake and talk to me."

"I have nothing to report," he told her with his eyes shut.

She heard the telephone ring distantly, and without thinking of anything but Patrick she said, "Santino, would you get that for me, please?" He started down the hall toward her room. "There's an extension in here," she called after him, but he was gone.

"Now, Patrick, I want you to sit up, please, and don't give me a problem. Just sit up slowly and lean against these pillows."

"I want to be left alone," he said.

She watched him.

"Oh, all right." He sat up and pulled the covers to his shoulders.

"Can you move things for me? Move your hands and feet, now your legs. That's good. Now look at me." She looked carefully into his bright blue eyes, not knowing what she should expect to see. "You fox," she said. But she knew something was going on.

"What is that fiddle player doing in my house at dawn?"

"It's nearly nine-thirty, and you called him."

"I won't fall for that story, Merce."

She watched him for a moment. "Why don't you tell me what happened?"

"I don't know," he said. She heard Santino come back into the room. "I woke up and I was in the wilderness. I didn't know how to get back."

"Your bell is right there by the bed. I would have come."

"Bells don't carry that far."

"Well, you could shout, then."

"Merce, I was not in this room! Get that straight! I was not here! I was on the way to somewhere else, and plans changed. I lost the trail back. You were not in the picture, or this house."

"But the phone was here. You managed to call Santino."

"I don't remember calling this bum."

"Well, you did, pal," Santino said. "You're going to ruin my marriage."

"Santino brought me back," Patrick said.

"While I slept," Mrs. Medina said, getting up.

"While you slept the sleep of the just," Patrick said. "Santino, how about helping me to the head? My pins are shaky."

Santino helped him out of bed and put one arm around his back. Seeing them together, Mrs. Medina realized that Patrick had lost more weight. Santino could probably have carried Patrick to the bathroom. She watched them go, her hands on her hips. Then she retied her gown, which had loosened.

"Oh, Mercedes," Santino said over his shoulder. "Phone message from a girl called Lennie. She says she's at work, if you want to call her."

"Piss on it," Patrick said.

"See?" Santino said. "He's okay."

Mrs. Medina went to make coffee.

She sat in the living room with her second cup of coffee. It was a neutral zone, and there was no telephone. Her own room had the sick aroma of failure about it. In it she felt childlike, her bed with the twisted sheets a symptom of a cloistered neurasthenia, a condition that would appeal to no one. She sipped her coffee. *Well, that's a little extreme,* she thought with a smile.

Santino had stayed a while to talk with Patrick about some old scores he had found on the piano. She wished he would stay all morning, but she heard him at Patrick's door, his voice in a cautionary tone of farewell. He had a real life, out in the world. He couldn't stay on in this confusion.

Patrick in the wilderness! She had a call in to Harry Max, but she had a feeling he was tired of these calls. In fact, she was tired of making them. *I'm in a wilderness too,* she thought.

She rose as Santino came to the door.

"On my way, Mercedes," he said, and kissed her on the cheek. "He's all right, I think."

She rubbed the back of her neck. "I've called Harry Max, just the same. I don't want you to think I'm a neglectful caretaker."

He drew back. "I would never think that." He got himself into his blue corduroy jacket. "I think he wants to shave. I told him he should rest."

She smiled. "I'll help him shave. It cheers him up."

"Right. I'll call you later."

"Love to Daria."

Now there was nothing left but Lennie.

She sent Patrick back to bed smelling sweetly of English lavender shaving soap. Back in her own room she threw open all the windows and stripped the bed. All the sheets, her nightgown and all her towels went into the washing machine, and on the way back she dragged out the vacuum and brought in her yellow rubber gloves. She was on her knees scrubbing the bathtub when Patrick appeared at her door. He had on his green cotton pajama bottoms and a blue-and-white-striped shirt.

It looked as if he had begun to get dressed but thought better of it.

"What's up in here?" he said.

"Cleaning." She looked up at him. "Aren't you supposed to be in bed?"

"If I shave, I get up. That's the way it goes."

She rose with a little groan and sat on the side of the tub and took off her gloves. She had put on a pair of old khakis and now she was too hot. "I think, Patrick, I would prefer that you lie down until Harry calls."

"What's in the washing machine?"

"Sheets. If that's all right."

"That is a suspicious tone of voice. Do I expect Nikki today?"

She had lost track of days. After a moment she said, "No, I don't think this is Nikki's day."

"She's bringing me some CDs. The Beaux Arts boys have taken on a female fiddler."

"That's nice."

"You're whirling around here like a deranged cleaning lady today. You're making me nervous as hell." He walked toward the door. "I'm going to watch the noon movie. They're playing *Thirty Seconds Over Tokyo*."

"I'll bring your lunch in after a while."

"Grilled cheese?"

"Grilled cheese, all right."

The afternoon drifted along, and later she sat on the chaise and calmly did her nails. She had not returned Lennie's call, and she had no idea what she was waiting for. She almost felt deflated, as if she had been unplugged from a giant generator. Her bed was still stripped, the vacuum was strewn across the rug, and the blue, pungent aroma of toilet bowl cleaner drifted out from the bathroom. *My deranged room,* she thought. *Patrick is right: I am a collapsing star.*

In the end it was her sense of propriety that propelled her to pick up the telephone. She did not like to leave calls unanswered.

But when she heard Lennie's voice, her mouth went dry. "This a bad time to call?" she said, and she had to swallow.

"No. No one here at all, in fact. Not even Guido."

Mrs. Medina took a breath to speak, but Lennie continued, "Guido told me you called."

"Yes, you were setting bulbs, he said."

"Right. I've got dirt under my nails that will be there forever."

Mrs. Medina thought of Lennie's hands. "Get them all in?" she asked.

"Yep. I had a lot of help. Two nuns and a priest."

"Well, I called," she cleared her throat, "I called to make sure you got home all right..."

"Sure. Home in half an hour."

"Good. But I also wanted to say that I enjoyed myself. Very much. The sole was wonderful."

"Yeah, the food is good there."

"I did like it." The hopelessness began to drag at her again, and there was nothing to do now but say goodbye, no reason to continue. She gripped the phone with two hands. "I miss you," she said, blindly stepping across a threshold into another room. Now that that was done, she tossed her entire life after it. She no longer cared how she would be received.

"I'll come by," Lennie said. "If you want."

"Yes. Come by."

"I'll come tonight. I don't know exactly when. I need to go home first, then I'll come over."

"Fine. It doesn't matter what time."

"Okay, then."

"Do you remember where I am?"

"Corner of Clarendon and Comm. Ave."

"The doorman will call me. Just tell him. Come anytime."

"I will, I will." There was the noise of another phone line ringing. "Gotta get that," Lennie said.

"All right. I'll see you later, then."

"See you later."

They hung up.

Mrs. Medina sat very still with the telephone in her lap. From a distance came the sound of Patrick's toilet flushing. Then, after a moment, the murmur of his late-afternoon television program. She heard him cough. The sound of his recliner sliding back.

She tried steady, even breaths and found she could breathe. It was four-thirty. She probably had three or four hours. Her room appeared dreamy in the twilight. Had she vacuumed? She couldn't remember. *Make the bed,* she thought. *Try to remember if you've vacuumed. Examine the rug.* She stood up. *I can't tell,* she said to herself, *whether I vacuumed or not. All right, feed Patrick.* There was no question of her eating. *Well first, TELL Patrick.* She put her fist on her forehead, gave it a little thump. *Tell Patrick. Take a bath... Iron. Flowers. Flowers?* She looked around. *There should be flowers. Food? Will Lennie expect food? Wine? Beer? What do I have?* She turned on the bedside lamp.

She put on her coat to go for flowers, then turned on the vacuum and thought, *I don't have time to look for lint or fluff, I'll just do it again.* So she vacuumed frantically in her coat, then took it off and threw it on the chaise. *Clean sheets,* she thought, and stopped the vacuum to rummage in the linen closet in the hall for some colorful stripes. She smelled them. Slightly musty. Never mind, it would never come to that. Put them on anyway.

"Merce!" Patrick called. "Time for a drink!"

She expected it was all right for him to have a mild one. Harry had not even volunteered to come by when he called. He had only said, "If it happens again within thirty-six hours, I want him hospitalized, and I will not put up with any foolishness from him."

She brought Patrick his drink, and said briefly, "How do you feel? Because my friend Lennie will be coming by for a while tonight, if that's all right. I'm going into the kitchen to see what I can rustle up for your dinner. How about one of those little steaks?"

"Mule carcass," he said. "Where's your drink?"

"I seem to have run out of wine. I'm going to run over to Boylston Street."

"Well, pick up some Black Jack too. We're running low."

"All right. Anything else?"

He had switched to the Weather Channel. "Nothing but mud in California," he said. "Why do people live there?"

Perhaps she should keep Lennie in the living room. But it was too large, they'd get lost. The bedroom, then. Her bedroom was as much a sitting room as a place to sleep.

"What time is this girlfriend coming?" Patrick asked.

She put her head back into his room. "Oh, seven-thirty or eight."

"I will be unavailable," he said.

By seven-fifteen Mrs. Medina had returned with wine. She had crammed the vacuum back into the pantry closet and made her bed and bathed in a tub scented with Madame Rochas and burned Patrick's steak. She sat with him while he silently chewed, and served herself some peas and rice to keep him company. She touched the nape of her neck. Her hair was still damp. She turned a glass of Merlot between her fingers, wondering whether she should change her clothes again. She had put on a beige cashmere sweater over a white shirt with a small collar and her Brooks Brothers denims.

"I smell you," Patrick said, looking up.

"Something bad?" she asked him anxiously.

"Over the odor of this burnt, mashed meat I hear your fancy perfume shouting at me."

"You do?"

"You have an assignation. That's what I'm trying to get used to."

"She's coming over for a glass of wine, Patrick, that's all. I wish you'd agree to meet her. You said you wanted to." She smiled at him.

"I am not in the mood for lighthearted banter." He wiped his mouth. "I am a grown man and well known in certain circles. I don't give a damn about rock music and drugs and whatever else the two of you discuss."

Mrs. Medina gave a quick look at her watch. "How about some more rice, then?"

"This is possibly the worst meal you have ever cooked, and I am finished with it." He got up, supporting himself on the table with his right hand. "I'm going to my room."

"Okay. I'll come in and see you after she leaves." She began to gather the plates.

"I think she should be out of here by ten-thirty."

She waited first in her bedroom, then in the living room, and then back in her bedroom again. She turned on two lamps in the living room and considered the bedroom carefully, finally deciding that her bedside lamp and her reading lamp were sufficient. But something was missing. She looked around. Flowers. She'd forgotten. She put her hand over her mouth. "Stupid woman, stupid woman," she chastised herself aloud, as she ran for her coat. If Lennie arrived while she was gone, she could wait downstairs with Constantin.

And when she returned, breathless, carrying the yellow tulips she had just managed to snatch out of Winston's before they closed the door, Constantin looked up and said, "For you, Mrs. Medina," as if he were presenting a telegram, gesturing to where Lennie stood with her hands in the pockets of her long black coat, smiling slightly, taking in the lobby mirrors, Constantin, all of it.

"Here I am," she said.

For it was indeed Lennie.

~ fourteen ~

"What is this cowboy coat?" Mrs. Medina said a little wildly. "Let me take it. You look like you just got off a horse."

"It's called a duster. Like it?" She took it off. "Not really cold enough for it yet."

Mrs. Medina decided on her own room. "This way," she said.

"Nice place." She heard amusement in Lennie's voice.

"Sit, sit," Mrs. Medina said, gesturing to her reading chair, the chaise. Lennie took the chair. "What would you like, some wine, beer? Have you eaten?" For a few minutes there was this little chaos, with Mrs. Medina making a quick trip to her bathroom to be sure she had flushed the toilet, straightening the pens and paper on her desk. Then she remembered she hadn't put the flowers in water. Lennie leaned forward in the chair, her arms on her knees, and waited, with a friendly look, for Mrs. Medina to slow down. Mrs. Medina eventually did, of course. She managed to open the bottle of San Gimignano that Lennie had brought and sank down into the chaise opposite her.

"Thank you for this wine," Mrs. Medina said.

"The guy in the liquor store told me it was good. It's Italian."

"Yes. I like it."

"Want me to take off my boots? This is a nice rug."

She sat back. "Well, the rug's old."

They smiled at each other. Lennie's skin had a dusty, summer color still about it, and her cheeks were slightly flushed from her day of planting in the Zen garden.

Lennie put down her glass. "I think I'll just take them off anyway, if it's okay. The Zen people are brainwashing me. They don't wear shoes in their house."

"Whatever you want." She imagined Patrick's ear pressed against his door, as the boots fell with a small thud.

"Now," Lennie said, and stretched out her long legs. She was wearing red socks.

Mrs. Medina learned everything she would ever know about longing during the first hour they spent together, and the inevitable feeling of loss that accompanies passionate encounters, as opposed to the perfect state of imagining them, in which anything can happen. At first she was in limbo, stretched over a chasm between what her mind had imagined and the real possibility sitting across from her. Still, she managed to talk. She fell back on her intelligence and it did not disappoint her; she even managed some humor, a little joke or two. But there were moments when they sat and looked at each other for long minutes without speaking. What did they mean, those silences? *She's thinking about my age,* Mrs. Medina decided. So she made an excuse to run off to the kitchen in order to rest her hand on Lennie's knee and ask, "What would you like? What can I bring you?"

She stood before the refrigerator, her hand on the icy wine bottle, shaking. And her mind was silently repeating, *What, what should I do?*

When she returned to the bedroom she found Lennie standing in front of the Whistler print, which Mrs. Medina had moved from the living room after its restoration. She had her little pigtail wrapped around one finger.

"Like that?" Mrs. Medina put the wine glasses on a table and came to stand beside her. They were almost exactly the same height.

"Where is it?"

"Venice."

"I guess I see a canal there along the side." She peered closely at the etching. "I was just wondering about this tree, what it was. Maybe—"

"Trees are precious in Venice. I don't know what kind it is. It's a Whistler."

"Whistler who had the mother?"

Mrs. Medina smiled. "The same one. I love it, I bought it there."

"It's nice."

She was aware of Lennie's complex accumulation of scents, a spice-like fragrance on the surface and then a faint aftershock of onion tonight, not in the least unpleasant, which all mingled with the unusual amount of body heat that Lennie seemed to generate. She felt it wrap around her, and swayed a bit.

They stood and looked at the print in silence for a moment.

Lennie took her hand. "So you missed me."

This was a move Mrs. Medina had not expected. Her hand lay motionless against Lennie's warm palm. Lennie's hand was bigger, she realized.

"I did miss you," she began, and stopped. She saw the open door over Lennie's shoulder, and imagined Patrick in the hall. *I've got to go on*, she told him silently.

She took Lennie's hand in both of hers and clasped it tightly. "Lennie, I don't know what I'm doing here, you know. I don't know what's happening, and I'm older than you by—well, by quite a bit. Maybe I'm assuming the wrong things. About you. Certainly about me. Except—" She realized she had been talking with her eyes shut, and when she opened them she found Lennie's face very close to hers, her lips slightly parted. Their clasped hands were between them, as if they were singing one of those pastry-puff Viennese love duets.

"Except—" Lennie repeated.

Mrs. Medina shook her head.

"It's simple," Lennie said.

"Don't make me look foolish."

"Just let go of my hand—there—and watch how simple this is."

Once, when she was about ten, Mercedes de Soares had returned early one evening from play at a friend's house and found her own home uncharacteristically in darkness. The big oak front door was locked tight. Puzzled, she searched around the outside of the house, but all doors, all windows were closed. The big black DeSoto was not in the drive, though she spotted her mother's smaller Ford tucked away in the garage as if it had been abandoned.

She called for the dogs. "Teo! Vita!" There was no answer. It was nearly dark, five-thirty on an October evening. Someone nearby was burning leaves, just finishing. It was growing chilly.

When she peered through the big front window, the rooms appeared to be completely empty. It was then that she decided her family had left her. In some way she had offended one of them, and as punishment they had all packed up and gone away, to California probably, and left her alone. She sat on the porch steps. This old familiar house, in which she had lived since she was born, now seemed to have withdrawn its love as well. She wondered what it was she had done, and if her family might have a change of heart and come back for her. Even as she had that thought, she imagined her father (by then nearing the bridge over the Hudson, no doubt) reversing the car, her mother beside him, pulling the large fur collar of her best coat up around her neck, saying, "We'll go back, Hugo. She's been punished enough." And as her father turned, his lights suddenly caught the glare of a massive truck, bearing down on them. Her brother and sisters in the backseat shrieked in terror, and then they all went up in a gigantic explosion, sailed off the highway trailing fire like a comet, and plunged into the dark waters of the river, sinking instantly.

She began to cry, already imagining herself an orphan. Hearing a noise in the house behind her, she jumped up in fright and ran across the broad expanse of lawn to stand shivering by the steps to the street. Abandoned, an orphan, unloved even by her family, even by the dogs.

Then, at the top of the street, a pair of headlights ponderously turned the corner and headed down the hill toward the house. And in a sweet rush of certainty she knew this was her family returning, safe, whole, all of them returning, and soon there would be warmth, light, the smell of dinner cooking, the clamor of the dogs, and her sisters and brother jostling around in their usual evening roustabouts. In one instant she knew all of this, even though the car was still some distance away and there was no logical reason to assure her that she was right.

But in fact she was right, and her mother gathered her closely in her arms, apologizing for all of them. They had all gone to meet her father's train, and it had been unusually late. Her mother smelled of Je Reviens, and the young Mercedes thought she had never experienced anything so wonderful as her mother's smell, the feel of her hard shoulder against her cheek, and the knowledge that—for a while, at least—she was utterly and completely happy and exactly where she belonged.

And as Lennie came into her arms, this sensation returned to her, for the first time since that long ago evening in the driveway, before life had sent her down so many other, darker passages.

It was light, coming back.

At first Mrs. Medina was afraid to move, fearful even of pulling back, of looking into Lennie's eyes. Afraid, afraid, she was sick of being afraid. She allowed herself to move her hands across Lennie's back, down to where her waist dipped deliciously inward, and she prayed that Lennie could not feel her own heart rattling against her ribs, her arms trembling like earthquakes. But Lennie began to kiss her, paying no attention at all. Her lips were skilled and pliant and had a sinuous movement that seemed to match the way her arms were tightening and loosening, tightening and loosening, around Mrs. Medina's body. Mrs. Medina sensed Lennie's breathing, rather than hearing it, but she heard it too and it was all she could hear.

Mrs. Medina thought, when she could think, *I don't want her farther than a foot from me, for the rest of my life.*

Lennie drew back and looked at Mrs. Medina with her eyes half closed, but smiling, and said, "Okay?"

Mrs. Medina raised her eyebrows and nodded, not trusting herself to speak.

"I see you thinking too much," Lennie said, and drew her down on the chaise. And then, after a long while, they moved to the bed, lying very close together on top of the spread. Mrs. Medina's heart galloped upward with no way of escape. How to please her? But she didn't know how, and was chagrined, at her age, to be as inexperienced with her own sex as she actually was.

And so they arrived at an uncertain place and stopped.

Mrs. Medina finally rose on one elbow. Lennie's hair was wildly mussed, and at her hairline there was a fine film of perspiration. Her face was calm, perfectly relaxed, and her eyes were closed. Her shirt was out of her black jeans and had ridden up to reveal a small section of her abdomen. Mrs. Medina dared to slip her hand under Lennie's shirt and place it on her belly, and this touch gave her such immediate pleasure that she shook herself and swung away to sit on the side of the bed. Her shoes had been thrown aside on the rug, and now she looked down at herself to find her sweater twisted around toward the back and her own shirt tail loosened. The sweater was intolerably warm, so she pulled it off.

And then faintly, through the wall, she heard Patrick cry, "Bench the son of a bitch!"

She looked up at the door, which she had quickly managed to shove closed before she and Lennie had moved toward the bed.

Lennie rolled over and put her hand against Mrs. Medina's back. "That your husband?"

Mrs. Medina nodded.

"Want me to go?"

"No." She got up to turn off the lamp by the chair and her legs almost gave way, as if she were descending a hill with knees that could not support her.

"Hey," Lennie said. "Come back here."

"We don't need both lights." When she returned to the bed, Lennie had propped herself up against the headboard.

Mrs. Medina sat down on the side of the bed and rubbed her hands together. "My hands are cold," she said, although they weren't.

"Give them to me." Lennie took them between her two palms and rubbed them vigorously. Now they could both clearly hear Patrick's television, which was playing at quite a loud volume.

Eventually she lay back down, and Lennie came close and with a sigh lay her head on Mrs. Medina's breasts. Mrs. Medina put her arms around her and for a long while they stayed that way, with the bedside clock ticking quietly, and the building creaking, and sounds from the street rising up from time to time. Eventually there was no more sound from Patrick's room and the house was still. She looked down on the top of Lennie's head, then lay her cheek against it.

Does she expect to spend the night? Mrs. Medina thought, looking into the dark corners of her room. *What is the next step?*

Much later, at the door, Mrs. Medina said quietly, "Should I call you?" because she couldn't help herself.

Lennie nodded. "Call," she said. She looked sleepy, standing in the hall in her long coat. It was one-fifteen. Would she be back? What would bring her back?

"I'm sorry—" Mrs. Medina began, imagining the possibility of Lennie's physical disappointment.

Lennie put her finger over Mrs. Medina's lips and shook her head. "The cab's gotta be down there waiting," she said.

Mrs. Medina put her into the elevator, casting about for something to say, something that would make things complete. "It was wonderful," she managed to say as the elevator door closed.

Patrick's room was in darkness. She checked his breathing, as one might a child's, and it was light and even. Mrs. Medina suspected he was awake, but she didn't think she could manage a talk with him tonight, so she made sure his bell was on his bedside table and pulled the door halfway to.

She gathered the few glasses and the plate that were in her room—she had finally made Lennie a ham sandwich about midnight—and cleaned everything up in the kitchen. Her hands moved mechanically over the dishes, and she watched them dreamily.

She fixed herself a small gin and bitters and took it to her room, put on her gown and got into the rumpled bed. A slight trace of Lennie's scent remained on the sheets, or so she imagined, and she burrowed down and shut her eyes. But she did not sleep. Not right away.

Just after dawn she stirred and turned over and knew Patrick was there, watching her. She kept her eyes closed, sighed. He came close to the bed and bent down to sniff her glass. Eventually he turned away. She heard his socked feet pad slowly up the hall.

fifteen

Mrs. Medina made sure she was up at her regular hour and made a point of not showering before breakfast, so as not to vary her usual routine. She took a deep breath and strode purposefully into the kitchen. Patrick was pouring his coffee.

"Good morning," she said. She pulled the belt of her robe a bit tighter.

"Raining," he said.

She hadn't noticed. "Sorry I didn't get in to say good night until you were already asleep. Sleeping quite soundly, in fact."

"Must've been pretty damn late."

"Yes, it was late. Do you want eggs?"

He gave her a patient look and sat down at the kitchen table. They spoke no more of it.

~

During the following days Mrs. Medina lived in a constant state of anticipation, and every part of her life was involved. But she didn't talk to Patrick at first, and oddly he didn't ask any questions. They spent their time together talking of ordinary things, walking carefully in circles. It was this walking that finally exhausted her, and made her say one afternoon after lunch, "I think we'd better talk."

"Uh oh," he said. "Here comes trouble."

She started down the hall with him toward his room, then turned and said, "Want to go for a stroll by the river?"

"I'm sedentary today," he said. "No walks."

"Well, come into my room, then. Stretch out on the chaise."

He pursued his path toward his own quarters. "I will not sully that sacred bedchamber."

"All right." She followed him in and waited until he was settled in his chair. Once again her senses deserted her, and now all she wanted to do was flee.

"I expect you know," she said. She began to pace a bit, she could not bring herself to settle.

"I'm not blind. And I'm not nuts, even if my brain is blowing out. I still have my ears. I am ousted. I secede from the union."

"Patrick."

He had his fingers clasped together and he loosened them, and shook his hands. "You have launched yourself into the sex arena, I gather."

"Well, if you want to call it that." She sat down. "You did encourage me to—pursue this…"

He tightened his face into a little grimace. "Maybe I should have thought twice about that little speech."

"And I want to continue to see her. I won't see her here, if it makes you uncomfortable."

"It would make anyone uncomfortable. But the old man has no say in the matter. Go ahead."

"Patrick—"

"What do you want, Merce, a formal blessing?"

"I guess I do."

"Well, I withhold it, pending the outcome of future days."

"Fair enough."

"Are you finished? I want a nap."

"I do love you, Patrick."

"We're not talking about love now." He turned and looked out the window. "I guess it's fair," he said. "I hate it, but it's fair. Considering what you put up with from me in past times."

She watched him struggling with this idea, flexing his fingers again as if he were about to pick up his cello.

"But I never had a fling when you were anywhere nearby! That's the thing. And goddamn it, it's natural for a man to succumb every now and then. Women are supposed to have more control." He knew what her response would be to this argument, and looked over at her out of the corner of his eye.

So she said nothing, and waited.

"But I can't stop you now, can I?" He took out his handkerchief and blew his nose. "You've always just rolled along like a steamroller, inscrutable as a cat."

"I was more like a trolley car, Patrick, in my life." She got up suddenly and went to his bedside table. "This handkerchief has blood on it." She turned to face him.

"I killed a big bug."

"I'm serious. What is this?"

"I took a wrong turn on the way to the head last night and ran into the corner of the bookcase. Conked me on the noggin." He pointed to a little cut on the side of his head that she hadn't noticed.

"Did you fall?"

"I sat down on the floor for a while. To think about what to do."

"Why didn't you ring your bell?"

"That little fairy bell was over on the table by my bed! I don't travel with it around my neck. Anyway, why should I drag you from your bed of passion?"

"Lennie wasn't here last night, Patrick, you knew that. And I will be angry if you don't ring your bell when you need me."

"Your anger flies by my door like the Passover angel. I don't care about your anger."

"All right." She walked to the door. "I'll try to think of some way to handle the situation that will work out for both of us."

"That's always been your problem." He hoisted himself out of his chair. "Trying to be the great compromiser. Doesn't always work, Merce. Someone's got to get the short straw. This time it's me. So just go on."

"I'll wake you at four," she said.

And so Mrs. Medina waited for Lennie with a bit of melancholy, imagining Patrick, alone in his room, with the short straw. She came to wish he had never put his situation into exactly those words, but she could not help herself. Lennie was there, like a deep lake, and Mrs. Medina had plunged in.

Dark nights. Early autumn wind, sucking at the windows. Mrs. Medina lay on the bed with Lennie's face against her belly, and Lennie moved her cheek against her, moved her hands up along Mrs. Medina's ribs to her breasts and back down.

How have I lived so much of my life without this? Mrs. Medina wondered. Lennie moved her head slightly lower, a small, deliberate gesture, and Mrs. Medina grew still. "I want to," Lennie said, and Mrs. Medina closed her eyes. She was still afraid of appearing the fool.

"I'm sorry," Mrs. Medina said. "I don't know why."

"It's okay," Lennie said, her eyes closed. Smiling.

"It's just, I suppose..." She shook her head. "I want to, it's not that..."

Lennie extended her body in a long, beautiful stretch. "Can I sleep for a while, then?"

"Of course." She thought briefly of Patrick, wishing him no harm, just out of the house for the night so she could learn Lennie's body in complete solitude, with all the air in the world to cry out into.

Just before dawn they woke (but Mrs. Medina had been awake for half an hour, watching Lennie sleep), and Lennie's body turned to her, moving against her like a marvelous, voluptuous machine.

"I've got to get back to Cambridge," Lennie said after a while. "The trains are running now."

"I know. I know."

Lennie dressed and left, and Mrs. Medina buried her face in the fragrant sheets.

It was six o'clock.

Then Patrick rang his bell, like a summons from another world. She threw on her robe and went to him.

"I heard a thump," he said, squinting at her, patting his bedside table for his glasses.

"Oh, that was me," she said. She handed him his glasses. *It could have been me*, she thought. *In fact, it probably was me. I shut the door after her.* But she busied herself opening his curtains, and then took some time to look at the light on the little patch of river that could be seen from Patrick's northwest window.

"You told me I could ring and I did," he said finally.

~

Mrs. Medina began to dream of Lennie living with her, the two of them together in an exotic place. This was the depth of her infatuation. She yearned for a place that would surprise her: coming across the crest of a hill and seeing the sea spread out suddenly like a glittering pool of spilt champagne; misty dawns in which strange birds cried; huge, deep beds with sheets that smelled of lavender; rich, fragrant coffee. She imagined them in grand hotels (which she liked) and in isolated mountain cabins (which she thought Lennie would prefer). The scenarios were long and intricate. In Mrs. Medina's mind they danced in nightclubs where it made no difference, or woke in an airy bedroom in a red-roofed Spanish villa, high above the sea. They had long meals by candlelight, and Mrs. Medina fed Lennie hearts of palm from a slender silver fork. She placed the two of them in a grand circle of her old friends, who related marvelous stories in which Mrs. Medina was the magician.

Hours would pass.

Patrick would creep by the door, watch her silently, and depart. "Can't you do anything else?" he muttered to her at breakfast. "Sex is sex. It doesn't have to take over your life."

She continued to care for Patrick. Her kindness to him became extraordinary, but she knew he was now suspicious of her motives. One afternoon she sat on the side of his bed, just as he was waking from his nap, and found herself saying quietly, "I'm so happy." She put her hand on his arm and her ring snagged a thread of his blanket. She carefully disentangled it. Patrick had given her this gold band set with five small diamonds several years before they were married. It was not a wedding ring. They had not exchanged rings when they married.

She picked up his hand in both of hers. "I don't want to breathe unless she is with me."

"Pretty risky," he muttered without opening his eyes.

"Yes," she said. "Yes, she makes me want to take risks."

The days that Nikki came to read to Patrick were always easier.

One Tuesday Mrs. Medina was making tea and Nikki appeared in the kitchen. Her wild mane of hair seemed to be multiplying, every week producing vaster quantities of curls.

"Something wrong?" Mrs. Medina asked.

"He wants to go for a walk."

Mrs. Medina turned to face her. "He does?"

"Just to the river and back. What do you think?" She looked at Mrs. Medina and smoothed her hands over her hips. Nikki was all in black today—black tights, short black skirt, black turtleneck. "Don't think it'll hurt for him to go out. Nice day and all." She edged up to the cookie plate. "Mind if I have one of those?"

"Of course not. Help yourself." Mrs. Medina went over to the window and checked the thermometer. "It's sixty-two. Sure, why don't you take him out if he wants to go."

They got him into his Chesterfield coat, and he was bustling with excitement. He took the carved ash walking stick she had bought him in Ireland. From the window in Patrick's room Mrs. Medina watched their slow progress along Clarendon Street until they disappeared, then her eyes lifted out over the river.

~

Her happiness was made up of yearning, gratitude, and intense sexual memory, an intoxicating cocktail. The imprint of Lennie's body was on her own, even when they were not together.

"The lover and the beloved," she said. "I am a monstrous cliché."

Her movement through the days was effortless, meals were cooked to perfection, she had the right words always ready. Even the little hall rug, over which she normally tripped several times a day, stayed out of her way. She thought that probably no one had ever experienced this accumulation of little miracles in quite the same way.

She did not allow herself to speculate about when this happiness would end, when the first cloud would appear. She even imagined she might keep this affair alive indefinitely, simply by her own will.

She was eating dinner with Lennie in an Italian restaurant on Hanover Street in the North End, not Mamma Maria's, Mrs.

Medina's favorite, which was closed for a private party. Here the pasta was watery. From the kitchen came the violent sounds of mallets pounding veal.

"Why so glum?" Mrs. Medina said.

"Who's glum? I'm tired. I'm thinking about my class tomorrow. Guido's was so busy today, I didn't have time to sketch any of my plans."

"Ever think of giving up Guido's?"

Lennie gave her a sidelong glance. "And live on what?"

"Well..."

"I've got to think about money. Unlucky me."

Mrs. Medina was silent. Finally, she said, "Lennie..."

"No. But thanks."

"Look, money is something I have. Not endless amounts, but I could carry you for a year or two, let you study officially, get a degree."

"I don't want a degree. I don't need a degree. Why does everyone have to have a degree? I don't want to design gardens for the fucking White House."

"Well, being in school gets you contacts, if you want to go into business for yourself. That's one reason."

"I don't know that I want to go into business for myself." She rubbed her forehead.

"What's bothering you?"

"There's too much going on in my life right now. I can't do everything."

Mrs. Medina's heart clutched. "Yes, yes, you're very busy." And before she could stop herself she asked, "Are you getting, I don't know, bored with me? With us?"

Lennie turned to face her. "No. Why?"

"I think it's difficult for you, being with me. I'm," she threw out her hands, "I'm new. I don't know how to handle things, to do things. You know what I mean." She took a drink of wine. "I'm just not usual for you, I imagine."

Lennie smiled. "No, you're not."

The waiter arrived with their meals, then took a long, slow time to grind parmesan on the pasta, relight the candle, brush crumbs from the table into his hand. Mrs. Medina sat with her hands in her lap, then picked up her fork.

Lennie began to eat. "Have you always worked?"

Mrs. Medina put her fork down and looked at her. "Of course." Lennie smiled slightly.

"I still work."

"Well, yes, I know that. Tell me about it."

"I teach Italian at BU, Italian literature. Not as much as I used to, because of Patrick, but usually a seminar during the winter. I've been teaching since long before I met Patrick. I taught English to Italians in Florence too, for three or four years. Then I met Patrick and sort of gave it up for a while." She was watching the movements of Lennie's hands, cutting her chicken. "To travel with him."

"You quit then? No work?"

Mrs. Medina drew herself up. "Not exactly," she said. "Should I be on the defensive here?"

"No. Why?"

"I've taught this course at BU for several years. And I've done some writing. I've finished the first draft of a translation of a lovely novel by Elio Vittorini, an Italian writer no one here knows much about. Someday I'll get back to it. Someday I'll teach more, probably." Mrs. Medina gave her a long look. "Don't put me down as a member of the idle rich," she said.

Lennie reached over and patted her cheek. "I don't. Sorry. I'm just pissed today, about all sorts of things. I'm just as broke as when I was twenty, for one thing. It seems like I've been working forever, and nothing ever changes."

What about me? Mrs. Medina thought. *Aren't I a change?*

"I just keep doing the same things, over and over."

"Well, life can become that way, if you're not careful."

"Yeah." She finished up her pasta and wiped the bowl with a small piece of bread. "All of a sudden you look up and there's the door to nowhere."

Mrs. Medina cleared her throat. "Do you want the rest of this wine?" she asked. She poured it into Lennie's glass, and poured herself some mineral water. Her hand was trembling a bit, and she wondered what possible attraction her own aging body, her aging spirit, could have for this beautiful young woman who had other things on her mind. The rest of her life, for example.

The busboy arrived and loaded his tray with their plates and glasses. After he had moved off Mrs. Medina said, "Don't be so unhappy with things." And then, hearing with horror the maiden aunt in her voice, she put her hand under the table and touched Lennie's thigh.

"I bet you'd like to take me home," Lennie said, finally looking up.

Mrs. Medina felt her way across this vast new territory. No one, ever in her life, had said that to her. She could not draw back her hand, and yet she thought, *Any moment I will stop this. People are here, they will see how much I want her.* But for this moment she saw clearly, straight ahead, and to reach that brief future she had only to remove her hand from Lennie's thigh and pay the bill.

She came in later than she had intended that night. Nikki had said she couldn't stay past ten-thirty, and Lennie had insisted that they go to her place in North Cambridge for a change, since Kenny was away. She had been to Lennie's only once before, to allow Lennie to change clothes one evening after leaving Guido's. Kenny had been there, fortunately involved in a loud, shouting telephone call, and they had gotten in and out in a hurry. In fact, Mrs. Medina had waited by the front door of the apartment, holding it slightly ajar, having no desire to come face to face with Kenny even for a moment. There were children's toys in the hall and the smell of cats.

Tonight they were blessed with Kenny's absence. Lennie's room was big and breezy; there was a thick futon on the floor and a rainbow array of candles on the table and windowsills. They lay on the bed holding each other, but the erotic impulse seemed to have disappeared somewhere on the road back to Cambridge, and Mrs. Medina's mind was distracted by thoughts of their dinner conversation, of the "door to nowhere" that now loomed like a large emotional hole in the wall. After a little bit they sat up against the wall and had some tea. Mrs. Medina watched Lennie's compact breasts rise as she breathed, her nipples erect.

"Want a smoke?" Lennie rummaged in a small tin beside the bed and pulled out a joint. Mrs. Medina shook her head. Sometimes things didn't work. This was one of those times, and she didn't know how to fix it.

When she came in it was well after eleven. She found Patrick padding around in the kitchen with a quart of milk in his hand. He had on his long striped pajama bottoms and a white T-shirt.

"Where's a damn saucepan, Merce? Warm milk is what I want."

"Let me fix it," she said, and was happy to do it for him. "Cup or bowl?"

They sat in his room together, he on the side of his bed, she in his television chair. The city outside was quiet. He sipped his milk noisily. "You put a dash of something in this, didn't you? Whiskey or cinnamon. Just right."

She sighed and leaned back. "Has Nikki been gone long?"

"Yes," he said. "Too damn long. I could have electrocuted myself while you were out tooting around." But he didn't seem really bothered.

After a moment she took a sip of her brandy and said, "Are we a couple of old fools?"

He snorted. "Well, I don't know about you, but I'm no fool."

"No, I don't think you are."

"She making you feel like a fool?"

"We don't have a lot in common, I guess."

"So what? You're not going to marry her."

"No."

"Think you can't keep up, that it?"

"I don't try to keep up, Patrick. I just feel like an adolescent, and I'm horrified of behaving like one."

"I like adolescents, myself," he said thoughtfully.

She smiled.

After a few minutes his mind settled in again, and he looked at her with a concerned frown. He leaned over and set his cup on the floor. "Come on over here," he said, "and I'll hold your hand."

She sat beside him and felt his hand, warm and dry and surprisingly firm, take hers.

"Now what?" she said.

"Well, we have held hands before," he said. "What're you worried about, Merce? With this kid."

"I'm afraid it will stop. I don't know what to do to make it stay."

He was silent for a minute, his breath wheezing a bit. "Stop worrying about putting concrete around it," he said finally. "It will go, that's the way of the world. And when it's time, let it go."

"I couldn't bear it."

"What's that?"

"You and I have lasted," she said. "It doesn't always go."

She sensed him struggling with the thought that she might be equating her relationship with Lennie with the one she had with him. She knew it hurt him. She squeezed his hand. "You see," she said.

"You love her?" he asked. "I thought it was just a fling."

"Oh, God, I have no idea, Patrick!"

He scratched his chin.

"But where can it go? I'm an old woman, fumbling with snaps and buttons."

"Bed her if you want to," he said suddenly. "But stop feeling sorry for yourself." He removed his hand from hers. "I thought I was the love of your life," he added, almost primly.

She turned to face him. "Of course you are. You always were." She felt him begin to shiver. "Come," she said. "Get into bed."

"Now, now I will," he said, and lifted his bony knees.

She helped him in. He smiled at her with his bright blue eyes. "Sleep with me for a while," he said. "Hold me so I don't float away."

She undressed to her slip and climbed in with him, taking his body in her arms. His head nestled at her shoulder and he sighed contentedly. She smiled over the top of his head. *How small he's become,* she thought. *Like a toy.*

"They won't come for me at dawn," he said clearly after a while. "So don't be afraid."

"I'm not afraid."

"Eggs," he said finally. "Eggs for breakfast."

"Yes."

"Breakfast with you. We do have breakfast, and we do have eggs."

"We do. We do."

She dozed, and later rose quietly and left him, stopping to listen for a moment to his breathing, which was coming in slow bubbly breaths. She gathered her clothes and went into the living room to the window. There was no sign of light. Along the avenue the trees had lost nearly all their leaves, and their branches were turning in a breeze she couldn't hear. A plane silently rose over the city, heading west, its running lights blinking roughly. *Where is everyone going?* she thought. *Night and day. It never stops.*

As she stepped into her own bed, the phone rang and she picked it up with a quick jerk, listening for Patrick.

"Hi," Lennie said. "You sound awake."

"I am awake. Where are you?"

"I'm here. I'm home." There was a laugh in the background and some music began. "Kenny's back." She laughed a little. "I'm feeling a little bit better now."

"Yes, I hear."

"Since you're awake, can I come over?"

"What, now?"

"I can't go to sleep. Anyway, I want to make up for earlier. I acted like a total asshole."

"Sweetheart, I don't think it's such a good idea. It's so late, and..." Then she asked herself, *What are you going to do that's so important? Read? Sew on a button?*

She heard Lennie groan and stretch, and imagined the length and stride of her body, her head thrown back, the delicious scent of her neck. She moved to the edge of her bed.

There was silence on the other end of the line.

"How will you get here?" Mrs. Medina said.

"I'll take Kenny's car. I'll be there in twenty minutes. Warn that guy downstairs, will you? He thinks I'm some sort of gangster." There was a click.

Lennie was there in less than twenty minutes, smelling of wine and smoke. "I guess you think I'm crazy," she said. Her eyes were unsteady, grazing on the air.

"No—"

She stood in the middle of Mrs. Medina's room, her hands on her hips. "I feel like a fucking baby."

"It's all right." Mrs. Medina shut the door.

Lennie began to unbutton her shirt quickly, as if she were very warm. "Now," she said. "Let's see what happens now." She pulled Mrs. Medina down and kissed her and made it very clear what she wanted.

Breakfast was years away.

Then it was breakfast, of course. The first time Lennie had stayed. Mrs. Medina introduced them quickly, as if this were not a momentous occasion. Patrick was a little confused.

"Eggs?" he queried Mrs. Medina, in a puzzled way.

"No, it's cereal, Patrick. There wasn't time for eggs."

He looked sadly at his bowl.

"Were you here yesterday?" he asked Lennie.

"Very late," she said. "What kind of eggs do you like?"

"Scrambled. That's it when I have eggs."

"There's time for that," Lennie said, getting up. "I'll fix you some eggs."

Patrick looked helplessly at Mrs. Medina.

"No," she said, following Lennie into the kitchen. "No, Lennie, don't. He wants me to do them. I'll do them."

"Why did you say there wasn't time?"

"I didn't think you were going to stay to eat." She broke two eggs into a small glass bowl. "Go on back now and talk to him. I don't want him to be alone."

"Are you moving in here?" he asked Lennie in the dining room. The day was overcast and monochromatic, the cool, smoky smell of the autumn morning outside was easy to imagine.

"I live in Cambridge," Lennie said. "North Cambridge, really, out beyond Porter Square."

"My wife was a real beauty," Patrick said, leaning his chin on his hand.

"She's still a beauty," Lennie said. She smiled. "They tell me you were a really great cello player."

"I am a great cello player."

"Will you play for me sometime?"

He looked at her as if he had suddenly remembered the nature of her relationship with his wife. He held up his index finger. "Listen to me. She's new to real passion. If you harm one hair of her head, there will be trouble."

"Why should I harm her?"

"Someday," he said, "I'll tell you what my grandpop did at the Battle of Second Manassas."

"All right." She drummed her long fingers on the table.

"That story's better than any cello."

From the kitchen came the sound of eggs being scraped onto a plate. "She'll be here soon," he said, smiling.

When Mrs. Medina entered the room his eyes greeted her with the happiness of a much younger man.

"Now, does everyone have what they want?" Mrs. Medina said.

Lennie finished her cereal hurriedly, took a drink of coffee. "Got to go now," she said, standing up. She shook Patrick's hand. "I enjoyed our talk."

"We didn't talk," he said. Then he quickly raised her hand to his lips. "You're a damned troublemaker. But I'm a gentleman."

"When will I see you?" Mrs. Medina said at the door.

"Soon. Call me." Lennie walked across the small marbled foyer to ring for the elevator. The sound of her boots echoed against the walls.

Mrs. Medina followed, ran her hand down the length of Lennie's back, and cupped her rear end. A daring gesture, for her. She prayed that the Lowes across the hall had already left for work.

She already missed Lennie grotesquely.

Just before the elevator arrived, Lennie kissed her lightly on the mouth. "He had you first," she said. "But I've got you now."

She cleaned up the dishes while Patrick fiddled with the kitchen radio. Since he'd stopped playing, it was difficult for him to listen to music sometimes, music he associated with himself, and sometimes he sat before the radio glaring at it, ready to turn the dial violently if something came on that disturbed him. The Dohnányi C Minor Piano Quintet was announced, and he turned the set off altogether.

She turned around suddenly. "Now, I like that piece," she said. "Could we have it, please?"

"That's that group from Chicago. They don't play worth a damn, never did, and their cellist is a fag."

"Jesus Christ!" Mrs. Medina dried her hands and walked out into the living room.

He followed her. "Nothing but the truth. I knew them all when they started out."

"You introduced me to Roger Waye. He is not a fag. And don't use that word."

"I've always used that word. Known many fags in my life. Liked most of 'em. How do you know Roger isn't a fag? You take him on?"

"That's ridiculous, Patrick. And what do his sexual habits have to do with the way he plays? You've told me many times how good he is."

"Those guys should hang it up before one of 'em pops off in the middle of a *presto prestissimo*." He was wandering around the living room, picking things up off the tables and putting them down again.

"Come on, Patrick," she said tightly. "Help me with my crossword."

"Don't give me that patronizing air! I can still fight. She may be a spring heifer, but there's still fire in my blood."

"I'm not going to argue with you about whether Roger Waye is a homosexual."

"She's gone. And you look like a dreary candle that's just been puffed out." He banged her large silver cigarette case down on the coffee table. "That's why I'm mad. I'm here too!"

"No, we're fighting because there's no music around here anymore! And that's why I'm mad."

"Well, that hurts me too," he said. "But I'm not mad about that now. I'm mad because I'm not enough."

She tried to put herself in his place, anything to end this pointless quarrel. She had no ammunition to fight it, because, in fact, he wasn't enough. Not anymore.

"I don't want you here for a nanny," he said. "Nikki can be a nanny. I want you here because you belong here. Because you want to be here." He had been standing during this exchange, and she saw he was a bit teetery.

She got up and took his arm. "Come on, Patrick. This morning's gotten off on the wrong foot. Since you're so full of energy, let's walk over to Legal and buy something for dinner. A nice halibut, maybe."

"Dinner? What about right now?"

He was absolutely right. What about right now.

She took both his hands and looked him in the eye. "I'm happy when we're together, you and I. I'm happy with Lennie too. They're two different things."

"Is there enough of you to go around? Smoke that in your pipe."

"Let me be sad a bit when she's left, Patrick. Why worry about what's enough?"

"Before you go into the sunset you'd better think of your declining years. Who's going to take care of you? Will she take care of you?"

"You will not divert me by shifting your attack to my declining years. I'll probably take care of myself. Now, go and get your jacket."

"I don't want halibut."

"Well, we'll see what they have."

He started off down the hall but turned back and said, "Play music if you want. I didn't know you liked the Dohnányi. Sweet little piece, really. We played it for fun once, Santino and Barbara and I, with another fiddle and a viola. But it's a quintet, we never did it in concert."

"Yes, I know."

"Just don't let me hear any Schubert. It hurts me. And no Ludwig von."

sixteen

Mrs. Medina and Lennie came out of Pignoli's about one-thirty. They stopped on the sidewalk, and Mrs. Medina looked up toward Arlington Street as if she were unclear about what was to happen next. Which she was.

"Twenty-four ninety-five for a few little shrimp," Lennie said. "That's totally ridiculous."

"Well, I hope it was good. I wanted to take you someplace nice."

"Yeah, it was good," Lennie said, and flipped her pigtail back over her shoulder. It was one of those mild November days that can fool you. The air was sweet. The street sounds had lost the edge of cold. Lennie was wearing a white silk shirt under a black blazer that was a bit too big for her. After a moment she said, "I don't have to go back."

"You don't? That's wonderful. Why?"

"Guido owes me some time. We don't have any big jobs today." She turned and pulled Mrs. Medina away from the center of the sidewalk. "Let's go somewhere," she said.

The traffic throttled its way past them out St. James Avenue. "Somewhere? Well, Nikki is with Patrick today."

"Okay, not your place. My place is populated today too. So."

"Why didn't you say something earlier?"

"Too many plans spoil things."

Mrs. Medina knew Lennie could easily have gone back to work and said nothing. Pretended. Or actually gone.

"Look there." Lennie pointed.

The massive hulk of the Park Plaza loomed across the street. Huge. Anonymous. A monolith of granite transplanted from Moscow, Mrs. Medina had often thought.

"Ever been in there? Your sort of place?" Lennie was holding Mrs. Medina's arm.

"You mean to get a room?"

"Sure."

"In the middle of the afternoon?" Checking into a hotel for half a day, in the middle of the afternoon, was something she had never done. It elicited thoughts of dreary, flaking walls, stained bedspreads, rust in the washbasin. Richard Widmark or Ida Lupino lurking in the closet.

"Why not?"

"Lennie—"

Lennie stood back from her and put her hands on her hips. "Come on," she said. And then, coming closer, whispered into Mrs. Medina's ear, "You want to get laid or not?"

"You see, my apartment's being painted. I thought I could tolerate the smell, but it seems not." Mrs. Medina smiled at the desk clerk out of a flushed face and lay some bills on the counter. "I believe that will do it."

"You have no luggage, then."

"Oh, no. I expect things will be aired out by tonight. Or perhaps not. Perhaps I'll have to stay on. If you'll just give me the key, no need for a bellboy."

The desk clerk's eyes returned again to Lennie, who was lounging by a small potted tree, watching. "Very well," he said, dropping the key into Mrs. Medina's outstretched hand. "Eleventh floor. I hope you enjoy your afternoon."

"That bastard," Mrs. Medina said in the elevator.

"Forget him," Lennie said. She put her fingers on the back of Mrs. Medina's neck.

The room smelled medicinal, and was too warm. But the heavy, flowered bedspread was clean, the bathroom spotless. It was one of two hundred rooms surrounding them, all alike, populated by people neither of them knew.

At the window Mrs. Medina looked down at the traffic streaming silently west through Park Square. All the people she could see, whose worlds did not include her! Life could go on without her for a while. No one knew she was here, no one but the desk clerk, and he had seen this sort of thing before, no doubt. And no one would walk in, no one would be calling for her. No one cared. She could be anyone.

When Lennie came to her and kissed her she could still taste the garlic, the wine, from the $24.95 plate of shrimp she had watched her consume not an hour before. She took one end of Mrs. Medina's paisley scarf in her hand and slowly pulled it from around her neck. "Let's take a shower," she said.

Mrs. Medina removed her own clothes slowly, folded them neatly, piece by piece, on the brocade chair. She wished for a robe, at least. Lennie was in the bathroom fiddling with the water. Mrs. Medina stood in her underwear close to despair, and actually made a move to put her sweater back on. And almost at the same moment realized this was not the real problem. "You ridiculous woman," she said aloud. "You've wanted this for months." She folded her underwear and added it to the pile. She wondered if it looked too matronly. "To hell with it," she said, and sat down on the bed.

"Get in here," Lennie called from the shower. Her socks were on the floor, her clothes thrown over a stool, and she was already under the water. Mrs. Medina stepped delicately in with her. Lennie had run the water so hot that the room was piping with steam. Mrs. Medina saw her own skin flush and darken, and smooth into softness. Lennie put her arms around her from behind and gently sucked the water from her neck, and the water roared over them with the force of a cataract.

"We're getting soaked," Mrs. Medina said weakly, for nothing else came to mind.

Lennie laughed and turned Mrs. Medina around to face her. Her hair, which she had recently trimmed, was glittering with sparks of water. Every part of her was streaming. With slow hands she soaped Mrs. Medina all over her body, and afterward rinsed her and toweled her dry roughly, and threw the towel onto the floor.

"Bed," she said.

Everywhere Lennie touched her at first seemed impossible to bear. "You have to understand—" she began, and her breath caught.

Lennie leaned over her. Her body, tall as it was, was compact and tightly put together, and her gold pendant swung gracefully between her small breasts. She gave Mrs. Medina a long smiling look, and Mrs. Medina reached for her and pulled her down. The long, firm weight of Lennie's body made Mrs. Medina dizzy for a moment, and she wanted to stop because she didn't think she could bear it. There was this furious tension. "I know, I know," Lennie said, her lips against Mrs. Medina's neck. And Mrs. Medina trusted that she did know. For it was not a matter of gentleness; Mrs. Medina, finally, did not want gentleness, she wanted to be touched so she would know she was in her body, what that meant, and she hoped Lennie would understand this. The sheet under her back was clean and wonderfully rough. When Lennie touched her breasts, her belly, the base of her spine, parts of her body to which she had been indifferent for so long, they began to open, one after another, revealing, revealing, as more of her fell away. She seemed to be chasing some violent movement, and yet she wanted to be completely still and to be still wasn't possible. But Lennie was perfect, she followed her, she did not lose her. Mrs. Medina thought of flying, of rising, of her breath, which was loud and insistent. Then she stopped thinking. And when Lennie brought her to the edge she thought she would never reach, she clung to her with her thighs, and gripped her hair tightly as if she were thirty-five and used to this, and begged Lennie to bring her over. And Lennie brought her over.

Later Mrs. Medina cried a little but hadn't the strength to wipe her face, so her tears trickled down her cheeks, into her ears, and dampened the pillow. Lennie drowsed against her side. "Thank you, thank you, I love you for this," Mrs. Medina whispered. She heard the shower dripping, like an echoing memory.

She waited for Lennie to wake, and drew her up and kissed her gently and then much harder. Lennie finally leaned back, laughing. "What, again?" she said.

"Yes. Yes."

Then they dozed again.

When Mrs. Medina woke again she felt Lennie curled around her tightly, with her mouth against Mrs. Medina's neck. She said, "Hmm," and Mrs. Medina smiled. After a little while she asked, with just the slightest hesitation, "When did you know you were a lesbian? Or do you say gay? I mean, were there—signs—to tell you?"

"I knew," Lennie said, smiling, her eyes closed. "You just know. It takes some people longer to get it."

"I guess some people never get it. Do you—can you tell about other people?"

"I knew about you." Mrs. Medina drew back in surprise. "You were easy."

"Nearly six," Lennie whispered in her ear.

Mrs. Medina opened her eyes.

Lennie smiled. "Nearly six," she repeated.

"Oh, God," Mrs. Medina groaned. She stretched, loose, aching. "Where's the phone?"

Nikki was still with Patrick, and she agreed to stay and fix him dinner. "Where is she?" she heard him cry out in the background.

"I'll be home by eight," she said. She lay back and watched Lennie in the bathroom, the curve of her body as it bent over the sink.

"Do we have time for room service?" Lennie asked over her shoulder.

Mrs. Medina was proud of the tangled bed, but she didn't want anyone else to see it. They settled for a drink in one of the dark bars downstairs, where Mrs. Medina sipped one of her rare scotches, a Chivas that clung to her mouth like golden silk, and Lennie asked the piano player to play "Stairway to Heaven," and looked very pleased with herself.

They stood on the sidewalk in the evening chill—the autumn city, the flowing blood of cars, the brains of light.

"Aha," Lennie said. "You missed a button on your blouse."

"Don't bother me with clothes. I'll just take it off."

"You'd get some serious attention going home."

"Don't laugh at me."

"Can't help it. You going to walk?"

"I'll just float."

"I'll watch you go."

"Will you call me?"

"Sure."

"You still want to go to that film at the ICA? Friday?"

"I'll see when Friday comes."

Mrs. Medina wanted to put her arms around Lennie to keep her from leaving, as if whatever had happened between them would leave with her. There was a chill wind blowing up through Park Square.

Lennie leaned over and kissed her ear. "Don't worry," she said, "it'll happen again."

Patrick was not happy, and he had not eaten his dinner. "He wanted to wait for you," Nikki smiled. "I'm outta here. See you next week."

"Thanks for staying, Nikki."

"Where were you?" Patrick said.

"Have you been sitting there waiting for your dinner since six?" she said, tucking a napkin under his chin. "Here, Nikki's fixed you macaroni and cheese."

"Don't want it. Sit down. What're you eating?"

"I'll have some too," she said, but she had no desire to eat.

He reluctantly took up his fork.

"I had a late lunch with Lennie, you knew that, and it became—extended."

"Will this happen all the time now? Is it more of my new reality?"

"No, of course not." As she raised the fork to her mouth she encountered Lennie's mild scent on her fingertips, and the wind pushed hard against the windows.

"Windy," she said, her throat dry.

He was chewing with some purpose. "Maybe Nikki should move in here," he said.

"There's no need for that." But she had thought about it.

When she looked up at him his eyes were full.

"Don't you think I want you to be happy?" he said.

"Of course I do."

"Why didn't she wait until I kicked off?"

Mrs. Medina smiled. "We can work things out, Patrick." She poured herself a little wine.

"Whose advantage?" he said, turning his head. "I don't want to be selfish, but whose advantage? I'm on my way out, but I need a little help."

She got up and went to stand behind him, running her arms down around his neck. "I will never leave you," she said.

"That's not the problem, damn it. I know you'll never leave me!" He leaned his head against her arm and breathed wispily for a moment. "I wish I didn't want you here so much. It leaves me without my armor."

She kissed the top of his head. "We'll play some gin tonight, how about that?"

He did not reply. Then after a few moments he said, "Peace! Peace! Shouldn't you be looking for peace at your age?"

"I've had peace for most of my life, Patrick."

He nodded. "And now you want a little war."

She helped him up, and they walked slowly back to his room, hand in hand. The wind was increasing; it beat and wound around the windows. She wanted to crawl into bed and lie awake, dreaming. Instead they played a few hands of gin, then he pointedly put on one of the Brandenburg Concertos and they sat quietly, she listening, he dozing.

Yes, this is peace, she thought, *and I'm not tired of it.*

But now she also knew about the rough texture of complication that could draw peace away. The rough texture of uncertainty, of possibility. And peace would never find her there, she knew.

But she might not miss it.

When she woke him in the morning he was confused, not at all clear about where he was, or who she was. He called her "Lily," a name he had never mentioned before, and insisted that she rub his feet and help him with his boots.

"Patrick, Patrick," Mrs. Medina said.

"Be quick," he replied. "I only promised you one night." His eyes were focused on the window, or something he saw beyond it. Then she saw that his pajamas were wet. She helped him to his feet and into the bathroom and stripped him down. "You're a coy little number," he said. "You're never satisfied, are you?"

"Into the shower," she said. Then he sagged in her arms and seemed to lose consciousness for a moment. She got him seated on the side of the tub.

"Just get me back to bed," he mumbled irritably. "My legs went."

She called Harry Max and fortunately got him between appointments.

"Well," he said. "I'll send an ambulance over."

"I wish you'd come by," she said, "to see if it's absolutely necessary. He's awake now, lucid."

"What did I say last week, Mercedes? I want him in the hospital and I want to do some tests."

"He won't agree to that, Harry. I already know."

"Well, then *you* must agree to it." And she knew she had to. "All right," Harry said with a sigh. "I'm leaving for the Brigham in half an hour. I'll come by."

When she went back to Patrick's room he was sitting up in bed. "Well, I've been somewhere," he said, "but where the hell was it?"

She laughed. "You've been with Lily," she said.

"Lily? Lily Conover from Little Compton?"

"Whoever she is."

"Well, can you beat that. Old Lil. Came to fetch me, did she?"

"She didn't get you this time. Harry Max is coming by in a while. You can tell him about Lily Conover."

"No need for Harry. I want my coffee. And why am I benuded?"

"Benuded is not a word."

"I am starkers, as Lil used to say."

She was desperate to keep his good spirits perking. "I'll bring you breakfast in bed. What would you like?"

"Eggs. Eggs and toast and a grilled tomato."

"Patrick, this is November. You don't like any tomatoes that appear after the end of August."

"Right. Taste like raw potatoes, don't they? All right. Eggs and toast. Here, feel my heart. Popping right along."

She put her hand on his chest and was startled, for what she felt was the fluttering of a small bird trying to escape.

~

"Well, he absolutely refuses to go, Mercedes," Harry said later. "He's happier here, so let him stay. These may be small strokes, but I can't tell unless I can test him. He has no paralysis. Right now he's perfectly lucid. I've given him my straight from the shoulder speech, and he understands it."

"Maybe you'd better give it to me."

"All right. He could go on for a while, or go in his sleep tonight. His heart is weak, his body is wearing out. There is some loss of mental function. He knows all this, it's not something new. But you're taking good care of him, and he has a will of iron. Those are the positive points."

"Yes."

He handed her a prescription form. "I want him to try a new medication. Might help with these little episodes." He put his arm around her shoulders. "Now I've got to go."

"Harry, you're gaining weight," she said. "You're beginning to fill out those beautiful suits you parade around in."

"And are you keeping well, Mercedes?"

"Yes, all right."

He shrugged himself into his raincoat. "Are you teaching this fall?"

"No, not until the end of January."

He kissed her cheek. "You can get me anytime. I can be beeped." He showed her the beeper on his belt.

"Quit making time with my wife, Harry!" Patrick called from his room. "I'll come out there and conk you with my Louisville Slugger!"

"He does have one," Mrs. Medina said.

"Well, so do I." He smoothed his little gray mustache. "Back in the closet somewhere. The old ones are quite valuable now, you know."

seventeen

Ｓhe finally got Valentina Bird to come by for tea. As Tina came breathlessly in the door, Mrs. Medina realized how cloistered her own love-struck world had become. She began to see Tina as both a perplexing link to a remote way of life she was beginning not to recognize and a representative of a new dark threat that could conceivably hurt her. But it was difficult not to delight at the sight of her old friend, and she gave her an energetic hug.

Tina held her by her shoulders and looked hard at her. "You are causing me much grief," she said, shaking her head. "You have been silent as the Sphinx."

"I hope you don't mind coming here, Tina. I want to keep an eye on Patrick."

"Of course not. How is he?" Tina asked, bustling over to the couch. "Do you mind if I smoke? Is there oxygen about? Well, I'm trying to stop anyway."

"Relax, stop pacing about. Sit down."

Tina was Antiguan, and was given to wearing dresses of red and gold fabrics that clung in long folds around her body. Her skin was the color of sweet, dark rum, and her earrings were always classy and usually enormous. She was fluent in seven languages and loved to tell the story of a Liberian tribal chief who offered to buy her for five goats when she was working there after graduate school. Patrick demanded this story from her every time they met.

"Where have you been?" she said to Mrs. Medina. "You promised to call me. Have you shot your answering machine?"

"I turned it off. I think it bothers Patrick."

"Yes, they bother me too." She opened a large schedule book.

"But here it is November, Mercedes. We do have a commitment from you for your usual winter seminar. You were talking about doing all women—Ginzburg, Deledda, maybe Marta Morazzoni..." She consulted her list. "I need to know about texts."

"I was thinking of that." She sat down on the other end of the couch. "I may change my mind, though." She looked up at Tina and found her watching eyes. "Want a cup of tea? There's water on."

"Let's take care of business first."

"I've lost my patience with Italian women writers. I'm tired of stories about families and husbands. All the sacrifices."

Tina made a note in her folder. "All right."

"I want to teach something lyrical, something joyous."

"Nothing wrong with joy." Tina closed her book. "Given this much thought, Mercedes?"

"Well, yes." She leaned back. "Well, no, not really. I know what I *don't* want to teach. I don't want to teach self-sacrifice and family history."

"And who could blame you?" Tina tilted her head. Her earrings caught the light, golden hoops with strands of colored glass. "So it's joy and lyricism. Who did you have in mind? Hard to find an Italian without some gloom in his soul."

"I'll do Calvino," she said suddenly, "an extended study of *Invisible Cities*." She imagined the delight of teaching this work every week. Like living with the music of Bellini.

Tina pursed her lips and reopened her schedule book. "I think I'd like to see you develop a theme here, Mercedes—and certainly do more than one work. Call it magic realism, Italian style. Whatever you want. Maybe start with your Vittorini, the realist of realists, for contrast; he starts gloomy, but he gets cheerier." She made a few notes, closed the book firmly and put it on the table. "Think about it for a few days."

"Fine, fine. I will." Mrs. Medina straightened the magazines on the coffee table. She felt she had somehow abandoned her Italian women, and had a twinge of guilt.

They sat for a few moments in comfortable silence.

"Well," Tina said. "How's your work coming along? Pulling the translation into shape? I have a visiting professor from Bologna here this semester. He'd like to see it."

"Actually, I haven't had much time to work on it, Tina. I thought I would, but Patrick…" She put her hand on her forehead.

"What are you going to do when you don't have him for an excuse?" Tina said. She put her hand over Mrs. Medina's. "I'm sorry, Mercedes. I worry about you."

"I know," Mrs. Medina said. "Now, just let me put the tea in to steep. Be right back."

When she returned to the living room Tina was standing by the window, looking out at the avenue. "Trees are bare," she said.

"How many students, do you think, Tina?"

"Oh, small, no more than fifteen." She returned to her chair. "I hope you're not having second thoughts about this seminar. Because we're stuck at the moment."

"I know."

"And yes, it has to be taught." She picked up a cookie and held it in her fingers. "We used to have lunch every other week, even when Patrick nearly died of pneumonia two years ago. What's going on here? Are you sick?"

"No, as a matter of fact I'm very happy."

"Try again."

"I am happy. It's just that there's a lot to fit into my life just now."

"Patrick and—"

"Patrick, and, and—"

"Mercedes, no one's heard from you in weeks. In over a month."

"I think I'm in love." Then, quickly, she did feel happy. Suddenly full of joy. Speaking of love clarified it, for the first time.

"Jesus and Mary, I should've guessed." Tina smiled. "And about time, lady. Can't get you off the hook for the course, though, if that thought crossed your mind."

"I don't care."

"Well, you want to talk?"

She looked at Tina cautiously.

"Okay, talk when you're ready." She laughed, shaking her head with a bright movement of gold. "I know how you are." She reached over and patted Mrs. Medina's knee. "Now I'll give you the lecture I give my girls. And I am dead serious. These are days of the plague, so you have to be responsible for yourself. I don't care how old he is, or how old you are. Sex is sex. Are you doing the safe sex thing?"

"What?"

"Well, now we're down to it. You and I have been having tea and crumpets for years now, and discussing books, and husbands, and places in the world, and politics, and you've been kind to me during some very rough periods in my life. I didn't think you wanted to talk about matters of the flesh, and to tell you the truth, except for my little fling with that madman Joseph some years back, I had no reason to bring it up. But I doubt if you've been out in the world this way for a while, so as a true friend I must advise you." She took a look at Mrs. Medina. "God! I suddenly look into my daughter's face! I have a feeling you're in grave difficulty. What do you need to know?"

"Is that my little bird out there?" Patrick's voice, croaky from his nap, called out.

"I'll talk to you later," Mrs. Medina said, and stood up. "Yes, Patrick, it's Tina. Do you want some tea? We'll come in there."

Tina gripped her wrist. "You're not pregnant, are you? Some freak accident? I assumed you were long past having to worry about that particular problem."

Mrs. Medina laughed, but it sounded shrill. "No, I don't have to worry about that." She had hoped for a sharing of joy, but now she was unsure. Safe sex! It really was ridiculous. "What do you have for me to sign? And I guess you'd better get me a schedule of meetings."

"Tina! Fly in here on the double! I have something to show you!"

"What does he have to show me?" Tina said.

"I can't imagine. Go on, I'll bring the tea in. And Tina, Thanksgiving? The invitation is still open. With whoever you want to bring."

"Wouldn't miss it. Let me know what you need." She kissed Mrs. Medina's cheek. "I'm glad you're happy. You're too young to hole up in here for the rest of your life. Patrick would understand."

"Oh, Patrick understands."

"Well, don't try to hide the happiness, then. You look a bit peaky just now. Look happy if you are happy!" She shook her hips. "And call me next week, no matter what else you're up to." She tripped off into Patrick's room in her three-inch pumps.

Well, I suppose I have been out of the world, Mrs. Medina said to herself. She stood at the window and looked down at the avenue.

There was the world. Perfectly ordinary people walking along: a telephone man, his belt sagging with mystery gadgets; a tall blond student with a red backpack, spiky hair, her feet in black motorcycle boots; two young men holding hands! And she, Mercedes Medina, had been separated from it as surely as the pane of glass in front of her separated her from the air outside she could neither smell nor feel on her skin.

"Merce!" Patrick called. "We need some tea in here!"

In a perfectly ordinary moment of an ordinary day, pulling Patrick's dinner out of the oven, or picking over green beans at the Star Market, the vivid sensation of Lennie's mouth moving toward her own would be before her and she would stop, motionless.

She woke in the night and lay quietly listening to the dripping of a soft, earlier rain. She put her arm out, knowing she was alone, but wishing to touch the spot where Lennie had been, might still have been. She wondered if it was time to make a decision.

"Don't be so serious," Lennie was fond of saying. About sex, about time that was falling away.

"Don't leave me," Patrick had never said explicitly, but she had promised anyway, that she never would.

She shook herself and sat up and turned on the light.

It was so unusually quiet that she heard someone pass, whistling, seven floors below. She loved this time of night. She turned off the light and walked over to the window.

It didn't matter about labels, what she called herself; she was past that. And it shouldn't matter whether someone would come after Lennie or if Lennie would be around for a long time. She would have to commit herself to the person, rather than to the idea and all its baggage. Without conditions.

She walked down the hall to Patrick's room. He was sleeping on his back, his mouth open, breathing slowly but without a struggle. She stooped and put her hand on his cool forehead.

"I'm sorry," she said. "I'm sorry, I'm sorry."

But she had given him a good life. They had had wonderful times together. And she would see him out.

Back in her room she picked up the phone and called Lennie's number, not caring who she woke up.

Kenny answered on the first ring.

"Is Lennie—" she began.

"Yeah, it's about time you called. Tell Ray she's on her way. But she'll wait for him at the other place. You got the street number?"

Mrs. Medina had no idea what to say.

"You got it?"

"No." Mrs. Medina said it.

"One-oh-three. One-oh-three Rutland, second floor. But tell Ray to haul his ass. I'm tired of fucking with you people, and she's not going to wait." They both hung up together.

The next night she and Lennie emerged from the ICA Gallery about nine-thirty. It had grown cold, and a raw dampness was in the air. They had seen *La Notte*.

"What was that all about?" Lennie said with a little shiver. "It went on and on. Too much talk. Too many complications."

"Why," said Mrs. Medina, "it's not complicated at all." She was almost defensive, for this was one of her favorite films. "Two people, who were once close, have grown apart. They're realizing this. It's a tragedy, but the tragedy is they don't care. No one cares."

"All black-and-white movies seem automatically too serious for me."

"Oh, come on." Mrs. Medina took her arm. "Go along to the Star with me. I have to pick up some things. Do you have time?"

"Yeah, I guess."

Mrs. Medina had looked forward to strolling casually through the aisles with Lennie, that most domestic of activities. But Lennie became stalled at the lobster pool, and Mrs. Medina quickly gathered her eggs, her cheese, her toilet paper, and went to pay. Then they walked down Boylston Street into a wind. After a few minutes Mrs. Medina began, "I called you the other night—"

"You did? When?"

"Wednesday, I guess it was. Last night. I got Kenny."

"Must have been pretty late. He didn't tell me."

"He thought I was someone else. You were out delivering something, according to him."

For a moment she was silent. Then she said, "He must have been wrecked."

Mrs. Medina stopped. They were on the corner, under the bright canopy of the Lenox Hotel, and the wind was fierce, coming up Exeter Street off the river. "I don't know," she said. "What is it you actually do for him?"

"On Wednesday night I was out late, I wasn't even home."

"Yes, I know."

"I think I'm getting a message here," Lennie said, with a half smile.

"No. No message." Mrs. Medina crossed Boylston and started quickly along Exeter toward the lights of Newbury Street.

"What's the problem, then?" Lennie said, keeping pace with her.

"I just wonder, sometimes, about Kenny. About you and Kenny. That's all. I wonder whether—oh, I don't know."

"You don't have to worry about Kenny. I told you."

"That's not what I mean. Never mind, just forget it." But she felt a bitterness rise up in her, a sense that Lennie could easily walk away from her, in spite of her own will or any other force. She could walk away for any one of a hundred reasons, and Kenny was only one of them. Her own vulnerability was very clear. So she walked on, silently.

"I'm not exactly blind to his bad points," Lennie said after a few moments. "I'd live alone if I could afford it."

They came to the corner of Newbury Street, and Lennie stopped, put her hands on Mrs. Medina's shoulders, and said, "Mrs. Prim and Proper."

Mrs. Medina irritably shrugged her off, looking across at the line waiting to get into Friday's. The rich, sickening smell of frying hamburger fat came clouding out of a vent. The little fairy lights hanging in the trees reminded her that she should think about what to cook for Thanksgiving. A duck, perhaps, this year? No, that might be too rich for Patrick.

"Okay," Lennie said. "I'll go on home."

"Off you go, then." She kissed Lennie lightly on the cheek and gave her just a bit of a push.

Lennie turned away and crossed the street. A car passed, thumping with rap. Mrs. Medina watched her go. The wind whipped into her coat and her bones ached. She clutched her little bag: eggs, cheese, toilet paper, ordinary consumables for an ordinary life. She pictured Lennie at her Thanksgiving table, a meal she loved to cook, the house full of fall flowers, candles lit. Patrick attacking the bird with a knife as big as his grandfather's Confederate sword. She knew this scene had been in her mind, waiting, for some time. The late afternoon sun slanting into the room, the city quiet.

She threw up her arm. "Wait!" she cried into the darkness, dodging across the street. "Wait!"

She could hear the Schubert trio playing before she put her key into the lock. Lennie looked at her quizzically. "Well, we won't wake him up, at least," she said.

He actually came trotting down the hall from his room as soon as he heard the door close, his little wisps of hair waving about over the top of his head. His eyes were bright. He frightened her.

"Merce, they've called for us again!" Completely ignoring Lennie.

"Patrick, aren't you cold?" He was wearing his faded Celtics T-shirt and a voluminous pair of green plaid boxer shorts.

"Santino called. They want us, they want the trio, they've summoned the old Riviera for the Thanksgiving reunion at Jordan Hall."

"The reunion of what?" She hadn't taken off her coat, and Lennie was standing behind her, still as a statue.

The second movement of the Schubert was moving sweetly through the house. "That's what we'll do," he said. "The B flat. Our signature piece, and that's what we'll do. Santino agrees."

Mrs. Medina finally realized he was talking about the annual marathon performance that the Conservatory organized, gathering together everyone they could dig up who had ever played or sung at Jordan Hall. It was a benefit, the Saturday night of Thanksgiving weekend. She was horrified. She must call Santino immediately.

"I guess you're worried about the condition of Old Bess." Old Bess was his favorite cello.

"No, I'm not worried about Bess. I'm worried about you."

"Me? I'm happy as a bridegroom. This will bring me back to life."

"Patrick, the trio has disbanded. Barbara has severe arthritis, you know that."

"And you think I'm too old to cut the mustard."

"The Schubert's a longish piece. I'll talk to Santino."

"I can make my own decisions here, goddamn it." He peered around his wife and finally noticed Lennie. "So she's dragged you home, has she?" he said, but not in an unfriendly way. "She wants to rain on my parade. What do you think of that?"

Lennie smiled.

"Well, I'm going to have a tot of Black Jack. Anyone want to join me? Merce, did you bring the eggs? I'm going to need a large breakfast." He teetered off toward the kitchen.

Mrs. Medina dropped her bag of groceries into a chair. "It'll kill him," she said.

"He looks pretty happy to me," Lennie said.

"Where is Ben's number, Merce?" Patrick called from the kitchen. "Bess has to have a tune up."

"You don't need to call him tonight."

Lennie went into the living room and pulled a couple of fading anemones out of a vase. She settled the remainder in their water and stepped back to look at them.

"Please don't do that," Mrs. Medina said.

Lennie turned around. "I guess this isn't a good night to stay," she said.

In a sort of numbness, Mrs. Medina gave her a brief hug and opened the door. She was angry, and although Lennie was not responsible for this sudden turn of events, she was angry at her. It was inexplicable. Half an hour ago she was wondering when Lennie might walk away from her. Now for the second time that evening she was pushing her out as if to beat her to the punch.

She did not wait with Lennie at the elevator, and without taking off her coat she went into her room and closed her door. But the Schubert moved through the walls, music she had once loved, and eventually she sat down on the side of her bed and stared into the darkness. Patrick's life was ascending again, and it would take her up with it, whether she wanted to go or not.

~ *eighteen* ~

"**S**antino, I am very angry with you," she said on the phone the next morning, very early, while Patrick was still shaving. "I can't imagine why you've decided to torture him like this."

"Torture, Mercedes? I thought it would be a nice thing to do, people will be very happy to see him. I don't suppose he told you—so many are coming they only want us to do the allegro, only the first movement, and we can do that in about eleven or twelve minutes."

"They waited a bit late to call you, didn't they?"

"Well, it's sort of been brewing."

Her hand twisted the coils of the telephone cord. "I'm not worried about the actual playing, although that will be risky enough. It's what happens to him before. You know how he is. He paced around all night—he's already so excited. And then being there, backstage, with all those people who knew him...how can we control it?"

Santino was quiet.

"You know, Santino, he has his good days and his bad days, but he could die at any moment."

"He misses his playing."

"I know that. He's also very proud. Do you want him to make a fool of himself?"

"He won't. He knows this piece so well he could play it asleep."

"Well, not to make a point—"

"When it comes to music, his mind is fine."

She sighed.

"Do you know, Mercedes, how happy this will make him?"

"Yes, of course I do. But I'm not willing to risk his life to make him happy."

"That's an odd way of putting it."

"I'm responsible for him."

"So am I. So is Barbara."

"How are Barbara's hands?"

"Painful. But she wants to play."

"It seems I have no say, then."

"Of course you can forbid it. I'll do whatever you want."

"Santino, you have your own solo career now. We heard you do the Berg at Pittsburgh a couple of weeks ago. On the radio. It was splendid."

"Thank you." He paused. "I would regret it very much if anyone ever told me I couldn't play. Even on my deathbed."

"You're young. Patrick and Barbara—how will you pull them through it?"

"I won't have to pull them through anything. Once we start, no one will think of anything but the music." He laughed. "Like sex, you know. You don't think—you move forward until it's finished."

Mrs. Medina blushed. She heard Patrick come out of his bathroom, and she knew she should make some sort of decision quickly.

"But you will have to help us, Mercedes. He'll want to practice, and he should, but you should be there, and listen, and notice if he gets frustrated. Barbara and I will come over when it's time for us to practice together."

"I'm supposed to keep him calm, Santino."

"Well, you know best how to do that."

"I'll have to take out a gun and shoot him."

Santino laughed. "I sometimes wanted to do that myself. On the road."

"You've put me in a bad situation. I'm saying he may die if he goes ahead, and you're saying he's as good as dead if he doesn't."

"No. I'm simply saying it would make him very happy."

She heard Patrick whistling in his room, the clatter of hangers in his closet.

"I'm very dubious about that word, Santino. People use it as an excuse for all sorts of things."

"Maybe."

"What can I say? Tell them yes."

"Thank you, Mercedes. I'll call you soon. I'll call you tomorrow."

She sat there quietly, her hand on the receiver. This would not be a job for Nikki. It was clearly her job, and she ought to be happy for Patrick. But she was thinking of Lennie. She wanted to call her, but what could she say? See you in two weeks?

My two children, she thought suddenly.

"Eggs!" Patrick shouted, coming down the hall.

He sat at the breakfast table waiting for her, smelling nicely of Equipage, his knife and fork held upright between his fists. He gave her a bright, sly smile.

"Don't give me that army barracks routine," she said. She put his plate in front of him and sat down with her own cup of tea.

"Where's your grub?" he asked. "Don't like to eat alone."

"I'm drinking tea, and that will have to do. Eat your eggs before they get cold."

"Where's my coffee?"

She gave him a startled look. "Well, I suppose you forgot to set it up. I'm not accustomed to doing it. You arrange things for breakfast coffee. I've been forbidden many times to do anything but cook the food. So there, you see, there is no coffee."

He scraped at his eggs. "Well, so what."

"Serves you right, banging around all night singing, and Figaro is not your role, my dear Patrick."

He put down his fork and gave her a close look. "Your nose is out of joint this morning. What happened to your little chickie? She run off last night?"

"I sent her away. I couldn't deal with both of you at once."

"Aha." He took out a large red-checked handkerchief and blew his nose loudly. "I was going to offer both of you a drink and send you off to bed."

She watched him for a moment. His eyes were clear, he was managing to eat without spilling much, he actually remembered that Lennie had been in the apartment last night. He was dressed in a favorite green-and-black-checked shirt and had put on a black tie that went rather well with it. Less than a week ago she had carried him, almost, to the shower.

She rose and got his several bottles of pills from the mahogany buffet behind him.

"Can't take those without coffee," he said, crunching a toast crust.

"You will take them. You won't drink juice, but I'll get you some water."

When she returned he said, "You know it's wonderful that I still have most of my teeth. I was thinking about that while I was chewing on my toast. False choppers spoil the taste of things, and people can hear them clicking all the time. Charley Eagle was one. Click, click, click. Drove me crazy. Wigs too. Never bothered me that my hair flew away. Girls find that sexy, a bald head. What do you think?"

"Take these pills, please."

"I have good genes, I guess. Both my grandpops virile as bulls and bald as watermelons."

She stood, waiting.

"Let's see," he said, "two reds and a green for breakfast, right?"

"Two reds and one yellow."

He swallowed them all together.

"Thank you," she said.

"I think of these as my pep pills. Why are you fasting this morning?"

"I'm not fasting. I'm just not ready to eat yet."

"You should eat when I eat. We should eat together."

"Stop it, Patrick!" She was shocked to realize she had hit the table with her fist. She sat down and put her head in her hands.

After a few moments he said, "I knew you would call Santino, but I thought you'd wait until after breakfast. He has a young child, you know."

"Tony is nearly twenty, Patrick."

"Is that right? What does he play? Not the fiddle like his old man, probably."

"I did call Santino. I was angry, it couldn't wait."

"Susan Hayward said that line once. It was in that movie about the B-girl—"

"Will you reconsider your decision to play at this Thanksgiving concert?"

"Why should I? They've asked us. It's an honor. Barbara and Santino are counting on me. In any case, Santino has already said yes."

"He could easily cancel. They've got a lot of people coming," she said.

"Did you ask him to cancel?"

"Yes, I did."

"What did he say?"

"He said it was my call."

"*Your* call? He told you that? He told you you could cancel *for* me?"

"Well, Patrick, I assumed it was a decision we would make together."

He stood up, shaky for the first time that day. "I am not a corpse yet, even if I have a leg in the grave, Mercedes. You keep your ass out of my music. If I want to play, I will play, and you will not tell Santino to cancel. In my entire career I only canceled twice. I have a reputation."

Her job was beginning. She had to calm him, and calm him quickly.

"If you tell Santino to cancel, I'll throw all your mother's Minton out onto Commonwealth Avenue," he said in a quavery voice.

So she laughed. "Sit down, Patrick." She stood up and eased him back down into his chair. Then kissed the wisps of hair on top of his head. "No one will cancel for you, least of all me. But I'm very worried. I can't deny that. We've both been realistic about your health."

"We're only doing the first movement, Merce. I know that piece as well as my own pecker. I can play it in the dark. We'll knock it off in about ten minutes."

"Twelve minutes, Santino said."

"Well, Santino likes to drag it out. He loves to show off. But he's thinking of making it easier for Barbara too. Easier on her hands. Now, Barbara is the one we should be worrying about."

"All this worrying. Is it worth it?"

He gave her a look and she was instantly ashamed. It was certainly worth it to him. If it was not worth it for her, it was for reasons that probably had little to do with him. Could that be true? Was she worried that this concert would kill him? Or was she hoping that it might release them both?

He took a sip of water and dabbed at his forehead with his handkerchief. "I must practice, you know," he said, without meeting her eyes.

"Yes."

"I have to ask you to help me, Mercedes. I don't want to, but I have to."

"We'll get you through it, Patrick."

"It may get in the way of your other life."

"My other life?"

"Your new passion."

"Oh, yes. My new passion."

"But after Thanksgiving, back to normal. Less than two weeks."

She nodded. Two weeks. *Two weeks.*

"Maybe you can think of it as a business trip. You know, you'll be unavailable for a while, something like that."

"I have never thought of your music as a business trip of any kind."

"Let her sit in, if you want."

"No, I think this is for you and me to do." He was so elated, she could see that he would promise anything. His life was coming back to him, and her sense of fairness told her she should be happy too, happy for him. Instead the prospect of the weeks ahead fell upon her like the sound of a gavel. And she would not allow herself to deny that was what it was.

"Listen," Patrick said, leaning toward her, "if you help me do this, you can have your girl, you can run off into the sunset and I'll ask no more of you. Nikki will see me out. She needs the money. I want this concert like you want your girl. I understand that. You've stuck by me, and I'm a selfish son of a bitch. But if you help me, you can take our money, anything you want, and just go away with her. I will not look for you, and I won't send the police."

She wanted to laugh, but she knew it would hurt his feelings, so she simply patted his arm and got up. "Why don't you rest up for a little while?" she said.

"But I do think Ben should look at Bess right away," he continued tentatively.

"I'll take care of Ben, Patrick. You go on. I'll take care of everything."

nineteen

The Thanksgiving menu was settled finally at turkey with chestnut dressing, additional mashed potatoes for Patrick, cranberry and apple relish, warm green beans with dill, cornbread, an avocado salad, and Indian pudding. Tina would bring yams and Santino his special creamed onions, neither of which Mrs. Medina liked to eat or make. There would be plenty of champagne, cider, and wine, and for hors d'oeuvres she would put out nothing but an enormous bowl of shrimp. Patrick would have to deal with them.

She had presented Patrick with the menu several times, but on Thanksgiving eve he approached her in his socks in the kitchen, where she was chopping celery for the stuffing. In the oven the chestnuts were baking in their pan of water.

Patrick peered into the oven. "What are these little things?" he asked.

"Chestnuts. For the dressing."

"These are for the turkey dressing?"

"Yes. You like chestnut dressing."

"You're very busy tonight, Merce."

"I thought I'd make some of the dressing ahead of time."

"The Weather Channel just issued a warning." He walked over to the refrigerator and opened it. "If you stuff a turkey too soon, bacteria will grow and kill all your guests."

"That seems an odd thing for the Weather Channel to be concerned about. Shut that door, Patrick, unless you want something."

He slammed the door. "Do those nuts cook forever?"

"I'm just about to take them out."

"Then what?"

"Then I have to peel them, after they cool a bit."

"You'll be up all night."

"Well, then, you might help me." She removed the chestnuts from the oven and shook them gently.

"Think of what you're saying, Merce. I can't burn my fingers!"

She turned around to face him. "Patrick, what is it? Is there something you need?"

"To hell with Thanksgiving. I'm thinking about Saturday night."

"First we have to get through dinner tomorrow." She wiped her hands on her apron and sat down at the counter. "Saturday night will be here soon enough."

He came softly up behind her and put his hands on her shoulders. He had on his old brown tweed practice jacket, loose and comfortable.

She smiled. "You shouldn't be wandering around here in your socks," she said. "It's gotten cold."

"There's a part of the Schubert that's bugging me," he said, coming around to her side. "I don't understand it. This piece is in me like my blood. But I come to these few bars and I can't remember. My mind goes as blank as cow's eyes."

"You haven't played it in a while, Patrick." She was using a small sharp knife to peel the chestnuts, which were still steaming. "Maybe it would be a good idea to use the score."

"Out of the question. I don't need the score. I would be laughed out of the hall."

"I doubt it." She popped one of the chestnuts into her mouth, where its heat rose pleasantly into her head.

"When did you get to be such an unfeeling woman? This is big trouble."

"Have you looked at the score?"

"Yes, I've looked at the score."

"And that doesn't help?"

"Anyone can play with a score, Merce."

"What would you like me to do?"

"I'd like you to stop all this slicing and stirring about in the kitchen and come to my room and try to figure out what's happened." He paced in circles around the kitchen.

"All right. You must just let me finish here, though. And I'm not stuffing the turkey tonight, so there will be no bacteria growing."

"Maybe we should cancel Thanksgiving."

"Patrick! Why?"

"Because I have a performance Saturday night! This problem must be solved."

"We will not cancel Thanksgiving."

"It is a holiday for gluttons."

She laughed.

"Well, tell me," he said, "who is coming to my house tomorrow to eat all my food?"

"Tina's coming, and her daughter Sandra. You like both of them. Santino and Daria, and also Tony after some football game he must go to. And..." She paused for a moment. "And also Lennie may come by."

"Who is that?"

"Patrick, I'm going to finish up here. Go on back to your room, and then we'll work on the troublesome part."

"I'll stay and watch you finish up."

"All right. But if you can't be pleasant, keep silent."

"You're on your high horse."

"You're acting like a prima donna. Your problem is probably temporary. I've listened to you practice for nearly two weeks now. You've breezed right through it."

"Until yesterday. And male persons cannot be prima donnas."

"Well, then don't try to be the exception to the rule."

"Ha!" He gave a croaky little laugh. "You sound just like the old days, Merce. Have I ever had this trouble before?"

"Probably. I don't remember." She returned to the celery and the onions.

"Yes. Brussels, maybe, the Haydn, 1971..."

She began to wonder whether it was too late to call Lennie. Lennie had not said definitely that she would come for dinner, but Mrs. Medina had read something in her voice that gave her hope. And she had sent over some flowers, a beautiful arrangement of red and cream-colored lilies, which Mrs. Medina was pleased to imagine Lennie had created herself. But it had been a week since they had seen each other, briefly, here, with Patrick practicing furiously away in his room. They had held each other in the living room, while outside the sun slanted low against the bricks across the avenue, turning them a muscular rose. She had held Lennie and looked over her shoulder and saw this glowing color.

Well, Mrs. Medina thought. *It's almost winter.*

Lennie had allowed herself to be held, and the contours of her body were soft against Mrs. Medina's, but there had been some reticence in her that day, some drawing back, some distraction.

"What's the matter?" Mrs. Medina had said, drawing back.

Lennie shook her head. "Nothing. Tired, I guess." She looked at her watch.

Mrs. Medina's blood was quickly drawn up and out of her arms, leaving them icy. *That's it,* she said to herself. She had been looking for a sign and this was it. It had arrived, appeared like a long, dark car slowly making its ominous way along a silent lane toward a lighted, unsuspecting house.

After a moment of shock, she had drawn Lennie tightly against her, rubbing her hands across her back, reaching down to pull her hips closer. There might be no more of this, then. No more of anything, no weekend on the Cape, no trip to New York. Lennie had looked at her watch, and in that gesture vanished, and there was nothing to do. Or there was too much to do, and her mind searched frantically for where to begin. They had established no personal language that might explain what was happening, so she held Lennie at arm's length and looked into her eyes. Lennie smiled.

"Do you really think I'm entirely responsible for this situation?" Mrs. Medina said. "Why are you smiling? You'd better go on to wherever it is you're going."

"All right," Lennie said. She put her scarf around her neck and pulled it back and forth. "I'm tired," she repeated. "Don't make anything more out of it."

"If something's wrong," Mrs. Medina said, "we should talk. It sounds like something's wrong."

Lennie sighed and looked up at the ceiling.

"I don't want to let you walk out of here like this."

"Like what? What is it?"

Mrs. Medina stepped back. "All right, if you have to be somewhere, fine," she said. "Go on."

"You're tired too."

"You're right. I am."

They waited, looking at each other.

Then the doorbell rang. "Door!" Patrick shouted from his room.

Santino came smiling in, and there was nothing she could say to Lennie. She had to just let her go.

"Thanksgiving," she said to her at the door, not able to stop herself. Lennie was buttoning her coat. "We'll eat about three-thirty. Come earlier, of course, if…"

"I said I'd come if I could."

"Do come, Lennie. I'm sorry about today."

"I'll try. I said I'd try."

Now she was crying, but surely it was the onions. *What's the difference?* she thought. Perhaps she had overreacted.

"I've got it!" Patrick said suddenly, and started for his room. He had never recognized her tears, the difference between onions and grief was of no concern to him, and she was grateful for that. "I've got a plan! Bring me my Black Jack when you come, will you, Merce?"

~

Thanksgiving dinner went smoothly enough. Afterward Tina went into the kitchen to help Mrs. Medina put things more or less in order before dessert. Mrs. Medina stood with her hand on the coffeepot until she realized it was getting hot. She peered back around into the dining room. Lennie and Patrick were sitting at the table alone.

"She's cute," Tina said, shutting the refrigerator. "One of your students? Some lonely waif far from home?"

Mrs. Medina took the Indian pudding out of the microwave.

"You didn't eat much," Tina continued obliviously. "You made the rest of us look like pigs at the trough. Where are your cups?"

Where are my cups? Mrs. Medina thought. *Where are my cups?*

"Here they are on the tray, right before my eyes. My, these are nice." Tina held them up to the light. "Minton, right? I'm never wrong about china."

"My mother's," Mrs. Medina said. "I want to defrost the ice cream a bit in the microwave. Is five minutes about right?"

"Five minutes? You'll have soup." She came over and put her arm around Mrs. Medina's shoulders. "You don't have to cook ice cream, remember?" She stopped. "Hey." She turned Mrs. Medina to face her. "Hey, I said. You're shaking like a sparrow in the wind."

Mrs. Medina shook her head. "I seem to be cold," she said. She turned away toward the steaming bowl of pudding, which she was suddenly convinced Lennie would dislike.

"In this kitchen you're cold? I thought you had your love to keep you warm. Oops! Where's Patrick? I guess I don't need any more wine, do I?"

"I'm going, I think I'm going..." Mrs. Medina began.

Tina was quickly serious.

"I'm going to..."

"Be sick?" Tina drew her toward the kitchen door.

"No! No, I'm not sick. Just..."

"This is a sudden illness, what do you need? Here, some water." Mrs. Medina drank while Tina watched her carefully. Then Tina said, "Let me reconnoiter the field of battle, see if we can put off dessert."

Steam was now puttering out of the coffeepot, but oddly unscented. And there was the coffee grinder, still full of unground beans, behind the bowl of cooling pudding. "God *damn* it," she said.

"Now," Tina said, coming through the swinging door, "Sandra and Tony are getting to know each other rather quickly. They're having a heavy philosophical discussion about the evolution of Pearl Jam. Santino is asleep. It sounds as if Daria is still on the phone with her mother. So—"

"Patrick? Lennie?"

"Nowhere to be seen."

"Nowhere to be seen." Mrs. Medina nodded. "Yes," she said. "Of course."

"You want to rest a bit?"

"No, I don't. Sorry, Tina, I seem to be a bit disorganized. Look at this—I forgot to put coffee in the percolator. I must be losing my mind. I have to do it again."

Tina unplugged the machine. "Not just now you don't."

"I guess I should use one of those Mr. Coffees, but we've had this machine for so long. Patrick hates new things."

"Who is this kid?" Tina said. "She comes in and you fall apart. She's no lonesome student. She got something on you? Where'd she come from?"

"Out of the blue," Mrs. Medina said, turning away.

There was a small pause. "Aha," Tina said. "So that's it."

Tina made an attempt to take her arm, but Mrs. Medina turned quickly away and reached for the coffee grinder.

"Well," Mrs. Medina said in the door to the living room. "Coffee will be slightly delayed, but it's on the way." Tina brushed by her and sat on the arm of one of the sofas.

"A great meal, Mercedes," Santino said. He nodded at her, sleepy, smiling.

"Mum," Sandra squared herself on the sofa to look at her mother. "Tony wants me to go to a movie. Can I go?" Sandra was a somewhat larger version of her mother and with Tina's sense of style. She had made concessions to her age, however, and had shaved her head almost to the skull. Tonight she had on tiny round glasses with yellow lenses. Mrs. Medina watched Tina watching Tony (Sandra's elder by two years), who was gazing dreamily at her daughter. Tina was watching him carefully. Tony was dark and beautiful, shorter than his father, but with the same hooked Florentine nose.

"Where is it?" Tina said. "Jesus, I wish I could have a cigarette."

"If you start up again, you owe me fifty dollars," Sandra said.

I'll give them five more minutes, Mrs. Medina thought. *Then I'm going in after them.*

"Fifty? Never did I say fifty."

"It's nine-thirty at the Kendall," Sandra said. "Come on, Mum, we'll have to run to make it."

"Let them go, Tina," Santino said. "Tony will see that she gets home."

"To Wellesley?" Tina said.

"I've got my Jeep," Tony said. "No problem."

After a moment of silence, Tina said, "Well, let's send them off,

Santino. Tony, I want her back no later than one-thirty. And I will be up, believe me."

Tony stood up and raised his hand. "Promise."

They clattered out into the foyer.

"Well," Mrs. Medina said, "I smell coffee. I'd better round up Patrick and Lennie."

Daria joined her at the door. "I'll set up," she said.

Mrs. Medina was halfway down the hall when Patrick's door flew open with a crash, and to her astonishment Lennie came backing out the door. Patrick followed, his grandfather's Confederate sword raised shakily in front of him. "I see through you and I always have," he said. "You have slipped like Cleopatra's asp into my wife's bosom. You have brought a lovesick circus into my house!"

"Jesus Christ, calm down," Lennie said, giving a wary glance over her shoulder.

"Patrick!" Mrs. Medina said.

"Stay where you are, Merce. I must settle matters with this person."

Everyone was now gathered at the head of the hall.

"So what do we have here?" he continued. "Is it love or are you just dabbling in the water?"

"That's enough," Mrs. Medina said, starting toward him.

"Not until I'm satisfied," he said.

At the sound of Mrs. Medina's footsteps, Lennie began to turn toward her and the tip of the sword came to rest against the middle of her back. "This person must speak," Patrick said.

Mrs. Medina paused, unsure which of these two was in greater danger.

But then Santino moved quietly around her and took the tip of the sword in his fingers and carefully lifted it away from Lennie's back. "Come on, buddy," he said. "Battle's over."

"Speak!" Patrick shouted.

Santino took Patrick's arm and turned him back toward his room. And then before the entire company, Mrs. Medina took Lennie in her arms for a moment and held her tightly. "Are you all right?" she asked.

"I'm fine," Lennie said. "He was just fooling around."

"That's not the point."

"Both of you need a cup of coffee," Tina said. "Come on in here."

"What was he *saying* to you?" Mrs. Medina asked Lennie.

Lennie stepped away from her. "No harm done."

"That was inexcusable," Mrs. Medina said. "He's in a state, you know, about the recital."

"I said, no harm done."

"Well, then—"

"I think I need a walk," Lennie said. She stretched her shoulders.

"Your dessert is here. And coffee."

"Just for some air."

"I'll go with you."

"No."

Mrs. Medina stepped away. "You mean you won't be back."

"Well," Lennie said, "I guess I won't be back. Not today." She put on her coat and kissed Mrs. Medina lightly on the cheek. "Look, it's just getting a little tight for me in here. I need to get out for a while. Anyway, I promised Connie…" She opened the door. "It was a great meal. I'm glad you asked me."

"But you didn't eat a thing."

"You know me. I'm never hungry when I'm supposed to be."

Mrs. Medina followed Lennie into the foyer. The Lowes' door was shut, and she was thankful for that. They waited as the elevator made its interminable approach. Lennie tapped one toe of her boot.

"Can you at least tell me what happened back in his room? Did you say something—anything—to him that I should know about?"

"Not really," Lennie said.

"But when? When will I see you?" Oh, how she loathed her desperation.

Lennie gave her a smile, nearly affectionate; her eyes reflected a sort of wry resignation. She looked older suddenly.

"The concert, Saturday, do you want your ticket now or—"

Lennie tilted her head and her eyes touched Mrs. Medina's face. "You're really beautiful, you know," she said.

The elevator arrived, Lennie stepped in, and the door shut. As the sound of the departing elevator diminished, Mrs. Medina felt her blood following it down. Descending, falling, like a root, like a root. *This is just the first sixty seconds,* she thought. *The rest of it will go on forever.*

"Mercedes," called Daria, who seemed to be moving about in the apartment behind her, "I'll just pour the coffee. No need for you to bother. Spoons? Oh, here, I've found them."

Tina stepped up behind her and put her hands on her shoulders.

"Well," Mrs. Medina said. "Lennie has gone for a walk. We'll save her some Indian pudding."

"Good," Tina said. "Let's do that. Come on in now, why don't you."

Had the Lowes across the hall heard her exchange with Lennie? She imagined them crouched on the other side of the door.

She put her hand against the door frame to steady herself and straightened the little doormat with the toe of her shoe. "This marble should be shined," she said. "I do my best, but the Lowes are pigs, I've often thought it. On garbage days they leave their trash all over the hall, instead of on the back stairs. The superintendent should talk to them."

"Mercedes—" Tina said.

"Mercedes, I think the cream's a bit off," Daria said, suddenly beside her.

"We'll tend to it in a minute," Tina said.

"There's a new one in the icebox," Mrs. Medina said vaguely. "I think. I think it's behind the—"

The light in the foyer was hurting her eyes. What an ugly place. Too small.

The red marbled veins, throbbing.

"Straighten your spine," Tina said to Mrs. Medina. "Come back in and I'll be right beside you."

"There's more dessert," Mrs. Medina said later. "And more coffee."

Santino stretched. "I'm ready for bed. Soon we'd better—"

"Yes," Daria said.

They all smiled.

"I should check on Patrick," Mrs. Medina said after a moment.

Santino jumped up. "I'll do it."

"Such a nice girl, your friend," Daria said. "Sorry she had to leave. Are you friends with her parents?"

"Well, not exactly," Mrs. Medina said quickly. "She's a florist.

She works for Guido Pittino at his shop in Cambridge. Quite knowledgeable, really, quite a way with flowers. She did that arrangement on the dinner table." Here her throat went dry.

Daria glanced into the dining room. "Oh, yes. Nice."

"Do you travel much with Santino?" Tina asked.

"Sometimes. I don't like it much, though. It's hectic. I'm happy to have the time to myself at home, to tell you the truth. I've just finished a portrait of Tatiana Popp at the Conservatory. She's retiring."

"You don't say," Tina said. "So you paint."

"Saves my life," Daria said.

Who will save mine now? Mrs. Medina thought.

Tina gathered herself together and at the door said, "I want to see you, and I want to see you soon. I'll call you tomorrow."

"All right," Mrs. Medina said.

Now all she wanted was to be alone.

Santino came down the hall from Patrick's room with his overcoat over his arm. "He's resting," he said.

"Yes, rudeness takes a lot out of one."

Santino shrugged himself into his coat. "Patrick's on edge, I guess. Maybe she said something to annoy him."

"No, she wouldn't do that, Santino."

"Well, you know her best, I guess."

"What do you mean?" she said sharply.

"Well." He gave her a glance. "Nothing. It doesn't take much to get Patrick lit up."

"I do know her best," Mrs. Medina said. But she knew this was as far as she could go.

"Patrick is the issue here now, isn't he? He's sort of puffing, I guess, in there. Maybe you'd better look."

She stared down the hall toward the darkness of Patrick's room. She wondered how Santino had managed to check on Patrick without causing him to reignite.

"I think he imagines he's fought another battle," Santino said. "Or something."

She nodded, and rubbed her lower lip.

"Maybe—"

"Tomorrow he won't even remember what happened."

"I'm concerned. You must watch him."

"I do watch him," she said. "I do nothing but watch him."

"Let's keep him alive, Mercedes."

She turned to look at him. "He's keeping himself alive," she said. "The thought that he challenged someone with that damned sword, if he remembers, will only invigorate him, it won't kill him."

Santino looked at her solemnly.

"You think I'm heartless?" she said. "Well, now, as it happens, I probably am." She looked bitterly back toward Patrick's room. "He's had his life," she said.

Daria appeared at the end of the hall. "Santo, are you ready? Leave Patrick in peace."

At the door Mrs. Medina embraced them both.

"Call me, Mercedes," Santino said, "if anything should happen."

"Nothing will happen," she said. "I'll have turkey sandwiches for all of you tomorrow when you come to rehearse. And lots of Indian pudding."

She stood at the door to his room and heard him breathing in the dark. The smell of roasted turkey clung heavily in the air.

"You are a spy," she heard him say after a moment. "Come out of the shadows."

She moved toward the desk to turn on the lamp and suddenly found her feet entangled in the sword, which Santino had propped against Patrick's desk.

"This sword!" she said, and finally managed to kick it into a corner, where it fell to the floor with a clatter.

"Who's approaching?" Patrick rose on his elbows.

She turned on the desk lamp and faced him. "You were not a gracious host this evening," she said. "And I'm going to put that sword somewhere where you can't get at it."

He sank back down on his pillow. Santino, it seemed, had put Patrick into bed fully clothed. His red bow tie peeked over the top of the blanket. "I'll go through the woods," he said, "circle round, quiet as an Iroquois brave. Then I'll say, 'Lieutenant, sir, no need to worry about Jackson! He's lost by the river!' "

"Jesus Christ," Mrs. Medina said, and sat down on the desk. "Help me, help me."

"Follow me. Follow me," Patrick murmured. "I'll lead you out."

"I will not follow you," she said.

Suddenly he opened his eyes and turned his head toward her. "Ungrateful woman," he said. "Why are you sitting there with that Joan of Arc look on your face? What's happened to the party?"

"You ran the party off, and quite nicely too." *She'll call,* she thought. *She may call. She can't leave because of Patrick's silliness— that would be stupid.*

"Are you going to confront me with something? Did I hurl the cranberries to the floor?"

"You have taken my life from me," Mrs. Medina said, and stopped abruptly.

Patrick's eyes widened, then he reached for his glasses, which Santino had placed on his bedside table. He studied her for a minute or so.

"You look ridiculous," she said, laughing just a bit, "in bed with that bow tie on."

"Is this something to do with your little tootsie?"

"Patrick, you threatened her with that ridiculous sword."

"My grandpop's sword? That was Santino, we were just fooling around."

"No, that was Lennie."

"She must have provoked me, then. I've only brandished that sword seriously three times in my life."

"Well, you're not going to do it again."

"I'll do what I want in my own house." He turned on his back and regarded the ceiling. "But I am a gentleman. When she appears again, I shall kneel and apologize."

"She won't appear again." Then she said, "What were the two of you talking about back here? What did you say?"

"This and that. I'll try to think." He was silent for a long time, and Mrs. Medina thought he had gone back to sleep. Then finally he said, "Should I apologize to you, then? I'd better know this."

She watched him, not comprehending. "What for?"

"For taking away your life."

"No. No, you asked for it, but I gave it to you."

"Well, I humbly apologize anyway."

She was silent.

"You mean I ran her off?"

"She was going anyway, I think. You just shoved her out the door."

He swung his legs out of the bed. "Come get me into my night apparel. That might give you a lift."

She helped him off with his clothes and into his green pajamas. As she tied the cord at his waist, he leaned his frail body against her—frail, but still slightly taller than hers. She wanted to lean on him at this moment, she was longing just to feel his body as it had been twenty years ago, always firm, always strong, clearing up the confusion. And then, miraculously, he put his arms around her, as he might have then. "I'm a bastard," he said. "Go after her, why don't you?"

She shook her head.

"You're going to have to learn to jump for what you want after I leave. You can't just sit around on a toadstool and expect things to drop into your lap."

"You're beginning to shiver. Let's get you into bed." She pulled the covers up around his neck. "Santino and Barbara will be here at noon. Will you be ready to play?"

"Oh, hell," he said. "I'm ready now."

She kissed him on the forehead and went to turn off the desk lamp. She thought about things dropping into her lap.

Then Thanksgiving was over and it began to feel like the end of the year.

Outside, the sky had cleared and a bright full moon lit her room with the cold light of a lunar fire. She sat on the edge of the bed and rubbed her eyes, then undressed in the dark. She didn't want a light, she didn't want to see herself, her body, her eyes. The night spread out ahead of her like a vast field of battle. She consigned herself to this wilderness.

The house was settling, emitting various groans and ticks, and the wind had picked up, with the clearing sky. Sometimes she thought she could hear the wind brush across the piano wires, away in another part of the house, a sound that had always made her feel content. She clenched her fists and curled up against herself.

The moon had become so bright she could distinguish the hands on her clock. She turned onto her back. The sheets were freezing, too cold to turn over into; she lay like a corpse in the moonlight, her hands on her breasts.

Lovely little moon, stay with me until the sunrise...

That old tune her mother used to sing to her, an old show tune. Her mother would not understand her life now. Nevertheless, they had been able to talk; what would she say?

Keep me close to you, underneath the starry night skies...

Well, she was sick of this whole business with Lennie. It would be a relief not to worry about whether she would see her, if she should call her, where she might be, if she were safe. Safe! She laughed. Why would anyone want to be safe?

Leave my pillow touched with moonglow...

Her mother had sung the moon song to her before she went to sleep, and always said afterward, "You're growing like the moon. Soon you'll be big, soon you'll have your own beautiful life. Full of stars, and ships, and you'll dance the tango."

The clock finally said three-forty. She rose on one elbow and drank a little water. The moon was not so bright now.

One got through life by keeping it in order, not by falling in love. But Tina had said that loving was better than anything, even if you loved the wrong person. That was what Tina had said. And if you loved the wrong person, even that could be wonderful. And Tina was an adult person with a keen intelligence. But she wasn't like Tina!

What am I doing here, anyway? she thought. *Walking around on this strange planet.*

Ahead of her was the vast, gray ocean of the rest of her life. Hers the only ship. No stars, no tango. No moon.

~ twenty ~

The trio's appearance the Saturday night after Thanksgiving was a triumph, but Mrs. Medina sat in her aisle seat in the dark half expecting to have to rise at any moment and rush to assist Patrick off the stage. Although he had prepared himself. The hours had progressed toward this evening with the intensity of imminent battle. He continued to do his small morning routine of calisthenics (ten toe touches and a brief number of arm rotations that he said improved his shoulder flexibility) and his "fist preparation" (as he called it), which involved squeezing a tight spring in his hands. He ran the rehearsal on the day after Thanksgiving as he used to, pointing out missed cues, lecturing about dynamics. None of it was necessary. Santino sat with a smile on his face and allowed Patrick to go on. Barbara was quiet, obviously in pain, and once as Mrs. Medina had passed the living room she had seen the pianist's eyes, just as Patrick was saying, "And another thing that's bothering me..." Barbara was doing this for Patrick, and only for Patrick. It would no doubt be her last public performance. Mrs. Medina, who rarely interrupted rehearsals, put down the silver tray she was carrying with a clatter and said at the door, "I think it's time for some tea. Barbara, come help me, why don't you."

"Merce, get out of here," Patrick said.

Santino stood up. "No, let's take a break. I've got to use your facilities anyway."

"Lazy bunch of bums," Patrick muttered. "Always have been. Merce, late enough for a tot of Black Jack?"

In the kitchen she tried not to look at Barbara's gnarled, knotty knuckles and asked her instead about her grandchildren, momentarily removing the pain from her eyes.

I am a goddamned saint, Mrs. Medina thought.

Tina called twice, the Conservatory called twice, and a former student called and asked her out for coffee. Lennie was silent. At around five Mrs. Medina picked up the receiver with a sweaty hand and called Lennie's number, praying she would not get Kenny. She did not. Not in person, at least. His voice said, with a little snigger, "You've reached Lennie and Kenny. If it's business, leave your number, but don't tell me what you want. I'll get back to you. If it's urgent, call my cell phone. Those who need it have the number. If it's personal, tell me everything, tell me you love me, I'll come to you wherever you are. Wait for the burp."

"This is a message for Lennie," she said into the machine, swallowing dryly on the last part of her name. "Your ticket, if you want it, your ticket for Patrick's, the concert on Saturday night will—I'll leave it at the box office in your name. If you have—"

"Merce!" Patrick stuck his head around the door. "Is my penguin suit back from the cleaners?"

"Would you please call me?" she finished quickly.

"Who's that?" he said.

"Your tux has been back for three days. It's in the front closet."

"No need to be testy. Barbara has to leave. Santino and I are going to work on some rough spots."

"Patrick, there are no rough spots!" she said. "For God's sake, let everyone go home."

He came over and peered into her eyes. "Do you have a hangover?" he asked her seriously.

That night Patrick did a series of deep breathing exercises holding Bess against his chest. He talked to his instrument softly, caressed her curves, checked her tuning incessantly. "Ready?" Mrs. Medina heard him say to her. "Ready to go again?"

In the night Mrs. Medina heard him softly playing Bach, and she stared into the dark, understanding for a few moments why for a great part of her life this had been enough for her.

On Saturday night, when it became apparent that Patrick was leading the group toward a magnificent performance, that from some depth of his musical strength he was pulling the bow with the sweetness and sureness of a master at the prime of his career, she should have been relieved, completely happy for him.

Instead, the more masterfully he played, the lonelier she felt, until the expanse of the hall seemed to be a desolate planet somewhere in space, where her body had no substance. For several confusing moments she could not imagine why she was here, why she was needed here, when she clearly belonged, on this cold windy night, close in Lennie's arms in her bed, in any bed. From the seat beside her, Lennie's absence spoke with a grating, silent emptiness. She wanted no more of the tiresome Schubert now.

But here was her husband in the midst of the grand finale of his musical life. As she watched his body on the stage, so near to death, but gaining substance and power almost as she watched, she saw for perhaps the first fully recognized time her own substance in him, and the arid, empty universe that had remained within herself. This music, for example, reminded her of a time in Venice, ten or twelve years ago. The trio was there for a concert and was practicing in the church of Santo Stefano, playing this very piece, and she was sitting in a café across from the main entrance, waiting to take Patrick back to the Gritti for a bath and a drink and dinner. The music was drifting out, warm and rich, into the early evening. It was early fall. She eventually finished her espresso and wandered off through the enormous campo, filled with children and dogs and a variety of neighborhood dramas, down toward the Grand Canal. Just as the Accademia Bridge came into view, in the smaller Campo San Vidal, she looked up as the windows to an upper apartment were thrown open, and from within this room, which was lit with subdued light, a woman came to the window with a book in her hand and looked out, assessing the mood of the city, the progress of the evening.

I could live here, Mrs. Medina had thought suddenly. *I could be in that window, looking out, ready to chop my garlic, my tomatoes, make my evening meal. Perhaps I would be wondering whether I should put on a jacket and go out for a bit, walk along to San Marco, have a drink along the way. My books would be along the walls, my writing in neat stacks on the wide, rich slab of carved mahogany that serves as a desk. At night I could work late, and wake in the morning, deep in my soft bed, completely content.*

Work, food, wine, sleep. A beautiful city. I could live here. I could stop this traveling for months at a time, the packing and unpacking. I could find a place like that, a small comfortable place, it would be my place, I could stay here and work, I could put my book in some order, finally. She had actually stopped walking at that moment. She stepped aside by the flower stand where Patrick regularly stopped to buy a small rose for his lapel, and watched the woman in the window, her comfortable room behind her, already feeling as if she might belong in this city.

Back at the hotel it had all ended very quickly. She and Patrick were in the terrace bar, and the broad canal was busy with the changing lights of sunset and the evening business of the boats.

"Venice is central," she had said to him. "The months you play in Europe, I could stay here, and come to where you are periodically..."

"From time to time," he said.

"As often as you wanted."

"You're not talking about *buying* a place, are you? Don't be nuts."

"Of course not."

"How about another Campari?"

"Yes, all right."

He signaled the waiter with an abrupt movement of his arm and made eye contact immediately, in a way he always seemed able to do.

"Did you hear the practice today?"

"Most of it. I was in a café across the way."

"I count on your reactions. How did it sound?"

"Just as good as it always does, Patrick."

"You mean we're playing without thinking, that's it?"

"No, of course not. The three of you never play anything without thinking."

He nodded. "Are you in the mood for some squid tonight?"

"I am never in the mood for squid."

"You should try it here. They cook it in its own ink, with garlic and olives."

"Patrick, what do you think of my idea?"

"I don't like it. I'd miss you. But you do what you want. You're talking about going on with that book thing, or has an Italian playboy entered your life?"

"The Vittorini. I'm about halfway through the first draft now, and it needs some hard, steady work."

"Of course, of course. And you can't do it with me?" He flexed the fingers of his left hand. "My fingers went a bit numb today for a moment."

"I'd like to settle in one place for a while and just nail it down."

"And then what?" He continued to flex his hand.

"You mean when I've finished? Well, New Directions was interested in it. Once."

"And if they aren't now?"

"There are others." The Campari was bitter on her upper lip.

"Merce, Merce," he said, and reached across the table to touch her face. "I don't want you with me to keep me on schedule, to order my meals in the room, to handle the plane tickets. I want you with me because you're part of my music, part of the genius that I have. I don't have any other reason. I want you there."

"I know, Patrick. But I need to feel, at least for a while, that my life is being shaped from within, instead of from without."

"That is ridiculous female thinking. How can you be shaped from without? Am I without?"

"As close as we are, you are sometimes without."

"You have become one of those raving feminists," he said with a sigh. "What will be next?"

She laughed.

"Well," he said, draining the last of his whiskey from the glass, "at least let's wait until after the Salzburg recital. Erik and Annemarie are expecting both of us. Now, if you don't try the squid for dinner, I'm going to pop you in the nose."

And in Salzburg he had collapsed for the first time. A week after that they were back in New York. All she had to show from that brief run at the barricades was the wondrous little trial proof of a Whistler etching she had found in a small gallery near La Fenice. She had crept off and bought it for an outrageous price. It was a charming view of the courtyard of an anonymous Venetian palazzo, outside steps ascending to a loggia, a tree peeking over a high wall, a bit of a canal seen through a gate. She thought of it always as a house she would come to live in.

But now she was free, if she wanted freedom; Patrick had promised her that. Knowing, of course, that she would not go.

The trio concluded the allegro movement with force and brilliance, and there was an immediate explosion of applause, and everyone rose to their feet shouting, and Patrick also stood up, with Santino's help, and raised his bow above his head. Barbara stood away from the piano and bowed with both hands clasped in front of her. *There is the real courage,* Mrs. Medina thought, applauding with the rest. As she made her way back up the aisle to get quickly backstage, elegant in black silk—a long dress that still fit her after fifteen years—several people caught at her hands, congratulating her as if she were Patrick. As if she were Patrick!

In the hallway leading backstage there were two pay phones, both out of order. She paused, then pulled her coat around her and ran out to Huntington Avenue, to a phone by a lively Pizza Hut. Kenny answered.

"Well, what a surprise, Mrs. Mercedes. I was going to call you."

"Why?"

"Well, we've become great friends, haven't we, during our many, many telephone talks?"

"We've never had any telephone talks. If Lennie is there, could you please call her?"

"That's the problem. She may have, you know, split, it looks like. That's what it looks like."

"She's gone?"

"You got it. She with you? I made a note of all your messages, by the way."

"I wouldn't be calling if she were with me. How do you know she's gone?"

"Let's just say it looks like she's got some business ideas of her own. She took some stuff of mine and some cash too. That's the shit. Petty little thief on top of everything else."

"I don't believe it."

"I'm just reporting the news here."

"Did she take any clothes?"

She heard the shrug in his voice. "Don't know. I never looked at what she wore."

"Well, what are you going to do?"

"I'm doing *nada*. What can I do? I've made some calls. What else? She'll turn up one of these days, then we'll settle. Tell her that when she shows up on your doorstep."

A bus rattled by.

"Hey!" he said. "Hey!"

She hung up and stumbled back up Gainsborough Street, where the remains of the concert crowd were milling about. She pushed through them into the lobby, then into the auditorium. Just on the off chance. There was no one left, save the ushers, students, who were collecting fallen programs and shouting to one another about something called Radiohead.

Backstage there was pandemonium and Patrick was in the middle of it. Santino ducked through the crowd and embraced her.

"My God," she said, "look at the flush on his face. We've got to get him out of here. Is he drinking champagne?"

"Well, a little. People keep handing him glasses."

"Foolish, stupid man."

"Let him have his fun. Some of these people he hasn't seen in years."

"It isn't fun, Santino!"

He looked at her in surprise. "You want to go on home? I'll get him back in a cab."

"I don't trust him with you."

She would come to me, Mrs. Medina thought. *If she were in trouble. She might come here, even.* She craned her head around. *All these cackling people, blocking every view.* A lovely, blondish young woman appeared suddenly at Santino's side, and Mrs. Medina's heart lurched. But she wanted Santino's autograph, and she hung her breasts over the program while he obliged her.

"I don't suppose it's such a good idea for him to come to the reception," Santino said, when the autograph seeker had departed.

"Where is this reception?"

"It's here," he said. "In one of the bigger rooms." He looked at her for a moment. "You want to stay?"

"No, I do not want to stay. But Patrick obviously does."

"If you don't trust him with me…" Santino said.

"All right, I've changed my mind. I'll leave him with you. You got him into this situation—see that he doesn't die here, and I'll take care of everything else. Get him back to me with his heart still beating and I will thank you."

He drew her aside a little so they stood against a wall near a large fire hose, away from the denser part of the crowd. "Are you all right?" he asked her.

"I'm tired," she said.

"You want to—"

"I want to get away. Maybe for a week. Alone. Can you manage that? Can you and Daria take him in for a week?"

"After his last visit he swore he'd never come back, remember? He doesn't like to be away from home. Anyway, next week I'm scheduled for St. Louis, and then, of course, all the Christmas concerts begin..." He shook his head.

"Dad."

"Tony!" Santino kissed him. "Here's Mercedes too." Tony grinned and kissed her on the cheek. He smelled of smoke and his cheeks were cold.

"Dad, some people are waiting over there for you. Mom says you'd better come."

"Right. Be over in a second." Tony ducked back into the crowd. "Look, Mercedes, go on home. I'll see that he stays no more than fifteen minutes at the reception, then I'll get him back."

"Fine," she said.

"Okay, then." He helped her get properly into her coat.

"Merce!" Patrick had spotted her. "Where have you been? Come! Come here!" Eyes turned toward her.

"Mercedes Medina," someone said, coming out of the crowd toward her. She recognized his face, from New York, from London, from somewhere. "How did you manage to pull this off? You haven't changed a bit."

Santino slipped away.

She stayed at the reception with Patrick for an hour, until he went to sit down, missed the chair, and tumbled onto the floor. Six people rushed to pick him up, and she said, "We're going. I'll get your coat."

"Bess is locked up," Santino said in her ear. "I'll bring her by tomorrow. Get some rest."

In the cab she felt Patrick's vitality draining away from him. "I did it," he said. "Goddamn it. I did it. We were wonderful. They put us last. Most honored position. Erica Wirth was dying to go last."

"Erica played well."

"Erica's a flash in the pan."

"She's hardly a flash in the pan now, Patrick." But she didn't pursue the issue.

"You haven't said how well we did."

"Of course you did well. You know when you do well. You were magnificent. I've never heard you play that movement with so much feeling."

"That is a rehearsed remark."

She was watching the street. It had rained, and the pavement was slick with lights. "You were good. You don't need me to confirm that. You never have."

"But I like to hear you say it."

She took his hand. "I know. I love that piece, and you were wonderful."

He was satisfied with that. And it was true.

At home she undressed him, and he was half asleep and still excited, both, and insisted on his whiskey.

"Not on top of champagne," she said.

"You look beautiful," he said, "all in black like the Duchess of Frothingham, and I want my Black Jack."

"Just lie down, then, and I'll get it for you."

She took her time, and he was asleep by the time she got back. She tucked him in and turned on the low desk lamp he sometimes kept lit at night. "If you're going now, I don't know how to stop it," she said, almost inaudibly, as she bent to kiss him. "I just can't stop it now."

Without a backward glance she walked swiftly down the hall to her own room. She called downstairs. Constantin and Al had switched shifts.

"Al," she said, "if my tall friend with the little braid should appear, let her in, please. Call me. Anytime. It doesn't matter what time."

But when she hung up, she knew she needn't have bothered.

"She's gone, fool," she said aloud.

twenty-one

The city turned toward winter now, the days became spare of light, the sky clear and uncomplicated and pale over the black, grasping trees. Along the river the small sailboats were pulled in and stacked along the docks, and the Rollerbladers who whirled and pirouetted in front of the Hatch Shell had to dodge the workmen who were attaching the winter cover to the proscenium. Mrs. Medina would stop and get a cappuccino on Newbury Street and take it over the Dartmouth Street footbridge to sit by the river. She gazed across toward Cambridge, toward Memorial Drive, the MIT boathouse, a part of Cambridge where she knew Lennie was not likely to be. Still, they were breathing the same air, perhaps, the time of day was the same for both of them, the weather.

One of the college sculls moved by, silently, smoothly. "Pull!" the coxswain shouted. "And stroke!" Behind her the traffic on Storrow Drive moved angrily westward.

It was mild for early December. There was still a hope of something.

Before Lennie she had always fixed Patrick his whiskey at about six, and begun dinner while he watched some news. She had a Dubonnet or a small gin and bitters. They seemed to fall back into this routine now, and Patrick gave her glances out of the corner of his eye and tried not to look satisfied. His somber demeanor did not fool her, however. On the days Nikki came, they giggled together back in his room, and some evenings while she was at her desk, pulling notes together for her course, she heard him shout at the Celtics with obvious pleasure. But why should she begrudge him that? He had always been very good at making himself happy. He was happy now. So what?

Patrick's fish or his small piece of chicken would be prepared, and she made a small salad to go with it usually, and some rice, which he could have lived on exclusively, had it been up to him. She generally ate some of whatever she had fixed for him, often not remembering what she had prepared until she put it on the table.

They sat down to dinner at about seven, in the dining room with its view across the rooftops to the rear windows of the apartments on Beacon Street. By seven the worst part of the evening was past, the dead hours between four and seven, when the day was over but the night not old enough to hold excitement. *Is that right, though?* she thought one night, remembering these same hours at the Park Plaza with Lennie, the delicious evening after their afternoon in bed. They had dressed each other, and the air had been charged with a sort of sexual lassitude. And they had descended in the elevator to the dark bar, where someone had played "Stairway to Heaven" on the piano.

Now Patrick was talking. For some reason his memory was particularly keen at this time of day, and he often spent the meal reminiscing, in vivid detail, about the various adventures of his life. She listened quietly, and asked a question every now and then.

"I was with Howard," went one story, "and we had left Danny Steel at Albany with his wife and we were going to our place farther upstate near Lake Placid, on Cranberry Lake that was. The place we had all bought together just before the war started. Did you ever see that place?"

"Pictures of it. Before my time."

"We were bringing the booze. Dill Berman was bringing the girls." He giggled, then looked up quickly and straightened his face. He attended to his piece of haddock with great concentration.

"And the rain began," she prompted him.

"Like the devil." He grimaced. "And the only way in to our place was by water. Halfway across the lake..."

She lifted her mind away.

After dinner they would sit for a while in his room with the television on, sometimes watching it, sometimes not. He yelled at the Celtics and dreamed over the women in the commercials and didn't care about the sound. She could read, or write letters for a while.

One night she had overcooked his chicken (which he ate anyway, silently, indignantly) and had shown little interest in a story he was recounting about his one personal encounter with Anne-Sophie Mutter, a tale she had heard often enough. When he cleared his throat, she knew he was going to ask about Lennie.

"You should call the police," he said.

"Whatever for?"

"Find this, this—"

"I'm not sure she's gone anywhere."

"What are you doing here, then? Go get her. You're making me feel like Simon Legree."

She gave him a look.

"Well, I'll go get her, then, if you won't," he said.

"And what would you do with her?"

"I'd tell her to pack her bags, and bring her back for you."

"That's not how this works, Patrick."

He rubbed his hand across the top of his head. "Women are mysterious angels," he said. "I don't understand a one of you. Why do you complicate your lives?"

"It's very uncomplicated now, as a matter of fact. For me, that is. And it's my life." She stood up. "Now I'm going to work for a while. Anything you need?"

He clutched at her hand. "You must forgive me, Merce. Whatever I did. You're like a granite cliff. Your spark is gone. Where is it? Give me that goddamned sword, I'll chop my head off."

"You didn't run her off, Patrick."

"But you do forgive me?"

"Of course. Let's forget it."

Dear Lennie (she wrote, for she had to speak), *Darling Lennie, someday I will take you to Rome. Please let me dream of this, because I suspect Rome is not a place you particularly want to go. You are longing always for someplace hot, with beaches and oceans. Someplace that won't surprise you with age, or trouble you with an unfamiliar language or art that insists upon being seen. Well, never mind. We need not see anything or anyone but each other.*

We'll go in the autumn, she thought. The days will be dusty and the city will be exhausted from summer heat.

I'll ask Patrick's old friend Renato if we can use the apartment he keeps just off the Campo dei Fiori; field of flowers this means in Italian. Now it is a flower field of market awnings, bright reds and yellows, and the cries of garden birds have been replaced with lilting calls to buy. The curving language of the vendors, full of juice, wraps around the things it names and enters the heart of meaning. Renato's building is around the corner from this piazza, under a frescoed archway; it's over a small local bar, which shares a door with a furniture restorer, so the air is always redolent with the aromas of coffee and turpentine. I close my eyes and I can feel the presence of this building in front of me, the shouts in the street ring in my ears, the barking dogs, the sly, prowling cats. I remember the feel of the plate-size doorknob, the damp smell of plaster in the echoing foyer, the ponderous, clattering little elevator. Oh, and the happiness as we used to ascend! Such wonderful meals awaited us!

Renato's rooms are on the top floor, away from most of the noise from the street. His entrance hall is laid with diamond-shaped green and white tiles, and the walls are covered with mirrors. Off the living room is his long terrace, with many vines, always full of little chattering birds, sparrows. At night the lights of the city spread out like a pan of coals, and the bells of Sant'Andrea della Valle sound at regular hours.

We will dress and go down for dinner, and at Da Pancrazio's in Piazza Biscione we will sit inside away from the tourists, away from the fountains and children and the sly-eyed boys who lounge about in the evening, and the waiter will bring us first a bottle of Brunello, and open it with a flourish. The table linen will be flawlessly white, the silver satisfyingly heavy in the hand. The wine the impossible color of rubies and fresh, flowering bruises.

We will begin with bread, for life. Then tagliatelle with porcini mushrooms and fresh artichokes and asparagus. Tangy parmesan. And afterward a grilled bistecca, bloody, or a roasted chicken, its golden crusty skin dripping with fat, and long, thin green beans, with olive oil. Last a salad: radicchio, arugula, celery root, marinated tomatoes.

And after a while we will walk out through the cooling October night, through the Roman streets, heavy with the smell of exhaust fumes, an old city at the end of another day, and we'll go for coffee at a small bar I know in a quiet corner near the Pantheon. When we speak you will incline your head toward mine, and I will catch your scent, and then a fist will grip my aging heart, and I would take you in my arms right there except it would not be enough. Instead I will lean back and look up at the black sky and feel the coffee start my blood up.

Back in the apartment, on the terrace, the night birds and bats will swoop around and we will sit next to each other and sip a Montenegro and look for the stars, which we can see now and then above the haze. This haze is leaden with golden light, reflected from streets that are slowly falling asleep. And after we have made love I will hold you while the night breeze, scented with statues, turns the translucent curtains in and out and cools the sweat on our bodies. And finally we too will sleep, profoundly, as if we were in air, and if I wake in the night I will only have to breathe to know that you are there with me, nestled in the sheets against my side or flung on your back lost in a dream, and I will only have to move slightly to grasp your waist and pull you toward me. And although you will never hear it, I will promise never to allow you to feel any fear or to venture into any place where I cannot protect you.

Mrs. Medina put down her pen. This letter was for herself, not Lennie, she knew, and it was an indulgence. She could have taken Lennie to Rome, but there wasn't time. She could have had Lennie and Patrick both perhaps, but there wasn't time to figure out how. She could have spoken to the woman in the gray suit, but it was time to leave for Los Angeles. At any moment she could have left Patrick, in New York, in London, in Zurich, in Munich, and gone back to Venice, to find her little place. But she had thought there would always be time; she was younger than he was, there would always be time.

She picked up the letter. The grazings about of a foolish woman who now had nothing but these daydreams, old bottles in the trash, a fish and a bit of potato for dinner, the news, the weather, stale-smelling rooms, early winter twilights, lists—things to do, little items to buy—shorter and shorter lists. *Now I have plenty of time*, she thought. *Plenty of time now.*

~

She finally called Guido, because she had no wish to speak with Kenny ever again. *If she's there*, she thought, *I'll just say*—

A strange voice answered. A young man. "You want who? Oh, yeah, that girl that used to be here. Don't know where she went."

"Could you ask Guido, please? This is a friend."

Guido came on the line. "Madam, hello. She is gone, I am disappointed to tell you."

"But where? Is she coming back?"

"There was some problem in the school. I don't know what. She is upset about it and she quits with me."

"She quit? What do you mean?"

"She does not explain."

"When did this happen?"

"I give her what I owe her, plus a little extra. She goes off. I am sorry."

"You don't know where she is?"

"At this moment I truly do not know." He paused, as if wanting to go on.

"Is there some trouble too? Some other trouble?"

"I hope not. And now I must go. Please forgive me."

"What for?" she asked a dead phone.

The next day he sent her a box of flowers. Blue lisianthus.

It was the telephone that woke her, and she reached for it blindly, to absorb its clamor. But even in sleep she already imagined Lennie's voice in her ear, at last explaining everything. Her bedside clock said five-forty. It was still dark.

At first she thought the voice on the phone had asked for Patrick. So she said, "No, he's asleep and I won't wake him at this hour. Who is this?"

"No, it's you I want, I believe, if you are Mercedes Medina,

Mrs. Patrick A. I'm Detective David Lopes, Cambridge Police, Narcotics."

She sat up quickly, reaching for the lamp. "I'm Mercedes Medina. What's happened?"

"Good. Good." She heard him shuffle some papers. "I need to speak with you about Lennie Visitor, of Rindge Avenue, North Cambridge. You know her, I believe."

"Yes. Is something wrong?"

"I need to know, Mrs. Medina, whether she's with you at the moment."

"No, she isn't."

"All right. When was your last contact with her?"

"My last contact? Thanksgiving Day."

"You haven't talked with her or seen her since then?"

"No!"

There was a confusion of noise in the background.

"Now. Sorry," he continued. "We have in custody here Kenneth L. Barrett and Spiro Stratas, both saying that this Ms. Visitor may be able to explain some certain activities that have occurred at their residence."

They raided the house, she thought. *Whatever they were doing.*

"Do you know something about this?" he asked.

"No. Nothing."

"Well, we'd like to get hold of this Ms. Visitor, to corroborate or not corroborate some of the statements being made, very loudly, if you can hear, by these two gentlemen."

In the background she thought she heard Kenny shout, but could not understand what he was saying.

"I'm sorry, officer, detective, I can't help you. I haven't seen her, or talked with her, as I said, since Thanksgiving Day."

"Yes." She heard the strike of a match. Was he really with the police? How did she know? "Now, I wonder, I'd like to come by and talk with you, just briefly, if you wouldn't mind."

"What, do you mean *now?*"

"No, no, later. Maybe around ten, if that's all right. Won't take long."

She rubbed the back of her neck. "Well, I suppose that's all right."

"You are at—"

"I'm on the corner of Commonwealth Avenue and Clarendon Street. In the Back Bay. What is it exactly that you need to know? I haven't seen her, I said."

"Well, better to talk face to face, don't you think? I'll be by about ten."

She hung up slowly.

Well, here was some excitement. She realized she didn't know whether what she and Lennie had done in bed was illegal. She supposed it was. Did he want to ask her about that? What bearing could that have on Kenny's drug dealings? If that's what they were. She took a sip of water. The window was beginning to lighten.

Patrick must not be frightened. That was important. Patrick must not be frightened. *Well, Patrick will probably love every moment,* she thought. But Patrick would not be dealing with this—had he said his name was Lopes? She would. This was her business, and Patrick would not be present. Yes. She sat up straighter in bed. This was her business, it had something to do with Lennie, and Patrick would not be present.

At breakfast Patrick said, "Did I hear a bell? Did someone call in the night?" She looked up from her crossword, over the top of her glasses. "If I'm hearing gongs, I should know whether it's a social communication or a bacteria has invaded my ear drum."

"No, it was the phone," she said. "Sorry if it woke you. Oh—oops!" He had missed his mouth with his cereal spoon, and she reached over quickly to wipe his lips.

He brushed her hand away. "You're giving me these tiny doll spoons again for my cereal."

She smiled. "Sorry."

He chewed his cereal carefully, as if it were a piece of beefsteak. "Soon it will be my birthday," he observed thoughtfully.

"Yes, in about three weeks."

"And after that, you?"

She nodded.

"Are you catching up with me yet?"

"We both keep on, Patrick, at the same pace." She looked at her watch. It was nine-twenty.

He struck the table with his frail little fist. "You must have been nuts, Merce, to marry an old coot like me. Why did you do it? You were always younger." He tossed his head against the back of the chair. He was less subdued today, less on his guard. Perhaps he thought the phone call had been from Lennie, and he was exonerated.

"I married you because you pursued me with such a vivid imagination. How could I help it?" She got up and began to stack the plates. "Now, Patrick, I must talk with you about this phone call. At ten we will be having a visit from a Cambridge policeman."

His eyes widened. "A cop?"

"Yes. It looks like Lennie's housemate Kenny has gotten himself into some trouble, and they want to talk to me."

"To you? What does it have to do with you?"

"I don't know. I suppose I'll find out."

"I won't have a flatfoot in my house."

"He's coming, and he's coming to talk to me. That's it."

"Has your girl been up to no good?" She watched his mind reel through the possibilities, all of which were beginning to excite him.

She set the plates down firmly. "Don't talk to me about her, Patrick, or I will get very, very angry. This is my business, and you will not interfere this time. I will talk to him and you will not interrupt us."

He leaned back. "Well," he said. "I see I have lost all authority in my own domicile. Are you about to go to jail? Is that it? You have turned belligerent over these months, now I see it. That young chickie has led you down into the dark paths of crime, and this morning they are coming to take you away. Just like Susan Hayward in *I Want to Live!* They will drag you away, they will grill you—what will I do?" He was fluttering and red faced.

"Patrick, calm down, will you, please. I've done nothing wrong, I promise you. They won't be taking me anywhere."

"You can count on me," he said, rising shakily to his feet. He marched into the kitchen and picked up the phone. "Are you that Greek?" she heard him say to the doorman. "Well, who the hell is it, then? What is your name?"

"Patrick—" she came up behind him.

"Al. Okay, Al, this is Patrick Medina upstairs. Soon a cop will be coming in to see my wife, and I want him frisked. He will be packing a piece, and I want you to get it from him. I want no firearms under my roof."

"Patrick, please." She tried to pry the receiver away from him.

"I don't care. If he tries to take my wife away with him, you are to stop him. I will pay you one hundred dollars to stop him from taking my wife away to the slammer."

"That's it," she said, and forced the receiver out of his grasp. "Al, this is Mercedes Medina. A Detective Lopes will be coming by shortly, and it's all right to send him up. Thank you."

She hung up. "Now," she turned to face him, "this is Nikki's day to come to read to you, so why don't you go shower and shave and get dressed. I've put some clothes out for you. Let me handle the policeman, please, Patrick, will you?"

"Do what you want with him," he said, turning away from her. "I warned you about that girl. What's she doing with a man's name anyway?" He went off toward his room.

David Lopes was late. She stood in the living room, not knowing what to do with herself, her heart scrabbling about her chest. She heard Patrick moving clumsily about in his room, "cleaning" it, for Nikki. This routine consisted of wiping down all the glass in his picture frames with a Kleenex, and it usually amused her; today she was angry. From the window she could see several potentially dangerous events unfolding: a DC-10 straining for altitude above the Prudential Building; two motorcycles, racing each other, running a red light at Clarendon Street. The world seemed ominously tenuous.

"What?" Patrick called from his room. "Was that the bell?"

"Not yet!" she answered, and her voice broke.

David Lopes reminded her of a comfortable sofa. He was a big man, with a modest paunch, but he walked with a graceful sort of shuffle in his loafers, and she saw him straighten his tie as he entered the living room. She knew he was a smoker before she smelled it on his clothes, by the way his hands moved about, touching his breast pocket, feeling around in his jacket. The hair that remained on his head hung in dark crescent moons above his ears. His eyes were tired; Mrs. Medina guessed he had been up since long before he had telephoned her. But tired or not, she could see him forming an opinion of her apartment. He walked about slapping his pockets until she asked him to sit down, then he suddenly seemed to remember why he was there.

"What has Kenny told you?" she asked him. "What I mean is, does he have any idea where Lennie is?"

"Just a moment, just a moment," he said, opening a small zip around briefcase. It was old, and the zipper stuck, and Mrs. Medina sat and twisted her hands while he fiddled with it. He finally drew out a sheaf of papers. "Did you know her well?" he asked, as he shuffled through them.

"What is it? What is it?" Patrick screamed from his room. "Where is Nikki? I'm coming out there!"

She stood up and smiled apologetically. "My husband. I'll be right back."

On her way back she stopped and pulled on a sweater. Perhaps it would stop her shivering.

He shook out a pair of half glasses from his top pocket. There was a little piece of adhesive tape across the nose bridge. "We were speaking about Lennie Visitor on the telephone," he said when she was seated again. "I believe you said you hadn't seen her."

"That's right. Since Thanksgiving Day."

"Several weeks, then."

She nodded. "Yes. Fifteen days."

"Any idea where she might be?"

"No. I've been trying to find out myself, to tell you the truth." She twisted her ring. "Her housemate doesn't know?"

"Kenny? Says not. But I'm not inclined to take what he says as gospel, if you know what I mean. He's not exactly a stranger to us."

"Well, what does he say she's done?"

He scratched his ear. "Well, we moved on their house, found quite a stash of various controlled substances. Quite a little operation going on there. He *says* it was hers, her business. Claims complete innocence. It's a real fancy story, but the stuff was all in her room. He says she went out to meet a client, so-called, a couple of days after Thanksgiving and didn't come back. Supposedly she took off with everything she was delivering and some of his money as well. And that," he removed his glasses, "is what he says." He looked at Mrs. Medina for a moment. "This surprise you?"

"That sounds like a preposterous story," Mrs. Medina said.

"Does it? This isn't the sort of thing she would do?"

"Well—" Mrs. Medina put her hand to her throat. "Of course, I wasn't familiar with every aspect of her life, but"—*I must be loyal*, she thought. *I must be loyal*—"she was very happy with her work, I believe. She loved working with her plants and flowers. Why would she..." She wiped her palms on her skirt.

He pursed his lips and nodded. He didn't appear to be making notes, but he was paying great attention to the papers he had extracted from his briefcase. "No one's immune to drugs," he commented, almost as an aside. "So," he continued, looking up, "are you worried? Did you try to find out where she disappeared to? Kenny says you saw a lot of her."

"A lot—well, not exactly. Not recently, that is. She—well, yes, I wondered where she was, but we didn't always see each other. In fact, I did try to call Kenny once or twice. He told me she was gone, but I thought when she wanted to see me she would call. She was very busy. Well, what could I do? Perhaps I should have called the police, but that seemed a bit silly. I didn't really think she was a missing person. It never occurred to me that she might be injured in some way. Do you think that's possible?" She put one hand to her temple. Her voice sounded like a sewing machine, like a harpsichord, tickety, tickety, tick.

"Don't know," he said. "She ever done this before?"

"Done what?"

"Run off."

"I'm sure I don't know."

He waited.

She rubbed her upper arms. "People go off all the time, don't they? For different reasons?"

"They do, yes."

"I wouldn't believe Kenny, if I were you." There, she had taken a stand.

"You know Kenny, then."

"I've never met him. We've talked briefly on the phone. But I get the feeling that Kenny is very unpleasant. Just from talking to him."

"He's not a sweet person."

"And I don't believe Lennie was running any drug business, or whatever it was. I just don't think so. Would you like some coffee?" She half rose from her chair. "There's some made."

"No, thanks. I'd like to just continue here." He rubbed the back of his neck. She had no alternative but to sit back down. "How close were you, you and this girl? Were you friends, or just exactly what?"

Mrs. Medina felt her bowels contract. She seemed to hear the beating of wings in her ears, and felt a flush rising in her neck. She shook her head. He would never believe "friends."

"Just—friends, would you say?" he asked.

"We were friends, yes."

"Okay." He returned his eyes to his papers. After a moment he looked up and said, "It's hard for me to imagine her in this place, that's the thing." He swept his arm out. "You know." There were a couple of loose strings hanging from his jacket sleeve.

"She's been here. She's fine here."

"All right."

"What bearing does this have on your investigation of Kenny Barrett?"

"I'm investigating Kenny Barrett, Spiro Stratas, and your friend Lennie. All three."

"Well, I think I've told you all I know. I've never met Kenny, I've never heard of Spiro Stratas, and I have no idea where Lennie is at the present time."

"Yes. Well, then, any little thing she said lead you to think she might've been about to take off?"

She thought about what Guido had told her on the phone. "No." She rubbed her hands together.

"She have money problems, do you know? Ever ask you for money?"

"Never."

He unwrapped a stick of Juicy Fruit and folded it into his mouth. He chewed quietly for a minute. "Now, Mrs. Medina, I'd like for you to be just a little more precise. It would help me if I knew what, exactly, was the nature of your relationship with Lennie

Visitor. You're not required to answer, but she's in some trouble here. It may help me, you know, figure out what she might be up to. You could help her, possibly."

"I don't see how." And it was none of his business. She realized she was sitting forward in her chair, her hands now clenched into fists. The living room seemed to be flooded with a painful, unnatural brightness.

"You want to stick to friend, then?"

"No."

He gave her a weary look. "It makes absolutely no difference to me, you know. I just want to finish here."

She would like to answer him. She wanted to answer him. But any response, she felt, would have to be explained. She had been proud to be Lennie's lover. But she had an anxiety about the assumptions that would be made about her simply because of that one fact.

She drew herself up. "Don't cheapen me," she said. "We didn't meet in sordid bars or in dark corners somewhere."

He chewed his gum and the muscles of his jaw, peppered with a little stubble, swelled and receded.

"It was not trivial," she added.

"Love," he said surprisingly, "is never trivial. How much time exactly did she spend up here?"

"We saw each other maybe three times a week, at the most."

"Always at night?"

"No, not always. Why?"

"She—spend the night?" He didn't look up.

"Stop right there," Patrick said. He emerged dramatically from the hall and marched directly to David Lopes's chair, from which the detective began to rise to his feet. "My wife will have a lawyer present before you interrogate her further. Merce, call Gertrude Springer."

"Patrick, there's no need, please. Mr. Lopes, Detective Lopes, this is my husband, Patrick Medina."

David Lopes finally managed to stand up. "Pleased to meet you," he said.

Patrick ignored his hand. "You're not talking to a hillbilly here, you know," he said. "I know all about rights. Don't pursue that line of questioning any further."

"What line would that be?" David Lopes said.

"Patrick, please leave us alone. We're almost finished here."

"What line?" the detective repeated.

Patrick glared at him through his tiny glasses and stepped back a few paces. "My wife has broken no law," he said firmly.

"I'm not suggesting she has," David Lopes said, cocking his head.

"I know all about you boys," Patrick continued. "You want to know everyone's lurid sex details because you can't get it up on your own any longer. Well, that's not my wife's fault!" He staggered backward and caught himself on an arm of the couch.

"Patrick!" Mrs. Medina moved toward him.

"I don't believe I was attempting to elicit anything lurid from your wife."

"Elicit! That's the word! Merce, let go of my arm and go call Gertrude."

"No. No, I will not." She turned to face David Lopes. "Yes, she spent the night. Yes, we had a sexual relationship, although it's none of your business. No, I don't know where she is, but I wish I did!"

There was a pause.

"You'll spend the rest of your life behind bars," Patrick said finally. "Don't say I didn't warn you." He turned and walked shakily out of the room.

David Lopes returned to his seat and began to reorganize his papers. After a moment Mrs. Medina got up and walked over to the window. "She spent the night three or four times," she said. "Total."

"All right. Did she ever get any calls here, that you remember? Ever leave suddenly, in the middle of the night?"

"Never."

"She carry a pager, cell phone, that you noticed?"

"No."

"Now, I don't mean to offend you, Mrs. Medina, but was there any—" he searched for a word with great effort "—trouble there, with your relationship? She seeing someone else, maybe? Sorry to have to ask this. And there's no legal problem for you, by the way. If you were worried."

"She never mentioned anyone."

"Well, she might not have."

Mrs. Medina shut her eyes. "We never fought. Our relationship was fine."

"Perfect? Would you say?"

She looked at him angrily, blood pushing against her temples. "No, I would not say perfect. Perfect would be very dull."

"I guess I'd settle for perfect," he said, rubbing his eyes.

She looked at him with greater interest. He had not judged her, and that made her grateful. She put her hand on her forehead. "She's just dropped completely out of sight."

"She'll turn up," he said. He put his papers away. "I know where she lives, as the saying goes. I know where she works, or used to work. Kenny made bail, but we'll watch him. Find some of her friends. If she gets in touch with you—" He rose to his feet and handed her a card.

She opened the front door, and there, with her hand on the bell, was Nikki. "Well!" she smiled.

David Lopes stepped back a few paces and put his hand up to smooth the hair he no longer had. *I will not introduce them,* Mrs. Medina thought. "Hi, Nikki," she said.

"Nikki!" Patrick came down the hall. "Damn fuzz is still here, I see," he said. "Pay no mind. Come on, toots."

Nikki swept past, leaving a wake of floral perfume.

"Busy place," the detective said.

She nodded.

He stepped into the hall. "Just curious, Mrs. Medina," he said, "but if you could think of one place your friend might be, anywhere in the world, what place would come to mind?"

And quickly it came to her for the first time that Lennie might truly be in serious trouble. "Hawaii," she said, naming a place as far away as she could think of.

~

"This shrimp tastes like it was scraped up out of the sludge of Boston Harbor," Patrick said.

"That's iodine. It's good for you."

He put down his fork. "It is not iodine, it is filth. Bad shrimp."

"They don't catch shrimp in Boston Harbor."

"Don't lecture me."

"Eat your rice, then, and forget the shrimp."

"I must have some sort of protein or I'll fade away. Or maybe that's what you'd like."

"Patrick, don't be difficult, please. It's been a very unnerving day. Don't make it worse."

"I didn't ask that cop in here, did I? This business is playing havoc with my nervous system, if you don't know it. What have you done to our life? Why can't I have a little peace here!"

The telephone rang.

"This is what I mean!" Patrick shouted, throwing his napkin on the table.

Mrs. Medina was not in the habit of answering the telephone during dinner, but these days she was always hoping. She picked it up in the kitchen.

"Merry Christmas, Mrs. Mercedes," Kenny said.

She turned her back to the door leading back to the dining room. "What do you want?" she said. "I'm having my dinner."

"What did you tell that cop?"

"More to the point, what did *you* tell him?"

"You mean that you're a fucking dyke?"

"Who is it, Merce?" Patrick said from the dining room. "Dinner's freezing up in here!"

"I haven't time to talk with you now. I'm hanging up."

"Where is our little friend? I'm in a lot of shit here!"

"I have no idea where she is, and whatever trouble you're in, it's your problem, so deal with it yourself. Leave me alone."

"Merce!" She heard Patrick get up.

"Why did you call me?" she said quickly. "You want to find her, but I want to find her more than you do."

Patrick was suddenly beside her, his hand on the receiver. But she was too strong for him. She kept her hand out of his reach and hung up.

Patrick stood with his hands on his hips, staring at her. "You are prostituting yourself," he said. "I never thought I'd see it. Organized crime has entered our house." He turned around and walked back into the dining room. "If you were going to do this, why didn't you wait? Why didn't you wait until I wasn't such a goddamned burden, until I was gone with the wind? You are evicting me from the hacienda, just like Batista!" She heard him land in his chair with a crash. "And my dinner is cold!"

The lamplight lay on the desk, the familiar book was open, the darkness quiet around her. Her hand lay across her pages of notes, her skin already acquiring the brittleness of winter.

Io ero, quell'inverno, in preda ad astratti furori, Vittorini wrote. "That winter I was haunted by abstract furies." Mrs. Medina sat at her desk, in her dark room, the book in a pool of light. "I was shaken by abstract furies, but not in my blood; I was calm, unmoved by desires. I was calm, as if I had not ever lived a day, nor known what it meant to be happy; as if in all the years of my life I had never eaten bread, drunk wine or coffee, never been to bed with a woman; as if I had not thought all such things possible..."

Tricky grammar, she thought, tapping her pencil against her cheek. Vittorini was deceptively simple. "*...e come se mai in tutti i miei anni avessi mangiato pane, mai stato a letto con una ragazza...*"

As if I had never eaten bread, never been to bed with a woman.

twenty-two

On the last day of the year Mrs. Medina sat in an orange leatherette booth in a coffee shop on South Street and nursed a cup of Red Rose tea, which was rapidly cooling. She had been to one of the galleries to see new work by a former colleague, who had abruptly left his teaching job some years back to make lithographs in an unheated loft along the water on Fort Point Channel. She was startled to see that his prints were quite good, and this had surprised her, for she had always considered him a bit dull. One in particular she liked: hills, a small house, a vineyard falling away down a hill, vines cut back, waiting out the colder season. Fine lines, delineating contentment.

"Is this somewhere in particular, Frank?" she had asked, peering closely at it. It was Frank's day to be around the gallery premises.

He had approached the picture rubbing his hands. He was hunched inside an old leather jacket. They were both bundled up, in fact. The room was freezing. "California, I think," he said. "Yes. On Sarah's family's land, up near Mendocino."

"I do like it," she said.

He gave her a close look, pulling nervously on the corner of his graying mustache. "You do? It's sort of uninspired, I think, I never liked it much. It should sell, though. People buy landscapes."

She went over to a small hot plate where some mulled cider was steaming. "How is Sarah?" she said, taking up a paper cup.

"Sarah is back teaching at Milton. Loves it."

"Do you want some of this?"

"No, thanks. Had enough."

She walked around his work again, not knowing now what to say. The gallery was empty. It was cold. Frank had done what he wanted to do. It was simple, and people either bought his work or they didn't. He kept on working because that was what his life was about.

"Well, Frank," she said, taking off her glove to shake his hand.

"I don't feel much like talking today," he said. "Sorry, Mercedes. These huge crowds, you see, they make me nervous." He gave her a wry smile. An artist. His life was about this, working when no one would buy, working because he could not stop. It was an honest life.

"Still teaching?" he asked her.

"My usual winter course is coming up." She put her shoulders back.

"Why don't you quit? You don't need the money. Why go on with it? You must have better things to do."

"In fact, I'm hoping to finish off my Vittorini translation by spring."

"Good, good." He pulled a crumpled pack of Marlboros out of his shirt pocket and extracted one. "I think I'll go to Florida for a while," he said. "I'm getting sick of the cold already. Or maybe New Mexico." He turned the cigarette over in his crusty hands.

The weather was bitter. Outside the raw, sooty day had drawn down into an early darkness. The coffee shop windows were steamy, she could see only shadows passing, could only hear the dull slip of traffic against the wet street.

At home, high above the avenue, the greens were still fresh on the mantle, and the red candles, the many red candles, were still pungent and only half consumed. The little tree by the window still sparkled in its brilliant lights, as if it were covered with snow.

Patrick claimed to hate it all, yet when she had suggested they not decorate, not have the usual small gathering of friends in on Christmas Eve, his face had fallen. So she had pushed through it. She herself could have forgone the entire season.

Soon she must find a cab and get back to him, back to the lights, to the fresh smell of pine, the bayberry candles, the crowds of cards standing attentively on the side tables.

In ten days she would be sixty.

A torn corner of the leatherette gouged at her arm. She raised her hand for the check.

Beside her was the little package from Shreve's that held Patrick's birthday cuff links, thin silver triangles with a narrow border of twisted gold. She would present them at midnight, if both of them could stay awake.

She smiled, thinking she had caught the waitress's eye.

A short man with frowning, creased eyes entered with a gust of damp exhaust fumes in his wake. In spite of the cold his leather jacket was open and the collar of his orange-and brown-striped shirt was stretched wide over his trunk of a neck. He rubbed his hair furiously, and water flew like sparks. The waitress, suddenly alert, ran forward, and they began to converse at the cash register. He took a paper napkin and rubbed at a ketchup stain over her right breast.

"Miss," Mrs. Medina said, smiling, gracious.

The waitress shot her a look.

"My check, please?"

"Yeah, in a second," the waitress said. She returned her attention to the man, who frowned and glanced over his shoulder.

No melodrama, she thought, getting up. She counted out exactly what she thought she owed. No tip. She didn't want to waste another moment in this place. Now she could hear the freezing rain falling harder against the glass. Something wasn't fair. Yes. Something wasn't fair.

She gathered up her bags and walked pointedly to the door, shoulders squared.

"Happy New Year," the waitress said with a snicker as she passed.

On the sidewalk outside, a respectably dressed middle-aged man was lying face down in the rain, apparently unconscious. His finely manicured hands seemed to be grasping, trying to grip the cement. A few people had stopped; several faces had appeared in the lit windows of a nearby office building. Curious. One old woman was holding a battered umbrella over his head. Mrs. Medina joined those in the street for a moment, jostling among all the other umbrellas. No one spoke. *I can't do anything for him*, she thought. *Someone else will have to take care of it.*

A siren approached. The rain beat down. It was New Year's Eve.

At about ten-thirty Patrick asked her sleepily, "Time for the marches?"

She smiled. She had been thinking of whether she had the energy to put the kitchen in order before she went to bed. She pulled her heavy, flowered robe tighter around her. "Just about time."

He had the television tuned to an old Bette Davis movie, and she turned down the volume. She got the worn Sousa recording from its dingy sleeve and started it up. He smiled in contentment as the "Liberty Bell March" started up, and took a shaky sip of whiskey. For a man who claimed to have swum against the current for most of his life, he had a number of firmly observed traditions.

She walked to the window and looked out to the apartments across Clarendon Street, where several lively parties seemed to be in progress. The sky had cleared, and she could see the stars, and the world appeared to be happy. Someone was waving a sparkler from a balcony.

"Come here, Merce," he said. She came to sit down on his bed. He studied her face from his recliner. "Year-end blues?" he said.

"I can barely hear you, Patrick, for the music."

"Well, turn the damn thing down!" He watched her. She didn't lower the volume much; he wouldn't be able to hear. "Now," he said, "will I get my present soon? Better give it to me before you pass out."

"How was your afternoon?"

"You asked me that at dinner."

"So I did. Sorry."

"Couldn't remember then, can't remember now. They're all the same." He looked at her silently for a moment. She prayed he would not mention Lennie. She hoped he had forgotten Lennie. But he said, "Do you ever think of that place, where was it, where we spent New Year's and they threw all of that riffraff out the windows and I thought it was an earthquake? Where was that?"

He was combining several memories, but it didn't matter. "It was pots and pans they threw out the windows, Patrick. We were in Naples. Or maybe Palermo. That's a custom, I think. They throw all the old pots and pans out the windows and start the year with new."

"A great waste of kitchen instruments."

She did remember that night, but the strongest memory she had carried away with her was the firm feel of his back under his shirt where her hand had rested as they stood on their chilly hotel terrace.

The pots and pans had clattered and crashed into the streets, and they had stood listening together, not understanding for a few moments, her hand resting on his back. He had laughed and turned to her and said, "New year, new age." Because it was his birthday. January first. He had been sixty-one, she recalled, she just about to be thirty-six.

She turned away from him suddenly now, appalled at the time that had passed. They had had such fun together. The years had been filled with music, his music, his cities; they had waltzed together in Vienna and shared beans and franks in a blizzard in a freezing motel room somewhere in Michigan. She had to smile, remembering that night. He had been a delightful partner. She had been well taken care of.

But what was hers now, hers alone? What had she gathered close to her heart, what was *hers* now? What she had that was hers alone was a dried gardenia, pressed in a scrapbook, and a new, fresh wound that threatened never to heal, inflicted by a woman half her age who had now vanished.

She turned to him with tears in her eyes, tears she hated, and found him asleep, his head to one side. So she pulled herself together, knowing she could never be angry at him for any of it, for this year, for what could have happened but didn't.

The record concluded with the sound of the first fireworks. She checked her watch. Time for champagne. But she didn't move. She sat for a while until the noise outside had diminished to small pops, then rose and pulled his blanket up around his shoulders.

"New year, new age," she said, and kissed his forehead. If she told him in the morning he'd had champagne, well, he'd think he had.

twenty-three

M

rs. Medina closed the door behind her and locked it. The oranges in their plastic bag hung heavily from her hand. For a moment she stood and watched the remaining snowflakes melt against her coat, then she raised her head. The silence was immediate and vivid, and the shapes of the furniture took form in the darkness of the living room and imprinted themselves on her skin. She saw the dim reflection of the kitchen light over the sink, glowing like a voice, waiting, with a message.

Patrick's light was the only other one.

Outside, the wind gave a mighty gust around the corner of the building.

She felt a wave of grief, of release. She noted the date in her mind: January third. She hoped he hadn't fallen, but she sensed he hadn't. *What is it that flies steadily under all the events of our lives, carrying us, carrying us? Sometimes we can feel the speed with which we are being borne toward our destination!*

She put the bag down, pulled off her gloves. For an instant a great chasm threw itself open before her and she trembled in fright. This darkness had no boundaries and held the terror of vast, shapeless space. The terror of release from carnal form. Birth to death: an instant.

He is part of the air I am breathing now, she thought, and drew him in. And this act calmed her.

In her mouth the taste remained of the ham they had eaten for dinner. Those dishes would have to be done, she mustn't forget.

She walked firmly down the hall, still in her coat, to his room. The television played silently; the Celtics were at it. He was seated in his chair, reclined, his head to one side, jaw slightly adroop. No breath. No life. His eyes were closed. His brown blanket with the tiny gold threads was pulled up across his chest, his beautiful, long fingers holding it in a grip that had loosened slightly.

She knelt beside his chair. She wished she had been here, but she had always felt he wanted to do this alone. This was a vast, momentous moment, and she was lost in it, a speck, clinging to the hand that had so often pulled her through. In a way she wanted to stay right where she was for the rest of her life, if she could not go with him now. For now, while she was next to him, death held no fear for her, no mystery.

She squeezed his hand. "Oh, Patrick," she said aloud. "How I shall miss you. My mate. My truest friend." She kissed his palm. "Thank you. Thank you."

What had their last words been?

"Just going up to DeLuca's for some oranges for breakfast," she had called. "I won't be long."

Had he responded?

Leaving the dinner table he had remarked, "It's raining now in Rome. I watched the Weather Channel all afternoon. Just ask me for the weather, I'm your man." Was that the *last* thing he'd said? No. He'd said, walking toward the kitchen, "I guess there are worse ways to spend the rest of your life."

She had taken the long way back from the market; she must try not to think of the significance of that decision. It had been innocent. She loved to walk in the snow, so she had gone across Fairfield Street to Marlborough, and then slowly east. The snow was soft in the streetlights, and the brick sidewalks were just dusted. The air was still, and at one moment she thought she had heard music, a piano, but when she stopped there was nothing. A sudden little gust swirled around her, as if someone had passed by her shoulder. It was then she had become alert and quickened her steps toward home.

She knew that once she began to move there would be much to do. So she sat there for a while, holding his hand, with no thought in her mind. On the television screen the Celtics and Knicks moved silently up and down the court, the Celts in their home white uniforms.

Once she thought she heard him sigh as Antoine Walker missed a three-pointer.

Finally, her knees, still mortal, were in such pain that she had to stand up, and that done, she released his hand and picked up the phone. After she had spoken with Harry Max and Waterman's, she rolled up a little towel from the bathroom and placed it under his chin, gently closing his mouth as she had watched the nurses do for her mother. She saw he was in his clean blue pajamas, so that would be all right. His handsome bone hairbrush, part of the set he had bought in London, was on his bureau, and she took it and straightened his wisps of hair as much as was possible. Under the circumstances, she thought he would like a little cologne, so she picked up the bottle of Equipage that was his current favorite and put a little on his cheeks. Then she tucked a few drops behind her own ears to keep him close. She looked around. A robe would not be necessary, probably. Would they take him away in one of those ghastly rubber bags?

"Oh God, Constantin," she said aloud, and picked up the phone. In a calm voice she said, "Constantin, it's Mercedes Medina. Mr. Medina has died, I'm afraid. Soon some people from Waterman's will be here, and I hope you will help them in the elevator in any way you can." As Constantin began to lament loudly, as Greeks often do, she held the phone away from her, saying, "Please, please." Then she hung up.

She went over to the desk and put her hand flat on his large book of addresses. He had told her long ago that he had put red checkmarks next to the names he wanted her to call immediately, but Santino would be first, and she would call him for herself because she needed his help.

She turned to Patrick. "Where is that obituary you wrote for yourself a couple of years ago? Comparing yourself to Helen Hayes. I'm sure you kept it." She found she was shaking, and she didn't know when it had started, but she couldn't stop it. She heard his voice say, "Take a sip of my Black Jack, Merce. That'll calm you down." She saw a glass on the table beside his chair—he had poured himself a little drink and hadn't had time to finish it. So she sat down and tasted it, watching him curiously for some sign. Gradually a kind of peace came over her, but she knew it was temporary, and she accepted it as that. Patrick was hers now in a way he had never been; he was a part of her and yet he had truly set her free.

The phone rang. "Mrs. Medina," Constantin said. "They are

coming. If they need me, they will call me. Also your friend the doctor will come up."

"Fine, fine," she said. "Let them come."

She kissed the top of Patrick's head. "Here you go, darling Patrick. I wish I could go with you, but you must do this alone. I'm sure they will be gentle." Then her eyes filled with tears, for she knew what might happen; if one died at home, was an autopsy required? She didn't know. But that would not be gentle at all.

There was a short, quick buzz at the door.

She straightened up. She put her hands on Patrick's shoulders as if to protect him. It was all happening too quickly, she could think of nothing more to say to him. They were rushing her. Rushing her.

"I'll take care of Bess," she said. "I'll keep her waxed, and whatever else is called for. I'll ask Santino. Don't worry." She paused. "I'll call Nikki too. And I won't forget 'Dangerous Dan McGrew' at your service. I'll read it myself. And I won't wear black. I'll wear the mauve suit you love so much, with the peacock scarf you bought me in Salzburg. That scarf is a little much, though, Patrick. Why did you buy it? We'd had that fight about my coming back to New York. We never settled that, did we? You never really knew why I wanted to come back. I was tired. It was November. I was cold." She imagined the men from Waterman's standing about in the hall in their black suits with their black gurney, shifting from one foot to another, exchanging small talk with Harry Max. The peacock scarf had been a little bribe. "But I'll wear it," she said.

The door buzzed again, and she moved toward it without looking back.

twenty-four

She scattered Patrick's ashes off the coast of Duxbury Beach, where they had friends with a house he had loved. It was not easy to rent a boat for this purpose in January, but she did it. One of the Plymouth fishermen took her out, and she went alone, although Santino and Tina and even Nikki offered to go with her. The boat reeked of cod and haddock, and the deck was slippery with fish debris and a thin coat of ice, but the captain's wheelhouse was warm and there was plenty of coffee. When the time came to scatter Patrick about, the captain quickly stopped his gab, and when she returned from the icy deck she thought she heard him mutter something, a prayer perhaps. Some of the ashes had blown back onto her coat; she had thought they were snow, but they didn't melt. He took a small clean rag and brushed her off. When they parted back in the harbor he gave her a small package of fish—cod, or whatever they caught in the winter.

She had not been able to think of what to say as she opened the box that contained most of what was left of Patrick. She stared at the ashes and chunks of bone, expecting Patrick's voice to emerge, but there was no voice and she had no feeling in her except bitter cold. The wind was frigid, blowing hard out of the northeast, and the sea was throwing spray that iced up immediately on the windows and on the deck. Her mind was as dull as the leaden sky that was threatening to unload more snow, and so she finally just took a handful of his bones and gravel and flung it away over the water. The dust blew right back in her face—Patrick, obstinate as ever. She slid over to the lee side of the boat and managed to fling most of the contents of the plastic bag out, and they clung like scum for a moment on the choppy water and then were pulled under. She folded the bag neatly, returned it to the box, and went back toward the cabin.

But she should say something!

So she turned, desperate in her inability to connect with him, and said, "I just hope I've done this right, Patrick." These insufficient words haunted her for many weeks.

Valentina Bird insisted that Mrs. Medina carry on with her Italian course. It seemed like a good idea. But she suspected her lack of enthusiasm was apparent to all but the most insensitive of her students.

"Well, I'm sorry I missed my Friday class," Mrs. Medina said to Tina, the first week of February. "I just assumed that classes would be canceled because of the snow."

"Mercedes, the students are all on campus. They walk to class," Tina said. "And it wasn't much of a storm. I can't remember the last time we closed for snow. The blizzard in seventy-eight, maybe." She put her arm around Mrs. Medina's shoulders. "Come on, now."

Her students were intelligent, eager, all the good things, and they all looked alike. She had no reason to dislike them, but when she thought of Vittorini, of Calvino, of their language, of the joy she usually had in teaching their work, she was angry at these children whose identical eyes stared at her and expected her to relate these works to *their* lives, to *their* knowledge.

"Listen to this," she said to them one day. "*Io ero, quell'inverno, in preda ad astratti furori...la vita in me come un sordo sogno, e non speranza, quiete. Ero quieto, non avevo voglia di nulla. Pioveva, non dicevo una parola agli amici, e l'acqua mi entrava nelle scarpe.*" Will someone talk to me, please, about this man's state of mind?"

They looked at her uneasily. One of the bright ones said, "He's depressed."

"Let me read it in English to be sure we all know what we're talking about. 'That winter I was haunted by abstract furies...my life was like a blank dream, a quiet hopelessness...I was calm, unmoved by desires...and all the while it rained and I did not exchange a word with my friends, and the rain seeped through my shoes.' "

Mrs. Medina looked up.

"He's depressed," the bright one repeated.

At that moment, Mrs. Medina felt the buzzing of Vittorini's abstract furies, the dampness from his shoes climbing her legs. "This is a very short novel," she said. "Your assignment was to have read it all. I want to know about Silvestro's state of mind. Someone. Please."

The bright one continued her analysis of Silvestro's depression, which devolved into an argument among several class members about the efficacy of various antidepressants in treating the disease, and the presentation of details of personal reactions to these drugs. It all got quickly out of hand.

Mrs. Medina finally stopped them. "Listen to me," she said, and held up her hand. "Grow up. Look at Silvestro's life, what he has lost, as Vittorini has presented it. Silvestro's life, not yours. Think about the difference between anguish and depression, think of it. Vittorini will not relate to your lives. You must relate to his." Then she dismissed the class.

Tina got back to her about that incident.

On her days off she stood at the window and watched the street. The cars passing, the people walking along the mall, the Baptist ◀ church across the way on the corner of Clarendon Street, with its ridiculous angels, crowned with snow, trumpeting earthward from the top of the spire. Patrick used to refer to it as "Our Lady of the Pea Shooters."

She watched for snow. Around four o'clock she would begin to see her own reflection in the glass, shimmering, translucent.

She tried to think of a reason to make a cup of tea but could find none. She turned off the telephone. The door to Patrick's room was closed.

The snow stopped and started again, and if she got hungry she would go out to the Women's Industrial Union on Boylston Street, where she could have an English muffin and nurse a cup of tea for an hour or two. Silly women, below the mezzanine restaurant, chattered on about embroidery and stitching.

Then one day on a circuitous route home she passed the Ritz Bar.

The hours between four and seven, winter afternoon. Now all her days seemed stuck in these gray, haunted hours. The Ritz looked warm and comfortable from the street, and she felt a sudden urge for a martini. "Don't seat me by the window," she said to the headwaiter.

The harsh, skeletal tang of gin. The cut-crystal bowl of mixed nuts. The muted lights, the dark, plush armchairs. She had always loved hotel bars. They were comfortably anonymous, and you could be anyone; you were not always expected to be in the company of someone else.

In the distance she heard the clear ping of an elevator bell and the tap of a woman's heels on the marble floor, the low murmur of voices, a light laugh. Someone passed close behind her back, brushed her chair even, trailing a delicate wash of perfume. Mrs. Medina stared hard in front of her, at the tastefully painted wall, at the print of an old schooner in Boston harbor. She did not turn her head.

She ordered another drink. After the third, she said to herself, *The dreary day lurked outside the windows, like a pouting, uninvited guest.* She took out her notepad and wrote it down. Perhaps she should mail this to Taylor Bond. Maybe he could explain it. What was the party, to which the pouting guest had not been invited? Was she the pouting guest? She looked at what she had written, how she had put the sentence together. She found it balanced, syntactically correct, the proper use of the word *like;* the flaw was in the pathos of it. It was not objective. There it was.

The waiter appeared at her side. She glimpsed his tuxedo in the corner of her eye and thought he was a shark.

"May I bring you something else?" he said.

"No," she said, fumbling in her bag. It suddenly occurred to her that she might not have enough money. And then she realized that her hair seemed to be standing up all over her head and she had buttoned her sweater wrong. Her tacky maroon cardigan, a color she hated. And now she was probably drunk. Perhaps *he* thought she didn't have enough money. But she did.

It began to snow lightly as she approached the apartment building. She sometimes imagined that Lennie might appear out of the darkness by the door or be sitting by the elevator talking to Constantin, as Mrs. Medina had found her once. She imagined this happening, and was anxious to get by this moment, the moment when she saw that the darkness concealed only the snowy firs, and that Constantin was hunched over his *Herald*, as usual, that everything was as usual.

"Better drunk than sober, for this," she said, and opened the door to Patrick's room. The air was still, unmoved for weeks. Without turning on the light she could see the glint of the gold threads in his blanket, folded on his chair. She could see his address book still open on his desk, from which she had made the final calls the day after his death. His bed was still turned down. The cello in its case leaned in a great shadow against the far wall, where Santino had placed it months ago. This was all she could see through the darkness. The sink in Patrick's bathroom was dripping.

She was tired of being alone. And it was just beginning. She had no sense of Patrick's presence anywhere, just as she had feared.

"So, better sober than drunk, then, I guess," she said, and closed the door.

Later she sat by the phone in her room, thinking of someone she might like to call. While she was rejecting names she switched on the Weather Channel, as Patrick had regularly done at this hour. There was a major storm in the Midwest, moving swiftly east. She pressed the mute button. Perhaps her Thursday class would be canceled. What was she talking about on Thursday? What assignment had she given? She looked at her briefcase, thrown against her desk chair. On the television, innocuous swirls of white were paused over Chicago, and a silent sheet of brilliant green rain fell in Seattle. On the map of the West Coast a bright sun stood over Los Angeles, and tomorrow it would be seventy degrees. Flashing red thunderstorms snarled along the Florida Keys.

The gin had given her a headache. She wandered into the kitchen, where the breakfast dishes had tumbled over themselves in the sink, and looked into the refrigerator. Two shriveled oranges stared out at her like the breasts of a mummy, a package of gray hamburger, half an onion, starting to smell. She was lucky there was nothing there to cook, for she had no energy for it. She settled for some cereal with a little milk, the same meal she'd had twelve hours ago, and she ate it standing by the sink. As she finished she noticed she still had on the old maroon cardigan. *I should have thrown this away years ago*, she thought. *Who invented maroon?*

But it was too cold in the apartment to remove it.

She put the bowl in the sink with the other things, and ran water over it all.

The answering machine light was blinking, but she ignored it.

She knew something in these evenings would eventually kill her.

Lennie had sent her a note once. A postcard, depicting a lonesome black kitten gazing forlornly out a window. The message was, "Missing you." Lennie had signed it on the back. This was the type of card Mrs. Medina ordinarily would have been embarrassed to receive, much less sent herself, and yet because it had come from Lennie she had found it oddly touching. And oddly exciting, to receive such a childish communication from someone with whom she was so intimate.

Back in her room she retrieved the card from a portfolio of letters and clippings she kept in her desk. And there, under the portfolio, was a small shiny box with a bit of lavender tissue showing. The gold bracelet, purchased for Lennie in a much happier time. The sight of this gift she had never given brought a sudden clench of pain to her chest, and it surprised her so that without thinking she clasped the card to her heart as if to ease the ache. This pain was like fear. It was the ache of gin, and black, bitter, nights, and a profound sexual loneliness, not for Lennie in particular, or Patrick, but for what they both, separately, had brought to her: the joy of the human spirit, the delight of the human body. It seemed now that she was unable to sustain these feelings alone, nothing worked alone. She was unprotected, diminished.

"Patrick," she said aloud.

She walked to the door of his room and stood on the threshold again, not going in, but saying angrily, "Where in the hell are you?"

After a moment she sensed some warmth in the room she hadn't noticed before. She realized she hadn't turned Patrick's thermostat down, and he had always kept it set very high. So with this excuse she went in, finally, and went directly to his chair. She forgot about the thermostat; the heat felt soothing, and it calmed her.

Gingerly she settled into his recliner and eased herself back. Her legs rose smoothly, her body sank gratefully into the contours he had established over many years.

Still holding Lennie's card to her breast, she reached down and pulled Patrick's brown blanket up over her. His familiar scent clung to the threads, and she hesitated, but it seemed perfectly right for her to be there in the chair, with his blanket, holding a card they both would have laughed at, at one point in their lives together. She could allow herself no specific memories of him yet, and she was worn out with specific memories of Lennie; in any case her memory of Patrick was total and did not need the accents of time and place. Here she was warm for the first time in weeks.

And so she slept.

~

On the seventeenth of February a blizzard moved in from the northeast, and it snowed for twenty-one hours without a pause. This time Tina did call to say that classes were suspended, and Mrs. Medina spent most of the day seated by the living room window with a pot of tea, watching the avenue disappear under a fierce onslaught of snow and wind. The afternoon grew dim by three-thirty, and she could think of nothing to do but go to bed.

And under the blankets, while the winds tore at her windows, she curled up and felt consciousness ebb away and prayed that she would not dream. But the dream came. Out of some tangled undergrowth Patrick appeared, looking as he did when she had first met him, lithe and bright. He was wearing his tuxedo and a red cummerbund. She moved toward him. "Wait," Patrick said, and held up his hand. And from behind him, emerging gracefully from under a low branch, appeared a tall, handsome woman, short gray hair swept back from her face, dressed in an opaline green, sarong-like garment that revealed the classical white shoulders of a Botticelli Venus. She recognized her own face with a shock.

"Patrick," she said.

"This is the lady that's known as Lou," Patrick said. "She will stay with me. I've come to tell you."

"Patrick, that's me!" Mrs. Medina said. "Look at her, it's me."

"I died alone," he said. "And you let me go."

"That's not true," Mrs. Medina said. "You were not alone."

"You'll see me no more," he said, straightening his tie. "C'mon, toots. Time for a new life." The two Mrs. Medinas eyed each other across a universe of jungle.

She opened her eyes into the darkness. The wind had dropped, but snow was still coming down, and she wept as if Patrick were actually alive and had deserted her for this phantom version of herself. At this thought something clawed at her stomach, and she threw back the blankets and ran for the bathroom and vomited some brown fluid into the toilet.

Afterward she felt as if she had completed a treacherous journey and been washed up on a beach. She felt no hunger, no thirst; she was simply exhausted and wanted to rest. She imagined if she lay on the beach long enough her body would become formless, and she would simply disappear, like an image on a movie screen. She felt herself drawn toward that moment.

The next morning she called Taylor Bond. In the afternoon she took a cab that crawled out Beacon Street between four-foot snowdrifts.

"I'm glad you called, Mercedes," Bond said. "I was going to give you another week." He lowered the blind behind his desk and turned on the lamp.

"What do you mean?" She didn't want to sit on the couch, so she went over to the oversize studded leather chair by the desk.

He sat down. "I told you at Patrick's memorial service that I wanted to see you. I was waiting for you to call."

"Sorry. There was a lot going on then."

"Yes, I know. How are you?"

"Well, I'm keeping busy. My course is keeping my mind occupied."

"Good. Good." He rubbed his hands. "Too cold in here for you? My heating isn't working too well today."

"I'm fine."

"Bad storm."

"Yes."

He picked up a long red pencil and turned it over in his fingers.

She smiled. "What I wanted, Bond, was...I think I'd like something to help me sleep. Help me sleep at night, that is. If you can give me something, I don't care what."

"Problems sleeping?"

"Problems with dreams."

"Aha."

"And no, I'm not going to talk about them."

He smiled. "Sure, I can give you something for sleep. Might not help your dreams, though." He looked at her. "We could have taken care of that on the phone."

She blew on her hands. "It is cold in here."

"Sorry. They're working on it."

"If I'm having problems, they're just the same as you might expect after the death of—someone. A spouse. I've read about the problems. I wasn't expecting to feel happy."

"No."

She realized she would have to sing for her sleeping pills. "I haven't been able to tackle Patrick's things yet," she said. "I guess that will happen sometime."

"Big job."

She nodded. They looked at each other. "I just want to sleep soundly at night," she said. "So I can concentrate during the day."

"Perfectly understandable." He unlocked a desk drawer and got out a prescription pad. "Eating all right?"

"Oh, yes, I'm eating."

"And your health. In general. All right?"

"Yes. All right." She turned sideways in the chair. "This chair, Bond, is meant to accommodate a four-hundred-pound man."

"It's not too comfortable. Want to move to the couch?"

"No." She looked at her watch.

He bent his head and wrote out the prescription, tore it off the pad. "Now, I'm going to give you some Ativans, just a few, but there's a condition. I want you to come back again and talk with me."

"Why?"

"Because I think it would be a good idea. Just a couple of times."

"I don't need to talk. I just want to sleep."

He watched her with the prescription in his hand.

She stood up and took the prescription from him. "You've never been one for conditions."

"I'm not, usually."

"I'm not suicidal, Bond."

"I'm not suggesting you are."

"I guess I'll have to come back, then."

The pills helped a little, but still she was only able to drift off for two or three hours a night. She usually woke around two-thirty, marked the hours of the desolate winter night, and finally slept again at dawn. One morning she was so exhausted that she called and canceled her class. Valentina Bird telephoned late in the afternoon.

"This is not good," she said. "It's the third time you've canceled."

"Yes, I know. I'm sorry, Tina. I think I'm getting the flu."

"I'm coming over there," she said. "And I'll bring you some dinner. Chinese all right?"

"I wish you wouldn't. The apartment is a mess."

"That is of no importance to me whatsoever."

Tina bustled in about an hour later, laden with containers of spicy bean curd, mysterious chicken, and rice. She put them on the kitchen counter and opened the refrigerator. "What," she said, turning to face Mrs. Medina, "have you been eating? There's nothing in here but an open can of tuna and a couple of eggs."

"I told you I'm getting the flu. I have bread and cereal in the cupboard."

"Well, sit down. I'll make some tea."

Mrs. Medina watched Tina at the stove, her hair peeking out above a gold-and-green-striped silk band. She shook her beaded ear hoops and slammed the door to the microwave. Mrs. Medina thought, *I should be doing that,* and felt ashamed. She ate a little rice and chicken and some vegetables, to be polite. After dinner they sat with their cups of tea, and Tina looked at her carefully.

Finally, Mrs. Medina raised her head and said, "I'm awfully tired, Tina..."

"Listen to me, Mercedes." Tina reached across the table and grasped her hand. "You have twelve eager students who expect you to appear twice a week at your appointed hour. More to the point,

I expect to see your gracious body in that classroom when it's supposed to be there. If you're having problems, let's lay them out."

Mrs. Medina didn't know what to say. The kitchen seemed to be
filled with a harsh, white light that hurt her eyes.

Tina still held her hand. "This is a bad time for you, I know it.
I'm not inclined to let you off the hook, because I think it's better if
you go on. But something can be worked out if you can't continue."

"I can continue," Mrs. Medina said, removing her hand from Tina's.

"I wonder," Tina said. She watched Mrs. Medina for a few
moments. "Mercedes, you are one of my dearest friends," she said
finally.

Now she had to cover her eyes, the glare from the kitchen light
was so painful.

"What's happened to your friend with the flowers who was here
at Thanksgiving?" Tina went on. "Any word from her?"

Mrs. Medina uncovered her eyes and gave Tina such a look of
anguish that Tina immediately rose and came over to her. "Come on,"
she said, "let's get more comfortable."

Mrs. Medina sat propped up on her unmade bed, and Tina
enthroned herself on the chaise. They had brought their tea with
them. Tina had on a long black skirt and a green V-neck sweater with
sparkles of gold in it. She tucked her legs up under her. "How long
has she been gone, then?"

"Thanksgiving. Thanksgiving was the last time I saw her or spoke
to her."

Tina sipped her tea. "Know where she's gone off to?"

Mrs. Medina shook her head.

"Or why she went? You have a fight?"

"No, it wasn't a fight."

"Patrick and the sword? That might have done it."

"I'm not really sure what happened back in that room."

Tina reached around and put her teacup on the table. She looked
at Mrs. Medina and tilted her head. "You're not too comfortable
talking about her, are you?"

Mrs. Medina raised her eyebrows. "I don't know. I talked to
Patrick."

"You know, Mercedes, it doesn't matter to me a bit. I've never had a passion for a woman, but I certainly understand why people do. It seems perfectly natural. Gorgeous creatures, some of us. You're not the only lesbian I've known in my life."

"Is that what I am, then, Tina?" She pulled her cardigan up around her shoulders.

"That's a complicated question. You need something to call yourself?"

"I don't want to be called anything right now. Not even my own name."

"No little slots."

"Right." She put her teacup on the table and closed her eyes.

Tina raised her hand to adjust her headband, and her bracelets clattered down her arm. The wind was blowing hard from the northwest, and it rattled against the window glass. "May I turn the heat up?" Tina asked. "I'm an island girl, and it's a little cool in here tonight."

"The thermostat's in the hall."

When Tina came back she was carrying a bottle and two glasses filled with ice. "I just happened to have this in my bag," she said. "Fancy that. Barceló Gran Añejo, dark, dark rum from down around Santo Domingo. Nice to sip on a cold night. Cheaper than burning fuel in the furnace."

"This is pretty strong," Mrs. Medina said. She shook her head as the sweet fumes rose burning into her sinuses and a flush crept up her jawbone.

"I don't want to cry," Mrs. Medina said half an hour later. She had flung off her cardigan and was pacing around the room. "I'm sick of crying and I'm sick of talking."

"You haven't been doing much of either this evening," Tina said with a laugh. "Why don't you just continue."

Mrs. Medina circled around to the chaise and sat down at the foot, near Tina's feet. She swirled her ice around in her glass. "I am just high and dry on a rock," she said. "But I feel like I'm in a cesspool."

"A troublesome situation indeed," Tina said. She poured Mrs. Medina a little more rum and gave herself a bit as well.

Mrs. Medina sipped from her glass. "Something is stalking me," she said. "It's why I can't sleep. I hear it in my sleep and I hear it in the snow."

"What's it doing, Mercedes?"

"It's just waiting." She shook her head. "It's waiting for me to let down my guard. I'm now sleeping with Patrick's sword under my bed." She pointed.

"I know a grandma from Port-au-Prince who can rid you of that duppy," Tina said. "No kidding. She lives out in Malden now."

Mrs. Medina gave her a smile. She got up and walked across to her reading chair, the chair Lennie had sat in and kicked off her boots. Months now. "The first time Lennie came here," she said, "she had on red socks."

"Hot ticket," Tina said. She yawned behind her fist.

Mrs. Medina sat down. "Go home if you have to go," she said. "I'm all right."

Tina settled herself more comfortably on the chaise. "Did you love her, then?"

"I don't know. Yes. Of course I loved her. I still love her, I suppose."

"You should be happy for that, then."

"No, I'm not happy for that. She let me fall in love with her, and then she just walked off. Patrick was dying, and she just left me."

"Maybe she was confused. You and Patrick both had your eyes firmly fixed on the end of his life, we all saw that. Maybe she bolted because she didn't know how to handle it."

The rum had briefly warmed her up, but now Mrs. Medina felt herself shiver. "No." She walked back to her bed and picked up her detestable maroon sweater. "This is a horrible color, isn't it, Tina? Maroon?"

"Maroon is the absence of life, in my book," Tina said, pouring herself another tot of rum.

"It was just a fling. I was stupid not to have seen it."

"You're not the first to ride that ride," Tina said. "She was a sweet kid. Maybe she'll come back."

"She's in trouble. I don't think she'll come back."

"They're all in trouble, honey. You do remember the night I had to go out to Jackson Square and help the transit cops free Joseph from the fence along the subway track? Some fool had handcuffed him to it."

"His troubles didn't bother you?"

"I was crazy for that man. I still miss him. Troubles are part of it."

For a moment Mrs. Medina struggled to see how Tina's affair with Joseph was comparable in any way to hers with Lennie. Two people. Trouble. That was as far as she got. And yet Tina seemed to have no regrets.

"Everything is gray now," she said. "The sky gets lower every day. I lie down and words fly past me like shooting stars. Sometimes I feel my brain's going to break into pieces."

"No wonder you can't sleep." Tina brought over the bottle. "You know what I'm going to do? I'm going to get you ready for bed, and then I'm going to settle right down on that comfortable throne over there and bore you to death until you pass out."

"No, Tina."

"And then, if you'll find me a nightgown and a couple of blankets, I'll watch over you for tonight."

Mrs. Medina shook her head.

But Tina would have her way. She tended to Mrs. Medina as if she were a child, got her washed and into her flannel nightgown, remade the bed and put her into it. "Not so bad, is it?" she said, sitting down on the side. "Being cared for?"

Mrs. Medina lay back and closed her eyes.

"Now," Tina said, "I note these pills here with a recent date. Have you been to see that headshrinker with the gorgeous eyes?"

"Yes."

"You going back to see him again? Anytime soon?"

Mrs. Medina nodded. "Next week."

"Good. I think it would be a good time for you to bare all."

"I just want to find a way out, Tina." She opened her eyes. "Oh, don't look so alarmed. I'm not thinking of that."

"You and I will speak further about your teaching. I just want you to relax now. Don't think about sleep, just be still, and I'll tell you about the time my mama took my evil brother and me to Carnival in St. John's."

"Patrick asked me to hold on to him one night so he wouldn't fly away. A long time ago."

"I'm a pretty substantial anchor. You won't fly away."

For days Mrs. Medina had felt as if she were on an elevator, descending slowly but inevitably, past darkened floors into an abyss she couldn't see. Now for this one night the elevator had paused, the hum of the cables had abated, and all she could hear was Tina's low voice describing the heat of the islands. "My mother picked a beautiful flamboyant flower," she said, "and wove it into my braid. That's how the day began, just after dawn."

~ twenty-five ~

In the end Mrs. Medina told Bond about Lennie because she was too exhausted to keep avoiding it.

"She was an obsession, a weakness. I'm ashamed of it.

"And I don't want to talk about her personally. You should just know that this thing happened."

"I don't know how I can be a lesbian because I've never had any other experiences with women. I don't think I had looked at other women before I became involved with Lennie. But of course I must have! I just didn't realize why. There was a woman in San Francisco, on my honeymoon. I looked at her. I did look at her, and I thought about her, what she might be like, nothing specific. I've never forgotten her, I suppose that's significant. But I'm not thinking of a future here, I'm not thinking of anyone else.

"It would never have worked out, though, with Lennie, not as a long-term thing. How could it? We were separated by our entire lives. By more than that. Do you have any lesbian patients? Anyone my age?"

"Are you looking at me as a specimen now?"

"People can just disappear from your life. I think Lennie was gone before she actually disappeared. I think I could see right through her. I thought Patrick might hang around, but he is absolutely gone as well. He came in a dream to tell me."

"Yes, I loved her. But I had a life before she came, some sort of life. And let's not talk about love just now. It's irrelevant, really."

"She was passionate but indifferent. I see it now."

"I don't know what will happen to my work. I don't know whether I can go back. Now I wonder about my life and my work—they seem to have no connection. As opposed to Patrick's music, which was inseparable from his life.

"I did envy him that.

"The world was rolling by me like a patrol of tanks, and I was behind a curtain, my back to the window, not even watching the spectacle. Patrick, at least, was always interested in the spectacle."

"And I'm drinking too much."

~

Back at the apartment Tina was in the lobby chatting with Al, who was standing with a plastic bucket of salt crystals. Al was big and slow-moving and genial, as opposed to Constantin, who was small and tense and easily excitable.

"Drop your stuff," Tina said. "I'm taking you over to Bob the Chef's. I smell ribs cookin' on this cold, cold night."

"I'm not hungry, Tina. Really, I thought I'd just fix some soup."

"Let's go out for some soup, then. Anyplace you say."

"Gonna snow again tonight, Mrs. Medina," Al said. "Constantin's mother fell and broke her hip."

"I'm sorry," Mrs. Medina said.

"Let's go," Tina said.

They made it as far as Copley Place, where the bitter cold drove them into Legal Sea Foods. Mrs. Medina ordered a piece of scrod and a double martini.

Tina tilted her head. "I never thought of gin and scrod," she said. "That a good combination?"

"Try it."

Tina had some grouper and a Caesar salad. "You see the shrink?" she asked as they began to eat.

Mrs. Medina nodded.

"What did he say?"

"He said, 'See you next Thursday.' "

"Did you talk to him about Lennie?"

"More or less."

"Feel better?"

Mrs. Medina put down her fork. "No, I don't. And I appreciate your concern, but I've just gone on like an idiot for an hour, and I'd like to be quiet for a while."

"Fine." Tina took a bite of fish. "So I'll talk, if that's all right, and this will be good news, I hope. Bill Polito has agreed to take over your course for the remainder of the term."

Mrs. Medina leaned back. "Bill Polito? He's new, isn't he? He's just a baby."

"Very wet behind the ears. But enthusiastic. Thinks highly of you. He's willing to do it just for this year. The job is still yours, as long as I'm head of that department. But for now let's give you a little break here, lady. Take some time, put your life back in order. Or better still, let it all go to hell and find some new road to take."

"You're firing me," Mrs. Medina said.

"No. I'm giving you a temporary leave."

"What will I do?"

Tina leaned back and regarded her solemnly for a moment. "This is what you've been waiting for, if you'd just open your eyes."

"What I've been waiting for? I need to work, Tina. Don't make me beg for it."

"Work is not what you need right now. It's the last thing you need."

The waitress gathered up their plates brightly. "Coffee for anyone? Dessert?"

"No," Mrs. Medina said.

"Yes, please," Tina said. "Coffee for me. Black."

"It's just that I can't bear to be in that house any longer," Mrs. Medina said. "The snow, the darkness..."

"The snow is outside, Mercedes."

"No. No, it isn't."

"You have the money. Get out of here for a while. Beat it. Lose Boston, lose Patrick, lose the flower girl. Just temporarily. Stay away until the spring has come."

"Where would I go?" she said.

The waitress arrived with the coffee. "Anything else?" she said.

"No. Thanks." Tina did not take her eyes off Mrs. Medina.

"How about a dessert menu?" the waitress asked. "How about some key lime pie?"

Tina looked up at her and said, "No. Thank. You." The waitress quickly departed.

"I have too many things to decide, Tina. I can't go now."

"You buy a ticket and you pack. Those are decisions you can make."

Mrs. Medina caught movement out of the corner of her eye and saw an elbow strike a glass of water at the next table, watched the glass tilt, sway, and slowly lift into the air while the conversation that had been rattling about in her ears, the clash of plates, suddenly ceased. The glass described a graceful arc, trailing a veil of water, and silently fell toward what would surely be the violent conclusion of its existence. The black-and-white tile floor waited ominously. Mrs. Medina watched it in fascination, in an extended moment of complete silence.

And in the next second her legs were covered with water, and she felt the sting of glass fragments against her ankles. People seemed to be shouting, and Tina was busy wiping down the sleeves of her jacket and laughing with the woman at the table next to theirs. Everyone seemed to be laughing, in fact. Mrs. Medina sat very still. She thought of the dark, waiting apartment, of the ceaseless filthy snow, of the unrelenting cold. Spring would make no difference; there would be sunrise, sunsets, it wouldn't matter what time of day she ate or had a glass of gin. Sunrise, sunset, spring, summer, it would never be any different.

She watched Tina laugh.

"Mercedes, are you all right?" Tina said. "I've just had a bath!"

"Yes." Mrs. Medina looked out the window. "It's snowing again."

"I'll get the check," Tina said.

~

That was her last meal for several days. She made up for the absence of food with gin. When she felt hungry she ate dry cereal out of the box, and once she warmed up some chicken broth. She spent her time in Patrick's chair, facing the window, watching the snow stop and start. She slept there, sometimes during the daylight hours, sometimes at night. In the evenings she tried once or twice to find a Celtics game; she thought if she watched the Celtics perhaps Patrick would come back, but she couldn't locate them. So she watched old movies, she watched reruns of *The Beverly Hillbillies* and *Andy Griffith* and *Golden Girls*. Some of the shows she had never heard of. She watched talk shows and the news and the Weather Channel. Her eyes ached and she shivered constantly. But if she turned the sound off, the room seemed to scream at her.

She finally became tired of trying to decide what to wear, so she kept on her denims and the hateful maroon sweater, and over all of that she threw on her heavy flowered robe.

The second night she heard dogs barking in the bathroom, barking and snapping. She decided it was the answering machine. When she got up to go to the bathroom, her knees buckled and she had to sit down on the floor and while she was there she imagined a large bird was on its way to carry her off and so she had to count to keep it at bay. She was on the floor counting until the room grew light, and she crawled to the bathroom on her hands and knees.

This can't go on forever, she thought at one point. But she knew it could.

On the fourth day she ran out of food and gin. At ten-thirty in the morning she sat at the kitchen table trying to decide what to do. The problem of getting food into the house, and liquor, seemed insurmountable. If she went out, what would she wear? Was there ice on the streets, could she make it to DeLuca's? Should she send Al? Did she have any cash?

She put her head in her hands.

Everywhere she looked she saw filth, dust on the moldings, soot on the windowsills, unwashed glasses on every table. After a while she looked up as if she had heard a voice. "Patrick?" she called out.

When the door buzzer sounded she thought she had sent Al for supplies and he had brought them up.

"Just leave them, Al," she whispered through the door. "Leave them on the mat."

"Mercedes, open the door." It was Tina. Mrs. Medina closed her eyes. Did Tina have the groceries? "Open up, honey, or I'll break it down."

Tina was there, in the hall, and right behind her was Taylor Bond. Right behind Bond was Al, with his keys. None of them had groceries. Mrs. Medina stared at them all and pulled her robe a bit tighter around her.

"Mercedes," Tina said. Then she turned and said to Al, "Thanks, we'll do fine now. On your way."

"I'd ask you in, you see," Mrs. Medina said, straightening up, "but my house is a bit of a shambles. Perhaps another time."

"What can we do for you?" Bond said, stepping forward. "I think we'll come in. Is there something you need?"

"Yes," Mrs. Medina said. It was suddenly clear to her what it was she needed. "I'd just like someone to cook for me for a few days, if you think you can manage that. Someone I don't know. Someone who doesn't want to talk."

"Yes," Bond said with a smile. "We can manage that."

{ III }

IN TRANSIT

When it began to get light, Mrs. Medina abandoned any hope of sleep. She rolled over and smelled the unfamiliar sheets and the air was warm and for the first time in months she had no blanket over her. From the pier outside her window came the sound of two men's voices in patient argument, then the low grumble of an inboard motor firing up. A burst of music from a radio. The light was pink behind the louvered shutters. And in that growing light rain fell.

She opened the top half of the Dutch doors and made herself some coffee and took it out onto the deck. She could almost walk right out of the door of her little apartment into the water. The rain had stopped, and the sun lay across her face like hot planks. The coffee was bitter.

Halfway out the little pier a plump black boy in blue shorts was pouring the remains of his grape soda into a bobbing dinghy. He looked up at her and smiled. She lowered her sunglasses from atop her forehead and walked past him with her coffee cup and went on out to the end of the pier. The big green ferry marked PETER ISLAND was just arriving, and cut its powerful engines suddenly and wallowed about in its own massive wake before turning toward a marina across the harbor. Its passengers were already waving frantically. Why does everyone always want to wave? It was like the small boy at the airport in St. Thomas yesterday, running round and round his mother chanting, "We're here, mummy! We're here, mummy! We're here! We're here!"

Much more interesting now was the small wooden motorboat

that was slopping along in the chop toward the next dock up. In the bow of the boat a small white terrier hung forward as if he were a smiling bowsprit. Dog and owner tied up at Recardo's Paradise, where a band had lulled her to sleep last night with a long, repetitive rendition of a song she didn't know but now would never forget. She had heard drums and a bass guitar and keyboards, and every minute or so a chorus of voices sang out, "Baby, can I hold you tonight..." which were the only words she could understand. It beat against her head like a migraine, and like a migraine the tension of *feeling* it had sent her into sleep.

She tossed her bitter coffee into the water. Tina had assured her that Tortola was a perfect place. But she wasn't sure perfect was what she wanted.

When Tina had collected her from the hospital ten days ago she had not broached the subject right away. She waited until they had returned to Mrs. Medina's apartment, and Mrs. Medina had exclaimed over the flowers and the clean kitchen and the food in the refrigerator.

"The Merry Maids helped a bit," Tina had said, "so calm down."

"I'll repay you, of course," Mrs. Medina said, walking around her bedroom as if she had been away for a lifetime. "It was a real mess, Tina. I'm so grateful."

"Now, don't begin," Tina said, raising her hands. "Let's have some tea."

Mrs. Medina didn't know what she would do with all these empty rooms. She put her hand on the window in her bedroom. It still felt like February.

"Oh, look here," Tina said from the kitchen. "Chocolate cake."

They sat in the living room, more formal together than they had been for a long while. Mrs. Medina was beginning to remember with unpleasant clarity the state she had been in when Tina and Bond had come to find her. The days of dishes in the sink, her unmade bed, the accumulated trash. She swallowed, examined her nails.

"So," Tina said, "do you think my derriere is too large for these pants? The daughter says yes."

"I think you have a wonderful figure," Mrs. Medina said, then stopped, flustered, fearful of being misinterpreted. She must remember now that Tina knew everything. Mrs. Medina put down her teacup.

"I don't wear them to class, of course," Tina went on, oblivious.

Mrs. Medina picked up the little mother of pearl frame that held an old picture of Patrick on a sailboat, Lake Constance, summer of 1975. He had his mouth open singing "Vesti la giubba," she remembered. She could almost hear his voice.

Tina fiddled with her last bite of cake. "Oh, what the hell," she said. "Listen to my idea."

Her idea was this. One or two members of Tina's enormous family had made their way up the chain of islands from Antigua and settled in Tortola. Her second cousin Cyril Recardo owned a restaurant in Road Town, and his wife, Marianne, was a nurse in the hospital.

"He's always been a bit of an entrepreneur, Cyril," Tina said. "He and some others of the local gentry have bought some real estate, and they're renovating vacation condos. He's got a couple right on the harbor in Road Town. Can't vouch for them, never seen them, but they're newly done over, and clean for now, and the season's drawing to a close down there. So he says to send you down. Friend of the family. Stay for a month or so, and they'll keep you busy or leave you be, whatever you want."

"I've never been there," Mrs. Medina said.

"A good reason to go."

"You've done too much, Tina." Mrs. Medina stood up. "It makes me a little uncomfortable." She walked to the window. Dusk had crept down the avenue, and rush hour lights were streaming west through a raw March evening.

"Lady, you are one tough nut. Funds are not the point." She finished her tea. "But I am exhausted from arguing with you over these months. I want you to think about it and make a decision. It is a gift freely offered. Cyril hasn't anyone in one or two of those places right now, and he'd love for you to be there. Stop thinking about paying everyone back. Just do it or not, and now I'm going home."

Mrs. Medina walked her to the door, thinking of warmth, of returning sunlight.

Yesterday they had descended into St. Thomas through a squall, a sunlit deluge that hammered against the plane wings in a brief tattoo, then shot them out of the clouds into a steep bank over a sea that was as close to air as water, clear enough for Mrs. Medina to see through it, as if it were a transparent piece of sky, to the bottom, to the dunes that rippled a hundred feet or so beneath the surface. When she stepped off the plane the heat wrapped itself around her in an intimate sort of way, invasive, insistent. Like the child: *I'm here!* In Boston it had been thirty-one degrees at dawn, and an early spring snow was falling.

She went over to the Air Tortola desk and asked about the one-fifteen flight to Tortola.

"It will leave shortly," the young woman behind the counter said. She was sucking on an orange soda. She had on a short-sleeved light blue shirt with a pair of metal wings pinned over her right breast.

"Shortly—when?" Mrs. Medina said. "I don't want to miss it."

"You wait in Rita's there. You won't miss it."

Mrs. Medina crossed the cavernous, airy terminal and went into Rita's Rum Bar. On the other side of the rattling aluminum wall of the terminal, a big jet hurled itself down the runway with an agonized roar, charging the hill at the eastern end like a giant crazed pelican. The plane left an intense pall of kerosene in its wake, which mingled in the terminal with a smell of warm disinfectant that reminded her of the hospital.

"One of these days something's going to hit that hill," a man on another bar stool said to her. He had on Day-Glo orange shorts and a T-shirt that read I AM THE SKIPPER. His thick calves were muscled like tree roots, and he had them wound around his bar stool. His dark glasses were perched over his forehead, resting in sparse blond hair. He was working on a Caribé beer.

"Quiet, man," the Rasta bartender said with a sweet smile. "We got a traveler present."

Her glass was sticky and not too clean, but the rum punch was good and she could actually taste the rum.

At one-fifteen she went back to the airline desk. There was now a young man behind the desk, thin as a pencil and drinking a Coke. He wore a short-sleeved white shirt with black boards on the shoulders, and had a small number four shaved very closely into his otherwise nearly hairless scalp. Mrs. Medina asked whether he was the pilot.

"No, ma'am," he said. "The pilot has some business in town."

"Well, someone is meeting me in Tortola," Mrs. Medina said, hoisting her carry-on bag higher on her shoulder. "When will he be back?"

"Our next flight to Tortola is at—" he consulted an enormous wristwatch with many small dials "—five-thirty. I will write you a chit here for Rita's. You will be happy there with her rum punch, I bet." He smiled hopefully.

"I have had Rita's rum punch," Mrs. Medina said. "And it was very good, but I don't want another. I need to get to Tortola. Someone is expecting me at the airport, and I don't want to keep him waiting."

The young man smoothed the sparse, dark fuzz on his upper lip.

"And I'm tired," Mrs. Medina said with a little smile. She didn't want to be rude, after all.

"And you're hot in those winter duds too, probably." The man from the bar in the Day-Glo shorts stood beside her. "That five-thirty flight isn't likely to go either. It's the same pilot. Our friend Abercrombie. And he does have troubles in town. I'll vouch for that."

The youngster behind the counter straightened the boards on his shoulders and shuffled some papers.

"I'll ride you over," the man said.

"Who are you?" Mrs. Medina asked.

"Bobby Curtis. I've got my little Cessna here. She's just about loaded, but I think I can fit you in. How many bags have you got?"

"I expect Abercrombie will be back soon, Bobby," the young man said.

"I wouldn't count on it, Charles, you little bugger. Come on," he said over his shoulder to Mrs. Medina. "Thirty-minute flight."

Fortunately, the plane made so much noise that there was no need for conversation. They flew due east, with the sun behind them, and the nappy green hills of St. John floated slowly beneath them. The air was cooling, and the colors in the sky shifted dramatically from red to orange to lavender as they flew toward a pale quarter moon that had emerged above the darkening sea. Mrs. Medina's large piece of luggage was jabbing her in the back of her neck, her carry-on bag was crammed into her lap. The rest of the plane was loaded with cases of engine oil, two outboard motors, a propeller, several boxes of machine parts, and what appeared to be a small white coffin.

"Down we go," Bobby shouted suddenly, and cut the engines.

There was a shock of silence in the cabin. They dove through this silence toward the hills ahead of them, which were just beginning to twinkle in the dusk. After a minute or so Bobby kicked the engine in again and gave Mrs. Medina a sly look out of the corner of his eye. Ahead of them were the runway lights.

Cyril Recardo was standing around on the tarmac with some other men in animated conversation when Bobby's plane chugged up to the small terminal. Mrs. Medina lowered herself out of the cockpit, her legs stiff, her ears roaring, and Cyril spotted her immediately. He walked over quickly and ducked under the wing.

"I'm Cyril," he said, extending his big brown hand. He was well over six feet tall and wore a blond Panama tilted rakishly to the back of his head, which made him look even taller. His red shirt flapped out over a satisfied stomach, and a small pair of glasses sat uneasily on the end of his nose.

"I'm so sorry about the delay," Mrs. Medina began.

He lifted his hat and ran a white handkerchief over a very bald head. "We always expect Abercrombie when we see him." He looked over his shoulder. "But you seem to have caught another ride. Yo, Bobby."

"Hello there, Cyro. I brought you a customer."

"No customer, Bob. She's a welcome guest, a friend of my cousin Tina, up north. Valentina, that is, the professor."

"Thank you for the ride," Mrs. Medina remembered to say. She opened her bag and felt for her wallet. "Please let me pay you something."

"Forget it." He flapped his hand. "I was coming anyway."

Another plane fired up its engines and set the palms by the terminal door clicking in its hot diesel wind. Mrs. Medina looked across the airstrip and saw water, red runway lights, and an island twinkling beyond. The moon was clearly visible now, the color of crème brûlée, on its tropical back. She imagined the air was cooler.

"Come," Cyril said, taking her elbow. "We got to do the customs." He picked up Mrs. Medina's luggage in his other hand.

Two customs men were playing cards around a rickety table just inside the door. They were playing cards, but they had on their official caps with the black-and-white-checked hat bands.

"Who's winning there, Malcolm?" Cyril called.

"Oh, we not scoring, Cyril. How's things?"

"Fine, fine. This lady's a friend, came over with Bobby Curtis from St. Thomas. She got nothing to declare."

"All right, then, Cyril. Need to see her passport, though."

Cyril took it over to the table, and Malcolm stamped it with a great flourish, then returned to his cards. "All right, we see you later, possibly."

"Good band tonight, man. Better come by."

Cyril's large Buick was parked out in the warm evening in a small grove of palms across from the terminal. Now Mrs. Medina could smell the sweet wind off the water and hear the halyards from some nearby sailboats clanking lazily in the dusk. She took a deep breath, suddenly exhausted.

They rattled across the narrow bridge linking the airport island to mainland Tortola.

"You must tell me about Tina," Cyril said. "How's she doing? And her girl, she gettin' big now? Do they like the snow?"

~

Mrs. Medina considered the many places in the world she had been and angrily thought, *Why did Tina send me here? Nothing is organized. The planes don't run. The sun is too hot. There are large beetles in my shower. There are no museums, no opera. I don't belong here, I have only ever belonged with Patrick. I miss him, and he is everywhere around me, so it won't get any better.*

In the streets here there was color. The people lived in color. She had lived so long in grays and browns that the colors seemed noisy to her at first, the colors talked too much. They were an extension of the water: blue, green; an extension of the sun: orange, yellow, violent shades of pink. They were not subtle. They did not stay out of her way.

two

Mrs. Medina came to Cyril Recardo's Paradise Bar and Restaurant for lunch and ordered conch fritters for the third day in a row; they came with a tangy cabbage salad. The fritters were sweet, slightly chewy, and the batter was peppery hot. For three days she had depended upon the predictability of their taste. She had a Heineken to drink. On the wide, wooden terrace of Cyril's place she could drink her beer and watch the boat traffic. It was a short walk from her little apartment. Lunch was one high point of her day; the other was just after the sun fell behind Mount Sage, when she could begin to think about having a drink and watching the lights come on around the harbor.

The lunch crowd had cleared out, and Mrs. Medina sat with her warm beer and wondered whether she should go and nap. She should try to do something. A breeze had picked up off the water and it smelled of salt and heat, but it had a little coolness in it.

"Want another beer?" the restaurant manager asked her. She put her pencil behind her ear and picked up Mrs. Medina's plate.

"No, thanks. I'll leave if you want."

"No need to go. Just thought you might like another." She stood by the table and watched the harbor. "There goes Sidney. I guess one of the Princess ships is out in the channel."

Mrs. Medina smiled.

The woman looked down at her. "Sidney is the harbor pilot. He brings the big boats in."

Mrs. Medina took one last sip from her glass.

The woman put down the plate and took out a pack of Camels from her breast pocket. "Want a smoke?" she said.

"No, thanks."

After a moment the woman said, "I'm Dori Kite. From L.A. originally."

"Mercedes Medina."

"You a friend of Cyril's?"

"I'm a friend of a cousin of his. In Boston."

"Yeah, he has a lot of cousins." She drew on her cigarette. "I've got no family. I'm what you call an expat. You on vacation?"

"For a while, I guess."

"That's how I came down here too, for a vacation. Ended up staying, married an island guy. Didn't work out. You know, black and white, we just couldn't deal with it. Too different states of mind, know what I mean? Two rails going in the same direction that never meet. Now I'm fifty-one. Unless I'm lucky. I'll die alone in my solitary bed." She flipped her cigarette over the scalloped wooden rail into the water.

"Fifty-one isn't so old," Mrs. Medina said politely.

There was a low musical sound, and Dori removed a telephone from a holster on her hip. "Six cases, and get them here before five," she said into the phone, and paced away between the tables, touching her forehead with her fist. Her face was lean and lined and dark from the island sun; her hair that used to be blond was pulled up off her neck and pinned on top of her head.

Mrs. Medina reached for her purse.

Dori finished her conversation and flipped the phone shut. "I need a vacation from here," she said. "Well, nice to talk to someone from home. You ought to come by here at night. The guys from the cruise ships come in sometimes. We have a time."

~

Cyril Recardo's "vacation units" were right on the main highway to the west end of the island, just before the curve where cars picked up speed after leaving Road Town. A wrought iron gate led directly into a small red-tiled courtyard, which was surrounded by a tall wooden fence on which Cyril was trying to start some morning glory vines. Here lizards paused for long moments in the sun, drunk with heat, and Mrs. Medina sat under the bougainvillea in the wicker chair and sipped tea and tried to read *The End of the Affair,* which she had chosen from the collection of musty paperbacks in the house. Up three steps was the entrance to the smaller of her two rooms, louvered shutters, more red tiles, a telephone, a small television, a bright canvas-covered couch. On the wall was a picture of a scantily clad young woman swimming through a coral reef, accompanied by numerous glowing fish.

From this room three steps descended to a larger living area, spacious and new, in which were a couch and several chairs covered in colorful flowered chintz, a glass-topped table for meals, and, behind a screen, a double bed with a green-striped spread. The kitchen and bath were adjacent. The Dutch door led to the deck.

It was not a place one could get lost in.

Cyril came by one evening as she was cleaning up the dishes. He had a friend with him.

"This is Sam Brathwaite," he said. "Taxi man hereabouts." They both grinned. "He does some work for me in addition." Sam Brathwaite's hand was gnarled and dry, as if he had been working with turpentine. His teal shirt was covered with a confusion of multi-colored flying fish. His tight curly hair was completely white.

Mrs. Medina asked them to come and sit on the deck. They declined beers, but Cyril got right to the point.

"We worry about you," he said. "Me and Marianne."

Mrs. Medina smiled. "And why?"

"You seem to be declining here with sadness," he said. He threw open his large hands. "I promise my cousin Valentina I would cheer you up."

"Well," she said, "no need to cheer me up. I've been ill, you know. I do get out, I have my daily walks, but I'm just getting back on my feet."

"Tired a lot," Sam offered. "Know well what that is."

She nodded. "Yes, that's it."

"Marianne says we take you to dinner tomorrow. Not at my place, too ordinary. We will go to Mrs. Bobb's, up on the mountain."

"Never tire of seeing those pretty lights on the road up the hill across the water there," Sam said. "See how regular the cars go up, back and forth, zig and zag."

"Yes," Mrs. Medina agreed.

"Good island food. You will like it and we will have some fun," Cyril went on.

"I almost marry that woman, you know, Cyril," Sam said.

"Who, man?"

"Coral Bobb. We was engaged for many years."

Cyril smiled at Mrs. Medina. "And Sam here, this old roué, he will be your escort."

"If I not be too old a guy for you," Sam said earnestly. "And my time with Coral Bobb is over, so don't let that trouble you."

"And another thing," Cyril said, wiping the top of his head with his handkerchief, "hard to get to know this isle without leaving town. So Sam will give you his top taxi tour, you know, two or three hours, plus a drink at Bomba's Surfside over at Apple Bay. What do you say to that?"

Mrs. Medina's heart sank. She thought of all the conversation she would have to make, and her head began to ache. But there was nothing to do but be gracious. "I would be most pleased," she said.

Cyril stood up and hitched his pants up over his belly. "Fine. Fine. Settled, then." He shrugged his shoulders more comfortably into his jacket. "Now," he rubbed his hands, "I do have a restaurant to watch over. Big party from one of the Princess ships in tonight."

Sam jumped up and grabbed Mrs. Medina's hand. "Madame," he said, bending slightly at the waist. "I will be honored to accompany such an elegant lady. I call for you at two."

"See you then," Mrs. Medina said.

She was doing her best not to think of anything that had occurred over the last six months or so. And she was succeeding, more or less, though she wasn't particularly proud of her success. What she couldn't keep away was the ache that sprang into her chest at moments when she wasn't prepared, that surprised her, that didn't seem to be focused on Patrick or Lennie, but on—it was the only way she could describe it—"the door to nowhere" that beckoned her forward.

Drowsing after lunch in the wicker chair in the courtyard, the heat still and thick, with soft teeth in it that chewed languidly on the brain like a cat taking its time over a dead mouse, she imagined Lennie coming through the iron gate. She was not asleep, but she heard Lennie's footsteps, heard her come across the courtyard and pause by the chair, felt her lips against her mouth. She ran her hand over the contour of Lennie's hips, down the back of her thighs. *Such a relief to feel her body again.* Mrs. Medina's shoulders sagged against the back of the chair, and she exhaled a breath she had been holding for many weeks. Putting her hands around Lennie's waist, she drew her down, so she could feel the full weight of her body, and Lennie's head fell against her shoulder, her mouth against Mrs. Medina's neck.

It grew still then, the insects rested, the traffic outside her gate ceased momentarily, the lizard paused in the sun, just near a morning glory vine. Then the moment shifted back into the afternoon, and when she bent to retrieve her book, which had slipped off her lap, she felt her heart plunge suddenly into an abyss and stop. "Nerves," her doctor had told her when this happened once before. She stayed very still and tried to breathe slowly for a while, and to keep her mind occupied she concentrated on the instructions about hurricanes that she had read in the telephone book that morning. Rule number one: Stay calm.

Mrs. Medina had organized her days into segments. She generally woke early, because Sidney, the harbor pilot and her neighbor, had duties that took him out just after dawn, and his boat was not a quiet one. By nine her breakfast was completed, she had showered, and had locked her gate and begun the half-mile walk along the road into town. Beyond the Yacht Club there was a sidewalk of sorts, and she could get off the sandy verge and walk more easily. After she passed the hospital, set back from the road at the foot of the mountain, the road became a divided carriageway, and if it was the day to do the laundry, she crossed the road to Key-Linda's launderette, put her clothes in, and went to the terrace of the marina at Village Cay for a cup of coffee. If it was the day for the post office or the bank, she crossed the carriageway and went up one of the small grassy alleys leading into the main shopping street of Road Town. If it was the day for shopping, she passed the launderette and the shops attached to Village Cay Marina and continued straight on past the filling station to the rear entrance of the All-Rite Shopping Market, up at the traffic rotary. There was never too much she needed: bottled water, irradiated milk, cereal, bananas, coffee. Sometimes bread. Tonic. Limes. She could buy her gin there too. She took a cab back to her apartment and was usually home by noon.

She went up to Cyril's for lunch about two, and took her time (for time was what she had). A nap after lunch took care of some of the afternoon. She had a gin on the deck while the sun went down, and then went back into Road Town for dinner, usually at Village Cay or at the Carib Gardens, where one went up a rickety set of stairs off the street and emerged into a rather flung-together multi-terraced garden with a goldfish pool and several bubbling streams running off from it. The palms were strung with colored Christmas lights, which turned lentil curry or saffron rice or cold peanut soup, odd shades of red and green. She sat at her metal table one night waiting for her check and had the choice of craning her neck to look up through the Christmas lights into the night sky or staring directly into the kitchen, where her waitress and a friend stood laughing with a young man in a square African hat who had just come up the steps from the street. He had his arm around both of them, and that night Mrs. Medina had felt a little left out of everything. She had returned to the apartment and got a gin and sat on the deck watching the beetles crawl up from underneath the pier. She decided to go back to Boston early the next morning.

But that was the night before her date with Sam, so of course going back to Boston was impossible.

Mrs. Medina put on her green-and-white flowered sundress and stretched out on the bed. On the ceiling, water moved the light. The air was still with heat. The slap of water against the pilings. She tried to think of smiling.

At two precisely, Sam Brathwaite knocked three times on the iron gate.

Sam drove carefully in his old but clean Rover, with an air freshener shaped like a vanilla bean swinging from the rearview mirror. "Sorry, no cold air in this bus," he said. "But when we get up on the mountain we feel the trades and it will cool down some."

He drove slowly through the center of town. "We just pass the courthouse," he said. "And there is the prison. Room for thirty-six and the gallows."

Surprised at having the prison pointed out, Mrs. Medina looked at the plain, white structure with no windows. "Why don't they paint it blue?" she asked. "Or yellow? Like everything else?"

"Not like everything else," he said, making a wide turn to the right. "It's a serious place. There they hang people. They do give it a red door," he added.

She wondered about the crimes. She could not imagine murder on this island; the place did not seem complex enough.

They began to climb the hill in steep switchbacks, the Rover groaning in second gear, passing poor shacks in the heat, with dirt yards, an occasional pig or goat snoozing in the shade. Along the road the concrete shoulders were often crumbled away, their remains strewn down the hillside amid a confusion of vines and flowers. Mrs. Medina took off her straw hat and fanned herself. Above them coral and cream stucco villas with arcaded loggias looked out placidly over the water.

"Emancipation came to Tortola in 1834," Sam said, glancing up.

The air was growing cooler. They passed children with books slung across their backs, fooling around in the road, and several men on their way down the hill leading sad little donkeys. Many carried machetes, which they raised in grim salutes. After some time they arrived at an intersection marked Ridge Road and Sam turned right, toward the east. They were up quite high, and now the channel could be seen, long and dark, on their right, and Peter and Cooper Islands, and away through the haze, the humps of Virgin Gorda. She could hear the boom of the Atlantic surf below on their left, although for the moment it was out of sight. Sam drove on and didn't seem disturbed by her silence.

"I been everywhere," he remarked presently. "I been to Russia and I been to Australia. In Russia they confiscated my radio."

And then quite suddenly the broad Atlantic was beneath them, pounding in from the north with its great rollers.

"Beneath us is Josiah's Bay. It is serious water," Sam said with a smile, and pulled off the road slightly to where several benches had been strategically placed. They both got out of the car and walked to the edge of the cliff, and then, by silent assent, sat down. "These benches are here so that anyone can pause and look anytime they choose."

"That's a beautiful beach down there," Mrs. Medina said. "I wonder why it's deserted?" The surf was slamming into the piles of rocks that guarded the bay and flinging mammoth gouts of foam twenty feet into the air. But the inner beach was deep and white and quiet. The ocean stretched off to the northeast in three different shades of blue: aquamarine close to shore, then a blue that could have been the sky, and finally, in the far distance, the profound ink-blue that suggested bottomless places.

Sam frowned and peered over. "Surf's comin' in hard today. Those are what's called northern swells. Big waves, start from a storm in the north Atlantic and don't stop until they run into these islands."

Back away from the water was a small palm grove, and Mrs. Medina now observed that the beach was not completely unoccupied. Someone was down there, someone had risen from a beach chair and was walking toward the rocks.

"There's somebody down there, it looks like," she said, shading her eyes. "He's about to climb up on the rocks."

"That's no he. I can tell without lookin' that's Mrs. Vitti-Fraser," Sam said. "Didn't know she was back. How she love to do that, stand on the rocks and let the water fall all around her like a shower bath. Big wave knock her off once. Didn't stop her."

A distant figure in yellow emerged on the farthest rocky promontory and disappeared into the cascades of water.

"Will she be all right?" Mrs. Medina said.

"Oh, sure. She know this beach." He stood up. "Now, we better get underway. I still must take you to Long Look, where the Quakers came, and then all along the north shore road to see some interesting road improvements."

"I'll tell you what, Sam," Mrs. Medina said, starting for the car, "why don't we divide this tour into two parts and finish the north coast another day. Let's just go up—to Bomba's, is it?—and sit down and have a drink. What do you say?"

"Fine with me, if that what you want." He started the car. "Not because I am failing as a guide, I hope."

"Certainly not."

He made a U-turn and headed west across the Ridge Road, but after a few minutes he couldn't resist one last fact.

"Largest marlin ever caught in these parts was off Anegada." He pointed back over his shoulder. "One thousand one hundred and forty-five pounds. Ten feet long."

~

Coral Bobb's restaurant was perched on an outcropping of rock three quarters of the way up Mount Bellevue, looking southwest over Road Harbor and the channel. A squall had passed through as they were leaving Bomba's and rain had fallen in a tumult for ten minutes or so. Then the light had risen like a great outstretching of arms, and above them was the salmon palette of sunset.

"We got a jolting road here," Sam said. "This one so steep they can't get machinery up to fix it. Hold on."

Mrs. Medina was thrown about the front seat and finally rolled her window completely down and grabbed the roof of the car.

"Oh, boy," Sam said, "here come a big crack in the road." As he slowed, Mrs. Medina heard the dripping world around her, exuding aromas of earth and the deep green of plants, and through the tangle of trees and vines she saw the town appearing below.

Sam made a one-eighty turn and proceeded along a smoother, flatter gravel driveway, which led into a small courtyard.

"We have beat Marianne and Cyril," he said with some satisfaction. "You have time to powder your nose before we commence, if you like."

They walked around the outside of the house and entered the dining room, and though they heard clattering from the kitchen, there was no one else about. The red-tiled room held about fifteen tables, each set up with brilliant white-lace place mats atop a linen tablecloth of an arresting carmine color. She walked out onto the terrace, which ran the width of the building, and looked at the town below and the darkening water, and the lights beginning to come on.

"I make you a rum punch better than Bomba's," Sam said, handing her a glass. "See those twinking lights, over there in the far distance? That's St. Croix, thirty-five miles over the water."

Mrs. Medina sipped her drink. It was, in fact, much better than the rum punch at Bomba's.

"You see why I almost married Coral Bobb," Sam said. "I almost married her for her view." Mrs. Medina laughed. "There, that got a laugh from you."

"A view is a good enough reason to marry someone," she said. "As good as love, maybe."

"It depends," he said. "Love is okay, but brings its own troubles. Me, I'm glad to be in the pasture now, not lookin' for adventure."

The breeze blew sweetly against their faces.

"You must love it here," she said to him.

"Well," he said, "you ain't seen the bad spots."

"The lights at night would be enough for me."

"I wanted to be a waiter in London. My brother has a restaurant there, in Ladbroke Grove. You familiar with that neighborhood?"

She thought about the places she knew in London. "No," she said, "I'm not. Why didn't you go?"

He set his drink down on the railing. "I was too old a man when the idea struck me. Comes a point in life when change is disagreeable. You want to wake up in the morning and know what to expect."

"I suppose that's true."

"And that is a sad, sad moment. Because life is very dull when you don't get hit with an unexpected thing every now and then. Adds the color, adds the hot sauce to gettin' on from day to day." He sighed. "Now I feel often like I'm lookin' from afar, you know, just like you're lookin' down on these harbor lights, not knowin' what's goin' on in Wesley Potter's place halfway down the hill—is he once again about to blow up his outhouse? Overhead, there comes Abercrombie, maybe, flyin' the six-fifteen in from St. Thomas, and has he been partaking of the weed? Will he put his wheels on the runway or in the scrub? Across the way there, that villa with the light that just went on. There live Mr. Jack Hitchcock, who for two years has deeply loved Raffi, young man up from Dominica, who works down at the Moorings in the office of the dockmaster. This boy is the love of his life."

Mrs. Medina became alert.

"And so I watch now," Sam concluded. "And I suppose it is for the best. But it's gettin' hard to keep my spirit up."

"If—" Mrs. Medina began.

There was a loud roar from beneath the terrace and a ferocious tearing of gravel.

"Oh, boy," Sam said. "That's Cyril in his big boat tryin' to make that turn. I go direct him."

The dinner had been very good. Mrs. Medina had eaten "nonendangered" dolphin in a Creole sauce and some spicy rice, and they all had drunk too much rum, except for Marianne, who was due at the hospital at seven in the morning. Now it was nearly ten, and there were only a couple of tables left, finishing coffee. The jitney bus back down to Road Town had just departed. Coral Bobb came out of the kitchen to join them.

"You all ain't tired yet?" she said. She was a short, ample woman of about sixty-five, with strong forearms. She was wearing high platform wedgies, and her hair was up in a small, tight bun. "Time for my special dessert," she said.

"Oh, Coral," Marianne said, "I cannot eat another bite." She was sitting with her hand on Cyril's back.

Cyril sat with his fist under his chin, smoking a thin cigar. "I wonder," he said, "whether that beef was delivered. Could be I should call."

"Nothin' to be done about that now, Cyril," Sam said.

"He likes to worry," Marianne said. "Let him worry." She moved her head in a way that reminded Mrs. Medina of Tina, with a small smile, as if someone had just paid her a compliment. Marianne was a quiet woman, serious, almost stern. She had her hair bound up in a green silk scarf, whose tails trailed down her back.

Mrs. Medina closed her eyes. She thought she was probably drunk, but she wasn't sure. What should she do? If Patrick were here, he would order another round of drinks for everyone and start one of his long "tales of the trail," as he liked to call them. Now she felt it was time for her to do something. She must stand in for Patrick. These people had been very kind to her, but she didn't think she could laugh again; she had tried too hard and her face hurt. So she must do something else. Was this what her life would be like? Always thinking about what to say, having to respond and listen and say the right things, and not offend? *Not offend.* If Patrick were here, he would tell his tales and listen to the tales of others, and ask the questions that would draw the others to him and not go home until dawn.

"Here is my piece of resistance," Coral said, returning with a tray. "Banana flambé."

Sam sat up straighter and kissed his fingertips. "Bananas from heaven," he said.

Coral passed around the plates, each of which contained one banana, sliced lengthwise, reclining in a pool of dark rum sauce.

"My special sauce," Coral said. "But she needs to be lit up. Then the nuts go on."

"Matches, Coral, you forget them?" Sam said.

Coral pulled a large box of kitchen matches from her apron pocket. "Who will do the honor?"

Mrs. Medina, who had always had anything flambé delivered to her table already ablaze, said, "I will." She took out a long match.

"Now, careful," Marianne said. "Coral is known for her strong rum sauce."

"Well," Mrs. Medina said, extending the match toward Marianne's plate, "it's simply a matter of just touching the tip of the fire, like this—"

And with those words Marianne's plate ignited in a brilliant flame that rose with a great whoosh at least three feet into the air. It was gone in an instant, but Mrs. Medina and Marianne fell to the floor with a great clatter of chairs, and there was the distinct odor of scorched hair. When Mrs. Medina peered up from under the table, the banana was burning merrily, and she and Marianne began to laugh.

A voice from the door said, "I see I'm not too late for the games."

"Diana!" Cyril said, and scraped his chair back.

Mrs. Medina thought about getting up, but for the moment couldn't coordinate her legs and knees, and the woman in the doorway gave her an amused look over the flaming banana as if the two of them had made an appointment and one of them had missed it. But then she smiled and removed her small round glasses, which seemed to be tinted lavender. "It looks like Coral has been busy with the rum sauce again."

"Miscalculation," Coral said, moving about the table and lighting up the remaining bananas, all of which caught fire in an orderly manner. Mrs. Medina and Marianne brushed themselves off and sat back down.

"Coral," Diana said, "I've just come from popping Jeremy onto his flight to Antigua, and I'm in need of a proper drink. I do not want a flaming banana, thank you. Am I too late?"

"Don't be foolish, woman," Coral said, waving out the last match. "Come over here and sit down."

Cyril gathered himself together for introductions, but the woman walked up to Mrs. Medina and shook her hand. "I'm Diana Vitti-Fraser," she said. "You're from under the table, the only one I don't know."

"Oh, yes," Mrs. Medina said, brushing some bits of ash from her forearm. "We saw you on the rocks today."

"You did?" She looked down and smiled. "Who did?"

"She was worried about you," Sam said. "I tell her you know well what you're doin'."

"Mount Gay fine with you?" Coral said from the door to the bar.

"Perfect," Diana said. She sat next to Marianne, who leaned over and kissed her on the cheek. "You were worried about me on the rocks? I'm so pleased. No one thinks to worry about me on those rocks anymore. Oh, thank you, Coral dear." She sipped her rum. "Now, would someone tell me the name of this gracious lady who was so concerned about my safety?"

Mrs. Medina colored. "Oh, sorry," she said. "I'm Mercedes Medina. I've been trying to set fire to the table, I think."

"Well, I'm glad I happened upon this exciting company," Diana said with satisfaction.

Diana was decidedly British, with darkish blond hair that had been casually pushed behind her ears but was already showing a tendency to fall down over her cheekbones. Her chin narrowed to a determined set under a wide mouth that—when she smiled—lifted a bit higher on the left side, as if she were thinking of a private joke. She was wearing a longish flowered skirt and a low-cut white shirt that, despite their simplicity, had a distinct air of chic about them. Mrs. Medina was startled to see earrings of coral and shell swinging from her ears, startled because for the first time they looked very right. It was difficult to tell how old she was, because her body was what Patrick used to call "healthy and volupt," and the only lines Mrs. Medina could detect were several small ones on each side of her mouth. Early fifties, perhaps.

She's too cheerful, Mrs. Medina thought. *I can't bear it. And I can't be nice to anyone else tonight.* She suddenly missed Patrick painfully.

"Excuse me," she said, and walked out onto the terrace.

Outside it was cool, and a breeze was coming in off the channel. Road Town harbor lay in a horseshoe of quiet light, and she could see the running lights of a couple of boats passing just in front of where her little apartment should be. Her bed was there too. She wished she were in it. She wished she were in it with Patrick, not talking, simply listening to his breathing, touching his back from time to time.

"Not something I said?" Diana had come out to join her. "Sorry, that's a tired old remark."

Mrs. Medina wiped her eyes with her handkerchief. "Just a long day. I thought some air might help."

"So right. It's been too long a day." She sipped her drink, and Mrs. Medina heard the companionable jostling of ice against the glass in the dark. "I can't say I'm sorry to have my growing lad out from under my feet. I think I'll probably sleep nicely tonight, thank you very much."

"How old is he?" Mrs. Medina asked politely.

"Jeremy? Oh, seventeen or so," Diana said. "I can never remember exactly." She laughed. "He was with me today, down at Josiah's Beach. Out in the water."

"You mean swimming? I didn't see him. That was quite a surf."

"He had his surfboard, actually. He's rather good. I've nearly ceased to worry about him, to tell you the truth." She brushed her hair back from her face. "You still worry about your children? Or have you given up?"

"Well, I don't have children." She started to go on, but thought, *Damn it, I don't have to explain anything.*

"Smart move, that," Diana said. Her voice was low and pleasantly supple.

"I—" Mrs. Medina began.

"You—" Diana spoke at the same time.

They laughed. "You first," Mrs. Medina said.

Diana turned to face her. "I've been thinking about your name," she said. "It rings a very distinct bell. Some years back, ten or so, I heard a wonderful cellist named Medina. Can't think of his first name. In London it was, not Albert Hall. It must have been at the ghastly Barbican Center, with the London Symphony, I think. An older man, utterly sublime."

"Patrick Medina."

"Yes! That's him. Don't tell me—he's your father."

"No. My husband."

Diana put her glass down on one of the tables. "Not a day of it," she said. "Why, this is wonderful. Is he with you?"

"No, he died in January. I'm sure he would have loved being here, though."

"Ah," Diana said. "I'm sorry." She put both hands on the terrace rail and stretched her arms. "That was a truly memorable evening. Dvořák, I believe it was. Were you there?"

"Yes, I guess I must have been." She laughed. "He wasn't fond of the Dvořák."

"Well, it wasn't apparent. It was a very moving performance."

"You're very kind. He didn't do a lot of solo work. He always preferred playing with his chamber group."

"Then I consider myself fortunate to have heard him."

Mrs. Medina, to her astonishment, burst into tears. And quite suddenly Cyril, Marianne, and Sam all thronged onto the terrace, ready to depart. She turned her face away.

Diana took over. "You lot finally ready to call it a night?"

"I've got him on his feet," Marianne said, her arm around Cyril's waist. "Now I must get him across the mountain."

"One more drink?" Sam said brightly. Coral Bobb came up and removed the bottle of rum from his hand.

"Sam, I must work at seven A.M.," Marianne said. "And our guest must be exhausted with you lecturing at her all the long afternoon."

"She love every word," Sam said.

Mrs. Medina blew her nose and turned around. "Yes, I did," she said. "It was a grand tour."

"The best," Sam said. With that he sank onto one of the low couches and spread his arms out across the cushions. "And now, good night."

Cyril moved forward quickly. "None of that, Samuel," he said. "You have to escort your lady to her door."

"He's out," Coral Bobb said. "I know him, he's out for good." She went over and fanned his face with a large red napkin.

There was a moment of silence.

"I can run you home, Mercedes," Diana said. "Where are you staying?"

"I will wake that man," Cyril said.

"No," Coral said, "you will not be able. The drink has overtaken him." She shook her head sadly. "He no longer have legs for it."

"It's no trouble for me to take her," Diana said. "Cyril, don't make a fuss about it. Let Sam sleep it off here." She threw her sweater around her shoulders.

"I'm at Cyril's waterfront apartments," Mrs. Medina said.

"Perfect," Diana said. "Right on my way."

"Cyril, you just help me lift his feet up," Coral said. "There, that's fine. I get his shoes off, and he sleep the night here. Won't be the first time."

In the gravel parking area the air was thick with the sweet scent of frangipani. Diana got into her Austin Mini and threw a canvas bag into the backseat. "Hop in," she said. "Just toss your hat in back. Lucky the surfboard's back at the house."

They bumped and lurched down the hill in silence until the conditions of the road became so treacherous that they demanded conversation.

"Sorry," Diana said. "Am I going too fast? Road's a bit of an axle breaker."

Mrs. Medina shook her head. "If you go any slower, we'll never get to the bottom. The air's nice, anyway."

Some overgrown vines whipped in through the window and smacked Mrs. Medina in the face.

Diana shifted down in one of the switchbacks and her left hand brushed Mrs. Medina's thigh in the darkness. "Well," Mrs. Medina said quickly, "I should practice driving something with the wheel on the right, like this."

"Not driven here yet, then?"

"No. I thought I might like to get out to that beach where you were today. I thought I could rent a car."

"Yes. Lovely beach. Tremendous surf." She swerved to avoid a pig that was trotting along the verge of the road as if he had business to attend to. Shortly after that the road smoothed out a bit and the incline downward became less precarious.

"So," Diana said, glancing sideways at her, "you here for long?"

"I've been here for two weeks almost. Another two, probably."

"You here alone? Stop me if I'm getting too curious."

"Quite alone. And happy to be alone. Cyril and Marianne see this as a sign of a terminal personality disorder."

Diana threw back her head and laughed. Mrs. Medina looked at her. *Patrick would like this one,* she thought.

They finally came to the bottom of the hill just past the gas storage tanks and turned toward Road Town.

"Are you a permanent resident?" Mrs. Medina asked.

"More or less. Some months here, some months not. I own some jewelry shops—*boutiques* is the fancy word, I suppose. Native artists, that sort of thing. One here, one in St. Martin, another in Antigua. I have to go check up on those from time to time, and then I usually go back to London for longer spells. My London branch, the size of a breadbox, is all set to open."

"It sounds hectic."

"It suits me." She was driving faster now, and they sped past the roller arena, a large, screened, open-air building in which a convention of freight trains seemed to be shifting tracks to a reggae beat. A silver ball rotated slowly from the ceiling, illuminating for a moment the figure of a tall man with a head full of white curls who was just emerging from one of the palm groves outside. He crossed the road behind them, and Diana gave her horn a squeak and raised her arm.

"Jack Hitchcock," she said, glancing in her rearview mirror. "Going to pick up Raphael."

Mrs. Medina looked back at him. *He's the one with the boy,* she remembered.

"Know him?" Diana asked.

"No, no," Mrs. Medina said quickly.

"Looked as if you might have," Diana said with a smile. "Nice fellow."

Diana pulled quickly into the little gravel parking area in front of Mrs. Medina's iron gate.

"Thank you so much," Mrs. Medina said, opening the door. "I'm sure Cyril and Marianne were glad not to have to make the trip down the hill."

"Pleasure." She gunned the engine and looked across at Mrs. Medina with a quizzical smile. "Nice to have someone new to talk to."

Mrs. Medina unfolded herself from the tiny car and stood up. "Yes. Well, I'll say good night."

"Say," Diana leaned her head across and spoke out the window, "if I decide to take a run over to Josiah's Beach again, I'll give you a ring. Maybe you'd like to come along."

"That might be nice." She would deal with it later. Diana was too damn nice.

Diana backed onto the road with a spray of gravel and sped off westward. One of her rear taillights was out.

Mrs. Medina undressed without turning on a light. She opened both windows to the deck and fell into bed without bothering to search for her nightshirt.

three

Sometime in the night it rained briefly, and Mrs. Medina came half awake and heard the downpour, which began and ended as if someone had opened the great valves of a giant tank then shut them off abruptly. In the dripping aftermath, the boats tied up at the pier slopped about quietly and a small breeze meandered through the louvers and touched her cheek, bringing with it the smell of damp creosote from the pilings and the increasingly familiar aroma of engine fuel. She was actually surprised that she was still here, in this disorienting country of color and water, the passage of days marked only by the sun. She had even lost track of what day of the week it was.

Odd that Diana had been at that London concert.

Patrick, Patrick, she thought, *that Dvořák will haunt us forever.* She curled up around her pillow in an odd aura of relief, as if someone were behind her, holding her.

Dear Tina, she began, and put down her pen. The morning was already hot on the deck, and she went inside for her straw hat. She stood by her bed and remembered it in the back of Diana's car.

Well, that was stupid. No hat. She took the old blue-and-green baseball cap she had seen hanging in the kitchen and put it on. It seemed clean enough.

Cyril and Marianne have been extraordinarily attentive, and I feel very well taken care of. I'm becoming addicted to the conch fritters at Cyril's restaurant, which is a few steps up the road.

She looked up. "I might as well say, 'Having a wonderful time. Wish you were here,' " she said aloud.

Irritably, she swept her paper aside. Next door, on the cement steps leading down to the water, an older black man, shirtless, was cleaning fish with a large knife, chopping against the cement in a regular rhythm. The heads and guts he tossed into the water. A damp, unlit cigarette hung from his lips.

"Oh, come on, Mary," he sang out suddenly. "Come on and take me home."

"Shut up, Camden," a woman's voice called from the apartment above the steps. But in a friendly way. Then, "Camden? You want a soda?"

"Time for town," Mrs. Medina muttered to herself.

She sat at her usual table on the porch at Village Cay Marina and tried again to write to Tina. This time she had picked a postcard with a view of Cyril's restaurant. She had asked for some orange juice because it was really, this time, too hot for coffee. Across the harbor a tender from one of the big cruise ships was disgorging a group of pastel-clad tourists.

Several tables down was the man she now knew was Jack Hitchcock. In spite of the heat he had on a light blue seersucker jacket and a white shirt open at the collar, and he did not look uncomfortable. His spectacular head of white curls started an inch or so above his ears and ended in windblown confusion. He was carefully working a crossword puzzle with a pen.

One of the largish waitresses sauntered out to him with a plate of fried eggs and bread, and a bowl of melon slices. She circled his table once, as if to get his attention, and from back under the awning, at the bar, Mrs. Medina heard the giggles of the other girls.

"Here is your breakfast, Mr. Jack," the waitress said, leaning her ample breasts over the table.

"Thank you very much, Naneen," he said, looking up.

Mrs. Medina hadn't expected him to raise his head so quickly, but he did and caught her watching him. She was grateful for her sunglasses, and took a quick sip of her juice, then bent over her card to Tina.

Dear Tina, This is Cyril's restaurant. I go there every day for lunch, conch fritters very good. She tried to call up some memory, some point at which she could begin to speak to Tina in a spontaneous way that would reflect their genuine friendship. *Everyone here asks about you and Sandra. Weather fine. Love, M.* She got a stamp out of her billfold and put some coins on the table. She had an odd, sudden inclination to speak to Jack Hitchcock but couldn't think of how she might approach him. So she was surprised when, as she rose to go, he looked up and gave her a wry little smile. She smiled back.

~

"Now, this track isn't nearly as bone cracking as the road down from Coral Bobb's," Diana said, "but then again we're not in a bloody Jag either, so hold on." She turned the Austin down into a steeply inclining grass road and Mrs. Medina heard the sound of the surf. "Oh, your hat's in the back there. Didn't notice it till this moment."

At the bottom, past Josiah's Pond, Josiah's Bay opened out in a broad arc, armed at each distant point by the massive piles of rocks. The surf again was beating loudly in, foaming high against the rocks, but on the inner beach the water made a long bubbling run in and receded gently.

Diana parked in a grove of palms. There were two bicycles leaning up against the trees, but no one seemed to be about. She stepped around a couple of small cacti and walked away through the scrub to the sand.

Mrs. Medina took a bite of the orange she had peeled. It was blood red. "It looks like you can walk out pretty far into the water," she said. "Before the surf starts to agitate." She spat out a pip into her hand, then tossed it aside.

Diana nodded. "Yes." She leaned back in her beach chair. "But it's tricky." She was in blue shorts. Her full breasts hung nicely within a snug, ribbed white tank top, and Mrs. Medina gave her a quick glance. *Perhaps she isn't in her fifties,* she observed. *Perhaps she's forty-five.* She wiped her hands on a saturated towel. Diana had put on Mrs. Medina's straw hat.

"You don't seem the type to lie about on beaches," Diana said, turning her head to look at her. "Did you bring a bathing costume?"

"No, my shorts will be fine for now."

Diana leaned back and closed her eyes. After a little while she said, "It's nice and peaceful here with you. Thank God you don't want to talk. Jeremy was driving me barmy." She sat with one leg straight out, the other up, bent at the knee. Mrs. Medina, dreamy in the heat, allowed her eyes to rest on the flesh of Diana's thigh as it emerged from beneath the cuff of her shorts, the graceful way the ridge of her thigh muscle made its way down the plane of her leg and followed the contour of her calf to her ankle. All in one gesture, as it were. Just to the side of her knee there was a small blue bruise.

Mrs. Medina looked, remembering Lennie's legs. She took a deep breath. Something stirred.

Diana sat up and began to rub some cream on her skin. Although they were more or less under the palms, there was no escaping the sun; the brilliant light seemed to be blown in by the wind. Diana's skin was the color of blushed apricots, and her chest was attractively freckled under her tan. Mrs. Medina looked at her own white flesh with dismay. She lay back on her towel and closed her eyes.

They walked along the top of the surf line, and the cool, incoming water slithered under their bare feet. The sand was white, the sun was white. The wind was hard in their faces. Mrs. Medina stooped and picked up a small pink stone.

"I call this the white hour," Diana said. "Between one and three. Complete absence of color. Except for the sea."

Back under the palms, Diana unscrewed a thermos of rum punch. "This will probably knock you on your bum," she said with a laugh.

"Thanks very much. I didn't think to bring anything."

"And cold chicken and cucumbers on white bread. Unsophisticated, but you'd better have one if you're going to drink the rum," Diana said. "Here. Crisps in the bag there."

"Is it time for lunch?"

"Does it matter?"

The punch was icy, and Mrs. Medina quickly drank half her cup.

"Like my specs?" Diana asked. She held them up to the light. "Purple lenses. They're Jeremy's. He left them in the car."

"I noticed them the other night. Do they really keep out the sun?"

"Not much. He's trying to project an attitude, I think they call it." She put them back on. "How's the punch?"

"I'm used to it warmer. But this is perfect, more refreshing."

"Good."

They lay back in the heat that the steady wind off the water could not completely dispel. A bee flew low over Mrs. Medina's face, and she sat up and brushed it away. She felt a bit out of sorts; the rum had enlivened her for a while, but now she was thinking about her cool bed off the deck, the afternoon routines she had abandoned.

"Does anyone else ever come here?" she said.

Diana sat up also. "You looking for entertainment?" she asked with a smile. Then she shaded her eyes and looked off down the beach. "Well, fancy. Here come Jack and Raphael. Just in the nick."

Jack Hitchcock had his trousers rolled up above his ankles and was carrying his seersucker jacket over his arm. He squinted into the palm grove.

"Come on over," Diana called to him. "We still have some punch."

Jack walked toward the palm grove with Raphael trailing behind him. Diana made introductions.

"I saw you at breakfast," Jack said, bending to shake Mrs. Medina's hand.

"Sit," Diana gestured to part of the enormous towel on which Mrs. Medina was already perched.

"Sorry, Raffi has to get back to work," Jack said. "And we're on our bikes."

"Hey, Jack, I could use a little drink. Long ride back, man." Raphael squatted down, and Diana handed him the thermos. Jack remained standing, leaning against the tree. He had a pleasant, weathered face, with an odd nose that looked as if it had been pinched at the end.

Raphael Dicken was tall and slender with a hard, flat chest that showed his ribs. But his shoulders were broad, and his skin was the intoxicating color of dark, shined mahogany. He was about twenty-five, Mrs. Medina guessed. His full lips broke into a boyish smile as he contemplated his cup of punch. "This will hit the spot," he said.

Jack had picked a blade of scrub grass and was sucking it. "You're at one of Cyril's places, aren't you?" he asked Mrs. Medina.

"Yes, for another couple of weeks."

"Jack, old thing, you have a book of mine that I need back rather urgently," Diana said.

"Oh, yes, the Hazan cookbook. I have one more small dish I want to try."

"Did you try the vitello tonnato?"

"I did indeed. Raffi pronounced it splendid."

Raffi smiled at Mrs. Medina. "Good stuff," he said. "Cold veal with a tunny sauce."

"I've had it," Mrs. Medina said. "I love it too."

"I don't understand, Raffi," Diana said, "how you can eat Jack's meals and stay so bloody thin."

Raffi raised his chin in a superior smile. And as he did so, there was a sudden crackling of brush behind them and a hail of stones sailed past his head. One, in fact, glanced off his cheek.

"Hey!" Jack said, straightening up. Diana leapt to her feet as well.

Behind them three teenage boys stood on the edge of the scrub, their hands full of rocks. They simultaneously began to shout, first in English, and then in patois as they grew more furious. Another rain of rocks clattered through the palm fronds.

Raffi stood up now, and Mrs. Medina scrambled up as well. Raffi held his hand against his cheek.

Jack started through the scrub toward the boys. "Piss off, you sodding bastards," he shouted at them. This enraged them even more, but then Diana stepped up beside Jack and said, "Othman Potter, I know your mother well. You should be ashamed of yourself. Now, take your friends and go. Leave us alone."

The boys glanced at Othman Potter, who gave Diana a dark look. Then Jack picked up a large piece of driftwood and started toward them. They turned and ran back up toward the pond. "Faggot!" the last one called over his shoulder.

"Raffi," Diana said, returning to him. "Are you all right?"

He raised his hand. "No harm done." Jack came up beside him and looked closely at his cheek. "No harm done, man," Raffi said. He leaned his elbow on Jack's shoulder, and Mrs. Medina could see his arm trembling.

"No harm indeed," Jack said. "Ignorant buggers."

"You know those nice lads, then, Raffi?" Diana asked him. "Here, have the last of the punch."

"They're just kids," he said. "From Cripple's Rest." But he sank down onto the towel.

Mrs. Medina was profoundly shocked. She had never in her life been attacked like that. And yet they had not been attacking her. She had just been there, in the line of fire. Jack was attending to Raffi, and he finally turned around and said, "It'll just be a bruise, I think."

"I'll have a talk with Othman's mother," Diana said.

"No! No, don't do that, Diana," Raffi said. "It will make things bad."

"Things are bad now," Diana said.

Jack stood up. "He's right, of course."

"Is there something I can do?" Mrs. Medina asked helplessly.

"Yes," Diana said. "Help me pack up all this baggage. We'll try to sardine everyone into the Mini."

"The bikes," Raffi said. "My bike is new."

"I'll get my car and come back for the bikes," Jack said. "Come on now. Diana's right."

"Pay attention, Jack," Diana said, folding up the towel. "They were after you too, you know."

The Mini groaned up the grassy road, and there was no sign of the boys. Mrs. Medina was crammed into the rear seat thigh to thigh with Raffi, and his body shuddered from time to time as if he were very cold. Jack gave him occasional looks as if to assure himself that he was all right.

Diana patted the dash. "If this little baby makes it up the hill, I swear I'll never malign her again." She had put on a lightweight denim shirt, rolled to the elbows.

They finally achieved the Ridge Road again, and Diana turned west, into the lowering sun.

"Don't go down through Cripple's Rest," Jack said. "Take the cut through by the bait shop."

"Right."

Raffi ran his hands over the top of his head and then put his head in his hands.

After a little while, Jack said, "What do you hear from Lily, Diana?"

"Not a word. Well, one small card to let me know she got back to Paris all right."

Jack put his arm across the back of Diana's seat and patted her shoulder. "Nice of her."

"Thought so." Diana took the turn by the bait shop, and soon they were heading down the hill again at an oblique angle, skirting the northern fringes of Road Town.

"You're knocking about in that house, I imagine, now that she's gone," Jack went on. "You should close it up, move into town."

"I love that house. Anyway, it's half Nigel's."

"Well, you must come to dinner, then."

Diana lifted her chin and tilted her head, as if to remove a stray lock of hair from her face. "That sounds like a better alternative."

"When are you off to London?"

"I don't know yet. There's a bit of a cock up with the books at the West End shop here. I've been trying to straighten it out. Hilarene's living in a dream world out there. She's developed a passion for one of the blokes who drives the St. John ferry, and she has no mind for anything else. Last week she rang up one hundred forty dollars on the till, no sale. Took me a while to figure *that* out."

Jack laughed.

"Ah, here we are, then, safe and sound." She pulled into a short paved drive leading up to Jack's bungalow, the shaded coral house that Mrs. Medina and Sam had observed from Mrs. Bobb's on the other side of the harbor. The sun was just below the tip of the mountain behind them now, and was casting long, peaceful shadows through a grove of avocado trees behind Jack's house, in which a group of sparrows was making preparations for the evening.

"Well," Jack said, shaking Mrs. Medina's hand, "next time a more pleasant outing, let's hope."

Mrs. Medina continued to feel as if she were walking in space. No one had chosen to explain the incident at the beach to her, so she didn't know if she should express her dismay, be solicitous to Raffi, or even acknowledge that it had happened. But she felt oddly allied with Jack and wanted to let him know that. She searched unsuccessfully for appropriate words, and finally just leaned forward from the backseat and shook Jack's hand and agreed that the next time would be better.

"The plumbago seems to be doing nicely now," Diana said, examining the pale blue flowers of a line of shrubs beside the driveway.

"Yes. Carleton Smith came up and pruned some of the branches from the old tamarind there. They were blocking the sunlight."

Raffi had gone into the house and now ran down the steps with a small canvas bag. "Lady Di, may I ask you to run me down to the Moorings? Must be to work by five."

"Don't be disrespectful to the deceased, Raffi. Of course."

Jack kissed him on the cheek. "Chin up," he said. "See you later."

Mrs. Medina looked discreetly away, but she was certain Jack didn't care whether she saw or not.

"My place is nothing fancy," Mrs. Medina said later. "And I only have gin. But you're welcome to come in for a drink."

Diana switched off her engine. "That would be lovely. The Mini could use a bit of a rest. And I could use the loo."

On the deck their feet shared the rattan hassock, and they sat with their drinks and watched the harbor begin to light up. Then, improbably, the lilt of a band playing "Easy to Love" drifted across from the deep-water harbor, where a massive cruise ship with its dress lights ablaze lay in an aura of imminent festivity.

After a moment Diana asked, "Ever dance to Lester Lanin?"

"Many a time. Did you? I didn't know his band got out of the States."

"He had several that he sent about, I think. Wonderful music. My old dad took me out dancing to Lester Lanin the night before I went up to university."

Mrs. Medina remembered a rainy evening at the Rainbow Room in New York, with Manhattan lit up like an undersea city beneath them. They'd danced to one Cole Porter tune after another, and the hair on the back of Patrick's neck lay under her fingers like soft eider down.

"I suspect," Diana said, "you're wondering about that little incident back at the beach."

Mrs. Medina straightened up. "I was, a little. I couldn't imagine what they were doing—it didn't seem to matter who they were throwing at."

"It didn't. It's a pity you were there, actually. They're tormenting Jack and Raffi, but anyone in their company is fair game."

Mrs. Medina sipped her drink.

"Most of the people in town have more or less accepted Jack's relationship with Raffi," Diana said, "although they don't understand it. They're willing to let them go their own way. They are never, *never* asked to the governor's house for dinner, however—well, I joke, but Jack used to be. He could care less now." She paused for a moment. "The people here love Jack. He came to Tortola twenty years ago to teach in the school for ten months, and he never went back. He's a wonderful teacher and the kids loved him. He helped some of the bright ones go off to university. The older people here remember that."

"Then who are the kids with the rocks?" Mrs. Medina said.

"The kids with the rocks are from Cripple's Rest—most of them—it's a poorer settlement just north of the main part of town. The ones we saw today aren't the real problem. They're put up to it by the older blokes, the ones who want to get off the island and go to Miami or San Juan and get rich. But they can't because they don't have the money, so they stay here and take it out on everyone else. They cause all sorts of aggro. It's not a large group, just a few punks with nothing to do who've been influenced by bilge from the States, if you will pardon me. And there aren't so many left at the school who remember Jack. I'm sure Othman Potter has no idea Jack used some of his own money to help Othman's sister, Key-Linda, start up her launderette at Village Cay."

"Will you talk with his mother?"

Diana ran her fingers through her hair. "I don't know. She'd just beat the shit out of Othman and troubles would multiply, I'm afraid."

"Would you like another drink?"

Diana drained her glass. "One more. Then I'm off."

"So what will happen?" Mrs. Medina said, when she returned. Now it was nearly dark, although high above the hills the skies still held a wash of blue and coral, striped with long fingers of black cloud.

"I don't know. It may all just stop, if we're lucky."

Mrs. Medina turned and watched the lights come on at Cyril's up the way.

"Does it bother you?" Diana asked.

"It seems like a troublesome situation," Mrs. Medina said.

"No, I mean the relationship between Jack and Raffi. Does that sort of thing disturb you?"

"No," Mrs. Medina said quickly. "It's their business."

"A lovely, liberal point of view," Diana said with a smile.

Mrs. Medina stood up. "And now," she said, "it's been a long day."

"Yes, indeed," Diana said, finishing her drink. "I've overstayed and you must forgive me."

"No, you haven't overstayed," Mrs. Medina said. "I didn't mean that at all."

At the iron gate Diana turned to her and said, "Unless, of course, you'd like to join me for dinner. Out at my villa, so-called, in which I am by all accounts knocking about. Even without the Hazan cookbook I can cook up a mean pasta."

"I don't think so tonight, thanks," Mrs. Medina said.

"How about tomorrow?"

The two of them were standing quite close in the gateway, and Mrs. Medina was suddenly aware of the complex chemistry of fragrances the heat was drawing up from Diana's body, a combination of fresh shampoo and sweet perspiration. Mrs. Medina was surprised to find herself mildly aroused, and she abruptly remembered that it was April 18, Lennie's birthday.

She shook her head, as if to clear it. "Tomorrow, you mean?" she said to Diana.

"Or some other day." Diana had made no move toward her car.

"Tomorrow might be all right, it might be…"

"Good enough for me," Diana said. "I'll pick you up about six. You can practice driving my car."

Mrs. Medina shut the gate behind her and locked it, tension released from her shoulders. Then as she crossed the terrace she heard the telephone ring.

If I'd just stood with Diana five minutes more, she thought, *I wouldn't have to deal with it.*

But it was Tina, and Mrs. Medina was happy to hear her voice.

"Cousin Cyril taking care of you?" Tina asked.

"Yes, wonderfully." Mrs. Medina pushed the outer door shut with her foot. There was a large beetle staring at her from the middle of the tile floor. "You're sweet, Tina, to call and check up on me."

"That's not the only reason I called."

"My replacement can't handle the course, is that it?"

"No. In fact, I've had a call from your young friend."

Mrs. Medina bent her head and grimaced as if she had been struck with a sudden pain.

"Mercedes? You there?"

"Yes." She put her hand on the desk to steady herself.

"She called me, wants to know where you are."

Mrs. Medina watched the beetle waddle casually toward the couch and disappear underneath it. She became aware of the smell of damp canvas and the scent of lime on her hands. A motorbike accelerated outside on the road. She sat down on the chair by the telephone desk. "What did you tell her?"

"Nothing. Told her you weren't teaching, so she shouldn't come to the classroom. That's what she had in mind. I don't know whether she believes me or not."

Mrs. Medina rubbed her temples with her thumb and forefinger. "Did she say what she wanted?"

"She didn't tell me, but I'm sure I'll hear from her again. Should I give her this number?"

Mrs. Medina felt a little sick. The gin, probably, the emotional events of the day.

"Yes or no, Mercedes. I can't read your mind from this distance."

"Not just now, Tina. If you could just tell her I'm away for a while. Ask her to give you a number or an address."

"All right."

"Would you mind doing that?"

"Not at all. I have to wait for her to call me, you understand."

"Yes."

"Meeting some nice people there, Mercedes?"

"A few. I don't really fit in, but it doesn't bother me."

"You're down there for the quiet and for the sun, honey. It's not a social gig."

"I do miss you, Tina. You, I would love to see."

"Not a chance. End of April's looming. Papers, exams. Panic time for us all."

Mrs. Medina smiled. "Thanks for calling me."

"Cold as hell still up here, Mercedes. That should make you feel better."

Later, waiting for sleep, she realized she had grown comfortable with the vacant ache of Lennie's absence, even the more urgent ache of physical memory that ambushed her from time to time. She found she had been released in some way by the knowledge that Lennie had attempted to contact her; it was an intimate gesture, and one that had, oddly, loosened her feelings up a bit.

She wondered what Jack and Raffi were doing, whether they were driving back up the mountain, making love. There was an almost silent thrumming in the air outside as the cruise ship reversed out of the deep-water harbor and headed out for the overnight run to St. Martin.

And who, she wondered, *is Lily?*

The full moon fell across her pillow at about two-thirty, waking her. She had been dreaming of Patrick, a dream she couldn't remember, and she lay for a while thinking of him. She thought of what they had been doing in April of last year—nothing much, if memory served. *That was before Lennie*, she thought. *Long before.*

She rolled over on her stomach and lay her head on her folded arms, in the moonlight. She should probably think about leaving soon. She could not stay here forever. Back in Boston she would have to find some possibility in the emotional desolation that surely awaited her, but her sense of possibility—if it had ever existed—was now somewhere on the other side of this desolation, and she would have to find a way to get through it.

In the meantime, she had dinner with Diana to deal with. She turned onto her back. What should she wear?

~ four ~

"Y̶ou want to drive now?" Diana said the following evening. Mrs. Medina was locking the gate. A bottle of French merlot wrapped in a paper bag was tucked under her arm.

"No, I feel more like watching. I've never been much farther on this road than the bend up there."

"Off we go, then." The Austin rattled into the line of cars heading west. Great hot clouds were piling up above them in shifting explosions of shape.

"Squall coming," Diana said.

They sped past Prospect Reef Resort and then turned abruptly inland, skirting Sea Cow Bay where St. Paul's Episcopal Church, under its brilliant red roof, stood like a small Church Militant beside its overgrown graveyard. Beyond it rotting shacks hugged the side of the road, and tangled undergrowth climbed the hill behind. Just inside a broken wooden door an old man was preparing his dinner, frying a bit of something on a gas ring. They turned back toward the water and continued westward, past the Starving Man restaurant shack, with the darkening channel on their left. A magnificent ketch with light blue sails was making for the marina at Nanny Cay. At that point the road was so close to the water that Mrs. Medina could see clearly into the boat's cockpit, where drinks were being served to a group that seemed to be more interested in examining the great whorls of red and orange in the curdling sky.

Just past the cutoff road to the north side of the island, Diana turned left through a low, carved stone gate and drove in a cloud of dust along a drive lined with hibiscus and lavender crape myrtle, and just over the crest of a small rise she lurched to a stop. She sat back

and smiled. "I should have let you drive. I'm always in such a mad
rush to get back here. Welcome to Lone Palm. The lone palm is there,
down by the beach."

Mrs. Medina got out of the car, and a fresh wind off the channel
whipped against her skirt. Across an expanse of water, the lights of a
resort were appearing in the dusk, but they were not intrusive. Mrs.
Medina loved the place the minute her foot touched the sandy soil.

Diana's house was a low, two-story wooden plantation house facing the channel. Clean, neat, no extraneous jim-jam. A nearly flat roof.
Stairs to the second floor ascended the vine-covered exterior of the eastern wall, and facing the water was a long raised veranda under a deep
wooden overhang. The house had tall arched windows, in the island
style. The land surrounding the house was surrounded by low stone
walls, which extended down a shallow incline toward the water and out
of sight. The land had obviously been thoughtfully landscaped, but
with a casual sense of botanical style. Mrs. Medina recognized frangipani and flamboyant, and an enormous tulip tree in full bloom stood in
magnificent solitude about halfway to the water. Nearer the house was
a waterfall of yellow that Mrs. Medina thought might be an Indian
laburnum.

"A goddamned botanical riot," Diana said from the terrace.
"This cultivation is all Nigel's doing. My ex. Or soon to be. I myself
have a thumb black as a coal miner's lung. Come along up to the
veranda. Lovely time of evening."

Diana was rolling up several of the side canvas awnings. "Let's see
if the wind's too blustery."

"It's fine," Mrs. Medina said. "Leave them up. This is heavenly."

The veranda was furnished as if it were an extension of the main
living room, with plump upholstered wicker furniture spilling out the
three large doors, and there was every evidence that Diana spent much
of her time out here. A copy of *The English Patient* lay on a glass-
topped table, a page marked with a feather, and there were stacks of
paperbacks and magazines. Near the far end a woven hammock swung
lazily in the breeze.

"What are you drinking, then?" Diana asked from a small bar
against the rear wall. "Gin, right? Splash of tonic?"

"Fine, yes." Mrs. Medina seated herself on one of the sofas.

"So," Diana said, putting their drinks on the glass coffee table and tossing her hair off her cheek. "What do you—"

And as if those words were a cue, a loud, high-pitched whining sound began over the channel to the west, and came toward them quickly, growing painfully louder.

"What in the hell?" Diana said. She walked to the edge of the porch. Mrs. Medina joined her.

Right down the middle of Drake Channel, about a hundred feet above the water, came the evening flight from St. Thomas, its two propellers screaming. The top-mounted wings seemed to be yearning for vertical space, but the small plane continued in a horizontal path, past them in a shot.

"What is that fool Abercrombie up to now?" Diana said. They both walked off the veranda and toward the water. "I'm waiting for the explosion. He'll hit Mount Bellevue this time unless he goes straight on to Virgin Gorda."

Toward the east the stars were appearing, and the squall Diana had predicted had blown away somewhere else. From across the water came the sound of a steel band. They waited for disaster and watched the stars, and the wind, which had calmed, was sweet against their cheeks.

Then far down the coast they saw the plane rise at an unbearably steep attitude, and when it got high enough it leveled out, described a graceful circle, and disappeared in a slow descent toward Beef Island airport.

They stood silently in the dark. Then Diana said, "I don't know why they don't fire that stupid bugger. He's a peril. He pointedly abstains from alcohol, but he does love his marijuana, and it makes him happy, very happy indeed."

They walked back toward the house. "Does anyone complain about him?"

"No one who matters," Diana said. "My friend Lily was about to, but then Abercrombie offered her a discount rate on his special herb, as he calls it, so she conveniently lost interest in his other antics. I was tempted to offer my own services, in fact, at one point. I used to fly a bit. Nigel and I had a little Piper to get me about to my various island shops. Let my license lapse, though. Too expensive. Come on into the kitchen with me while I make the salad."

In Diana's house one airy room led gracefully into another, through a series of wide, arched doorways. They were finishing dinner at an oval mahogany table, by the light of several candles. Pale yellow walls ascended into darkness. A ceiling fan turned lazily above them.

"Wonderful pasta," Mrs. Medina said. "Where did you get all these different mushrooms?"

"Free ranging," Diana said, and laughed loudly. "Sorry, a private joke with my friend who's no longer here." She pushed her hair back out of her eyes and then rubbed them as if to extinguish a fatigue. "Some grow on the island," she said. "Some I borrowed from the kitchen of my accomplice Remy Tour, who runs the French restaurant out on the eastern coast road." She ate the last forkful of tagliatelle. "Your merlot goes very well with this. Thanks."

~

"The important thing," Diana said, "is to have as many windows as possible, and just as many ways to shade them all during the hottest part of the day. Of course, they can be a bit of a problem in a hurricane." They were standing in her bedroom, where enormous French doors were open onto a small porch. Soft curtains undulated in the breeze that had picked up again off the channel. Diana had switched on the small bedside lamps.

"You must sleep well in here," Mrs. Medina said.

"Yes," she said. "One can."

The bed was wide and made up with white sheets and a spread of cream-colored linen. The gauzy mosquito netting that fell down from a great hook in the ceiling gave the room a dream-like quality, which was intensified by the array of mirrors on the walls and the dim bedside lamps. On one of the bedside tables was a photograph in an ornamental silver frame. Mrs. Medina moved casually closer. The woman in the picture was in her late thirties, with short dark curls. She was slouched comfortably against one of the big trees in the garden, holding a tumbler of what appeared to be white wine, one long leg extended, the other crooked up. Her sunglasses rested on the end of her nose. She was barefoot and all in white, white duck pants and a flimsy white top that left her midriff bare and was loose enough to reveal the modest swell of one breast. She was looking seriously at the camera.

"That's Lily," Diana said.

"Sorry," Mrs. Medina said. Then, feeling she should say something, she added, "She's lovely."

"Yes, isn't she." Diana picked up the frame and studied the photograph. She wiped a smear off the edge of the glass with a corner of her shirt. "I can't take credit for her looks, however. But I am responsible for that look of barely controlled impatience she's wearing on her face."

"I see," Mrs. Medina said. "Well, perhaps we could have some coffee, if there's some available."

"There certainly is." Diana put down the frame. "And some Montenegro, if you're familiar with that concoction."

"Montenegro," Mrs. Medina said. "I haven't had that since Patrick and I were last in Italy."

"Memories for all of us, then," Diana said. "Come on. Outside stairs."

They sat on the veranda in the darkness, with two mosquito coils smoking into the air. The music from across the water had turned to something Latin, with occasional squalling trumpets, and it came in fits with the wind. It was comfortable when the wind came in, but when it died the air was warm and still. The stars were brilliant and strewn in handfuls across the black sky.

"There is no way to be anything but prosaic about stars," Mrs. Medina said.

"Yes. They're a damned nuisance that way."

"Do you mind living out here alone?"

"Not at all. Well, I wasn't alone, really, until about six weeks ago. I don't mind it. I adore the house. We've owned it for nearly twenty years, and it's survived hurricanes and attacks from various bugs and worms and growing children, and it's a comfort to me. It's an old plantation house, but God knows what it's doing on this land because there was never a plantation of any kind here. Someone had an idea, I suppose. It hadn't been lived in for years when we bought it. Perfectly rotten condition. Nigel fell in love with the land, and I fell in love with the house. Bought it straightaway. We eventually fell out of love with each other, but this house keeps us from completely severing our ties."

Mrs. Medina sipped her Montenegro and let the bitter sweetness remain on her tongue for a moment. She remembered the times she had drunk Montenegro with Patrick, in all sorts of places. It was their personal nightcap, a sign that the evening was about to draw to a peaceful close, that soon they would be in a room—somewhere—in the quiet of each other's company, completely alone. She could even feel herself slipping under the cool sheets, waiting for Patrick to finish in the shower, for the bed to sag slightly as he climbed in beside her.

"You're quiet," Diana said.

"This drink reminds me of Patrick."

"What a grand life it must have been, married to him."

"Yes. We had a good time."

"All that music. You could wake in the night and say, 'Give me some Bach!' And there it would be."

Mrs. Medina laughed. "Well, it wasn't always that simple."

"Did he die suddenly?"

"No. Well, in the end, yes. But it was a gradual wearing down."

"Sorry if I touched a bruise."

"You didn't. I don't mind talking about him. I constantly meet people who knew him, who want to talk about him. I miss him very much, no getting around that, but life goes on." She hated the cliché, but there was no other way to put it.

"Yes. One does go on." She picked up the bottle of liqueur. "May I refill your glass?"

"All right."

The wind was more or less steady now, and it blew the laughs from a small sailboat in to them, as it moved eastward along the shore. They sat in silence for a few moments.

"Will you marry again, do you think?" Diana asked her finally.

"No," Mrs. Medina said. *That's a bit too personal*, she thought, so she added, "Will you?"

Diana laughed, then let her laughter die. "I don't know why the hell I'm laughing," she said. "It would be far simpler if I did marry again." She rummaged around on the coffee table. "I think I'll have a cigarette. Want one?"

"Yes, why not?"

"Good."

They were in companionable silence again, the smoke from their cigarettes mingling in the dark.

"No," Diana said, "it's not likely I'll marry again. Lily, you see, the charming woman in the photograph upstairs, she and I were lovers. And I'd been involved with several women before her. So it's not likely at all."

Her words confirmed a fact Mrs. Medina had already known, in some part of her mind. A kind of terror shook her for a moment. Her body gave an involuntary shiver, and she leaned forward and put her glass down on the table.

"Have I spooked you? You ready to bolt back to town?" Diana asked her.

"No." She rubbed her forehead with the tips of her fingers and found it damp with a chilly sweat. "No."

Inside the house a clock chimed eleven.

"Lily came into Road Town on a big French schooner, hitched a ride up from Martinique with the captain. She's a botanist, she was doing some research there on the Empress Josephine's gardens, all those bloody flowers she had sent back to Malmaison. Lily's half French, half Dutch, and the best of both, more or less. I met her at a do at the yacht club here and fell for her as soon as she walked through the door. Never had that happen before." She smiled in the dark. "I swiped her out from under the hairy paws of the French *capitaine*, and there we were."

Mrs. Medina took a last drag from her cigarette and stubbed it out. It was an odd feeling to be smoking again, not unpleasant at all. She wondered whether she should risk telling Diana about the stoves in the basement at Malmaison.

"But love ran its course," Diana went on. "I guess. She gave me twelve delicious months, then went back to Paris to finish her book."

"Did you love her?" Mrs. Medina asked.

"Did I love her?" Diana repeated. "I was crazy about her. She's been gone six weeks, and I'm still a bit weepy. Lily, bless her, is the one who finally prompted me to ask Nigel for a divorce. He'd been living in Antigua for three years, but it never seemed worth it to get the lawyers involved. Now it did. I don't know why. I knew I was just a brief place for Lily to rest her wheels—she was thirty-nine and I was fifty, for Christ's sake."

"Well," Mrs. Medina cleared her throat, "that's hardly enough difference to matter, is it?"

"Oh, age always matters," Diana said. "In the long run." She paused. "There were a number of years between you and your husband, is that what you're getting at?"

"Twenty-five."

"Well, you understand what I mean, then."

"The age difference was never a problem between me and Patrick."

"Well, you were unusually fortunate."

"I think I was." She sat forward on the sofa. "Do you regret it?"

"Do I regret Lily? Not a moment of it. She broke my heart, but that will always be our bond. She knows she broke my heart."

"That sounds a bit overly romantic."

"Don't tell me you're against romance?"

Mrs. Medina stretched her arms above her head. "Perhaps I should be getting back to Road Town."

"How about a walk down to the water before you go? There's a small dock. The view at night is wonderful. And I think the moon's about to appear out of the sea."

They wandered through the gardens down toward the water, pushing through curtains of heavy fragrance, and night things skittered about under their feet. By the time they got to the dock the moon was already up.

"Soon it'll be full," Diana said, leaning on the dock rail.

"The moon looks different in this part of the world," Mrs. Medina said. "It's on its back."

"Yes. Now, where's Orion? Ah, there he is, sailing overhead. My steady constellation."

They watched the water for a while, the distant lights from the resort, the running lights from the boats out on the dark channel. Mrs. Medina was trying not to wonder about Diana's casual revelation, but she was losing the battle. She was suddenly freezing, and her jacket was back up on the porch. She gripped her upper arms. She thought about her time with Lennie, and it didn't seem to put her on any common ground with Diana and Lily, or Jack and Raffi, or anyone else. Perhaps Lennie was an aberration after all, perhaps she should not expect a destiny of women. *A destiny of women.* Highly unlikely. She wiped the corners of her eyes, then let her head fall back so her heart wouldn't ache so much.

"Another cigarette?" Diana said, from close by.

Mrs. Medina lowered her head. "I wonder," she said, "if it's possible to get through life without the possibility of love."

Diana turned her back to the water to light a cigarette and tossed the match away. After a few moments she said, "You can always find love if that's what you want."

"I guess I don't mean love, then," Mrs. Medina said.

Diana drew on her cigarette. "Are you looking for love?"

"No. How can you look for love?"

"How indeed?"

Mrs. Medina stared out over the water.

"Well," Diana said, "if not the possibility of love, what then? The possibility of what?"

Mrs. Medina dropped her head. "Are you happy in your life?"

"Ah. A loaded question."

"I mean it in a straightforward way. You're independent, you come and go, you live here happily alone, you have...involvements, you seem to be looking forward."

"Well." Diana brushed some ashes off the front of her shirt. After a moment she said, "I'm not sure what you're really asking me. I'm always a bit skeptical of people who talk about happiness. Happiness has become like one of those ghastly American malls. We'll tell you what you need, you come in and spend your money. All will be well. Eventually no one knows what they really want."

"You seem to."

"My dear." Diana turned to her. "You have made some wrong assumptions."

"I'm sixty years old," Mrs. Medina said. "I have no idea what I want, or even what the possibilities are."

Diana turned and tossed her cigarette into the water.

"And don't tell me," Mrs. Medina continued, "that I'm grieving over Patrick. Of course I am. But that isn't the answer." In the midst of her frustration, she realized she was talking to Diana as if she were an old friend, with whom she could be irritable and it wouldn't matter. She had a passing inclination to apologize but didn't.

"I don't have any answers for you, Mercedes," Diana said after a moment. "But don't go holding my life up as a model. Just last week I was considering stopping the divorce proceedings so I could persuade Nigel to move back in. Just so I would have someone in the house. But I'd get restless eventually and have to fly off somewhere, and what sort of domestic arrangement is that? Even when Lily was here I couldn't stay still for long."

"But while you're traveling about, does that make you happy? Forgive the use of the word."

Diana rubbed the back of her neck. "I love getting from one point to another. The process. When I'm in love I most like the chase. I adore reading timetables. In London sometimes I plan complicated routes by tube just for the pleasure of making the trip. Getting from Heathrow to a tiny hotel on the island of Mykonos is a great adventure for me. The airports, the buses, the boats. All of that I love. And in two days, I'm thinking of ways to get somewhere else." She paused for a moment. "If I'm in a city and I get an anxiety attack, which I do sometimes, I leave my hotel and spend the night in the train station. Or at an airport. Coming and going. It calms me." She turned so her back was to the water. "So I am not the perfectly adjusted woman."

"I'm not interested in being perfectly adjusted," Mrs. Medina said.

"Eventually I'd like to be at peace somewhere," Diana said. "But that seems too simple to hope for."

"Will you always be with women?" Mrs. Medina asked quickly, without considering her question.

"You mean romantically?" Diana said. "Yes, if I'm lucky."

"Well," Mrs. Medina said, "what I mean is, do you call yourself a lesbian?"

Diana laughed, and in the darkness Mrs. Medina could see her white hand reach up to move her hair off her cheek. "Rarely. I don't call myself anything but female and British, and I have to do that in order to match what it says on my passport. But for the most part my inclinations are toward women, if that's what you mean."

Mrs. Medina rotated her shoulders and felt a soft fatigue settle over her.

"But," Diana said, "I know several men around town who'd love to take you about, if that interests you. You're a very attractive woman. Very classy. Just a bit on the downside right now, so it might do you good to go out."

"No," Mrs. Medina said firmly. "Thank you."

Diana looked at Mrs. Medina in the dark. "I know you miss Patrick," she said. "But it will get easier in time."

"That's not the problem." She turned away. "That's not the problem."

Diana took a breath. "Let's go back up to the house, then."

When the clock chimed two-thirty, Mrs. Medina stopped talking and realized that, finally, she had nothing more to say, finally heard the Chopin nocturnes Diana must have put on the disc player half an hour ago. They were back on the veranda, and the wind had died completely; the air was warm and still. The lamps from the sitting room behind them cast intense shadows out across the tiles.

Diana repositioned her legs on the hassock. "And you have no idea why she took off?"

"Of course I have some ideas. None of them very flattering. She was playing around, I was a desperate old lady, she got bored. What else?"

"Well, she's looking for you now. That's something. And you're not an old lady at sixty, by the way."

"Yes, she's looking for me." She shook her head. "I can't imagine why I've been torturing you with this idiotic tale."

"Oh, please," Diana said. "Torture?"

Mrs. Medina turned her head and followed the movement of a small moth.

"They do cause us havoc, don't they?" Diana said. "These lovely women?"

Mrs. Medina heard the "us" and realized she was being included in a common view with which she was still uncomfortable. But she found Diana's remark oddly reassuring.

"What an experience for you," Diana continued. "Love and death, as it were. Sorry, couldn't resist. Patrick was extraordinary, though. I wish I'd known him."

"Well, let's just say he made everything more complicated. In this case, at least."

"More complicated but more entertaining, it sounds like." Diana took the last cigarette and crumpled the pack. "What will you do about Lennie? Let her know where you are? Get her down here? Sounds as if you'd like to."

"I don't know what she wants, why she's trying to find me."

"Well, that's hardly the issue, is it? Do you want to see her or not?"

Mrs. Medina never thought she would have to ask herself that question twice. "It could be just a whim of hers...I don't know."

Diana exhaled a mouthful of smoke. "Whims are gifts from the gods," she said. "Grab them as they go flying by."

Mrs. Medina sighed. She leaned back against the sofa cushions. Her eyes felt gritty with sleep she hadn't had and desperately needed, and she felt her mind changing shape with exhaustion, moving from one idea to another with no clear focus. "It's late," she said.

"Fancy a swim?" Diana asked.

"A swim?"

"We have a small beach just down from the dock. Mostly gravel, but I'll give you some rubber shoes. I know the water there, no danger this time of night."

"Danger from what?" Mrs. Medina laughed.

Diana got up. "Come on," she said. "I'll get towels."

"I don't have a suit."

"Well, I won't wear one either. Fire up that lantern over there on the far table, if you would. Feeble little light, but it doesn't draw the bugs."

Mrs. Medina lay on her back in the tepid water and watched the stars, the populated heavens floating above her. Among them a tiny plane was making its way through the night. Her breasts bobbed gently on the surface like twin, ghostly domes, and when her legs sank slightly from time to time she became aware of the colder current that was persistently attempting to pull her eastward.

They had undressed on the beach in near darkness, parking the little gas lantern over to the side by the end of the dock. Mrs. Medina had taken a quick look at Diana and felt immediately like a schoolgirl, peering up through lowered lids in the locker room to observe whose breasts were developing. That quick look in the moonlight, however, discovered a body richly curvaceous without being plump, and pendulous breasts that somehow had not lost their firmness. Diana casually threw her clothes into a heap and ran quickly into the water. Mrs. Medina followed, her long legs striding into the quiet surf.

The beach was shallow for about twenty yards, then dropped off abruptly. "Careful," Diana said, suddenly at her side. "The current gets strong without much warning. You're out rather far. Come on back this way."

Mrs. Medina realized with a start that she had been on the verge of falling asleep. And that had seemed like a perfect thing, to fall asleep; to cease her vigilance, to spend the night sleeping, carried by the currents, through one inlet and another, kept afloat by the salt of her own body and that of the sea—that larger living organism that supported her. Chance would wash her up on some shore, and where would it be?

Who would she find there?

She and Diana swam lazily back toward the beach.

"I've brought Nigel's terry dressing gown for you," Diana said as they were toweling off. "Hope you don't mind."

"Why should I mind? But I should probably get right back into my clothes, Diana. It must be nearly dawn." She threw on the robe anyway, because she didn't want to stand there with nothing on. It fit her rather well.

They started back up the path to the house. "I have a better idea," Diana said. "Just sleep here. I'll make up one of the other beds, and you'll be asleep in ten minutes instead of an hour. How about that?"

Mrs. Medina ran her fingers through her hair, which was rapidly drying.

"Come on," Diana said. "I'll give you a T-shirt to sleep in, or even a silk gown if that would persuade you."

They mounted the steps to the veranda.

"Oh, look," Mrs. Medina said.

Across the rim of the eastern horizon a band of intense coral had formed. It seemed as if it were on the rim of the world, hovering over a tremendous fall of water that was pouring out of the sea into darkness.

"Nigel was hooked on watching the sunrises from this terrace," Diana said.

"I can see why." But as she watched the east her eyes closed, and she almost fell asleep on her feet.

Diana extinguished all the lights, and they mounted the outside stairs to the second floor in the freshening air.

"Only one bathroom functioning now," she said. "Just have a seat on my bed, and I'll bring you some towels before I make up your room."

Mrs. Medina collapsed in stages, like a puppet gently released from the control of its master's wires. She remained standing for a moment, then rested briefly on the edge of the bed, then leaned back against the headboard, and finally slid down into sleep.

~

Mrs. Medina woke breathless in the growing heat, hearing the almost silent slip of the ceiling fan above her. A gauzy piece of mosquito netting brushed against her arm, and when she stirred a bit she felt Diana settle in behind her with a little sigh. Mrs. Medina opened her eyes quickly. She was lying more or less on her side, with her head on Diana's arm, just beneath her neck. They were not exactly sleeping spoon fashion, but slightly turned so that Diana's breasts were comfortably resting against Mrs. Medina's shoulders, her left arm on Mrs. Medina's waist. Outside the louvered shutters the sun was brilliant, and there was the distant sound of the surf. To her great relief she discovered she had on some type of large sleep shirt. Nigel's robe was thrown over the back of a chair across the room, and her own clothes had been neatly folded below it.

She held her breath and tried to determine whether Diana was awake. Diana was so close to her that Mrs. Medina wasn't able to tell where their two bodies became separate, and so she shifted slightly but found herself closer. Her heart quickened.

"I must just remove my arm," Diana's sleepy voice said close to her ear. "Sorry."

Mrs. Medina turned her body slightly, as if she were still asleep, and moved toward the edge of the bed. Her mouth tasted like bitter acid. Morning in the mouth, too much to drink, puffy eyes. Dark circles. After a certain age, one was meant to wake up alone.

Diana gave a long stretch. "Oh, blissful sleep. Thank God for it," she said. "Have you had enough? You passed out on me last night. I had to put you to bed in here." Mrs. Medina did not immediately respond. "Sorry," Diana said in a lower voice. "Thought you were awake."

"Sorry to have been a bother," Mrs. Medina said. "I guess I was just exhausted."

"No need to apologize. Turn over, I can barely hear you."

"What time is it?" Mrs. Medina asked, edging her body over onto her back. "I have to think about getting on my way."

Diana raised herself on one elbow. "Don't be daft, I'll give you breakfast. It's nearly eleven."

"I don't know." She lay straight and still. Diana was wearing a yellow T-shirt that said SAIL WEEK ANTIGUA, 1994, and Mrs. Medina could see her nipples pressing against the bow and stern of a blue, three-masted schooner.

"Mercedes, listen. Look at me. We had a lovely evening, a nice sleep together, and I'm not about to make a pass. I did get you out of your clothes last night, but I made every effort to avert my eyes."

"Oh, hell," Mrs. Medina said.

Diana fell back against the pillow. "You're an odd one. Forgive me if I've made you uncomfortable. But for my own selfish reasons, it was delightful to have a body in the bed again. You're an absolutely silent sleeper."

"I'm not really used to sleeping with someone else. Actually, you know, sleeping."

"Nothing to it. Just wants getting used to. Look, the pattern of the sun on the ceiling there, through the louvers. Like water, like sunlight in a cool pond. Watch it moving."

Mrs. Medina had noticed this too. Through the mosquito netting the room seemed without edges, soft and languid. They lay there in the undulating light and were quiet. Mrs. Medina felt the heat from Diana's body moving to her across the bedclothes, and Diana's scent was warm and musky with sleep. The wind rattled the shutters. The morning paused.

"The day is calling," Diana said. "I'll jump in the shower and you can catch forty winks. Then after breakfast you can come with me over to my shop at Soper's Hole, where I must check to be sure Hilarene isn't larking about with that ferry driver. Then I'll get some petrol and run you home. How does that sound?" She threw back the sheet, dodged under the mosquito net, and headed for the bathroom, pulling her T-shirt over her head as she went. Mrs. Medina watched her go, out of the corner of her eye. *I slept with that woman,* she thought. Then she smiled, a bit pleased with herself.

five

Later the day lost the sun, and the wind grew sullen and fitful; by three-thirty there seemed to be no air at all. Mrs. Medina rose from her bed, where she had been trying unsuccessfully to nap, and poured herself a glass of iced tea. She took it out onto the deck and walked out to the end of the pier. The sky had lowered, and a chorus line of wingless sailboats was motoring into port. She felt a few spits of rain against her cheek. She thought she probably still harbored a bit of a hangover.

When she and Diana had arrived at the smart blue and green painted shop at Soper's Hole Marina, there was a sign posted, RETURN IN 10 MIN., and no sign of Hilarene. The shop was unlocked. Diana stormed off toward the ferry landing and returned with the young shop assistant in tow. Hilarene gave Mrs. Medina a brilliant smile as she passed, and waggled her red fingernails. They disappeared into a back room, and while she was waiting for their muted argument to reach some sort of conclusion, a customer wandered in and asked about the coral and shell earrings.

"They're very popular," Mrs. Medina said. "They look good with just about anything."

"That child," Diana said back in the Mini. "I daren't fire her. Her grandmother would have my head. Her granny cared for Jeremy when he was younger." She pulled up to a lonely gas tank near the docks and filled her car up.

"So after I take you home I'm going to spend the afternoon out here," Diana said, getting back into the car. "We're going to straighten this out." She scribbled some figures in a small notebook and threw it back on the dash. "I'll settle with Corwin later. Now, let's get you back to your digs."

"No need for you to drive all the way back into town," Mrs. Medina said. "Let me call a taxi."

"Wouldn't think of it. I'll keep your company as long as I can."

Mrs. Medina watched Diana's hands on the wheel as she accelerated eastward into the coast road. They were slender and tan, with trim, even nails.

"You almost sold some earrings, I noticed," Diana said, turning to smile at her.

Mrs. Medina laughed. "Yes. Like the ones you were wearing the other night, up at Mrs. Bobb's."

"You like those?"

"They're growing on me."

"I'll call you later," Diana said at Mrs. Medina's door.

"Why?" The question was out before Mrs. Medina considered it.

Diana laughed. "Well, maybe I won't call you, then." She pursed her lips. "It's a real treat having you here, Mercedes. I've longed for someone with brains in her head to talk with. You're a godsend. Gets my mind off my girl who walked out on me."

"Sorry," Mrs. Medina said, stepping back from the car so she could see Diana more clearly. "That came out wrong. Certainly, call if you'd like." She looked at Diana and was touched by her candor, her easiness with herself, her guileless expression of friendship. "In fact, do call," she added.

"I'm concerned about you too," Diana said, gunning the engine, which responded with a modest backfire. She smiled. "You're a winner, but you've given up the race. Think about getting that bird down here. Maybe what you need is some time with her. In a new place."

Mrs. Medina turned her head aside. "We'll see," she said.

"Well, do *something*, then. I demand it." She backed out into the road, and headed westward with a grand wave.

Mrs. Medina puttered around the little flat, refreshing the orchids—pale lavender and white—in their bowl with water, straightening the cushions on the couch. She stood at the window and watched the Peter Island ferry come roiling in and Sidney take his pilot's launch and head out to the channel. She got some clean sheets and changed the bed, and got together some laundry to do in the morning, and by that time it was way past the hour when she usually went up to Cyril's, but she still felt pleasantly satisfied from the breakfast Diana had fixed. Diana had given her homemade scones with jam and fresh butter, and orange juice the color of a fiery sunset.

She wondered what would happen if she asked Lennie to come to the island. It was difficult to imagine. She lay down on the bed. A nap, perhaps, to calm her restlessness.

She tried images. She and Lennie at the Park Plaza, the afternoon that had begun with lunch at Pignoli's and ended with "Stairway to Heaven" in the bar. And all that came in between. Mrs. Medina looked at the series of triangular ceiling beams and waited for the rush of excitement. Outside, a voice cried, "Calvin! Come get this mess of grouper here!" and a plane buzzed slowly by, leaving the sound of a piano in its wake, someone up at Cyril's, picking out an aimless afternoon tune. It was quiet then. She found herself imagining telling Diana about that day at the hotel, watching Diana's face as she talked. She had talked about Lennie in some detail last night, but she'd skirted the explicitly sexual. Perhaps that had been a mistake.

She remembered Diana's body against hers in the muted morning light, the movement of Diana's breasts against her shoulders. Now the excitement came.

With a groan she got up and poured herself some tea and went out to the deck. It was three forty-five. She wondered what time Diana would call.

But she didn't really want Diana, did she? Sleeping with her had been peaceful, and, in retrospect, adventurous—laughably so, for a woman of her own age. Would it happen again? Do *something,* Diana had said. Do something, *do* something. It was no longer an issue of making decisions for Patrick. Or for the pleasure of Lennie. She must move out of that child's world of hope, always hoping—for Christmas, for change, for time to pass—certain she could never put out her hand and bring events to pass herself.

Still, she was puzzled; she paced around the deck trying to formulate the question that was lurking about in an impending state. She longed to discover this question, whatever it was, for she now felt she could begin to answer it. But she needed to be asked. She walked about, feeling vaguely as if she were flapping her wings.

Across the way Calvin was cleaning grouper on the cement bricks. "Afternoon," he said, raising his hand.

"Good afternoon," Mrs. Medina replied.

"May have a storm," Calvin said.

"Yes, I see the boats all coming in. A hurricane, do you think?"

He laughed. "No, bit early in the year for a hurricane. Just a storm, is all. Might be a wild night, then it will blow away."

Mrs. Medina nodded.

"How about one of these fine grouper?" he said, holding one up by the tail. "Jus' caught. All cleaned. I see you pacin' about over there, and I think you're probably wonderin' what to cook up for your supper."

"Why, thank you." She was startled by his offer, but he added, "Be a gift, we got a fine catch today." He placed the fish on a piece of newspaper and stepped over and handed it to her. "Big fella," Calvin said. *Big enough for two, in fact,* Mrs. Medina thought.

There was a quiet grumble of thunder. "Uh-oh," he said, "here she come."

Mrs. Medina gave him a smile and thanked him again and went back into her apartment and directly to the telephone.

"What a delightful surprise," Diana said. "I'm sorting charge slips out here. Idiot's work. Something wrong?"

"I have just been presented with a rather large grouper, which I have no idea how to cook. If you'll come and advise me, I'll give you dinner."

"Done. Whoops, here comes the rain. I'll finish here, pop home, change, grab my mac, and see you about seven-thirty."

"This is actually quite a cozy place," Diana said. They were sitting inside at the small dining table, watching the storm blow itself out over the harbor.

"How do you like the flowered chintz?" Mrs. Medina asked her. They exchanged a look.

"Stunning," Diana said.

"I think I'll open the door to the deck a bit wider," Mrs. Medina said. "It's stuffy in here, with the heat from the kitchen." While she was up, she carried the dinner plates out to the sink. "Want some coffee? Tea?"

"Not just yet. I still have my wine. Lovely orchids there, in the bowl."

"Yes, aren't they? Sam Brathwaite brought them by."

"Sam is A-one." Mrs. Medina rejoined Diana at the table and attempted to think of a way to begin a particular type of conversation that would arrive at a point that was not yet clearly defined in her own mind. But Diana said, "Well, are you thinking of leaving for Boston soon? Can we entice you to stay around a while longer?"

"Cyril's letting me stay here without charging me," Mrs. Medina said with a little smile. "That can't go on."

Diana looked at her speculatively. "What, exactly, do you have to get back to?"

"A lot," Mrs. Medina said. "Too much. I probably should teach a summer course, to make amends to my friend Tina for leaving her in the academic lurch. I've got to begin sorting through Patrick's papers, and his former manager contends that he's already had inquiries about a book. About Patrick!" She laughed. "Well, about the trio, actually. Patrick wanted to write that book himself."

"He should've," Diana said. "Why didn't you get him to? While he was still alive?"

Mrs. Medina thought about that. "We talked about it," she said.

"Why don't you do it? You know as much as anyone about that group. And you certainly know Patrick."

"Never thought of it. I'm not any sort of a musician."

"Well, you can always find an excuse," she said. "Not to do something." Mrs. Medina gave her a look. "No offense meant," Diana said. She finished her wine.

Mrs. Medina got up and poured herself some more of the chardonnay, and filled Diana's glass as well.

"May we move over to the couch?" Diana asked. "My bum's a bit tired of these hard chairs, and I know exactly where Cyril bought them."

"Of course."

Diana was wearing white cotton pants and a bright coral blouse, with a circular pattern in the silk that you had to look for. On the way to the couch she kicked off her straw espadrilles, and when she sat down she pulled her feet up under her. After a moment of indecision, Mrs. Medina sat beside her.

They sipped at their wine simultaneously.

Mrs. Medina cleared her throat and made a move to get up again. "I think I'll just—"

"Oh, do sit down," Diana said with a laugh. "The air's fine in here now." She picked up Mrs. Medina's hand and simply pulled her back, and then allowed their hands to stay together, lightly, as one does when one wants to make a point. "What's in your future?" she said.

"What future?" Mrs. Medina asked stupidly, her heart quickening.

"You do plan to have a future? I hope."

"I'll go back—"

"That's not what I meant. What will you do? After paying your debt to academic society, after sorting through Patrick's things, what will you do in the long evenings?"

Mrs. Medina took her hand from Diana's and ran it through her hair. She noted that she needed a haircut. Where, in this town, would she go to get a haircut? "Well," she said with a flip of her hands, "I'll probably travel a bit."

Diana nodded. "Good idea."

"I haven't thought about it, to tell you the truth." And she felt the old darkness appear again; it was outside in the damp evening, it had come in on one of those geriatric cruise ships, on the dark tide, and slipped across the harbor on the dregs of the rain and was even now about to peer in through the top of the Dutch door. "I don't want to teach," she said suddenly.

"Well, that's decided, then," Diana said.

"In fact—this is Thursday, isn't it?—I should probably go back to Boston the first of next week."

"I'm disappointed to hear that," Diana said. "Because I'm making a serious attempt to persuade you to stay on for a while, in case you've misunderstood me."

Mrs. Medina got up and went to the window. The lights wrapped around the gas tanks on the other side of the harbor were undulating through a watery breeze. She had the odd sensation of having been let off a leash. There were decisions to be made here, but they only affected her now—not Patrick, not Lennie, and not Tina, at least not immediately. She felt a bit light-headed. "When are you going to London?" she asked.

"Don't quite know yet," Diana said. "I can go anytime. Within the month, probably."

"I've always loved London."

"Come with me, then."

Mrs. Medina turned to face her. Diana was smiling, that odd smile, with one side of her mouth upturned slightly. Mrs. Medina threw out her hands and took a breath. "How do I know—" she began.

And the telephone rang.

It startled them both. They looked at each other in silent shock for a moment, as if they had been surprised in an illicit activity. Diana laughed. "Go on," she said. "Could be your bird."

And, in fact, it was.

When Mrs. Medina returned to the living room ten minutes later she heard Diana cleaning up the dishes in the kitchen and did not protest. She sat in the single wicker chair and finished her glass of wine and waited.

"Well," Diana said, "the galley's shipshape. What's the matter with you? You're sitting there like a stone lion."

"That," Mrs. Medina said, "was Lennie."

Diana drew back. "Well. I was right, then."

"Could you get the brandy, please? Under the sink."

"Uncommon place to keep good brandy."

"It isn't good brandy."

Diana returned with the bottle. "You're right. Rotgut. Where did this come from?"

"It was here."

"Where is she?"

"St. Thomas."

"More to the point, what does she want?" She gave Mrs. Medina a large tumbler, with just an inch of brandy in it. "Sorry about the big glass. Alien kitchen."

"She wants to see me."

"And who wouldn't? Tell her to come on, then."

"She can't. She hasn't got a passport, and she seems to have used someone else's credit card to get down here. And she's probably broke. Damn that Tina. She promised she wouldn't tell her where I was."

"Look at it this way," Diana said. "It's clear you want to see her. Clear to me, anyway. I recognize the symptoms. So go to her and untangle. Or tangle further, but step out and do it. Don't let her go off missing again. Settle it yourself."

Mrs. Medina looked at her.

"This is where you are. Go find out."

"What time is it?"

"Nearly midnight. Abercrombie flies out at eight-fifteen."

Mrs. Medina laughed. "I should get on a plane with him?"

"Mornings are safer than evenings. How did you leave it with her?"

"I told her to wait at the airport. I would come or I wouldn't, and if I didn't, I would send over some money. With someone. Maybe I could get Bobby Curtis to take it."

"Take it yourself."

"How about—" Mrs. Medina said.

"Not me," Diana said. "No, thank you."

"I was going to say, how about coming over with me?"

"I'm not sure I want to meet this one."

"You wouldn't have to."

"Righto," Diana said. "I'll shop, then, while you decide the rest of your life."

~ six ~

Lennie was in Rita's Rum Bar, her long legs, in washed-out blue shorts, twined around the bar stool. Dusty black clogs, a colorful woven strap around her right ankle. She was drinking a Caribé beer from a clear glass bottle, talking to the bartender. Mrs. Medina stood in the door in her sharply creased khaki shorts and her new blue shirt with the colored shells, and wished she had simply thrown on a T-shirt. She had prepared herself for a momentous occasion that didn't seem likely to happen. As she looked at Lennie she almost felt as if she were examining an artifact from her extinct past. She was thinner. Her pigtail was still intact, although it was shorter, and her hair was curlier, as if she hadn't had it cut for a while.

She had left Diana back on the tarmac with Abercrombie, making sure he was clear about the fact that the one-fifteen flight back to Tortola must be flown today. Abercrombie, a small, bright East Indian of about thirty with a pencil-thin mustache, insisted upon saluting Diana every time she made a point, an impressive British salute, palm out. On the flight over he had talked loudly and incessantly above the nasal whine of the engines, all the time tapping his gauges and adjusting the throttle.

Mrs. Medina waited, watching Lennie with a hope that some memory would move her forward, but at the same time unwilling to have that memory shattered, precarious as it had become. Lennie was still in conversation with the bartender, who finally nodded to her and then to Mrs. Medina. Having been discovered, Mrs. Medina walked briskly over to the bar, as briskly as her shaky legs would carry her. The cement floor seemed to give like rubber under her feet.

"Well," she said, with a little smile. Then, almost as an after-thought, she kissed Lennie's cheek.

Lennie put her hand on Mrs. Medina's arm, just above her elbow. "Don't you look tan and terrific," she said. Her eyes were bright—too bright.

They looked at each other.

"Let's go to a table," Mrs. Medina said.

"May I serve you something, madam?" the bartender asked her. The same Rasta barman, smiling out of liquid brown eyes. "A beer? A rum?"

"Just an iced tea, please."

"You have what you want, young miss?" the barman asked Lennie.

"For now," she said.

They sat themselves down at one of the round metal tables. It was too early for the passengers from New York and Boston and Miami, so they had the bar to themselves. Above them a ceiling fan turned lazily with a little tick, tick, tick. The cement floor was still damp from an earlier swab.

"Are we going to stay here?" Lennie asked her. She rested her chin in her palm. It didn't look as if she'd had much sleep. Mrs. Medina hadn't either. She suddenly wanted to reach across the table and simply grab Lennie, to shake her furiously, or to embrace her; she needed some violent physical contact with Lennie's body, which was quickly assuming the shape and curve of familiarity.

"Well, let's start here, at least," Mrs. Medina said. "How did you find me? Did you call Tina Bird?"

"Your doorman."

"Constantin?"

Lennie scratched her ear. "Yeah, I told him it was a life-and-death thing. That's how I got your number."

Mrs. Medina laughed a little. "Yes, he's susceptible to situations like that."

"Do you mind? Are you glad to see me?"

"I'm surprised to see you."

"I read that Patrick died. I'm sorry."

"Patrick died in January."

"I was going to write you a note, but I thought that might be confusing."

"It might have been. I don't know."

They looked at each other, but Lennie seemed to have a difficult time focusing. "Sorry," she said, "I haven't slept in a while."

"Where did you stay last night?"

She leaned forward and put her palm on her forehead. "I camped in a shelter on one of the beaches."

"Last night was stormy."

"Yeah, it was."

"Where are your bags?"

She gestured toward the bar. "My knapsack is back behind the bar there."

Mrs. Medina sipped her tea, which had come already sweetened and had a nice spicy, fragrance to it.

"Can we go someplace?" Lennie said.

"We can find you a room, if you like."

"Where are your bags?"

"Back in Tortola."

"But I need a passport to go to Tortola. I don't have one."

Mrs. Medina reached over and took both of Lennie's hands in hers. "Why don't you tell me what you're doing here." She looked at Lennie's face, remembering it in quick jumps—tense with passion, abandoned in sleep, cocky, teasing. She was wearing a green T-shirt with SAN FRANCISCO printed in faded blue letters across the front. It looked as if it had been slept in.

"Are you in trouble?" Mrs. Medina said.

"I was. But Guido straightened it out."

"The police came to see me. Back in Boston."

Lennie took her hands back. "I figured they might," she said. "I didn't like to think of that, but there wasn't anything I could do."

"You could have called me, explained some things."

The terminal was heating up. One of the big flights had landed, and there was a quick decibel rise out by the gates. Two young men marched into Rita's stripping themselves of sweaters and down vests. "Beer," they said to the barman. "Beer, beer, beer."

Lennie gave her a look that said, *I will put up with anything you want to do to me.* Excessively patient. This look made Mrs. Medina smile. "What is it?" Lennie said, not smiling.

"What's your friend Kenny up to?"

Lennie lowered her eyes. "Kenny," she said. "They locked him up, but then they let him out."

"And you?"

"Why would they lock me up?"

Mrs. Medina tilted her head and opened her hands as if to say, *You tell me.*

The barman switched the ceiling fans onto a higher speed.

Lennie sighed. "Jesus Christ, I hate going over this. Do we have to?"

"No, we don't have to. But it would be helpful to me."

"I thought Guido would let you know that they kicked me out of that class."

"He did. And he told me you'd quit work."

"I did quit." She looked around. "I didn't see the point anymore. I was just arranging flowers. It was going nowhere."

"But it was your living."

"Not entirely." She reached down and adjusted her ankle bracelet. "Okay, I wasn't an angel, and I didn't talk to you about it because I knew you'd hassle me. I didn't want to deal with that. Yeah, Kenny and I were what you might call business partners, and so that's the way it was. I was making enough to support myself. It was never meant to be a permanent thing."

"But you loved working with the flowers."

"Well, that doesn't make any difference, does it?" She shook her head. "Does it? Look, when they kicked me out of that class it was no big deal. It was a sort of sign, you know, that I should just quit trying to shove myself upstream. That was the sign. So I did."

Mrs. Medina kept her eyes on Lennie's face.

"I wasn't selling hard stuff, if that makes any difference to you. Kenny was dealing hard stuff. He nearly killed some people with some bad crystal meth, and that's what got the cops going." She shook her empty beer bottle. "I think I'd like another beer." The barman caught her eye and brought over another Caribé. "I like these bottles," Lennie said, when he had departed. "With these two pink flamingos standing by the palm tree." She held the bottle up to the light.

Mrs. Medina clasped her hands under her chin. "Did you run off with Kenny's money?"

"It wasn't his. It was my stuff and my money. I had a feeling we were going to get a visit from the narcs, so I split. That pissed him off."

"Where did you go?"

"I was with the Zen people. I stayed there through the winter. I never went back to Cambridge, to my apartment, I never picked up any of my stuff, I never went back to Guido's."

The Zen Center was the one place Mrs. Medina hadn't considered, and it was logically the first place she should have called.

"And what, you were doing business from there?"

"I was only living there, working on their garden."

"I wish you'd talked to me about it. I didn't know where you'd gone."

"I thought you might come looking for me."

"I did look for you. In every way I could. You just walked out on me."

"Well, walk out, I don't know. Walk out from what?"

"Lennie, we were having a love affair. I thought we had some sort of understanding. At least."

Lennie rubbed her forehead with the tips of her fingers. "I should have just left you alone," she said. "From the beginning."

"I'm glad you didn't," Mrs. Medina said, and she meant it. "You were the most wonderful thing that had ever happened to me."

"Yeah, I figured that."

"You figured that? And how did you feel? I guess that's the issue."

Lennie sighed and leaned back in her chair. "You scared me a little. After a while. I felt like I was responsible for you, like you wanted me to cure your life."

Mrs. Medina nodded. Yes, that was probably true.

"Look, you wouldn't have wanted me to stay. There wasn't anything about me that fit into your life."

"Did you love me?" Mrs. Medina asked.

Lennie turned her head aside.

"Because I loved you."

Lennie twisted her pigtail around her finger in a familiar gesture, and Mrs. Medina saw that her face was truly haggard. There was dirt under her nails, and a smudge of grease on her arm. Mrs. Medina thought briefly of putting her in a shower somewhere, soaping her up, taking her to bed. Still she thought of these things. She shifted a bit on her chair. "I still love you," she said.

A wave of new arrivals jabbered into the bar like a happy herd of turkeys. Their faces held vestiges of the pale northern spring, chill rains, color still asleep. She wondered what Diana might be doing, whether she was shopping, sitting in another bar just like this one.

"He trashed my garden," Lennie said, her face dark.

"Kenny did?"

"Yeah, pulled everything up, did some other things I won't mention. A true asshole."

"That beautiful garden," Mrs. Medina said. "What an awful thing to do."

Lennie turned her head aside and looked at the people at the bar.

"Did you finish the garden for the Zen people?"

Her face brightened a bit. "Yes, I did. Not as spectacular as I wanted—they ran out of money. But they didn't really want spectacular, so that was okay. It looks great, lots of space and gravel walks, and Guido got me a new type of lavender from England."

"It's good you finished it."

They fell silent.

"Are you staying in one of those ritzy resorts?" Lennie asked after a moment. "Is someone with you?"

"I'm staying in a place that belongs to a cousin of Tina's."

"Is it more or less quiet and out of the way? Or is it a big resort?"

"I would say it's more or less out of the way."

"I need someplace to go, just to rest and be quiet for a while. To sort of get myself back on track. To think about some things."

Mrs. Medina thought for a moment. "And you want me to provide that?"

Lennie looked at her quickly, and then glanced away. "Look, everything can't be explained," Lennie said. "I wish you'd stop trying."

The arriving passengers had gulped their drinks and departed in search of their baggage, or connecting flights. Mrs. Medina wondered where Abercrombie was at this moment. She fanned herself with a menu. "Are you hungry?" she asked suddenly.

"I suppose I could go for a hamburger, if we're going to hang out here."

Mrs. Medina opened the menu. "Hamburger, cheeseburger, West Indian roti," she said.

"What's that?"

"A little fried dough pocket filled with different things. Meat, usually."

Lennie's eyes were becoming vague with fatigue. "I don't really know what I want," she said.

Mrs. Medina went to the counter and asked for a hamburger and a couple of rotis and got herself another iced tea. When she returned to the table Lennie's head was on her arms, and she appeared to be asleep. But she sat up straight when she heard Mrs. Medina sit down. "You're not going to tell me to get lost, are you?" she said.

"Do you want some money? I can do that." *I should say more,* she thought. *It breaks my heart to see her so...vulnerable.* She felt nights of anger, longing, begin to slip away.

Lennie looked at her and tapped her chin with her fist.

"What about Connie?" Mrs. Medina asked. "Could you stay with her for a while?"

Lennie shook her head. "I needed you. That's why I came down here. I don't want anyone else."

Mrs. Medina looked at Lennie and realized now that she did truly love her, as you always love those few in your life who have rearranged your spirit, and little pricks of tears appeared in the corners of her eyes. She had expected this meeting with Lennie to show her what to do, to present her with something dramatic, a sign, a jolt that would shove her into action, indicate which way to go. But it wouldn't happen like that, she saw now. What would happen would be more like a slow undoing, thread by thread, of the texture and weave of her life, much like a poppy with its roots deeply embedded in a stone wall disengages itself, root by delicate root, to begin a new life in the soil. It would be a slow and intricate process, *something like Diana's journey to Mykonos,* she thought: *a cab to Heathrow, a plane to Athens, a boat over blue water to the island, a bus to a small hotel, a restful sleep until the next sunrise.*

"My life is changing now, Lennie," Mrs. Medina said. "I'm going off to London in a couple of weeks, I think."

Lennie was struggling to stay awake. "I just want someplace safe," she said. "It doesn't have to be forever."

The barman arrived with the food and left them alone again.

Lennie devoured the hamburger and both rotis, barely lifting her head. Mrs. Medina watched her and sipped her tea. "These things are good," she said, wiping her mouth. "Thanks."

"I don't know how to handle the problem of a passport," Mrs. Medina said. "But there's someone with me who probably does." She stood up. "Get your bag and let's go find her."

But out in the terminal there were too many people milling about, and Diana wasn't at the Air Tortola desk where they had arranged to meet. But it was only twelve-fifteen. The terminal had become stifling, and Lennie finally said, "I can't breathe in here."

Outside, the sun beat down, but there was a breeze and it was somewhat cooler under a large anaconda tree, in red-orange bloom, not far from the main entrance to the terminal. Mrs. Medina sat down on one of the long benches beside the path and patted the wood beside her. "Lie down and sleep for half an hour," she said. "We can't do anything yet."

Lennie arranged her lumpy backpack on the other end of the bench and prepared to stretch out.

"Put your head in my lap," Mrs. Medina said. "More comfortable." Lennie looked at her in surprise. "It's all right. It's not forever, remember?"

Lennie settled her head, and Mrs. Medina felt her body become heavier as she sighed and fell immediately into sleep. She stroked Lennie's hair, looked up at the sky. "Don't be scared," she said. "You'll land on your feet." She smoothed the hair along Lennie's neck. The scent from the flowers drifted down.

The people streamed by, in swirls of blustery dust, with shouts, and bags, full of the excitement of going away, and of coming home. She sat with her arm across Lennie's shoulder and watched her sleep, and waited patiently for Diana to come back.